The
State
of Me

The State of Me

a novel

by

Nasim Marie Jafry

The Friday Project
An imprint of HarperCollins Publishers
77–85 Fulham Palace Road
Hammersmith, London W6 8JB

www.thefridayproject.co.uk
www.harpercollins.co.uk

First published by The Friday Project in 2008

1
Nasim Marie Jafry asserts the moral right to
be identified as the author of this work

A catalogue record for this book
is available from the British Library

ISBN 978-1-906321-05-5

Typeset by Wordsense Ltd, Edinburgh (www.wordsense.co.uk)

Printed and bound in Great Britain by
Clays Ltd, St Ives plc

Contents

Tell me right away if I'm disturbing you,
he said as he stepped inside my door,
and I'll leave at once.

You not only disturb me, I said,
you shatter my entire existence.
Welcome.

Eeva Kilpi
(translated by Börje Vähämäki)

for lizzie

Prologue

All you need to know is this: Coxsackie. Coxsuckie. Cock-a-leekie.

Three funny words that sound the same.

Can you guess what they mean?

I'll tell you: a virus, a sexual act and a kind of soup made from chicken and leeks.

Part One

1

A Lime and a Sofa Bed, 1998

WHEN SHE'S FALLING asleep, she rubs her left foot against her right foot. Stop that, he says, you're like a giant cricket. He deserves an acrobatic lover, a Nadia Comaneci. When she's got energy, she goes on top as a special treat.

*

Dragging legs, concentrating on every step, I feel like I'm wading through water. I take a trolley even though I'm only buying a few things. I don't want to have to carry a basket. I pick up some tea bags. My arms and face are going numb, my bones are burning. I stop the trolley and pretend to look at the coffee. The lights are too bright, there are too many shiny things to look at, too many jars and bottles. I don't feel real. I abandon the trolley and go to the checkout, picking up a lime on the way.

The woman in front of me places the NEXT CUSTOMER divider between her dog food and my lime. She has a pink pinched face and limpid blue eyes. You can't see her eyelashes. A mountain of Pedigree Chum edges towards the scanner.

I focus on the lime and hope my legs will last.

I'm wondering how many dogs the pinched woman has, and if her husband loves her without eyelashes, when a shrill voice punctures my head: the voice of the checkout girl. I haven't realised it's my turn.

D'you know how much this is? she says, holding up the lime. She's typed in a code, and PUMPKIN LARGE has come up on the till display.

It's not a pumpkin, I say. It's a lime.

She rings for the store manager, who appears from nowhere, brisk and important. He gives the girl the correct code and disappears again in a camp jangle of keys. The girl rings up the lime and I'm free. I go outside and sit on the wall. I feel spectacularly ill.

I make my way home with no shopping. It's only a five minute walk. I pass the dead seagull folded on the road. It's been there for three days. It has blood on it.

I reach the house and the smell of fresh paint hits me as I unlock the front door – we'd painted the bathroom last week, my arms left like rags.

I'll need to call him.

When he answers the phone, I try to sound independent.

I got ill at the supermarket, I say. Can you please get

some groceries on the way home?

What do we need?

Pasta, salad, bread. Basics.

I'll nip home just now. I need to get out of here for a bit anyway.

Can you get some Parmesan too?

Okay.

I'm sorry, I say.

It's not your fault, he replies.

That seagull's still there, d'you think I should call the council?

They'll be closed, he says, it's after four.

Someone's moved it into the gutter, at least it's not in the middle of the road anymore.

Call them tomorrow, he says.

I just feel sorry for it.

See you in a bit, he says.

I imagine him taking off his glasses after he's hung up, rubbing his eyes and sighing. When he gets home, I'll tell him I dreamt we had a baby made of lettuce, and he'll smile and unwind in spite of himself.

Things had been tense last night. Why d'you have to hack the whole head, why can't you just chop it normally? he'd said, frowning at the mess of skins and garlic cloves on the work-top. I don't do anything normally, I'd replied – did no one tell you?

I lie down on the couch. I can't get the seagull out of my head.

3

*

Why didn't you wait for me to come home? he says, handing me a cup of tea. I could've done the shopping. You really are your own worst enemy sometimes.

The fridge was bare, I say, I got you a lime for your gin.

I have to go back to work for a couple of hours. I'll make dinner tonight. You don't mind eating late, do you?

No, I say, I'm not hungry at all.

He kisses the top of my head as he leaves.

I dreamt we had a baby made of lettuce last night.

Tell me later, he says, I have to go.

I wonder if he's really gone back to work or if he's gone to fuck Lucia. I wonder if I'll have to call in sick tomorrow.

She'd stayed with us before Christmas when her central heating wasn't working. It was supposed to be for a couple of nights, but two nights had become two weeks. She'd given me a bag of Guatemalan worry dolls. For under your pillow, she'd said.

I know, I said, I've had them before.

She went on, girlishly, Tell them your worries before you sleep, and in the morning, they'll all be gone!

I'm worried you'll sleep with my boyfriend, I'd said into myself.

She'd slept on the sofa bed in the study. One morning,

4

I'd been woken by loud voices and laughing. I got up. The sofa bed was sticking up in the middle of the floor like a monstrous orange sculpture. It's stuck, said Lucia, giggling, I don't know what I've done! They'd wrestled with it for a while and finally managed to collapse it and fold it up. Sorry we woke you, Helen, he said. We didn't want to leave you with it all day.

I'd hated him referring to Lucia and him as 'we'. I'd watched them go out to the car. I grudged their intimacy, their shared knowledge of genes and proteins. She was beginning to annoy me with her skittishness, her smart coat and boots, so matching and groomed. I'd gone back to bed and tried to sleep more, but I couldn't settle: they had to go – I felt agitated, just knowing they were there. I'd scooped the tiny Guatemalans from under my pillow and thrown them in the bin, covering them with rubbish so no one else would see them.

NB. Helen's boyfriend and Lucia work together, their affair, however, may be psychosomatic, it's causing Helen pain, but it's not really there! Sometimes she sees them, Lucia, so eager to please in her short skirt and boots, him leaning over to kiss her.

She's so fucking fragile, Lu, he says, I can't take it anymore.

2

Rita and Nab

I<small>T IS MY</small> policy never to ask people what they do. If they want to tell me, that's fine, but I would never ask. I understand the dread of being asked.

*

stranger	What do you do?
me	I work one afternoon a week. I've been ill (for fifteen years).
stranger	You don't look ill.
me	That's good, isn't it?
stranger	You seem to have a lot of energy.
me	That's 'cos we're sitting down just talking.

stranger	Why can't you do a job where you can sit down?
me	Because it's not just my legs. If I overdo it my arms feel mashed up and my head shuts down. I can't think straight.
stranger	I see.
me	You don't believe me, do you?
stranger	No, not really.
me	I've got more fucking 'O' grades and Highers than you've had hot dinners, so please just leave me alone. (Into myself.)

It was the same when I used to go to the post office to cash my sickness benefit – the people behind the counter looked at me suspiciously, especially if I was wearing lipstick.

*

I am thirty-five, but I still depend on Rita and Nab. Rita works part-time as a librarian. She trained as a nurse and stopped when she had me. Nab's exotic, he grew up in Greenland. His Danish father taught there. Nab's a hospital engineer. He's high up.

They met on holiday in Tenerife: divorced Nab with his son Finn, and divorced Rita with me and my brother Sean. Rita'd used her savings to get a four-star hotel – we'd had a horrible three-star hotel in Alicante two years before, and my granny had spent the first day cleaning her room with Dettol. I still have my Alicante souvenir, a donkey with yellow nylon fur, peeling now, revealing the cheap grey plastic underneath.

Nab hired a car and took us round the island. Sean and I admired the bougainvillea and sheer drops politely. Finn was cool and wore black clogs. He was bored shitless. Volcanic rock didn't impress him. Nab was easy to love but Rita and I secretly laughed at his Scandinavian Jesus sandals.

My real father Peter had his own dental practice above a butcher's shop. He had minty breath and slept with his nurses. (*A little more suction, please, Denise!*) When you went through the close to get to the surgery upstairs, you could smell the meat from the butcher's delivery entrance. Sometimes there was blood on the ground. There was a fish-tank in the waiting room and the goldfish always had a string of white shit hanging from its tail.

Peter left when I was ten but we still went to him for fillings. I didn't find the divorce traumatic – I'd never really liked him. The only thing I have in common with him is that we both love raw onion.

Sean is four years younger than me. We grew up on the Bonnie Banks. Our house was right next to the park.

You nipped over the fence, jumped the ditch, ran past the Michael tree (a boy called Michael fell off it and died), through the rhododendrons, and you were at the top of a huge grassy hill, Loch Lomond spread out in front of you.

Every spring the park was carpeted with bluebells. We'd pick Rita giant bunches for her birthday, Mother's Day and Easter. She must've been sick of them – they're not exactly fragrant. In fact, bluebells stink. (Also, they are toxic to deer and cattle.)

And, there is Brian, I depend on him too, for his big wide love, Rita's youngest brother, brain-damaged at birth, not profoundly, but enough to make him happy.

3

Before

I HAVEN'T ALWAYS been ill. Once upon a time, I got lots of 'A's and played right-inner for the school hockey team. I wasn't very good but that's not the point. I loved the clatter of the game and the gorgeous bruises and the orange segments at half-time. I loved the adrenaline at the start, the jamming and locking of sticks when the centre-forwards fought for possession of the ball.

Ground, Stick! Ground, Stick! Ground, Stick! BALL!

We had to wear disgusting maroon hockey skirts. We envied the nearby private school whose uniform was deep lilac and much sexier.

When we left school, my best friend Rachel and I got summer jobs at the Swan Hotel. The staff had to wear tartan. Rachel and I wore mini kilts and flirted with the chefs. The bottle boy was always trying to get Rachel to go down to the cellar with him.

The local speed-boat owners came regularly with their beer bellies and Alsatians. Dogs weren't allowed, so the Alsatians clipped along the pier, barking at the swans while their owners devoured scampi-in-the-basket washed down by pints of heavy. Coach parties were a nightmare, tea and coffee for eighty. Josie, the woman who made the sandwiches, would test if the bread was defrosted by holding the cold slices against her hairy face. The tourists nibbled on their egg and cress and gazed out at Ben Lomond, blissfully unknowing. When it was quiet, I would sit at the bar, folding napkins, remembering how Peter used to bring us here on Sundays for chicken-in-the-basket. Sean and I would sneak into the ball-room and slide on the polished dance floor. Rita would be staring out at the loch. She hated it when her husband played happy families.

Sometimes, after our shifts, we would go up the park and hide in the rhododendrons and get stoned with the commis chefs. We'd talk rubbish, pissing ourselves laughing amongst the crimson flowers and shiny leaves. One time, we put dope in tea and watched *Yellow Submarine* at the bar manager's flat. Nothing for an hour then my elbows were made of cotton and my tongue felt like sawdust. It was a bit scary. I kept saying, I've got cotton elbows, but Rachel couldn't stop laughing.

In my first year at university, I commuted, thought nothing of the mile walk to the train station. *Why would I?*

I met Hadi, handsome and narcissistic, at the beginning of the second term. He was Libyan and had his own flat

11

and a fat black cat called Blue *because she liked the blues*. When Hadi had the munchies he would overfeed her, tipping Whiskas onto a saucer, tapping the spoon against the rim to get her attention: *Come on, fat lady, come to eat!* Hadi hardly ever went to his engineering lectures and got his friends to photocopy their notes for him.

His erection was bent like a banana and he rolled his eyes when he came. I thought this was normal. The third time we had sex he complained about using Durex ('stupid skins') and said I should go on the pill. I told him I wouldn't have sex without a condom because I didn't know his history. He pouted and accused me of being neurotic and clinical about love. When I finished with him at the end of term, he kicked over the rubber plant I'd got him and called me a prick-tease. I told him I was tired of his moods and tired of him shovelling cat food into Blue. I told him I was tired of his friends always being there skinning up, and tired of listening to J. J. Cale. When I tried to leave the flat, he said he'd kill himself. A couple of weeks later, I saw him with his arm round a girl in the Grosvenor Cafe. I half smiled, but he blanked me.

In my second year, I moved up to Glasgow into a student flat. My flatmate Jana was petite and fragile with a sexy, throaty voice and jet black hair that swung like a curtain. She'd grown up in San Francisco. Her mum was half American Indian and had died of breast cancer when Jana was fifteen. (It's sad, Jana'd say – she was beautiful but she was bi-polar and she was always going on crazy spending sprees, she got us into a lot of debt.) Jana's dad was Scottish and her granny lived in Anniesland. Jana had stayed with her when she first came to Glasgow. She loved Glasgow. The first time she'd seen well-fired rolls in Greggs' bakery she'd taken a photo because she thought they were burnt.

Ivan lived in the flat above. He was studying biochemistry and looked a bit like Adam Ant, but taller and more rugged. Everyone fancied him. We would eye each other up in the Reading Room, the dome-shaped library where you went if you just had a couple of hours and didn't want the palaver of checking into the main library. The Reading Room echoed with suppressed giggles and shuffled papers and books slammed shut. The librarian was stern and wore salmon pink twin-sets. You could feel her eyes stabbing you when you scraped your chair along the ground or dropped your pen and it echoed. Jana called her the salmon spinster and was always getting thrown out for carrying on.

In Week Eight, I got off with Ivan in the union bar to *Love Will Tear Us Apart* by Joy Division. I said I loved his blue eyes. He said he loved my green eyes. They're not really green, I said, they're more grey. When I told him I was from Balloch, he said he'd camped there once and someone had jumped on his tent. It wasn't me, I said.

You'll never guess who's been sleeping in my bed! I said to Jana the next morning. I told her it was Ivan and she screamed and went to check I was telling the truth. She peeked into my bedroom. He was still sleeping.

I wouldn't mind doing pelvic thrusts with him, she whispered to me back in the kitchen. Bring him to *Rocky Horror*. It's on this Friday.

I'll see, I said. I want to play hard to get. And by the way, we haven't done pelvic thrusts yet, we just dibbled and dabbled. (Dibbling and dabbling was Jana's term for non-penetrative sex.)

I bet he has a beautiful body, she said.

He does, I said. He's in the university tennis club. And he's in a band. And he wears contact lenses. He's as blind as a bat without them.

So if I climbed into bed with him now, he'd just think it was you? she said.

Don't even think about it, you cheeky wench!

When she'd gone to her class, I took Ivan tea in bed. Nonchalant and shaking, I asked him about *Rocky Horror*. Sure, green eyes, he said, peering for the cup. It's a date.

After that we were joined at the hip.

He was mature. He was twenty-one (I was nineteen). He'd taken a year out after school and worked in America. He'd gone to a private school. His parents lived in Dundee in a huge house overlooking the Tay. His dad was a surgeon and his mum was a part-time English teacher from Dublin. The first time I met her she got tipsy and maudlin. She showed me photos of Ivan's sister Molly who'd been killed in 1975 when she'd tripped up crossing the road in her flip-flops. Don't ever have children, Helen, she said. You'll only lose them if you do.

4

France

In September of our third year, Jana and I went to study in Caen, a town in the north of France. We'd been looking forward to our year abroad all summer.

I'd been to France twice before. The first time was a school trip to Paris, and we all had to wear red cagoules. A black man with broken yellow teeth and bloodshot eyes had tried to put his hand between my legs in the Eiffel Tower lift. I'd screamed and he'd pulled back, but part of me had felt sorry for him because of the Africans in the street selling trinkets that no one wanted. I'd bought a giant packet of paper hankies from one man. The second time was a couple of days in Nice during an inter-railing trip with Rachel. We'd sunbathed topless and felt cosmopolitan. Two sisters from Inverness had latched onto us because we spoke French, but they wouldn't take their tops off. They said there might be perverts.

*

Two weeks before we left for Caen, I had a going away/ passing my driving test party. Nab and Rita went up north for the weekend. It was Nab's birthday.

I was sexy at the party, I didn't know it would be for the last time. I could've walked out of Bananarama with my fuchsia mini dress, gold fishnet tights, pink shoes from Ravel and black chiffon scarf tied in a bow round my hair, which had been back-combed with half a tub of gel; I had heavy arches of pink eye crayon and fuchsia frenzy lipstick.

Ivan came with his new band and his flatmate Rez. He brought me a Matchbox Mini with a red bow round it.

Jana came with her summer fling, Piedro, a morose Portuguese student with bad teeth. He's not circumcised, said Jana. Things are a bit baggy down there. It creeps me out.

Rachel turned up on her own. She'd gone to St Andrews to do law. We still had our summer jobs at the Swan Hotel but we were drifting apart. She was in with a posh crowd and had changed the way she talked.

Richard from next door came with his Barbie-doll girlfriend, Clare, who worked in his dad's carpet shop. She kept giving me cold looks as if she knew that he used to touch my breasts when I was helping him with his calculus.

Callum, who used to sniff glue under Balloch bridge, brought his girlfriend, Roquia, an Asian goth who kept running away from home. Callum was now a photographer with the local paper.

Dribs and drabs of hippies and punks turned up. I recognised some of them from school.

Rita had made Sean promise he wouldn't drink and made me promise that I would confiscate whatever he did try to drink. His friend brought a quarter bottle of Pernod which he later threw up on the hall carpet. They spent the night shrinking empty crisp packets in the oven – you made badges by putting safety pins on the back of the miniature shrunken bags.

Jana and Piedro had sex in the greenhouse. Jana sat on some bulbs and came back into the house with mud on her white jeans. Shit, my good jeans are ruined, she said. D'you think this'll come out? That guy Callum's weird. He was watching us having sex. He had his head pressed up against the glass the whole time. And he had a rose between his teeth.

Don't mind Callum, I said. He's harmless. Weird but harmless. Are the bulbs okay? Rita will go mad if you've ruined them.

She grinned. I had to re-pot them but they're fine.

Jana, I hope you're joking! I said.

Later, I found Callum stoned, lying on top of the coats in Sean's bedroom. Why did you watch my friends having sex in the greenhouse? I asked.

Och, I was just having a laugh, he said. I couldn't really see much. It was all steamed up.

Jana said you had a rose between your teeth.

I stole it from next door, he said. It just tempted me. Do you mind?

You're mad, I said. Where's Roquia got to?

I think she's in the huff with me for flirting with Rachel. She's away chatting up your boyfriend to get me back. He's a handsome boy, by the way. I could shag him myself. Here, d'you fancy a draw? He handed me a soggy joint.

No thanks. (You could never be sure what Callum was smoking. It was probably mixed with dung or something.) I'm away to mingle. Don't be sick on the coats.

D'you fancy a snog before you go?

Behave yourself, I said.

Has anyone ever told you you've got a dancer's legs?

When the party started to fizzle out, Ivan and his friends got their guitars out. Callum kept requesting *Bohemian Rhapsody* but they ignored him so he paraded around singing all the parts himself. It's too operatic for you, he said. That's your problem, boys. Too fucking operatic.

We got to bed about five and Ivan and I had sex, jammed together in my single bed. He said he'd miss me like hell when I went away. Me too, I said. He hummed my favourite Leonard Cohen song and I fell asleep. The next morning I was up by eleven, opening all the windows and cleaning up. The others would've slept all day if I hadn't woken them.

Piedro had sleeping bag zip marks on his face and was mooching around the kitchen. Sean was pretending that he had a hang-over to act tough – he'd hardly drunk a thing

– and said he couldn't eat anything. He went into the garden to get some air and came back and said the hollyhocks were broken. I went into the front garden to check. It looked like someone had gone over them on a bike. I snapped off the broken flowers and tried to ruffle up the leaves to get rid of the flatness and tyre marks. I knew it was Callum.

Mum'll go mad, I said. And you can still see a stain where your friend was sick in the hall. You'll need to put more disinfectant on it.

It's stinking, said Sean.

I'm glad I'm going away next week, I said. Mum'll have her stony face for days after this.

I went upstairs to finish hoovering, and Piedro made omelettes for everyone. He wasn't as glaikit as he looked.

We'd filled six bin bags with rubbish from the party. I hoped the squirrels wouldn't get them. It was the only thing that made Nab angry, litter strewn in the garden when the squirrels chewed the bags. He was always shouting at them, You bloody rodents with no respect!

I loved the squirrels. I loved the way they'd skite up the trees and along branches and down again.

*

Diarrhoea the day before we left. Pain like sharp sticks. A heavy headache that hurt my eyes. You'll be fine, said Rita. It's just nerves. Drink lots of water so you don't get dehydrated.

*

Ivan and Rita and Nab saw us off at Central Station. I was worried the diarrhoea would come back when I was on the train. Rita went off to John Menzies to get me some Pan Drops. Peppermint's good for you, she said, it'll settle your stomach. You sound like Granny, I said.

A Polaroid snap of the occasion: me clinging to Ivan. See you at Christmas. I love you. Nab like a wall round me with his polar bear hug. Rita pressing the Pan Drops into my hand. Remember we love you. Phone us when you get there. Ivan whispering in my ear, Don't shit yourself on the train. My mother wiping a tear away as the train jolts out. Nab's arm round her. Ivan making a face, trying not to show emotion in front of them.

I was homesick by Preston and wanted to go back. You can't be serious, said Jana. We are going to have a ball over there, my girl. This time next week you'll be asking yourself, Who is Ivan anyway?

I doubt it, I said. Did I tell you we've agreed that we can kiss other people while I'm away, as long as we tell each other about it?

Jana rolled her eyes.

Won't you miss Piedro at all? I asked. Won't you miss his omelettes?

She started to laugh and couldn't stop. Speaking of Piedro, she said, snorting, how are your skitters?

Poor Piedro. He'll be pining for you all next term. And

since you asked, the skitters seem to have dried up for the time being.

Great, she said. Everything's just hunky dory. Yes, we are going to have a ball, my girl. A veritable ball!

We stayed overnight in Weymouth at a B&B. I cried in the toilet because I was missing Ivan. I was scared he'd get back with Gail, his ex. She was still after him.

We went out and had fish and chips, and scones with clotted cream. Jana found a hair in her cream. That's fucking gross, she said. I told her about the time I was wee and we were at a dentist friend's of Peter's for dinner and I'd found a hair in my fruit cocktail. I'd been too shy to say anything and had just eaten it. I could feel it in my throat for ages afterwards.

The next morning we missed the ferry to Cherbourg because we slept in. We got to the docks just as the Sealink ferry was floating off. We could have reached out and touched it. Looks like we've missed the boat, said Jana. I sent Ivan a postcard. I love you. Jana was scathing.

We got lodgings with a family in Caen. The mother Simone looked like Jeanne Moreau. She warned us that electricity was very expensive and we should never leave the lights on. She had a lock on the phone. Her husband Vincent was a lot older. He'd had a stroke and taken early retirement from his factory job. He shuffled around the house, eating grapes. Their son Jean-Paul had just done his army service and lived in the basement.

That'll have to go, Jana said, pointing to the poster in our bedroom – *Entre Les Trous de la Mémoire*, a montage of some anaemic girl and her memories, featuring a cruise ship with symbolic waves; the leaning tower of Pisa; a tree; a pile of books (one of them in flames); a hot air balloon and a mirror. It was horrible but I persuaded Jana to leave it there 'til we'd ingratiated ourselves a bit more with Simone.

We had to register at *la préfecture* and get ID cards. *Le préfet* was like a Peter Sellers character. He glared at us while he stamped our *cartes de séjour* with a hundred different stamps. We started to giggle and he glimmered us a smile.

We didn't have any exams and our attendance wasn't being checked, so there was no incentive for Jana to go to classes. I'd lugged over my huge Collins dictionary and planned to get through everything on next year's reading list. Jana had started sleeping with Jean-Paul in our third week and preferred to spend her mornings in the basement. She'd roll into the student canteen at lunchtime, boasting that Jean-Paul had asked her to *fais-moi la pipe*. At first she hadn't understood what he meant. Jean-Paul grinned. *Comme une sucette,* like a lollipop.

Louis de Funèz, a French comedy actor, had just died,

and they were showing all his films. We would sit around the TV, *en famille*, guffawing at his antics. Vincent would cry and snort with joy. It was the only time he was ever animated.

At the end of September, Abas came to lodge with us. He was from Morocco. He would invite me into his room to eat oranges and help him with his English. He said he was missing his wife. His eyes would fill up and he'd try and sit a bit nearer me on the bed.

In the evenings, we'd go to the Bar de la Fac and eat crêpes and get drunk on kir royal with Esther, a student from Cork. Esther was plump and breathless and beautiful. She wanted to lose her virginity before Christmas. Abas was at the top of her list. She thought he was lovely.

One weekend, we went skating. I could skate backwards better than I could skate forwards. I had more control going backwards.

Abas had never skated. He clung to Esther like a toddler, terrified to leave the side of the rink. Jean-Paul and his friend, a lorry driver from Ouistreham, with a thuggish crew-cut, sped round, pissing themselves at Abas every time he fell. I didn't like the lorry driver and wished someone would skate over his hands.

I had to sit down after twenty minutes because my legs felt weak. I spectated for the rest of the afternoon. The smell of the rink reminded me of learning to skate in Aviemore,

Nab skating round effortlessly with his hands clasped behind his back.

I shivered. I felt I was coming down with something.

*

Nagging pain in spine for last two weeks. Feeling stoned all the time. When I bend down, I feel dizzy.

I've only had one letter from Ivan in a month. I've written to him every week.

Something isn't right.

When I go outside, the light hurts my eyes.

*

Dear Ivan,

I am missing you so much, sweet boy. I think about you all the time and want to kiss you right now. Jana and Abas have gone to Bayeux today but I didn't feel up to going. I've been feeling ill and weird. I might have picked something up in the university canteen. The food is fucking horrible. I'm sure they gave us pigeon last week. They covered it with grated carrots to make it seem healthy. Did I tell you that Simone, the landlady, has arranged a wee party for my birthday? It's funny, 'cos she's really tight-fisted. We're not allowed to use her real coffee, we have to drink the chicory stuff! We're scared she finds out we've binned that poster she had up in our room. It was really ugly and the drawing pins kept falling out. We've also hidden the vase with the plastic flowers behind the wardrobe. We couldn't stand looking at them anymore. I don't have much more news, I told you everything in last letter. I'm sending you lots of kisses.

Helen xxx

PS. I am wearing your cosy purple tartan shirt and sandalwood oil. It makes me feel near you. PPS. How's the band going?

I put the letter in my bedside drawer. I wouldn't send it 'til I got a reply to my last two.

One morning during a lecture on Voltaire, it just came over me.

Hot twisting cramps.

I thought I was going to shit myself. I bolted out of the lecture hall and ran to the toilet. I sat there for almost an hour 'til there was nothing left.

I got the bus home and went to bed. I cried myself to sleep. Jana woke me up rummaging for cigarettes in her bedside cabinet.

There's something wrong with me, Jana, I said. I almost shat myself today in the Voltaire lecture, and the other weird feelings are getting worse. My head keeps going numb.

She came over and sat on the side of the bed. Maybe it's hormonal 'cos you came off the pill. We'll go to the uni doctor tomorrow.

*

The next day the university doctor took a urine sample and gave me antibiotics for a urinary tract infection that I knew I didn't have. He assured me that I didn't have appendicitis and asked if British people had their appendix on the left side like their cars. He told me to come back in a week if I wasn't better.

We picked up the prescription and Jana talked me into buying a pink lambswool sweater from Au Printemps that I couldn't afford. You need something to cheer yourself up, she said.

I felt dizzy in the changing room. The spot-light glared above me. It looks great, said Jana, swooshing the curtain back. You're so lucky you've got breasts.

You're so lucky you've got hips, I replied out of habit.

You're so lucky you're tall.

You're so lucky you don't feel as if you're dying.

Is it so bad?

Yes. I want to go home.

I'll come with you.

No, don't. I'm just going to go to bed.

She went to the Bar de la Fac to meet some Americans she'd befriended and I went home with the nagging pain circling me and the pink sweater folded preciously in floral tissue paper.

*

26

I took the antibiotics anyway, *Doctor's orders!* When I went back to see him he said my urine was clear and took some blood. He patted my head and said I looked pale. It's *inside* my muscle, I said, pointing to the nagging in my spine. I struggled for the correct French preposition. We'll know more when we get the blood results, he said. Come back in two weeks.

Later, I lay in the bath, scrunching up my eyes, wishing that when I unscrunched them I could be home with Rita and Nab – like Dorothy clicking her magic slippers.

Ivan phoned in the middle of my party and sang *Happy Birthday* down the phone. He'd sent a card too.

Simone had bought cheap pâté from Carrefour that looked like cat food. Abas had bought a cake with bright green icing. Simone's eyes lit up when he brought it to the table. She was like a magpie. He had made thick black coffee which he poured ceremoniously into tiny cups. It was almost undrinkable. When Abas wasn't looking Jean-Paul threw his in the yucca plant. I thought Jana would explode. Esther guzzled the sparkling wine she'd brought and told Abas his coffee was *très bon.* He beamed.

Why do you sound so sad? said Ivan.

I'm still feeling ill, I said. I've been staying in bed. The pain's still there and the funny feelings. I'm going back to the doctor's a week on Tuesday.

Hang in there, he said. You'll soon be home for

Christmas. By the way, I've got a surprise for you, I got my ear pierced. We used ice and potatoes. It was agony!

You're crazy, I said. You should have done it properly. It could get infected. Who's *we?*

Rez and me.

Abas had put on his favourite tape, an awful, wailing Middle Eastern woman. (He was always singing along to her in his room, completely out of tune.)

What the hell's that racket? said Ivan

Abas's music, I said.

Is Abas deaf?

Ha ha. Very funny.

Tell Abas to change it. It's shite. He laughed and sent a kiss down the phone before hanging up.

I went back to the party.

Ça va avec ton copain? Simone was blinking and beaming, hungry for details.

Oui, ça va, I said.

I hated Ivan for not believing how bad I felt and I hated him for being happy without me and I hated him for slagging Abas.

I wanted to phone him back and tell him how much I missed him.

Let's go out tonight. It'll cheer you up, Jana said, recently emerged from the basement. A couple of the Moroccans are having a party on the campus.

If I could go to a party that meant I was fine, so I forced myself to go just to pretend. I wore my new pink sweater. The hosts had made spicy hamburgers and boiled eggs. I sipped on a kir and tried to blend in with the noise, but it wasn't working. I wasn't part of this. I just wanted to lie down.

We got a taxi home. Jana went into the kitchen to get some bottled water. She screamed and jumped back from the fridge. Jesus Christ! Whatever you do, don't look in the fridge, Helen. Just don't look!

What is it?! Tell me!

The rabbit's in the fridge! The bastards have killed their pet rabbit, can you believe it?! She was a bit drunk and kept saying, *Pauvre fucking lapin* over and over again.

I trudged upstairs and started to pack. The rabbit had decided me, I was going home. I couldn't wait 'til the Christmas break. I was going now. I packed everything except my French dictionary and umbrella. My case weighed a ton.

Jana and Abas came to the station with me. Abas, mournful in his blue anorak, tried to kiss me goodbye on the lips. Jana said she didn't think I should be travelling on my own. I hadn't told Rita and Nab I was coming back. I didn't want to worry them. Remember to cancel my doctor's appointment, I mouthed to her from the train.

On the way to Cherbourg, I thought I was having a

heart attack. Chest pains, numb face, pins and needles in my legs. I kept staring at my feet to stay calm. I'd bought these blue desert boots for coming to France. I could see myself two months ago – a young woman in Schuh trying on a mountain of boots: *I can never get shoes to fit, I'm not a six or a seven, I'm really a six and a half.*

I met a French girl on the ferry. She was starting a job as a nanny in London. When she asked me where I was going, I told her I was going home for Christmas. But it's only the fifth of December, she said.

I brushed my teeth in a trickle of water and tossed and turned all night in the grey cabin. I slept for two hours and smelled of sweat when I woke.

I called home at half eight in the morning, hoping that Nab would answer. He did.

Nab, I'm in Weymouth, I'm coming home. I'm ill.

Calm and Scandinavian, he said he'd meet me in Glasgow. Nab didn't judge.

I got a taxi to Seaview, the B&B we'd stayed at on the way out. The landlady recognised me. You're the ones that missed the boat, she said. Is your friend not with you?

I booked in and hauled my case into room six. She grudgingly made me breakfast. I had just made the deadline. The dining room was empty, just me and the dirty tables. I felt sick and hungry at the same time and forced down some toast and half a glistening sausage.

I got to the toilet just in time. The cramps had come from nowhere, clawing into me. The toilet seat was freezing.

I was doubled over, groaning, my head in my hands, my gut in twisted loops. The toilet paper was like the chemical stuff you got at school. I must have used half the box. I was pulling up my jeans when I saw the spider on the ceiling. It was the size of a cup. I scraped my knuckles on the snib in my panic to get out. My jeans were still undone.

Back in the room, I sat on the floor, sucking my knuckles, trying to banish the image of what I'd seen, hoping no one could hear me crying.

I had to get clean.

I gathered up my toiletries and underwear and realised I didn't have a towel – all I had was the skimpy grey B&B hand-towel. I'd need to use my dressing gown. I locked the room and went along the corridor to the bathroom. The corridor smelled of bacon.

I checked for spiders before going in. The radiator was boiling hot. I piled up my stuff beside it and rinsed the bath with the shower attachment. There was a pubic hair stuck on the side. I imagined Jana's reaction: *Gross me out the door!* I climbed in and washed away the ferry and diarrhoea. I washed my hair with soap even though I knew it would give me dandruff.

I felt the cleanest I'd ever felt.

I dried off with my dressing gown and went back to my room, slightly cheered up by clean pants. I went to bed wearing Ivan's shirt. When I woke up it was four o'clock. I couldn't be bothered moving but my bladder was nagging me to get up. I pulled on my jeans and went along the corridor.

31

I opened the toilet door, keeping it at arm's length. I forced myself to look inside. The spider had fucking moved! It was halfway down the wall now, spanned and waiting. I fled to the toilet upstairs, still shuddering at the thought of it looking down on me before.

I went back to the room and made some coffee. There was a tray on top of the dressing-table with two damp sachets of Nescafe and a kettle with a melted handle.

When I stirred in the powdered milk, it floated in clumps on the top. I threw it away. I tried to drink the second cup black, but it was too bitter.

I was feeling hungry again and went to ask the landlady if I could have some toast. She said the kitchen was closed. I told her I wasn't feeling well. There's an Indian takeaway round the corner, she said. I asked if she could get rid of the spider in the toilet. She said they were harmless and that they ate flies. There are no flies, I wanted to say. It's winter.

I trudged back to my room and found half a packet of peanuts at the bottom of my bag. I ate them and lay down again. By six o'clock, I was starving. I got dressed and went round the corner to the Taj Mahal. They were just opening. I thought I could manage some pakora but they didn't have any. The flock wallpaper and Indian music made me think of Ivan. He loved Indian food. I ended up with chicken biryani and boiled rice and a plastic knife and fork. I went back to Seaview and sat on the bed and ate from the foil trays. I could only eat half of it. I got up and opened the window.

The air was cold and sharp. The room was stinking of curry and I'd spilled biryani on the bedspread.

I lay on the bed with my year-abroad boots on, wondering what Ivan would say. I was dying to speak to him but he didn't have a phone in his flat. I thought of calling his parents but his dad could be a bit gruff and I didn't know what to say.

I saw Nab before he saw me. I saw him from the window of the train. He was wearing his sheepskin jacket.

He hugged me tightly on the platform and said, You've been feeling a bit scruffy, Helen?

Scruffy. Nab's word for ill.

*

I scrunch up my eyes. When I open them I am in the bath at home, Rita and Nab in the next room.

Safe.

5

The Trial

I KNEW RITA would think I was pregnant. She'd made me an appointment with Myra Finlay, our family doctor.

Beginning of the trial.

Sitting opposite Myra, I presented my evidence.

She wrote it all down.

You're not pregnant are you?

I shook my head.

You haven't been taking drugs over in France?

No, I said.

Are you worried about anything?

I'm worried about what's wrong with me.

She took some blood and told me to come back in a week. On the way out, I peed into a tube and handed it in at reception. It was still warm.

*

Results all negative.

It's common for young women your age to have aches and pains. Being homesick's a terrible thing. Go back to France and stop worrying.

What about the diarrhoea?

It's anxiety.

What about the pain in my spine and the pressure in my head?

She smiled weakly and didn't answer.

I told everyone I'd go back after Christmas, I had to keep up appearances. I was trying to read Zola's *Germinal* without my dictionary. There were lots of mining terms that I didn't understand.

Ivan said, This year abroad's a great opportunity. Don't screw it up because you're missing me. Later, he apologised and said he'd been stressed by his end of term exams. He looked gorgeous with his earring. I'd been too scared to ask if he'd kissed Gail.

Rita took me Christmas shopping and I wandered round John Menzies wondering if I had something wrong with my kidneys. I shopped half-heartedly:

Boxers with red hearts and a sweater for Ivan;

Midnight's Children for Rita;

Stranglers album for Sean.

I didn't know what to get Nab. I'd probably go halfers with Sean on a bottle of Glenmorangie. Brian was easy. Whenever you asked him what he wanted for Christmas, he'd beam and say, A big giant selection box.

I helped Rita with the Christmas tree, trying to ignore the expanding headaches and ever-present gnawing in my spine. Our Christmas decorations had become Scandinavian since Nab: glass angels on the tree, wooden trolls under the tree, all white lights, and he'd taught us to curl the ribbons on presents with the edge of the scissors. (Nab's advent had also brought a Bang & Olufsen hi-fi, a huge chunky Lisa Larson lion, a couple of Greenlandic paintings, a set of orange and black almanacs called *Hvem, Hvad, Hvor* and duty-free Firkløver chocolate.)

Ivan had got me a ticket for Daft Friday, the all-night student Christmas ball.

I stayed in bed all day to make sure I could go, even though I knew I couldn't. I was cloaked in nausea, my head felt inflated with a bicycle pump. My fairy godmother whispered, *You shall go to the ball,* while the ugly sisters stuck the boot in, *Sick people don't go to balls, you're going nowhere!*

In the middle of the night, while Gail was tempting Ivan in her black cocktail dress, I was dreaming about bluebells: Ivan was an old man in a wheelchair. He was wearing a red leather jockstrap and I was pushing him through the bluebells in the park.

*

In and out of the dusty bluebells. I am the master! Helen's getting a bit dull, isn't she? She was hoping she could go back to France after Christmas and have an affair with one of those young Moroccans, put Ivan in his place, but alas she's going nowhere!

She's staying put.

*

It snowed on New Year's Day. I liked the way the snow blanked everything out. Ivan and Rez had gone to a friend's parents' cottage in Tighnabruaich for a few days. They'd invited me but I couldn't go. They got in a fight with some neds who called Rez Kunta Kinte, and Ivan ended up in Casualty with a broken nose. They'd been planning to visit me on their way back to Glasgow but the roads were too bad.

Jana had stayed with Jean-Paul over the holidays. She'd phoned me on Hogmanay. Abas keeps asking when you're coming back, she said. And your Frank Zappa compilation tape got mangled in the tape-recorder. I told her that I had an appointment to see Professor Pivot after the holidays. And Myra's doing more tests, I said. I'll write and tell you what's happening. That reminds me, she said, a letter came for you from the university health centre. I'll forward it with your other mail.

I didn't tell her that I'd sent her a poster of *The Orange Blind* by Cadell, one of the Scottish colourists. I thought she could do with a replacement and I wanted it to be a surprise.

Rita ran me up to Glasgow and waited in the Grosvenor Cafe while I explained my return from France to Professor Pivot, the Head of the French Department. (He was very angular and pivoted along rather than walked.) It was pissing down. We were late because of the slush slowing down the traffic.

I got drenched walking from the car and was dripping all over the professor's floor. He offered to get me a towel. His head was small compared to the rest of him.

I told him they hadn't found out what was wrong with me yet but were doing more tests. I hope I can re-do my year abroad next year, I said. I've sent this term's grant cheque back.

You're young, he said. Take time to think about things. We'll have another chat next term. You might know what's wrong by then.

He was so understanding that I was tempted to list my symptoms.

On the way out, I went to look at the noticeboard. I wished it was this time last year and all I had to worry about was an essay on Baudelaire.

The Grosvenor was packed as usual. It smelled of wet coats and smoke mixed with coffee and fried onions. The geology lecturer, who was always on his own, was there.

Rita looked worried. Well, how did it go?

He was really nice, but I was dripping all over his floor.

Can you go back to France next year?

I think so, I said. He was quite vague about things.

Ivan was dropping in before his three o'clock lecture to give me the keys of his flat. I'd hardly stayed with him since coming back from France. We'd only had sex once. Afterwards, I'd cried because I felt so crap and because I felt I was letting him down.

That guy over there's always in on his own, I said to Rita. It makes me sad, seeing him with his hamburger roll. I always want to invite him over.

You're being ridiculous, said my mother. He's probably quite happy eating on his own.

I don't think so, I said. He doesn't look happy.

I just ate on my own, and I was perfectly happy!

But you've got a husband, you're not on your own. That guy's not married.

Here's Ivan now, said Rita.

The rain was sliding off him. He squashed himself into our booth.

You're soaked! I said, kissing his cheek. You look like a hamster with your hair clapped round your head like that. I wished Rita wasn't there so I could kiss him properly, then I felt guilty for wishing she wasn't there. I squeezed his hand tightly under the table.

How's your nose? I asked. You said it was squint. It doesn't look squint.

It's okay, he said. It wasn't actually broken.

He'd just sat down when someone tapped me on the shoulder – a mature student from my English tutorial, whose name I could never remember. She had terrible facial hair. I thought it was you! she said. I thought you were in France doing your year abroad.

I was, I said, but I'm home for a while. I've been ill.

That's a shame. Well, I better go, my car's on a meter, I just thought I'd say hello. I hope you get better soon.

Thanks, I said.

Who was that? asked Rita.

She was in my English tutorial last year. I can never remember her name.

By the way, said Ivan, I got the Ian Dury tickets.

I hope I can come, I said. I'll be gutted if I can't.

Rez and his new girlfriend are going. Rez was saying he thinks you should get tested for brucellosis.

What's brucellosis?

Something you get from milk.

Myra'll batter me, I said, if I even *think* of suggesting it. I'm having soup, do you want anything to eat?

Nah, just hot chocolate.

I'll have another coffee, said Rita.

So what did your Prof say? asked Ivan.

I think he just thinks I'm anxious, but he was so nice about it.

So you're not chucked off the course?

I don't think so, I said.

The camp ginger-haired guy came and took my order. He'd fallen off a wall last year when he was drunk, and broken his back, but he was fine now, fully recovered.

He brought the soup straight away. I loved the comfort of being here with the two people who could make everything okay. I wanted this scene to play forever. I didn't want my soup to finish.

I have to go, said Ivan, I'm really late. He kissed me on the cheek (still shy in front of my mother). I'll see you later. Here are my keys.

I wanted to be like him, downing hot chocolate and going back to a class.

Normal.

When he'd gone, Rita said she'd have to be making tracks too. Are you sure you'll be okay?

Yes. I might go to the bookshop. I want to look at French dictionaries.

Could Jana not send yours back?

It'd probably cost less to buy a new one.

My mother frowned. Okay, I'm away. See you tomorrow. We'll pick you up from the station if you want. And don't be filling your head with what Rez says. Medical students are known for being neurotic.

She hugged me and left.

I sat there for a while wondering what to do next. Choices were: go and look at dictionaries and pretend to be normal, or go to Ivan's and lie down.

I chose to pretend.

It was still pissing down. The uni bookshop was only five minutes away but my arms were weak from holding the brolly by the time I got there.

I went straight to the medical section and looked up brucellosis. You got it from unpasteurised milk and dairy products. Symptoms were backache, fever and fatigue. I could easily have it, God knows what I'd eaten in France. I looked up brain tumours too and had worried myself sick before heading round to the French section.

I crouched down to look at the dictionaries. I knelt on the floor and looked up some words I'd written down from *Germinal*. As I scribbled down the meanings in the back of my chequebook, rain from my umbrella dripped onto a page of the dictionary. I snapped it shut, hoping no one had seen. When I stood up I felt dizzy and my face was going numb.

I wanted something easier to read than Zola. I quickly chose *Paroles* by Prévert. His poems were simple and quite easy to understand and it was a bargain for £1.50.

I had to get back to Ivan's flat.

It had finally stopped raining. I bumped into Gail coming up University Avenue, with her wide brown eyes, walking with her feet turned in because she thought it looked sexy. She looked like a knock-kneed foal.

Hi, she said in her fakey voice. I heard you'd come home. I heard you were ill.

I was just up seeing the Head of Department, I said. I'm

on my way to Ivan's now.

What do you think of Ivan's earring? He really suits it, doesn't he? It was such a laugh when we did it! Rez was standing by with the cotton wool and TCP for emergencies. He wouldn't let me do his though.

She could feel me wither – *she'd* pierced Ivan's ear, the bitch.

Yeah, he really suits it, I said. He should have got it done properly though. It's stupid to risk infection.

She gave me her foal eyes and laughed.

I better go, I said. I'm not feeling great.

I better go too. I'm going up to the Stevie building to sign up for an aerobics class. Say hello to Ivan from me.

I will, I said.

I walked to Lawrence Street wishing in spite of my numb head that I'd had eye-liner on when I met her.

Ivan was living in the same flat as last year above Jana's and my old place. The paint was still peeling off our front door. The Cocteau Twins were playing inside. I could hear laughing. It could've been me and Jana a year ago. I climbed one more flight up to Ivan's.

It was freezing in his flat. I chucked my umbrella in the bath and put the gas fire on in his bedroom. I moved his guitar off the bed (it seemed so bulky) and got under his black and white checked quilt, still dressed. I could smell him on the pillow.

My feet wouldn't heat up and I felt like I had a brick in my neck. I got up and looked for a pair of Ivan's socks to put over my own. His room was a tip. There were two dried-up oranges on his desk with half the peel bitten off. There would be others he'd forgotten, hidden under his books and clothes. He always ate orange peel when he was studying. I found some socks and put them on and went through to the bathroom to look for Anadin. I put the toilet seat down and looked in the medicine cabinet: one medical rubber glove, a bottle of sandalwood oil and a bottle of pink nail polish. I dabbed some of Ivan's oil on my wrists then soaked a facecloth in cold water and wrung it out.

I went back to the bed and put the facecloth on my head. I wondered who the nail polish belonged to. I tried conjugating subjunctives and somehow fell asleep.

Ivan woke me when he came home. (When you shut the front door the whole flat shook.) I could hear him taking off his jacket in the hall. He was singing. There was a damp patch on the bed where the facecloth had been.

He came into the bedroom and sat on the bed. You fell asleep with the fire on, he said, ruffling my hair. God, you'll never guess what the guy who sits next to me in Nucleic Acids' girlfriend did?

What? I mumbled.

She found out he'd slept with someone else and she threw all his notes in the bath!

The bastard must've deserved it.

You sound blocked up? Have you been crying?

My head feels weird. I met Gail. You didn't tell me she'd pierced your ear.

44

I know I didn't. I knew you'd get the wrong end of the stick. That's why.

Did you shag her when I was ill in France?

Of course not! Please not the third degree about Gail again. D'you want some tea?

Why does she walk like a foal?

What?

Why does Gail walk like a foal? I'm just wondering.

I don't know what you mean. D'you want some tea or not?

Yeah. I'm getting up. I need a drink of water. My head's killing me. Have you got any painkillers? I couldn't find any.

Maybe in the kitchen drawer. I'll go and look.

He came back through with a faded strip of Disprin and a glass of water. Will these do? he asked.

They look really old. Have they passed their expiry date?

They'll be fine, just take them.

I sat up and he put his arms round me. His face was cold and he smelled of rain.

I loved being held by this boy in his chunky white fisherman's sweater. He was forgiven for Gail. I decided not to mention the nail polish.

Someone's been dabbing my sandalwood, he said.

I love the smell of it, I said. It smells of you.

What d'you want for tea? he asked.

I don't care. I'm not really hungry.

45

We could get a takeaway.

He went through to the kitchen and I dissolved the Disprin, stirring it round the glass with my finger. The dregs stuck to the side of the glass when I drank it.

I trudged through after Ivan, utterly happy that he was back from his lecture even though the foal had pierced his ear.

I can't believe that girl throwing his notes in the bath, he said, shaking his head and dunking a tea bag in a mug.

Sounds like he deserved it, I said. Can I have a mug that's not chipped, please?

They're all chipped, he said, spooning the tea bag into the pedal-bin, leaving a trail of brown drips.

Maybe I should throw your notes in the bath.

What, because Gail pierced my ear?!

Yup.

You wouldn't dare! he said, laughing. He pulled a bright blue menu out of the kitchen drawer. What d'you fancy? Prawn bhuna? Chicken korma? Lamb patia?

I don't mind. Please don't read out the whole menu. Can we go back through? It's freezing in here.

We went back to his bedroom and he put Aztec Camera on. I'll keep the volume low for your head, he said.

I lay under the quilt, he lay on top. I was cocooned and safe.

So how are you, green eyes? he said.

They're not green, I said. They're more grey.

He smiled.

Ivan, you do believe me, don't you?

What that your eyes are really grey?

No. You believe that I'm ill, don't you?

Yup.

Are you sure? You don't think it's in my head, do you?

Nope.

You did at first though when you were being horrible.

I was worried you were homesick, that's all. But now I know there's something really wrong. I just want you to get better. I want things to get back to normal.

Me too. Can you pass up my tea, please?

Your hands are freezing, he said, handing me the mug.

They're always cold these days, I said. I clasped the tea against me, still lying down, and sipped from the mug, wedging it under my chin.

Watch you don't spill it on the bed, he said.

I will. This quilt's horrible, by the way.

I know, my mum gave it to me for Christmas. He picked up the blue menu again. I quite fancy a korma.

Anything you want. I'll just have a wee bit.

Will we get pakora?

If you want, I said.

Maybe not. It was a bit greasy the last time.

When I got back here and couldn't sleep, I was thinking about that geology lecturer who's always in the Grosvenor on his own. I bet he cries himself to sleep at night.

How can you leap from talking about pakora to the

geology lecturer?!

He's got greasy hair, I said. Greasy pakora and greasy hair.

You always do that, he said, leap from one thing to something totally unrelated.

That's what makes me interesting.

I think I'll go out for the food now, he said. I'm starving.

Can I stay here?

Yup.

You're an angel, I said. I put my tea down and leaned over him and kissed his ear. The earring felt spiky and cold.

The front door slammed and the record jumped.

That's Rez back. I'll see if he wants anything. Hey, Rez, we're in here, d'you want a curry?

Rez put his head round the door. Hiya! Is that you hiding in bed, Helen? How are you doing?

Och, hanging in there, I said.

I'd love a curry, he said to Ivan. I'll come with you.

They left and I stayed in bed for a bit thinking about where I could get a nice mug tree for Ivan.

I got up to set the table. I wanted to be useful. Three forks, a bottle of flat Irn Bru and half a bottle of Black Tower. I put the oven on to warm the plates and read some poems while I waited. *Alicante* cheered me up even though I thought it was about a lost love.

The flat shook and they were back. Sorry we took so long, said Ivan. The place was mobbed.

*

Three happy students having dinner round the table: Ivan, Helen and Rez. *Can you guess which one has a weird burning feeling in her head/neck/spine that she doesn't want to mention?!*

Yes, that's right. It's Helen!

*

Nab ran me to the station on the night of the Ian Dury concert. All my symptoms were trailing behind me. I'd taken four extra strong Panadol. I took *Germinal* to read on the train but it didn't come out of my bag. I watched the raindrops skitter along the train windows like sperm.

I got off at Partick and took the Underground to Hillhead where Ivan was meeting me. I used the escalators. (I'd always used the stairs before.) Ivan was waiting for me in his leather jacket. He was chatting to the guy who was always there selling the *Socialist Worker*. We waited as long as we could for the rain to stop before making our way up to the union. I was exhausted from standing at the station and got a seat upstairs on the balcony.

Ian Dury was brilliant. He came on stage, writhing and wrapped in tinfoil. He sang *Ban The Bomb*. Ivan was up the front with his friends. He kept turning round and looking up at me. When they sang *Hit Me With Your Rhythm Stick*, I thought of Rachel and an experiment we'd done at school in chemistry. Rachel had been trying to write down the lyrics of *Rhythm Stick* and I'd been trying to write down the experiment. Something about iron ions, something turning Prussian blue. The teacher had sent her to the 'sin bin', a solitary chair at the back of the lab and wouldn't let us sit together for the rest of term. Another time, in physics, we'd pinned crocodile clips all over each other's backs. The teacher was angry but trying not to laugh. His experiments never worked and we felt sorry for him. All that wasted ticker tape. I felt sad thinking about Rachel. I'd seen her at Christmas but she'd been dismissive of me coming home from France early. We'd been inseparable at school. I'd gone to recorder lessons for three months just because she went, even though I was crap at music and got mouth ulcers. I hated unscrewing the top of the recorder to shake out the saliva.

When they played *Sweet Gene Vincent*, everyone started to pogo at the fast bit. I looked down on all the jumping, dyed blonde/purple/spiky heads. I was outside all of this. My spine felt like it was being stretched and my hands were numb and tingling.

Ian Dury was glowing with sweat.

After the concert, Ivan's band friends came back to the flat. I wanted them to go away, I wanted him to myself. They were drunk and slagging off some girl that one of them had had a blind date with. Joe (from London) was saying, You get two kinds of red-head. You get the beautiful Irish kind with pale skin and you get the freaky, red-faced Scottish kind with freckles. This one was FREAKY!

They all thought Joe was so funny. They all laughed like they were choking.

I went to bed and lay awake waiting for Ivan. I could faintly hear the yelping of the Cocteau Twins from downstairs. I wondered if the girls who lived there got carpet burns when they had sex. (The flat was covered throughout with dark brown industrial strength carpet.)

I couldn't get rid of them, Ivan said when he finally came through. Joe's got a new song he's excited about.

Joe's a wanker, I said. He talks such shite. God, your feet are freezing!

You can warm me up, he said, rubbing his feet against me.

*

A bundle of mail arrived from Caen, the stuff Jana had forwarded: the blood test results and some Christmas cards. I ripped open the blood test. Now I would have a weapon against Myra, proof that I really was ill! When I read it my heart sank. It said there had been a mix-up at the lab, they'd lost the samples and they wanted to re-do the tests, could I please make an appointment? I read it twice to make sure I'd understood. I screwed it up and threw it across the carpet. Agnes batted it under the table. I had no chance now, I was at Myra's mercy forever.

The Christmas cards – so pointless in the middle of

January – were from people who had no idea I'd come home. All three had pictures of penguins with stupid smiles.

Agnes was curving her paws round the table leg, catching the twist of paper then batting it away again. I binned the penguins, took Agnes upstairs and cried into her.

More tests: a chest x-ray; an ECG; a kidney x-ray; a liver function test; a barium meal and a barium enema (beware the white shit that won't flush!).

Negative! Myra crowed, as each result came back.

But I'm getting worse. My legs are like jelly. The pain's burning into my bones. I feel sick all the time. My brain feels inflamed. Why don't you believe me?

Helen, there is nothing physically wrong with you. If this goes on I think you should see a clinical psychologist. Believe me, I'm the doctor.

(Believe me. Just for a change. I'm the patient.)

It turned out I'd already been tested for brucellosis. Rita, who thought it was a possibility, after all, had asked for me to be tested and was told I already had been.

I had to sign on now that I'd sent my grant back. Officially, I was no longer a student. Officially, I was no longer anything.

The dole office was a grim flat building with bits of grey roughcast falling off. Rita waited for me in the car. It was my first time signing on. There was a man arguing about his claim when I went in. He was saying that it was fucking daylight robbery. He had an Alsatian on a long lead and he'd dressed it in a white T-shirt. The dog's tongue was hanging out and it was panting.

I waited for my turn and was called to a booth. I recognised the girl behind the glass. She'd been in the year below me at school. Her brother used to scare people in the playground by turning his eyelids inside out.

I explained that I was out of uni for a while.

Are you looking for work? she said.

No, I'm ill. I had to come home from France.

It's all right for some, swanning off to France, she said. You'll need a sick note from your doctor if you're not available for work.

I don't have a sick note. They don't know what's wrong with me yet. (And by the way, your perm's fucking horrible, it's growing out and you don't even suit it.)

Well, if you want any money you'll need to sign on as available for work, she said, pushing a bundle of blue and white forms under the glass divider.

Since I'd come back from France Rita'd been dragging me out to the park in an attempt to pep me up. You're getting too peely-wally, she'd say. Just a short walk to get some colour in your cheeks. We'd wrap up and climb the fence and cross the ditch (funny to see your mother jumping a ditch), pass the Michael tree, and I'd be exhausted by the time we reached the castle. We'd sit on the bench and look down at the loch for answers.

One time we went straight to the bench after a bad appointment with Myra. You could drive to the castle and park there.

There were bursts of purple and yellow crocuses all around us.

I love spring flowers, said Rita. They're so full of hope, the way they push up through the hard ground.

They're lovely, I said, but you wonder how they can stand the cold. I turned to face her. D'you think I'll be better by next spring, Mum?

We're going to get to the bottom of this, pet, she said, putting her arm round me. I promise you. We won't give up 'til they've found out what's wrong with you. And as soon as we know, we can start getting you better.

I smiled and tried not to cry. Rita tried not to cry and smiled back.

D'you remember when you were small, she said, and you wanted to have your wedding reception at the castle, with cheese sandwiches and a giant pot of tea?

Yeah, and remember the time I put my hand in a hole in the ground over there and it came out covered in wasps?

You were screaming the park down.

And we went to Casualty and a nurse gave me a Jaffa Cake.

It seems like a lifetime ago, she said, sighing. Sean

54

wasn't even born. I must've been pregnant with him.

I just remember being curious about the hole and putting my foot in and when nothing happened I put my hand in, I said.

Maybe you were expecting a wee mole or something.

Maybe – d'you know what the French word for wasp is?

No. We never got to insects at school, she said.

It's *une guêpe*, pronounced 'gep'. I remember the first time I saw it, I thought it was pronounced 'gweep' and the French teacher was killing himself.

Gweep's a nice word, said Rita.

It's a lovely word.

We stayed there for an hour, both of us drawing comfort from the loch.

I think I need to go home soon, I said. I'm feeling really crap.

*

Brian was stroking his face with a pussy willow stem and giggling. I like this furry stuff, he said. It's lovely.

It's called pussy willow, I said. I got it for Rita for Mother's Day.

Is it real fur, he said, like Agnes?

No, I laughed. It just feels like it. What did you get your mum for Mother's Day?

I got her daffodils but I wish I'd got this furry stuff.

*

Two weeks later, I had a letter from Jana. I could just picture it: Jana, Esther and Abas, all steaming. Music blaring. Every light in the house blazing. Simone coming back from her country-house early, stomping round switching off the lights, calling Jana a slut for seducing her son. Abas hiding in his room.

I had a lump in my throat. Maybe I'd be able to go back after Easter.

Brian phoned on Palm Sunday – he got someone to dial for him, he could read and write but numbers confused him – to say he'd lit a candle and said a prayer for me. He went to Mass with my granny every week. My granny was devout: she'd tutted her way through *The Thornbirds*, and later boasted that my grandad had never seen her without her nightie on. My grandad went to Mass occasionally, to keep the peace.

Rita stopped going when she was sixteen. Sean and I were never christened, one of the few things Rita and Peter agreed about. They were both atheists.

Brian asked me if I'd be going up to the castle next weekend to roll my egg. I'll see how I feel, I said.

Valerie's coming, he said.

*

I sat on the bench and watched Brian hurtling his eggs down the hill, whooping every time. Valerie had bad circulation and her lips were tinged blue. She rolled her eggs gently, leaving them for Brian to retrieve. I'd painted one happy and one sad. I'd given them to Brian to roll. Valerie came and sat beside me, plumping herself down.

So is Brian your uncle then? she said, linking her arm into mine.

Yes, I said, but I don't call him Uncle. He's only six years older than me. More like a big brother really.

I think he's lovely, she said.

He has his moments, I suppose.

Have you got your flask with you for the picnic?

Yes, I've got it in my bag, I said dutifully.

My mum and dad have gone to get the tartan rug from the car.

That's good.

Did you know I got four Easter eggs and a chocolate rabbit?

That'll keep you going for a while, I said.

I ate the ears today. My mum says I've to share the rest. Did you get many yourself?

I got one from my granny and one from my boyfriend.

That's nice. Brian's my boyfriend.

I hope you don't fight.

Not really. I don't think so. No we don't.

I'm glad.

We watched Brian ambling down the hill to collect

the eggs.

I think he's really enjoying himself today, she said. Are you enjoying yourself?

Yes, thanks, I said.

During the picnic, Brian farted and Valerie told him to say 'Excuse Me'. He denied it was him and went in the huff.

Later, when I was lying on the couch he came over and said, I'm sorry about that thing in the park, Helen.

It's okay, I said, but it's polite to say excuse me. You know that.

Excuse me then, he said.

You're excused.

D'you think Valerie will still want to be my girlfriend?

I'm sure she will.

He sat down and put my feet on his lap. I think I'll just stroke these big feet of yours, if you don't mind.

If you want to, I said.

He loved stroking things.

6

Round Window

IF YOU LOOK at yourself through a window, it's not really you it's happening to, it's like watching yourself in a play. Today, 10th May 1984, we're looking through the round window. Rain's spitting on the windows of the health centre, Myra's smiling weakly.

You've got a virus called Coxsackie B4, she says. There have been recent sporadic cases in the west of Scotland. It can take a long time to burn itself out. We'll send you to see a specialist.

She passes me the tissues, her first helpful gesture since the trial began.

I told you I was ill, I say. I've been telling you for months and you didn't believe me! If that locum hadn't come out to see me, you'd never have done viral studies and you still wouldn't believe me. *He* could see I was really ill, he believed me, why couldn't you?!

I'm sorry, Helen, she replies. We doctors aren't gods. I was making what I thought was an accurate clinical judgement. Sometimes, we get it wrong. At least we're on the right track now, aren't we?

(Yes, Myra we're on the right track now, no fucking thanks to you.)

I'm giving you something for the pain and nausea, she says, reaching for her pad. And I'll give you a sick note for the next three months. Her hands twitch and scribble. She's like a giant insect.

As I leave her room, I see that a huge rainbow has come out.

Rita's in the waiting room. She hugs me tightly when I tell her what Myra has said. Everyone's looking at us, wondering what disease the thin girl has. When we get home, I go back to bed and Rita calls Nab to tell him the news.

Nab looked it up in a book at the hospital. He photocopied page 110 and came home from work early with flowers and strawberry tarts.

Coxsackie, he read out loud at my bedside: *an enterovirus first isolated in the town of Coxsackie in New York. Can cause a polio-like illness (without the paralysis) in humans; can cause paralysis and death in young mice.*

At least I'm not a young mouse, I said. Nab sat down on the bed and gave me one of his polar bear hugs.

When Sean got in from school, he galloped up the stairs and burst into my room. I hear you've got the cock-a-leekie virus! he said.

After tea, Rita called my granny to tell her about the diagnosis. I couldn't make out everything she said but I heard 'light at the end of the tunnel'.

The next night, Ivan called me from a payphone in the uni library to see how it had gone with Myra. He said he'd look up enteroviruses and call me back. Half an hour later, he told me that enteroviruses developed in your gut and could affect your muscles and nervous system. I bet I got it when I was working at the Swan Hotel, I said. He started to answer but his money ran out and we got cut off. I waited by the phone, hoping he'd call back but he didn't.

*

Shrouded in my pink candlewick dressing gown, crying with pain. Sean's friends walk past me with embarrassed respect. Square window.

*

Brian's coming on Sunday, Rita said to the grey-faced fixture on the couch. That should cheer you up.

He had asked Rita if I was going to die. Don't worry, he said, she'll go to heaven and heaven's lovely. It's the same as earth but you get less colds.

61

*

I heard Brian tramping up the stairs. My granny had already been up. He put his head round the door, beaming. Hello, how's my favourite niece?! He stood there for a minute before coming over and smothering me in his black mohair arms, planting himself at the side of the bed.

It's lovely to see you, Brian. I love your jumper.

Your granny knitted it for me. How are you, dear?

Well, you know I'm not very well. I have to stay in bed a lot.

He took my hand. Are you coming downstairs later?

Yeah, maybe I'll come down for tea, I said.

I've got a new girlfriend. Her name's Moira.

What happened to Valerie? I thought she was your girlfriend.

Valerie's not well. It's that heart of hers.

Poor Valerie. So what's Moira like?

She's just beautiful, he said, turning round to give Agnes a perfunctory clap on the head. I think I'll go back downstairs now, if that's all right with you?

Can you not stay up here for a bit?

I'm sorry, dear, but I don't want to miss the racing.

He clumped off downstairs and I lay staring at the black strands of mohair and the dent that he'd left in the duvet. Agnes yawned and licked her paws. She jumped off the bed and padded out of the room. Agnes was tired of the sick-bed too.

Clumping feet and padding feet, walking away.

I thought about the unbearable cliché I'd become: an ill young woman with a tortoiseshell cat that sits on her bed throughout her illness.

I decided to go downstairs for ten minutes. I wanted to make the most of us having visitors. I got up and put Ivan's polo neck on over my pyjamas.

I sat on the living room floor hugging my knees, my back clamped against the radiator. The heat was eating up the pain in my spine.

Don't sit so near the radiator, Helen, my granny warned from the couch. It'll dry up your lungs.

My grandad was eating marshmallows and watching the racing. I was jealous of him with no worries, focused on his horse. How are you keeping, dear? he asked. He swivelled round and offered me a sweet. I sank my teeth into the vile pinkness. He cleared his throat and I could hear the *hem hem* travelling up through his gullet. (When you make that *hem hem* noise, d'you ever think it's not really you, but another voice in your head? These are the things you think about when you've got a lot of time.)

I asked my grandad what his horse was called.

He didn't answer.

He's deaf, said Brian. It's called *Swizzle Stick*.

They should name racehorses after illnesses, I said. It'd give ill people a chance to be sporty.

No one was really listening.

You could put your money on *Viral Meningitis* or *Parkinson's Disease*.

That's a terrible thing to say, said Rita from behind her crossword, but she was laughing.

Brian joined me at the radiator and rested his head against my shoulder. His hair smelled of apple shampoo. My hair smelled of illness.

Come away from that radiator, Brian. It's bad for your lungs.

Och, Mum! he tutted. He put his arm round me. Are you all right, dear? His breath smelled of mallows.

I think I'll need to go back upstairs, I said. I feel awful.

D'you want the *Observer* magazine? said Rita.

No thanks, I said, my head's too clamped.

I'll bring tea up if you're not well enough for the table.

Okay, I said.

I trudged back upstairs, still thinking of names for horses. In years to come, *Gulf War Syndrome* could be the favourite at Cheltenham.

7

Marion

12th June 1984

Dear Jana,

Well, they've finally found out what the fuck is wrong with me! I have a weird virus called Coxsackie B4, which is why I've been feeling so ill. Apparently it can take a long time to burn itself out. I'm pleased to report that Myra was a bit sheepish. I'm so RELIEVED they've found out, but I'm worried 'cos I'm still getting worse. I have an Aladdin's Cave of tablets: anti-nausea, muscle relaxants, extra-strong anti-inflammatories. I'm going to see a specialist, just waiting for the appointment – so it doesn't look like I'll be coming back to France for the last term after all.

I've been helping Sean a bit with his 'O' grade revision, though I feel I'm forgetting all my French. I've been re-reading *Candide*. I love Pangloss, he's a cheeky bastard. Also got some Prévert.

Rita and Nab are being great and Ivan's been great too but I'm worried that he'll get fed up with me feeling so crap. I've hardly stayed with him recently. He comes here quite a lot but he must be getting so BORED. He was away on a field-trip at Easter. I am, of course, paranoid about the women who went. He got me a giant Lindt egg.

His band's still on the go, they might be getting a gig at the Halt Bar, which would be brilliant. Other gossip: Rez has a stunning new girlfriend. She's a Swedish drama student and he's head over heels. You know how he always goes for blondes. By the way, Ivan saw Piedro in the union. He was wrapped morosely round some poor girl like a stole. (Has she tasted his omelettes, I wonder?)

The highlight of my social life was rolling eggs at Easter with Brian and his girlfriend Valerie who has Down's Syndrome. She's a sweetheart and has a smile that would bring you back from the brink of suicide. Brian was showing off like hell as usual. We had a picnic in the park with Valerie's parents. It was freezing. I went to Brian's social club about a month ago. They all wanted me to dance but I just didn't have the energy. One woman wants me to teach her French. She says she's got a jotter.

What's your gossip? Still shagging Jean-Paul? Your French must be so good by now. I'm so jealous. Has Esther got into Abas's pants yet? Have you been skating again? And is Simone still bullying poor wee Vincent?

Write SOON, SOON, SOON!

Lots of love, Helen xxx

*

Can't sleep for the clenching pain in my spine and legs. The birds have started. They're like electronic gadgets set on a timer. They start off one by one and you can't switch them off: a pigeon, a woodpecker then the din of the crows. I hate them all. I can't stop thinking about Valerie's blue lips.

I think she will die soon.

*

Square window. *July 1984*

Helen's having her hair cut today! Rita knows someone from the library whose sister-in-law has her own salon. When Marion offered to come to the house and cut Helen's hair, Helen couldn't wait.

She's been rehearsing the conversation with Marion in her head all week. *Can you take about two inches off the bottom and give me a blunt fringe, please?*

And now Marion's late.

Helen's sitting at the window, waiting and waiting. She's getting a metallic headache. Marion has Wednesdays off and said she'd be round at two, but it's half past and she's not here yet. The terrier across the road's sitting up at the window like a cuddly toy, its head poking between the vertical blinds.

Mrs Blonski's coming slowly down the road. She's wearing pink velvet trousers and silver sandals. She always gets dressed up, even just to go to the bank. As she walks past, she pauses and waves to Helen. She's blossomed since her husband died. He used to say their Pakistani neighbours were bringing down the value of the houses. Now Mrs Bhatti and Mrs Blonski are best friends. Helen waves back. She's glad Mr Blonski's dead. He looked like a rapist.

Agnes appears from nowhere and miaows to be let in. When you open the window, she jumps onto the sill, pulling herself up with her front legs. Sometimes, her back legs buckle and you think she's going to fall but she makes it. When she jumps up, the terrier starts yapping soundlessly. Helen has just closed the window when Marion draws up in a gold Ford Capri. She gets up to answer the door. Her legs have strange buzzing feelings in them.

Marion is Amazonian, a gust of 'Hi's and 'Sorry I'm late's. She is plastered in make-up and Opium. You can smell that she smokes. Helen offers her a cup of tea. No thanks, she says, I just had a coffee at my sister's. Helen gratefully sinks back down into the couch. Marion sits down beside her. Now what would you like done today?

Helen's palms are sweating. Can you take about two inches off the bottom and give me a blunt fringe, please?

Marion puts her hands through Helen's hair. Maybe we could layer it through at the top? she suggests. It's very thick.

I'd rather not. I don't like my hair layered. I just want it tidied up. It feels like a heavy wig.

Marion seems slightly miffed. D'you think you could

wet it for me? It's easier to cut when it's so thick. Also, d'you mind putting the cat out? I'm not keen on them.

I'll just be a minute, says Helen. She scoops Agnes up and puts her out the back. She gets dizzy from bending down too quickly. Sorry, Agnes, she whispers, that scary woman doesn't want you in the house. I'll call you as soon as she's gone, I promise.

She goes into the bathroom and fills the sink. She dips her head in slowly, still dizzy. She has the taste in her mouth that you get before a nosebleed. She doesn't want layers. She wants to lie down. She wants Marion to go away.

When her hair's wet enough, she turbans her head and goes back into the lounge. Marion has installed a kitchen chair in the centre of the room. Helen sits down. Marion's a bit rough when she dries her hair but it's nice to have her head touched. Helen can smell the nicotine from her fingers.

How long is it since you had it cut? asks Marion.

About three months, says Helen. I went to the Hair Hut but I got such a bad headache when I was there I couldn't even wait for them to blow-dry it. I had to get a taxi home. It's great you could come to the house to do it.

How are you keeping now?

To be honest, I feel like I've got a new symptom every day. The headaches are awful, like a helmet you can't take off.

A couple of the women that come into the salon have got it, says Marion. It's terrible – you're so young.

Now that they've diagnosed the Coxsackie, I've to see a neurologist, says Helen. My appointment's in a month. I was lucky to get one so soon.

Marion doesn't speak for the rest of the haircut. Helen is relieved that she is exempt from the usual ARE YOU OFF TODAY?/ARE YOU GOING OUT ON SATURDAY NIGHT? (But since you asked, No, I've stopped going out and, Yes, I'm actually off every day.)

Helen wonders why Marion's arms aren't killing her.

When Marion's finished drying Helen's hair, she says, Maybe you can think about going short next time. It'd be less tiring for you to manage.

I'll think about it says, Helen. How much do I owe you?

A fiver'll be fine.

Helen goes and gets the money from her wallet. Her wallet's barely been used. It was a Christmas present from Peter (it came with a matching bag). It still smells of leather. She pays Marion. Thanks very much. It feels much lighter, she says.

I can come back anytime you want. Here's my number.

When Marion's gone, Helen can still smell her Opium. She goes to the back door and calls on Agnes. You can come back now, Agnes, it's safe, Hitler's gone.

Agnes doesn't appear. Helen wishes she'd come back in. She lies down on the couch for a bit. She wants to hoover up the hair before Rita gets back. She closes her eyes.

stranger   What did you do today?

helen   I got my hair cut in the living room and hoovered up the hair with the dust-buster.

She hears Agnes miaowing to be let in. She gets up to open the window. Come on, she says. Come upstairs with me and keep me company. I'll give you a mint.

Agnes has quirky tastes for a cat. She loves garlic sausage and if you give her an extra strong Trebor mint she acts like it's catnip – she licks the mint, puts her head on the floor and tries to somersault. (*Agnes dies, by the way – riddled with cancer – but don't tell Helen, she's got enough on her plate!*)

8

Bob

THE SPECIALIST LOOKED like Bob Monkhouse. He had Myra's letter in front of him. I tried to see what she'd written, if she'd admitted that she'd fucked up until the Coxsackie diagnosis.

You're very thin, said Bob. Have you got a boyfriend?

Yes, I said, but what's that got to do with the price of bread? (Into myself.)

He listened as I listed my symptoms: exhaustion, severe muscle pain, weakness, dizziness, skull-crushing headaches, palpitations, stomach cramps, nausea, diarrhoea. (Do you really want me to go on, Bob?)

We're going to do some tests, he said. The Coxsackie virus can trigger a syndrome called *blah-de-blah-de-blah*. This may be what you have. We don't know much about it. We'll need to do a muscle biopsy and some other tests. Go outside and wait. Thank you. Goodbye.

I went back to Rita in the waiting room. He looks like Bob Monkhouse, I said.

We waited for almost an hour, staring at the plastic orange chairs and the paint peeling off the walls. A junior doctor wearing a polkadot tie appeared. He wasn't much older than me.

I'm just going to take some blood. Come this way.

Another room. Legs shaking.

He drew my blood, put it into three different tubes and labelled them.

Do you know what's wrong with me? I asked.

He smiled at me but didn't answer.

Arched window. *Muscle biopsy, early September 1984*
I lay on the trolley and gripped the nurse's hand. The surgeon and student stood over me, green and gowned.

Elegant legs, said the surgeon. We're going to do a needle biopsy. You'll just feel a little prick and then some pressure.

I shut my eyes.

He checked the area was numb and cut into my leg. I could feel the blood dripping down the parts that weren't anaesthetised. Something pressed hard, down to my bone. I gripped tighter onto the nurse.

Hard then nothing.

Well done, Andrew, you've just done your first muscle biopsy! the surgeon announced triumphantly.

(Yes, well done, Andrew! A fanfare of trumpets for Andrew, please! I don't really mind that you used me as a guinea pig.)

The surgeon patted my arm. I'm going to do another one. Nothing to worry about.

More pressure. More skilled.

They gave me those stitches that melt away. I was limping for ages. Andrew's scar still gets in the way when I'm waxing my legs.

I think he was a virgin.

The yellow outpatient card on the kitchen pin-board had become my social calendar. My next engagement was an EMG – an electromyelogram. A needle attached to an oscilloscope was inserted into the muscle on the back of my arm and I had to move my finger up and down 'til my arm ached.

*

It's the beginning of October 1984, a new term! We're looking through the round window.

The Junior Honours students are waiting for the Head of Modern Languages to address them. They've all done their year abroad. They're grown up now. *But where's Helen?! We can't see Helen!*

That's because she's at home in bed. Or maybe she's on the couch.

Her symptoms have signed a lease behind her back and moved in permanently. They like living in her muscle tissue. It's nice and warm there.

Ivan comes to stay some weekends. He studies in the spare room. He writes essays on liposomes and leaves behind half-eaten oranges. It's his final year.

Jana's got a new flatmate, Beryl, who's doing French and English. She's a busty punk with a harelip, who loves cooking. She's an amateur opera singer.

She sounds like good fun, I say.

It's like living with fucking Puccini, Jana replies.

A week before my twenty-first, I was summoned to Bob's consulting room for the second time. He was expressionless as I sat down on the orange chair.

You have a whole range of abnormalities, he said. Your muscles aren't producing energy normally.

Why not? I said.

We think you have ME, *myalgic encephalomyelitis*. It's a post-viral syndrome, triggered by the Coxsackie virus, in your case. There's no cure and it can last for five years. We're doing some clinical trials which we would like you to take part in. We'll be in touch. Can you ask your mother to come in now?

I came out and Rita went in. Someone had left a *Daily*

Record on the chair next to mine. I picked it up and looked at the front-page photo of Princess Diana with her six-week-old baby.

When Rita came out of Bob's room, her eyes were watering.

On the way home in the car, I hoped we'd crash and that I'd be killed instantly and Rita would walk away without a scratch. I kept thinking of the David Bowie song *Five Years*:... steady drums, louder and louder and louder... high, violiny bit.

*

Helen has a diagnosis! *Hurrah! Hurrah! Hurrah!* She has *blah-de-blah-de-blah,* it's official! She's got Malingerer's Elbow! She's chronically fatigued! She's a yuppie with flu!

Whatever your point of view, she's fucked.

9

New Blood

TERRIFIED. GETTING WORSE. No one can help me. Even my hands feel ill.

Myra's given me amitriptyline for the muscle pain. Amitriptyline's really an antidepressant but in low doses acts as an anti-inflammatory. I'm scared it will make me artificially happy. I've dried up, I have no saliva and my eyes feel like stones – a side effect of the drug. When I tell Ivan, he says, You're losing all your juices.

*

Helen's twenty-one today. She's opted for a quiet do. In fact, she's decided to stay in bed! Let's join her on this happy day.

Her friends and family have come to her bedside, bearing gifts.

Jana's given her a red Yves Saint Laurent lipstick. Rita and Nab have given her a compact stereo. Ivan's given her a dressing gown from Miss Selfridge – a print of white cotton covered in red kisses – and a bottle of Rive Gauche. Sean's given her *Flaubert's Parrot*, Julian Barnes' new book. Granny and Grandad have given her £25. Brian's given her a table with squint legs that he made at woodwork. Peter's sent her a huge basket of Body Shop goodies. She has lots of cards with a dual message: *Congratulations on the key of the door! Get well soon!*

She thanks everyone politely. Her arms and legs are injected with poison. She doesn't have the strength to peel an orange.

Rita has made beef stroganoff (the cows haven't gone mad yet) and fresh cream meringues. Helen has her birthday meal on a tray in bed. She has a sip of champagne. Jana sits with her and makes her put on her new lipstick. Helen feels like a clown, a grotesque invalid wearing bright red lipstick and titanium earrings. She's had her hair cut short and layered (Marion came round last week).

Jana chats away about her dissertation on Zola and who her flatmates are sleeping with. Helen interrupts her quietly, I wish I was dead, Jana.

When Nab comes up with the meringues, Jana and Helen aren't saying much.

After the party, Ivan gives Jana a lift back up to Glasgow. They feel so sad and helpless about Helen. They just want her back.

Later, they comfort each other in Jana's bed.

*

I can't take this for another five years. How can you feel so
ill and not be dying?

*

I wish we lived in a house without stairs. Sean gallops up
and down them all day, his friends too. I don't know how
they do it.

*

Christmas passes and she barely notices. She is dipped
in nausea. She counts the number of cards they get with
penguins – eight.

Ivan stays for a few nights, but he goes back to Dundee
for New Year.

Richard's parents have invited everyone next door for
Hogmanay. Helen sags into a red cord bean-bag. She's
wearing her new dress from Miss Selfridge. It has sweeps of
purple and beige paisley pattern and a huge forties collar. It
goes down to her feet. She has fawn suede boots to match.
People keep coming up to her and asking how she is. Clare
looks at her with pity.

She feels swallowed up in paisley swirls.

Heather and Archie are there, their neighbours on the other side. Heather is pregnant after two miscarriages. She is thirty-six. She doesn't care if it's a girl or a boy. Helen tells her she'd like to knit something for the baby when her arms are less weak.

After the bells, Helen goes straight home. Rita wants to go with her but Helen says she'll be fine.

At home she lies down on the sofa in the dark and cries her eyes out. Afterwards, she puts the Christmas tree lights on and makes hot chocolate. After the hot chocolate, she lies on the floor and listens to Nana Mouskouri on Nab's headphones.

*

Helen's having one of her conversations. Her face is swollen from crying. She probably won't mind if we eavesdrop.

helen   What are you doing today?

stranger   I'm going to see *Dance With a Stranger* after work. What about you?

helen   Oh, I'm getting new plasma. I'm bored with the stuff I've got, so I thought I'd get some new stuff. It's all the rage.

stranger   Where do you get it?

helen   You get it on the NHS. I'm taking part in a

clinical trial. I have a mystery illness called *blah-de-blah-de-blah*.

stranger   Why's it called *blah-de-blah-de-blah*?

helen   Well, it's controversial, nobody really understands it, except for the people who've got it. Bob, my doctor, thinks the new plasma might flush it away. My own antibodies *might* be making me ill. The new plasma will be free of antibodies and might make me better for a while. My muscles should feel less weak.

stranger   I see. Well, good luck.

helen   Thanks. Enjoy the film.

stranger   You too, enjoy the clinical trial.

Everyone's hopes are pinned on the plasma exchange. *Out with the old, in with the new! Light at the end of the tunnel! Keep your chin up!*

February 1985

It was like being hooked up to a dialysis machine. Your plasma was separated from the blood coming out of your right arm, new plasma was spun in, and the blood went back into your left arm. The new plasma was from a Polish

81

donor. The technician told me I had great veins and that I might feel faint during the proceedings.

It took three hours. He told me what Highers his son was doing and what colour of carpets him and his wife were getting for their new house. When it was over he said, That's you, you're half Polish now. He handed me a see-through bag of my old plasma. It was the colour of dirty goldfish water. A porter wheeled me back to the ward and delivered me to Bob. I had the bag of old plasma on my lap.

How are you feeling? the game show host asked.

Like a rag doll with a brain tumour, I replied, handing him my old antibodies.

Dinner was a choice of scrambled egg or mince. I forced down some scrambled egg and threw up later in the shower, crouched down on the hospital tiles, crying onto the Pears soap. The sick swirled around the gleaming drain before clogging it up like sawdust. I had to press it down into the holes with my fingers. I didn't want the other patients to see any traces.

The girl in the next bed was called Fizza. She was a medical student. She also had the mystery illness and was getting new plasma. She'd missed most of her second year. We'd had similar symptoms but she'd been diagnosed more quickly because her dad was a doctor and believed her. I asked her if her dreams were more vivid and violent since she got ill. She said it was like being at the cinema. I told her I was always dreaming I was being chopped up or that I was chopping other people up until there was nothing left of their bones.

We shared a room with another two women. Karen had lupus and Fiona had myasthenia gravis. They were getting new plasma too. Karen's face looked like it had been finely sand-papered, and Fiona's right eye drooped. She'd been diagnosed after having her baby. We wondered if we'd all be related after getting our new plasma.

In the evenings, the television room was commandeered by old women wearing slippers with circles of pink fur at the ankles. They had no visitors and watched *High Road* with watery eyes.

Fizza's visitors were sad and serene. Her mum wore Asian clothes and sat by the bed knitting her sadness into a bright pink cardigan. The cardigan was to cheer Fizza up. Her wee brother Kashif was well behaved and polite. Her dad was wearing a tweed suit and had sad eyes. He smiled at me and asked how long I'd been ill. I hope the plasmapheresis will help both you young girls, he said. You will be back to your studies in no time!

My visitors seemed rowdy next to Fizza's.

The first night, Rita chatted with Fizza's dad about the prevalence of Coxsackie B4 in the west of Scotland while Nab padded around the corridors looking for a nurse to put the Asian lilies in a vase. Ivan had nicknamed me Looby Loo when I said I felt like a rag doll. Sean sat on my bed, moping because the girl he fancied had got off with someone else at the Owners–Occupiers Association disco. Brian gulped his way through the Lucozade.

Fizza's mum didn't speak, she just kept knitting. Brian went over and told her that his mum was knitting him a jumper too. His mouth was orange and fuzzy from the Lucozade.

At eight-thirty on the dot, Fizza's family said goodbye to her quietly in Urdu. Kashif smiled at me shyly as he left.

The nurse had to remind my family it was closing time. Ivan kissed me and said, Bye, Looby. Time to go back in your basket! Brian couldn't stop laughing. Did you hear what he said to you, Helen? It's time to go back in your basket! Did you hear him?!

Fizza and Fiona and Karen thought Ivan was gorgeous. The nurses thought the orange lilies were gorgeous, but they were like hallucinations on my bedside cabinet. They were too bright and hurt my head.

On my third afternoon, Jana and Ivan came in with Joe. They'd been out the night before and Joe had got drunk and told Beryl she looked like a haggis. She had wept most of the night. Jana had told me before that the kids in France where she had taught on her year out had slagged her rotten because of her lip. I wished Joe hadn't come in.

Two minutes after they'd left, Ivan ran back. I miss you, Looby, he said softly. I really miss you. I just wanted to tell you.

He lifted my hand and kissed it.

I wish you could stay, I said, but you better go, the nurses'll chase you.

He kissed my floppy hand again and left.

I had another two plasma sessions with the man with the new carpets, and Bob had put me on scary immunosuppressants – prednisolone and azathioprine – to reduce the new antibodies I was producing, and huge unswallowable potassium pills. Possible side effects were an increased appetite, a moon face and excess body hair.

Helen can't get enough to eat. She laps up bowls of cock-a-leekie soup like a greedy cartoon cat (with three slices of bread and butter!). She develops a craving for cream eggs, especially the ones wrapped in green foil. Her face grows round as the steroids circulate in her blood, protecting her new plasma. She thinks of them as minders, even if they are a bit toxic. For the first time in her life, she has acne.

She has to go back to the hospital weekly to have her blood monitored. One time they tell her that her white cell count is dangerously low, a result of the azathioprine therapy. Make sure she doesn't get a cold, the polkadot boy doctor warns Rita, it could be dangerous. That's a hell of a responsibility, Rita replies.

They reduce the drugs gradually. Helen can't stand the texture of chocolate in her mouth anymore or the smell of Pears soap.

*

The new Polish plasma had done fuck all. Rag doll dragged round the block by an Alsatian, spat out on the carpet.

stranger   What did you do today?

me   I had a shower and made a cup of tea.

stranger   Is that all?

me   I tried to wash my hair but my arms were too weak to lather.

stranger   That's a shame. Are you able to read to pass the time?

me   Sometimes, but my arms get exhausted holding the book. They feel like they're burning. And my head feels like it's being sawed... I'm reading *The Naked Civil Servant* just now. It makes me laugh. Quentin said he'd get really upset if the kettle wasn't pointing the right way.

stranger   They say laughter's the best medicine.

me   You must think I'm really boring.

stranger   Yes, but it's not your fault, is it?

me   I've been invited to Rachel's twenty-first but I can't go. I'm fed up not being able to go to things. I feel like Cinderella.

stranger   It must be so frustrating... [*searching for another cliché*]... after all, these should be the best days of your life.

*

We were all guilty of clichés.

Have to get worse before you get better.

Tomorrow's another day.

Light at the end of the tunnel was the favourite, but my symptoms continued to synchronise themselves in a vicious kaleidoscopic pattern and all I could see was black.

I felt afraid on my own and would listen for Rita's key in the door if I wasn't sleeping. She had most afternoons off from work. She'd bring me up lunch on the blue tray and tell me the gossip from the library. She'd massage my back and legs with deep heat treatments. I constantly smelled of camphor.

My daywear had long ago blurred into nightwear. Sweatshirts and leggings for all occasions. Occasions being:

1. Sleeping. Eating. Having shower. Having bath. Having to sit on toilet to brush teeth 'cos legs so weak. Having to change hands halfway 'cos arms so weak.
2. Crying. Wanting to be dead. Praying even though atheist.

87

3. Waiting for phone calls, visitors, letters.

4. Waiting. Waiting. Waiting.

5. Fantasising about: going to work wearing a suit from Next/being on honeymoon with Ivan/dancing, dancing, dancing/inter-railing/running on the spot in a red tracksuit like the athlete in the Lucozade advert.

6. Looking at photos of other self in other life. Tracing finger over old self, a smiling girl in a hockey team. My hockey stick lay like a corpse in the back of my cupboard, club foot poking through my clothes, reminding me of my frailty. I had tried to throw it out twice, but Nab had brought it back in.

7. Crocheting white squares. I'd started a baby blanket for Heather.

8. Conjugating French verbs when my head wasn't too skewered, so I didn't forget.

I listened to the radio a lot. There was one DJ I hated. He was always going parachuting or skiing and he took it all for granted. I liked the shipping forecasts and the fishing news. The price of whiting soothed me. I also liked classical music except when it got trumpety and bombastic – then I wanted to kill the people in the orchestra for being so military and noisy. If I moved the radio diagonally and bent the aerial all the way back, I could get French radio stations at night-time, hissing and fizzling.

Sean always listened to The Smiths in the mornings.

When I asked him to turn it down Rita said I had to cut him some slack.

In the evenings if I felt well enough, I'd go downstairs. I liked the social aspect of being in the living room. On Thursdays, I watched *Top of the Pops* and wondered where they got the energy to sing and dance.

I started watching wildlife programmes. I could enjoy the images without having to follow the plot (like an old woman in a nursing home, without the pink circles of fur).

stranger	What did you do today?
me	I watched a documentary about sea horses.
stranger	What did you learn?
me	I learned that male sea horses give birth by spurting out hundreds of bright red eggs, and that they are antisocial and don't like their neighbours.

At the weekends, I would sit clamped against the radiator or lie on the couch while Sean and his friends watched videos. Sometimes Ivan was there. The highlight of Saturday was watching *Blind Date*. I would fantasise about being chosen and worried sick about being sent on a date where you had to walk a lot.

Sean said I should write to Jimmy Saville: Dear Jim, Please can you fix it for me to be healthy? I'm twenty-one and live in Scotland.

I could see myself sitting in the television studio, with the medal round my neck, grinning idiotically at the audience. Rita and Nab would run on with tears in their eyes, thanking Jim for the miracle.

*

Sometimes, after school, Sean brings through the magnetic chess set. He sits on the bed and lays out the pieces. Pawns are always getting lost in the blankets. Helen's never really liked chess apart from moving the horses in L-shapes. She doesn't try and Sean wins every game, but it passes the time.

*

Back to see Bob.

He looked more plastic than ever. I told him how I was feeling.

Chin up, he said. We're doing another trial in a few months with evening primrose oil.

Goody, goody gumdrops, I said. I can't wait. (Into myself.)

Afterwards, we went to the hospital canteen. Rita was dying for a cigarette. She'd started smoking again. While she queued for tea, I asked the old man at the next table if he needed help opening his sandwiches. One of his eyes was sewn shut and he had golliwog badges on his lapels.

That's very good of you, hen, he said.

I opened the cheese and pickled onion sandwich by stabbing the cellophane with the end of a spoon. Thank you very much, hen. You're very kind, he said.

I liked feeling useful.

Rita came back with tea that was far too strong, and synthetic cream doughnuts. She asked me if I still felt like going to Next.

If you think we can park really near and if I can sit down in the shop, I replied.

I loved shopping with Rita. She was like a dragon slaying away all the junk to get to the bargains. I wanted to buy a dress for Ivan's graduation. I'd seen a sleeveless polkadot dress in their catalogue.

On the way to Next I kept thinking about the wee man and his golliwog badges.

Imagine him saving up his marmalade labels and sending away for the badges, I said to Rita. He must have had the whole collection on his lapels.

Poor old soul, she replied. He probably lives on his own if he had no one at the hospital with him. It doesn't bear thinking about, does it?

No, it doesn't, I said.

*

Square window. *June 1985. Helen's in the dining room, looking at the birds in the garden.*

stranger   What are you doing?

helen   I'm watching the birds. The bastards wake me up all the time and I can't get back to sleep.

stranger   You look very sad.

helen   I *am* sad. It's Ivan's graduation today and I felt too ill to go. And it's raining.

stranger   It's a shame you can't be there.

helen   He'll be so handsome in his graduation robe and I should be with him, wearing my polkadot dress – afterwards, they're going to the Ubiquitous Chip for dinner and I'll be stuck here counting rooks and crows.

stranger   What's the difference between a rook and a crow?

helen   A rook's a kind of crow – a gregarious Eurasian crow to be precise. They nest up high and are very noisy.

stranger   How do you know?

helen   I saw it in a documentary.

stranger   So what's a raven then?

helen   It's a large carrion-eating crow.

stranger   I see... so when will you see Ivan again?

helen   He's coming here at the weekend to watch *Live Aid*.

stranger   At least that's something for you to look forward to.

me   Rez and him are going to Greece for two weeks in September. Then he's going to Dundee for a post-graduate course. I'll never see him again.

stranger   I'm sure that's not true. By the way, how's the blanket? I see you've been crocheting.

me   It's only half finished and the baby's due next month, but it's boring as well as tiring. I was going to knit something, but I couldn't be bothered with all the 'knitting two backwards' stuff. Crocheting needs less concentration.

stranger   It's good to have a project, it gives you a goal.

me   I suppose so, but white gets grubby so easily. It'll look second-hand.

stranger   Well, it's the thought that counts, and you could always wash it. Oh, and before you go, I was just wondering, what's a jackdaw?

me   A jackdaw's a small grey-headed crow, noted for its inquisitiveness.

*

I wish a plane would crash into the house when everyone's out. Rita and Nab have got insurance. They'd be okay. I heard Rita crying in the toilet last night.

*

I love the sun. It burns up the pain in my muscles. I've been lying in the garden all week. Brian can't stand the heat. My God, he says, it's like Alicante here today.

I've painted my toenails red.

*

Back to see Bob.

He wanted me in his evening primrose trial. I should have been honoured – evening primrose oil costs a fortune. Bob explained that it contains an essential fatty acid called GLA that can inhibit inflammation, boost the immune system and improve circulation. Essential fatty acids have to be taken through diet as they are not manufactured in the body. He told me cheerfully that evening primrose oil had helped people with multiple sclerosis and eczema, and gave me a note for the hospital pharmacy. He also gave me a diary to record how I was feeling. I was to go back in a few months.

The pharmacist gave me two huge grey canisters. I opened them in the Red Cross port-a-cabin cafe. They were packed with translucent yellow capsules with a hospital smell. I had to take six a day. I hoped it was the real thing and not the placebo.

When I got home there were postcards came from Jana and Ivan. Jana was in the States, travelling round with an old friend. Ivan was in Greece but wished I was there. I pinned them up beside Sean's card. He was in Boston for two weeks with Peter.

Rita and Nab had a September weekend dinner party for people Nab worked with. I didn't feel up to joining them. I came downstairs when they were having coffee and felt like a child, allowed to join the adults as a treat. Heather had brought four-week-old Zoe over. She was scrawny with a rash. I lied and said she was lovely. She squirmed in my arms like a ginger kitten. I was scared I'd drop her. I joked she'd probably be five by the time I'd finished crocheting the blanket. Heather asked how I was and I told her about the yellow capsules.

*

Can't get back to sleep for the whistling and warbling and screeching. In a few hours there will be high heels on the pavement going past the house to the train station.

My family will be getting up.

Car doors will be slamming.

People with real lives will be doing real things.

10

Halloween

WE'RE LOOKING THROUGH the round window. *Helen's been ill for two years now, can you believe it?! How time flies!*

Rita and Nab have ordered her a double bed. They think she should have a bigger bed since she spends so much time in it.

Sean's started Glasgow Uni. He's studying psychology and politics. He's staying at home his first year. Helen would miss him so much if he left.

Ivan's gone back to Dundee to start his MSc.

At Halloween, I dressed up as an invalid and lay on the couch to welcome the other guisers.

Mrs Bhatti's grandson came round, chaperoned by his mother who had a long Rapunzel plait and too much mascara. She was separated from her husband. The story was he'd stabbed her because she wouldn't move to Karachi.

The wee boy was wearing a bin bag over his school uniform. He started to recite *To A Mouse* the minute he was in the door. His voice was shaking and he got quieter and quieter with every word. By the third verse you could barely hear him. Rita told him he'd done enough, he could stop. He looked like he was going to cry.

Brian was in charge of handing out the apples and oranges. When we'd finished clapping, he solemnly gave the wee boy a handful of monkey nuts and said, That was lovely. Would you like an apple too? The wee boy nodded and Brian handed him an apple like it was an Olympic medal. Then he said, Would you like some chocolate? The wee boy nodded and Brian put a handful of mini Mars bars into his plastic bag. He turned to me and said, Have I given him enough?

We'd fallen out earlier because I was leaving the broken shells in the bowl with the rest of the nuts. Don't do that Helen! he'd said, painstakingly picking out the old shells. You can't get the good ones if you do that! But I'd kept doing it and he'd told me to fuck off before locking himself in the bathroom and giving himself a row. When he came out he said he was sorry for 'squaring' and he wouldn't do it again. Where did you hear that word? Rita'd asked him. At my centre, he said. Martin stole Donny's girlfriend and Donny told him to fuck off. Well, said Rita, Donny's very rude to use that language and I don't want to hear it in this house again.

For the rest of the evening his presentation of apples

and oranges and mini Mars bars was flawless. Before Rita took him home, he hugged us all and said again he was sorry for squaring.

Ivan was supposed to phone at nine. The last of the guisers had gone and the minutes peeled away, but the phone didn't ring. By quarter to ten I couldn't stand it anymore and rang his flat but the phone rang back with the bleak, distant tones you get when you know no one's going to answer. He was going to a fancy dress party at the Art School. He was dressing up as a wolf. I imagined some art student tart unzipping his costume, *My, what a big cock you've got...*

He was coming at the weekend. I couldn't wait. I hadn't seen him for a whole month. The last time he'd visited he'd taken me for a drive up the loch. When we were feeding the swans he'd said, You're too pretty to be ill.

So if I was ugly, being ill wouldn't matter?

That's not what I meant, he said.

A hundred years ago it would have been romantic to be ill, I said – I'd be in a sanatorium in the Alps and I'd sit in a wicker chair and write you heartbreaking letters.

And you'd be spitting up blood in a clean white hanky, and the day you died I wouldn't get to you in time, and a rosy-cheeked nurse would run across the lawn with tears in her eyes.

And you'd fall in love with the rosy-cheeked nurse whose huge breasts would be bursting out of her crisp uniform.

He'd laughed.

On the way home, we'd gone to the Swan Hotel for tea and biscuits. They'd changed the decor and had new swan-shaped salt and peppers with intertwining necks. I'd looked out leadenly at Ben Lomond, wondering how I'd ever managed to carry such heavy trays back and forward – three summers in a row.

I'd watched Ivan come back from the toilet, weaving between the tables, so lovely and healthy and sure of himself. I could make jokes about Alpine nurses but I could never bring myself to ask him about the other women, the women I was sure he had one night stands with. He didn't even bother bringing condoms anymore.

I was hardly in a position to object.

When she hears Ivan's car crunch into the drive she gets up. She doesn't want to be in bed when he arrives. She's wearing lipgloss and new leggings. When he comes upstairs she's sitting on the side of the bed. He opens the door. She gets up and falls into him, leaning on him 'til her legs tire. She takes his hand and sits down again.

I like you with your glasses, she says. You haven't worn them for ages. They're sexy in a geeky way.

I was too knackered to put my lenses in, he says.

D'you like my new bed? she asks. Maybe you can sleep beside me tonight instead of in the spare room.

Maybe, he says.

He looks exhausted.

*

He'd slept beside me in the new bed and it had been delicious just pressing next to him in the dark. I'd told him how much I'd missed him and asked if he'd missed me.

Yes, but things have been hectic.

I would love things to be hectic, I said. I can't remember what it feels like.

I know, he said, stroking my hair.

How was the Halloween party?

All right.

Just all right?

Yeah. There was one guy there who was a pain in the arse. He kept saying that his favourite toy when he was wee was a sheep's neck bone painted green and black. He wouldn't shut up about it. Typical art student. He wasn't even dressed up.

What about you, did you enjoy being a wolf? I said.

It was too hot and itchy.

Did you huff and puff and blow any houses down?

No, but I gobbled up Little Red Riding Hood.

Is that why you didn't phone me?

Don't be silly! I already told you, I didn't get away from the lab 'til after nine. It was hectic.

He kissed my ear.

Don't be sad, Looby. I missed you, I wished you were there. Honest I did.

I hope so, I said.

It'd taken me ages to fall asleep and he'd woken me up in the middle of the night, sleep-talking. (*The plants are coming to get us!*) I'd teased him in the morning and told him he'd been moaning about a girl with a red hood.

At Guy Fawkes, Richard's parents had a firework display for the kids in the back garden. (His wee sister was only nine. His parents'd had a late baby to save their marriage.) I sat on the kitchen step, blanketed in Nab's sheepskin. The children were writing their names with sparklers. I wrote Ivan's name and it melted into the air before it was formed. I'd wanted him to come back this weekend, but he was writing an essay on leprosy and armadillos. You shouldn't have left it 'til the last minute, I'd said, and then you could've come, couldn't you?

We're not all like you, you wee swot.

I'm not a wee swot, I said, I just don't leave things 'til the last minute. (I knew I was using the present tense. I should've been using the past.)

He'd told me to dry my eyes.

From nowhere, I suddenly missed my father: he was holding my arm as I held a sparkler, guiding me to make shimmery zigzags.

When I went home I could see funny outlines on the ceiling for hours afterwards. My eyes always did this now after bright lights – like your retinas were hanging onto an image for too long.

*

Back to bed after lunch, I was thinking about a horse I might have killed when I was twelve: the riding school teachers were scary twin brothers with black fringes, who shouted at you when you couldn't do a rising trot. I stopped going after I accidentally fed Basil (a handsome chestnut) a plastic bag. I'd been feeding him sugar from a sandwich bag and he'd eaten the bag too. At the time he'd seemed unscathed, but I'd been too scared to go back the next week in case he was dead.

About four o'clock, Rita brought me up a cup of tea and a mini Swiss roll covered in chocolate.

Thanks, I said. I love these mini rolls. I could eat a whole packet.

So could I, she said, but they're so fattening. It'll take more than yoga to shift the calories.

I was thinking about trying some yoga, I said. I found your old book with the guy in the purple leotard who looks constipated.

I'd forgotten I had that. It must be falling to bits.

I sellotaped up the spine, I said.

Well, make sure you're careful and don't overdo it.

I thought the stretching positions might be good.

You need to learn to breathe properly before you can benefit from yoga. You should really try to meditate first.

I can't meditate, I said, it's impossible. I can't empty my head. There's always something cluttering it up. Today

103

I was thinking about that time I fed a horse a plastic bag. D'you remember?

It wouldn't have done it any harm, said Rita. They've got stomachs like iron.

How d'you know that they've got stomachs like iron?

I just assume they do.

I laughed. That's the kind of thing that Granny would say.

Well, they say we all turn into our mothers, don't they?

I don't mind turning into you but I wouldn't want to turn into Granny.

Right, I'm going into the garden for a bit if you want me. I'm going to rake up the leaves.

It's a shame about Ivan's granny, isn't it?

Yes, he was saying she might have Alzheimer's.

She keeps over-watering the plants and she tried to boil potatoes in the kettle.

He's quite close to her, isn't he? said Rita.

He is, and I can't help feeling jealous that she'll take him away from me. I hardly see him as it is.

I'm sure he'll manage to divide himself. It's not as if he's not going to be the one looking after her, is it?

I suppose not, I said. D'you think I'm being selfish?

Well, it's easy to be a bit self-focused when you're ill for a long time. It's not so much selfish.

Okay. Thanks again for the tea.

On her way downstairs Rita shouted up, I don't think

you should be listening to Leonard Cohen. He's not exactly uplifting, is he?

*

Today her arms and legs are being eaten by moths. (So much for the yellow capsules.)

The Tree and the Salutation of the Sun are out of the question. She likes the eye exercises and the Rabbit (you just kneel). She can do the Fish up to the part where you have to lift your legs. Her favourite is the one where you lie still and pretend you're dead.

After her yoga class she distracts herself by looking through the arched window at the athletic moments in her life:

1. Tap-dancing in a black leotard and black shoes: *I'm a pink toothbrush, you're a blue toothbrush, have we met somewhere before?!* Rita used to sew sequins onto her costumes.
2. Doing walk-overs and crabs in the back garden with Rachel. They were both in love with Nadia Comaneci.
3. Eight mile sponsored walk with the Brownies. The girl she was holding hands with threw up macaroni cheese.
4. Running for a bus at secondary school. They never sent enough. At four o'clock the whole school would run to the back gates and you'd try to cram yourself onto a

bus. You'd get lifted off your feet in the scuffle of wet duffel coats and Adidas bags.

5.   Scoring a goal out of fear in a hockey match after the teacher shouted at her at half-time for not playing well.

6.   Climbing the Ben with Richard, getting stoned at the top. By the time they got down they looked like they had mumps, they were so badly bitten by midges.

7.   Inter-railing with Rachel. They lugged their rucksacks from Glasgow to London to Paris to Nice to Geneva to Innsbruck to Munich to Wiesbaden. And back again.

8.   Marching with thousands of other students. *Maggie! Maggie! Maggie! Out! Out! Out!*

9.   Sex with Ivan in Zakynthos. He lay on the beach looking at the moon while she fucked him. He was drunk and wanted to throw his contact lenses in the sea because he had sand in his eyes.

10. Sex with Ivan.

11. Sex with Ivan.

12. Sex with Ivan.

Rita must be burning rubbish. Helen can smell the smoke from the garden. She crumples up her athletic moments and throws them on the fire, and the memory of sex with Ivan curls up in the smoke and disappears.

*

Helen may be moth-eaten but she still has her uses: her friends and brother sit at the end of her bed and ask her to fix their relationships.

Richard is having doubts about Clare. They've been engaged for six months. Helen thinks he could do better. (Clare is very sexy but she isn't bright enough for him. She just wants someone who'll keep her in Benetton sweaters and holidays in Corfu, and she knows he'll inherit his dad's carpet business.) Helen says she doesn't know how he can be with someone who reads the *Daily Mail,* but Richard defends her, saying, She only reads it 'cos her parents read it. She's really got a heart of gold.

Sean fancies Nellie, a girl in his psychology class. She smiles at him a lot but he doesn't know if this means anything. He wants to know what he should do. He's too shy to ask her out. She's always with a posse of admirers. He sat in the Reading Room for two hours one Friday, hoping she'd come in.

Jana's sleeping with a guy in her Rimbaud tutorial. His girlfriend's at Lancaster University. Jana feels guilty, but not that guilty. It's just a fling, she says. Anyway, I'm going to Barcelona next term.

Helen thinks she should start her own agony aunt column, *Dear Looby...*

*

Dear Looby,

I am terrified my boyfriend will dump me. I have a mystery illness and I've had to leave university. He lives ninety miles away and I can't visit him, he has to come to me. I only see him every three weeks but I write him lots of letters. He's very good-looking and kind and supportive and I'm worried someone else is going to snap him up. What should I do?

With best wishes,

Helen.

*

Sometimes I go to the supermarket with Rita. She tells me what she needs and I write the shopping-list before we go. I feel like a child pretending to help. Sometimes I'm in the car putting my seat belt on and I have to go back inside because I feel too ill.

I take her arm and we walk slowly up the aisles. I have to sit down at the checkout. I watch the groceries being nudged along the conveyor belt. You buy all this food, just to shit it out, *what's the point?*

*

Christmas again. Penguin count ten.

Ivan came for New Year. We stayed in alone and watched *Scotch and Wry* and ate too many Twiglets. Everyone else was at Richard's. After the bells we went to bed and I made him come (*comme une sucette*, like a lollipop!). He'd tried to make me come, but I couldn't, everything was too jangled and I was scared I'd wet myself.

He wanted to see *My Beautiful Laundrette* before he went back to Dundee. He'd been going on about it the whole holiday. It's supposed to be brilliant, he said. Rez has seen it. What's the worst thing that could happen if we go?

My head will stove in and we'll have to leave in the middle, I said. It's not fair to you, and we'll disturb everyone, climbing over the seats.

We'll sit near the aisle, he said, and if we have to leave we have to leave. Fuck everyone else! You were okay up the loch a few weeks ago, why won't you be okay at the cinema? It's only ten miles away, it's not Timbuktu.

I've told you. The loch's much nearer. I feel safe there.

Come on, Looby. It'll be worth it. It's two and half years since we went to the cinema, when you dragged me to see that shite film *Diva*.

That's not true. We saw *The Big Chill* after I came home from France. Please don't put pressure on me to go. And *Diva* wasn't shite!

I'm not putting pressure on you. I just want you to see this. I promise I'll look after you. You've managed to go into town to the hospital with Rita all those times. And that's a longer journey.

I know it is, but I feel safe with Rita. She really understands how crappy I can feel.

I'll look after you, he said. I swear I will.

When we came out of the cinema my legs were shaking and I had popcorn stuck to my coat. Ivan'd had to park a few streets away. I sat in the foyer while he went to get the car. I'd loved the film and was euphoric to be mingling with other cinema-goers. They didn't know that my head was shifting inside and that I wasn't going back to my flat with my boyfriend, but back to my parents' to hibernate.

*

One night, Helen hears someone on the radio say: *The eternal problem of the human being is how to structure his waking hours.* They are quoting the psychiatrist Eric Berne. These words fix themselves in her head. It comforts her to think that healthy people – who go to uni, who go to work, who go to parties, who go inter-railing, who trek in the Himalayas – are merely structuring their waking hours.

She just structures hers differently.

Stoic and Hellenic.

Nothing to do with Greece.

11

New Bras

ONE DAY, WITHOUT warning, a pension book arrived for me in the post. Since Bob's diagnosis, I'd been sending in six-monthly sick notes and filling in forms with humiliating questions, but I didn't know I was a pensioner. They'd just been sending me giros.

It was like the book my granny had for Brian, long and thin like a skinny beige chequebook. Euphemistically known as a Monday Book.

Front page: HELEN FLEET. PLEASE DO NOT BEND.

Inside page: SEVERE DISABLEMENT ALLOWANCE.

Contents: perforated weekly payments to be signed for at the post office.

But I'm not disabled! I wailed to Rita. I'm exhausted and dizzy and weak and my life's ruined, but I'm not disabled!

I think it's a good sign, said Rita. It's a confirmation of how debilitating your illness is. It's a slap in the face for all the detractors.

But I'm severely debilitated, I said, not severely disabled.

I was mortified and hid it in the drawer with my bras and pants and only took it out on Mondays.

*

The post office is a quarter of a mile. Sometimes Rita goes herself and cashes the slip for me. Sometimes she runs me there and waits in the car while I wait behind blue-haired women and liver-spotted men and my legs burn. Sometimes I see Mrs Blonski.

On good days we walk, me leaning on Rita, like an old woman. We pass the house of the Latin teacher who killed himself, and the house owned by Italians, painted lilac to cheer themselves up when it rains.

*

Rita came through and told me there was a boy on the phone. I was making cheese scones, sitting down to roll the pastry.

Hello, doll, how are you doing? It was Callum.

He told me the *Lomond Herald* was interviewing people with the mystery illness. If I agreed to the interview, he would come with the reporter and take my photograph.

It'd be good to see you anyway, doll, he said.

When I hung up, the phone had floury fingerprints.

That night I couldn't sleep. I'd need to get Marion to come over and trim my hair – I didn't want to look a mess in the local paper.

I was starving. I often was in the middle of the night.

I went downstairs to get a banana. There was a dead bee in the fruit bowl, on its back with its legs half folded. It was huge. Its death seemed staged, as if someone had placed it there for me to find. I lifted it out with the turquoise washing-up gloves and tons of toilet paper so I couldn't feel it. I put it in the bin and it fell into an old Whiskas can.

The birds hadn't started yet. All you could hear was the fridge buzzing. I ripped a banana from the bunch and thought about Mr Cummings' grocery van. Rita used to send us out with the string bag and the shopping list and Mr Cummings would always say, *Would you like some nice bananas for your mother?* The second syllable of bananas was elongated because of his English accent. We used to do impersonations of him.

After eating the *ba-nah-na* I brushed my teeth and went back to bed.

stranger   What did you do today?

me   I made cheese scones and put a dead bee in the bin.

When I eventually fell asleep I dreamt that Marion was cutting my hair and I had shrubs growing out of my head.

*

The journalist from the *Lomond Herald* was called Angus. He was wearing a worn-out hacking jacket with velvet elbows. When he spoke, beads of saliva formed in the corners of his mouth.

I sat on our new January sales Chesterfield, hugging my knees, while Angus asked me the usual questions. Rita and Nab sat obediently on the other Chesterfield, at right angles to me. Sean was moping in the kitchen.

I got pins and needles during the interview and had to slap my legs to get rid of them. This happens all the time, I said. Even after five minutes in one position. And I'm always waking up in the middle of the night with elephant trunk arms. My circulation's not right.

Angus jotted it all down in his spiral pad.

I felt like a tape-recording of myself, I'd described the onset of the illness so often.

He asked Rita some questions too. She told him how helpless she'd felt, seeing me so ill and not being able to do anything, and what a relief the diagnosis had been.

Afterwards, Rita made Earl Grey tea and breaded ham sandwiches while Angus chatted to Nab and Sean (who was now moping in the living room).

Callum took some photos and I tried to look pale and interesting. When he'd finished he sat down beside me and grinned.

Don't use those photos if they're horrible, I said.

They'll be lovely, he said. You should patent that neck of yours.

I'll put it on my THINGS TO DO WHEN I'M BETTER LIST, I said.

I like your hair like that.

Thanks, I said. Bobs are back in. I've got a woman who comes to the house.

So how's that handsome boyfriend of yours doing?

He's fine. He's in Dundee doing a post-graduate course in pharmacology.

I knew he was a bright boy. You must miss him.

Intensely, I said, but he's coming back to Glasgow to do his PhD. Are you still with Roquia?

Nah. She moved to Stirling but we're still friends. She's doing politics there. D'you mind if I have a rolly?

A what?

A roll-up. I'm dying for one. Will your mum mind?

No, she smokes now and then. There's an ashtray on the table.

Is that an ashtray? It looks more like an ornament.

It's Danish, I said. Everything here's Danish since Nab.

He took out his tin and his Rizla papers. He had long fingers.

You're not putting dope in it, are you?

I'd love to, he said, laughing. Have you got any?

Yeah, there's a stash upstairs, I said. So will you be developing these photos yourself?

Nah, the technician develops them but I'll bring you the contact sheet if you want and you can choose which one you want. I'll have a word with the picture editor. The article won't be out for a couple of weeks yet, Angus is interviewing a few people.

I'd love to be able to develop my own photos, I said. It seems so glamorous.

There's nothing to it. I could teach you sometime if you want.

I don't have a darkroom.

You can use any wee room, as long as it's completely blacked out. Have you got a spare room here?

There's an office cum boxroom upstairs.

That'd do.

What about the trays and chemicals?

I could bring those.

What else d'you need?

An enlarger. He sniggered and licked the side of the cigarette paper, rolling it up slimly and perfectly. I'd like to show you my enlarger some time.

What else? I said.

A safelight.

What else?

He grinned and said, Paper.

It seems like an awful palaver.

It's a piece of cake. You can be the next Diane Arbus.

Who's Diane Arbus?

She was from New York and took photos of dwarves

and transvestites. I've got a book of her photos, I'll bring it round if you want. She killed herself.

Why did she kill herself?

She was unhappy... why does anyone kill themselves?

Lots of reasons, I said.

Angus, d'you know why Diane Arbus killed herself? said Callum.

Never heard of her, said Angus.

That's journalists for you, said Callum. They know nothing.

Rita brought the sandwiches through. Angus didn't drink Earl Grey and asked if we had any 'normal stuff'. His saliva beads got worse when he ate, stretching into thin wires as he chewed.

When they'd left I told Rita I had something to confess.

What is it? she said.

Callum's the one who flattened your hollyhocks before I went to France.

She frowned. Doesn't surprise me. He seems a bit strange. He's a bit gangly, isn't he, all arms and legs? And he doesn't seem very clean. He got ash all over the new sofa.

I'm sorry, I said. He said he'd bring the contact sheets over and I can choose the photo for the interview.

God, Helen, it's not the front page of the *Observer*! The photo's not really important, is it? It's what we said that matters.

Why are you snapping at me?

Because you're preoccupied by something that's trivial, that's why.

I just don't want to look like a pie. My face always looks flat in photos. So does yours, you know it does. Our cheekbones don't come out.

Maybe you look like a pie because you *do* look like a pie, said Sean.

Shut your face.

Don't you two start arguing, said Rita. *Please.*

He said he'd teach me photography, I said.

Where does he live? said Rita.

Electric flats, I said.

What on earth are the electric flats?

They're the council flats with blue verandas next to our old primary school, said Sean.

Why electric? said Rita.

I think because the verandas are electric blue, I said.

That's shite, said Sean.

Who asked you? I said.

Can't you see that guy's totally acting it?! he said. He's not going to teach you photography. He's a head case.

He's not a head case!

He is. He's a drug dealer.

No, he's not!

You're so naive, Helen. He's a head case, so's his sister.

You're the naive one. You think he's a drug dealer 'cos he lives in a council house. Granny and Grandad must be drug dealers too then. And Brian.

You live in a bubble, Helen.

Why don't you go and play with yourself, you horrible little boy?

Piss off.

Sean, don't talk to your sister like that.

What, I can't swear at her because she's ill?! What'll happen, will she crumble and die?!

I can't help being ill! It's not my fault!

Enough! said Rita. Both of you go upstairs if you can't be civil to one another. Nab and I would like some peace if it's not too much to ask.

Now, people, let's calm down, said Nab. We don't need to fight, do we?

Happy Larry started it, I said.

I'm staying downstairs, said Sean. I want to watch *A Very Peculiar Practice*.

So do I, I said.

I looked at my family divided between the Chesterfields and wondered if the interview had upset them. I knew I was on a high because Callum had been flirting with me. I wondered if I was being solipsistic (it was my new favourite word, I'd found it when I was looking up soliloquy, in a panic 'cos I'd forgotten how to spell it).

Before going to bed Sean came through to my room. I'm sorry about before, he said. I'm pissed off because I asked Nellie out today when we were in the Grosvenor and she said no but she'd love to be my friend. She says she feels

119

really relaxed with me.

Tell her to fuck off, you've got enough friends, I said.

He laughed. Okay, I'll tell her to fuck off tomorrow.

You're too nice, Sean, that's your problem. You're gorgeous, you should have girls falling all over you. Where's all your confidence?

I don't know, he said.

So is Callum really a dealer?

I don't know. I just don't trust him.

The next day I told Rita about Sean's knock-back. He obviously hasn't inherited Dad's womanising genes, I said. Poor Sean, said Rita. Don't tell him I told you, I said. He'll kill me.

*

Callum didn't phone and he didn't come round with the contact sheets. I couldn't bear to admit to myself that I was disappointed.

When the article came out I didn't look too much like a pie. The other people Angus had interviewed had similar stories: full lives and then grey invalids.

Richard came over to congratulate me on being famous. I asked him if Callum was a drug dealer. I really don't know, he said. His mum was in buying a carpet last week. She's a dinner lady at my wee sister's school. She had a bruise on her face but she didn't seem embarrassed. She's quite attractive for an older woman.

Maybe it was an accident, I said. What colour of carpet did she get?

Lilac Heather Twist. Hard-wearing. Ideal for living rooms and halls.

I hope his dad didn't hit her, I said. I bet he hates his wife working at a private school. He's in the Communist party.

You should phone him.

Oh, yeah. Hi, Callum, I'm just wondering if your dad hits your mum and why the fuck you didn't bring my contact sheets round.

You look fine in the photo.

I suppose so. Anyway, how's the lovely Clare doing?

Fine. She's away to London on an electrolysis course.

Will we be getting the wedding invitations soon?

I don't know. Her mum's doing all of that. I think it's six weeks before.

Well, there's still time to change your mind if the invitations aren't out.

He laughed.

You're going to go through with it, aren't you? I said.

Of course I am. I'm just a bit worried that I'll want to go to college and we won't be able to afford it 'cos she'll need the money to set up her own beauty business. It's her dream.

What about *your* dream of art school? You've kept your

dad happy, working for him for four years. Now you should do what you want. You can keep seeing Clare. Just don't marry her. She'll get over it.

But I want to marry her and, even if I didn't, the wedding's like a typhoon, you can't stop it. Anyway, how would you feel if Ivan finished with you?

My heart would break, my world would end.

It would be the same for Clare.

Yes, but I've got a mystery illness.

Does that really make a difference?

I couldn't do aerobics or run away. Clare could and she'd have endorphins to mop up her grief. I have no endorphins.

You're crazy.

Or she could just have a facial.

You're terrible.

Actually you can't cancel it, I said. It's the next big thing I have to look forward to.

When Richard had left I phoned Fizza – we'd kept in touch since the plasma exchange – and told her to get the *Lomond Herald*. She was having a bad week, new symptoms of creeping, burning feelings over her legs. And not being able to breathe properly, like there was a giant cat sitting on her chest. I told her I got that all the time and was always going to the back door to get a deep breath of air. I tried to cheer her up with Angus's saliva beads and the woman Rita'd told me about who'd been coming into the library: she'd sit there until closing time, reading Jean Plaidy, talking to herself and pushing up her breasts.

Can't sleep. I am such a bastard, slagging off Clare, when she gives me half-price leg waxes. I just don't want Richard to make a mistake. He deserves to be happy.

I'd got an extra copy of the paper and cut out the article to send to Ivan.

Walking to the post-box, legs shaking.

I kissed the letter before it went in. The post-box looked beautiful, dusted with frost and bathed in lamp-post amber. On the way back, I fantasised I was jogging in pink Lycra leggings.

March 1986
Back to see Bob.

I handed in the diary and told him I hadn't felt any different with the yellow capsules. Bob revealed that I'd been on the real thing.

Sometimes I think my legs are a bit less weak than others, I said. And sometimes I think I feel a bit better when I wake up, until I try and do something, like make breakfast or wash my hair, and then I realise I still feel horrible. I still feel mashed up.

Chin up, he said. We're doing a trial with ACTH in a

few months.

What's ACTH? I said.

It's a naturally occurring hormone that stimulates the adrenal glands to produce corticosteroids, which are anti-inflammatory.

Oh, I said. Will it help?

Maybe, he said. We also use it in flare-ups of multiple sclerosis. Sometimes it helps, sometimes it doesn't. You'll just have to keep your fingers crossed.

I sat cross-legged on the floor in the living room.

What are you doing, said Rita. Are you meditating?

No, I said. I'm trying to keep my chin up and my fingers crossed but it's very uncomfortable.

D'you want to go to the bench later? We can drive. It's a lovely day.

Okay, I said. I'll go and get dressed.

*

The weekend after Easter, we went into town to change some bras that Rita had bought me. Jana was just back from Barcelona. I was meeting her in the Next cafe afterwards.

The bra-measuring woman had a flat, isosceles face. She told me I'd probably been wearing the wrong size (36A), flicked the tape round me and declared me a 34C.

That explains why I can never get them to fit, I said.

I hope you've got your receipts, she said. We can only exchange goods with receipts.

You could tell she was bitter from grazing other women's breasts all day, with no one to touch hers when she got home. Obediently, I looked for some 34Cs to try on. I hated the way the hangers locked together like antlers and you had to fight to separate them. It was such a waste of energy.

Three of the bras fitted perfectly and I exchanged them for the old ones. Isosceles didn't crack her face.

I wanted to look for a dress for Richard's wedding but my neck felt like it had been caned. I told Rita I needed to sit down.

We squashed into the lift to get to the store cafe on the fifth floor. I leaned into the corner, avoiding the jabbing eyes of old women with hunches, and young women with babies, wondering why I was taking up space. Rita got out again and said she'd take the escalator. The lift stopped at every level and went down when it should have gone up.

When I got there, Rita was already at the self-service counter of dimly lit pies and haddock. I sat down. There was sugar spilled on the table. When I asked the girl if she could please wipe it she glared at me and came back ten minutes later with a cloth the size of a nappy. Rita had brought tea and sweating hot-cross buns (the least harmful of the snacks). Can you shift your stuff, please? the girl said, wiping the table in circles.

When we'd finished, Rita lit a Silk Cut.

125

You had one an hour ago, Mum, I said.

These are very mild, she said.

You said you're only on five a day but you're not.

Some days I have more, some days less. Please don't nag me.

I'm not nagging. I just don't want you to get lung cancer.

You don't understand, Helen. You don't smoke.

I do understand. Relapse is the norm with addicts. I saw it on a documentary.

She took a last long drag and stubbed out the cigarette. Are you happy now? she said. Happy you've got your own way?

It's not about me getting my own way.

Let's go, she said. Remember your bras.

We got the lift back down to LADIES' FASHION. I'd rather go straight to Next, I said.

You might as well have a look here, she said, trying to interest me in the Jaeger sale rack. The quality's gorgeous.

I'm not forty, Mum.

You never know what you might find, she said. There's seventy percent off.

There was nowhere to sit down. I hung round her like a reluctant toddler while she whizzed through the racks until she was satisfied there were no bargains and we could head for Next.

I was disappointed. There was nothing I really liked there. Half-heartedly, I took three dresses to try on.

The first one, a Chinese print dress, hung on me like curtains.

It's horrible, said Rita.

I know, I said. It's like something you'd make at school.

We both laughed, defrosting in spite of ourselves.

The second one, a sexy black number, cut under my arms and the security tag dug into my neck. I didn't even bother coming out of the cubicle to show her.

The sleeveless navy one was a surprise. It made me look quite healthy. It stopped a couple of inches above my knees before my legs got too thin.

What d'you think? I said.

I like it, she said. It's lovely at the bust.

Yeah, I said. I like the wee bow.

You could always have it taken in at the hips, said Rita.

The clothes in here are always too big at the hips, I said.

A nip and a tuck is all you need. I'm sure the Italian woman Heather knows could do it.

I pulled the dress in where it was too big and tried to imagine it tighter.

It would be nice with red shoes and a red bag, said Rita.

Blue with red?

They're classic together, she said.

It's not the '60s, Mum.

She made a face. Are you too tired to look for shoes just now?

I think so, I said. I should really go and wait for Jana. She'll be here soon.

We can always get them in Helensburgh, she said.

No way! I said. The shops there are so twee. Fine if you want elasticated sandals for bunions, that cost a hundred pounds.

Don't exaggerate, Helen. I'm just trying to help. It's less tiring for you to go there than come here.

Sorry, I said, going back into the cubicle.

I took the dress off.

D'you really like it, Mum? I said.

I *do* like it, she said through the curtain, but I don't think you like it.

I might as well get it, I said. I don't know when I'll be able to come into town again.

Right. I'm away to look for a shirt for Nab. I'll be back in an hour. Will you be okay?

Yup.

Don't get the dress if you're not sure.

I won't.

D'you want me to take the others out? she said, poking her head through.

It's okay, I said. I'll take them.

I got dressed. My arms burned when I lifted them above my head and I panicked when I couldn't find the plastic disc they give you for the number of items you take in. (Whenever

I'd been shopping since getting ill I'd always had the feeling I might be shoplifting because I was so spaced out.)

Relief like Calamine lotion: the plastic circle was on the floor under my new bras.

As I watched the girl folding the navy dress in tissue paper, I felt guilty (again) for punishing Rita for caring so much.

It's a lovely dress, the girl said. Not too fancy. You could wear it to work too.

I smiled and colluded.

Have you thought about opening a store account? she said.

No, I said. I'm a student.

Your receipt's in the bag. Enjoy the wedding, she said.

Thanks, I said.

Jana was late. I knew she would be.

While I waited, I watched the other women in the cafe – taking it all for granted with their blonde highlights and black shoes with bags to match. I would've liked highlights but I'd need to go into Marion's salon and I couldn't face the noise of hair-dryers like helicopters.

Jana looked frail when she came in. You feel very wee, I said when I hugged her. I'm so glad you're back.

I'm fucking exhausted, she said.

Must have been all those upside down question marks.

What question marks?! I didn't open a book. Too much partying. God, I wish you could have visited. You would have loved it. What d'you want to drink?

Hot chocolate, please. D'you mind going up, my legs are like jelly? Let me pay though.

Jana looked sad when she was queuing, sliding the tray down the counter like she couldn't be bothered.

You look so thin, she said when she was sitting down again. What's the latest with Dr Bob?

It's all so boring. I've finished the evening primrose oil trial – the one I wrote to you about – and I'm starting another one in a few months, some adrenal hormone thing. But the good news is... I know my proper bra size. I'm a 34C!

I took the new bras out to show her.

Sexy, she said, biting her lip.

I'm so happy to have cups that fit, I said. The bra woman was so grumpy. She looked like an iron.

I'm really worried, Helen. I think I'm pregnant.

I *knew* there was something wrong! I said. I could tell the minute I saw you.

My period's two weeks late. I just keep hoping it'll start. I've got so much reading to do. All that fucking Rabelais. I can't face it.

Have you done a pregnancy test?

Not yet. I'm too scared.

You always think you're pregnant. Are you sure ?

Yeah. I've been really stupid. I think I could be this time.

You *have* to have a test. You can't be pregnant during your finals, you just can't. Promise me.

I promise. She took out a cigarette. I started again in

Barcelona. They all smoke like devils there.

You shouldn't be smoking if you're pregnant, I said.

Like I'm going to keep it if I am!

I know, I said. I'm just trying to make you laugh.

Let's talk about something else. How's Ivan doing?

He's fine. He's coming next weekend.

Still crazy about him?

Of course. And I'm famous. I've been in the *Lomond Herald*. Callum came to the house a few weeks ago and took my photo for an interview. He was flirting with me. He's quite sexy. We talked about photography.

That's good, she said, a girl needs to flirt now and again. So what else is new?

Richard's getting married at end of May.

Cool.

I got this for his wedding, I said, taking the dress out to show her. I hope I can wear it to your graduation too.

It's cute, she said, but she wasn't really paying attention. She was miles away, smoking like a bad actress.

Jana, you better not be pregnant, I said, folding the dress back into the bag.

I know, she said.

You have to do a test. Go and get one now. We can do it together.

I can't. I'll do it tomorrow.

Phone me as soon as you know.

I was thinking of going to Student Health.

Don't. They get all the reject doctors. You should go to

the Family Planning Clinic.

What if I get some judgemental old hag who's never had sex? She'll just lecture me like crazy.

Well, if you are pregnant you'll need to go somewhere for advice.

Is it hard to get an abortion?

I don't know. I think you need two doctors' signatures.

Fuck. Maybe I should just quit school and have a Spanish baby.

Don't even joke, I said. Then neither of us will have careers.

Don't say anything to Rita, she said.

I won't.

On the way home in the car I thought about Jana and how stupid she'd been and how I couldn't tell her how stupid she'd been because she had been so supportive and believed that I was ill right from the start: she was like gold-dust. I wanted to share the pregnancy scare with Rita but I knew I couldn't.

I wished I hadn't bought the blue dress.

Jana phoned two days later. She was crying. I'm okay, she said. I got my period this morning. It's gross, it's the heaviest it's ever been but I'm fucking glad of the pain. I deserve it.

Thank God! I said. Now go and study. Off to the library with you!

I will. Thanks for not lecturing me for being so stupid.

Just don't do it again. *Please!*

I won't. What are you doing today?

I'm trying to read *Midnight's Children*. It's the third time I've started it but I can't get into it.

God, you're so disciplined.

I hate not finishing a book.

Go flirt with Callum or something. Call him and ask him over.

Maybe I will, I said. My horoscope says I'm running on high-energy voltage and am capable of extraordinary things.

*

Clammy moths nibbling my face. I feel wrung out like an old cloth that's been left to dry and stiffen under the sink. I look outside at the daffodils bending in the wind and wonder how long this is going to go on.

*

One afternoon, when no one was in, I practised dancing for Richard's wedding. I put on *Rock The Casbah* and watched myself in the mirror. I felt like a marionette with weak legs being jerked on a string. I didn't like watching, self-conscious in front of myself. I had to lie down during the first verse. When I tried to stand up my muscles felt like elastic pulled to its utmost tension. I lay on the floor 'til the end of the tape. I wondered if I'd damaged my legs for good.

The phone rang around three. It was Callum. It was six weeks since the newspaper interview.

You sound funny, he said. Echoey.

I'm lying on the landing, I said. My legs are fucked. I was trying to dance.

I tried to phone you a few times, he said.

I knew he was lying. I was always in.

I'm sorry I didn't come round with the contact sheets.

You're a bad wee bugger, I said.

Listen, I could come round now if you want. I'm down at the Swan Hotel. I've been photographing swans.

Why? I asked.

Neds were throwing stones off the bridge. A swan was tangled up and they killed it.

That's horrible!

I know. It's fucking criminal.

Bastards, I said.

So will I come over or not? I'm just down the road.

If you want to, but I'm knackered. I can't entertain you.

I'll be there in half an hour, he said.

Okay.

Toodle pip!

I hung up and went downstairs slowly. I smelled of night clothes and sweat. I crouched down in the bath and washed under my arms. I tried not to think of the swan being stoned but it kept coming into my head. I wished I didn't know. I put on my pink baggy trousers, brushed my hair and put on some lipgloss.

I lay on the couch and waited. My heart was racing. I didn't usually get visitors during the day. I got up again and put on some eyeliner.

He turned up an hour and a half later.

Sorry I'm late. I had a smoke to calm me down. The swans upset me.

Did you have to photograph the dead one?

No. Just the vicinity and some healthy ones.

I hope they get who did it.

They're cunts. They ran away.

It's like something out of *Taggart*.

He laughed. So how are you, doll? You're looking a wee bit peeky.

I'm getting on with it. I have no choice.

Are you even a wee bit better?

Sometimes I think so, but there's still so little I can do. I just want to get back to uni but I still have days where I think I'm dying.

When d'you think you can go back?

Fuck knows. It's supposed to burn itself out in five years so I've got two and a half to go. Honours is out the window, but I only need one class to get an Ordinary degree.

What about Fizzy? How's she doing?

Horrendous. She needs a wheelchair when she goes out. I doubt she'll get back to her medical degree, poor thing.

What about Handsome Horace?

Same as last time I saw you. In Dundee doing his MSc.

That's right, I forgot.

You've got no memory, all the dope you smoke.

Have you got any biscuits? he said.

I think there are KitKats.

I wouldn't mind one. And some of that perfumed tea if you've got any.

Help yourself, laddie. I take it weak with a little milk.

Tea for two coming right up, he said. He grinned and went into the kitchen.

I couldn't decide whether I fancied him or not.

Where's your cups, doll? he shouted through.

In the cupboard on the left.

Where's the milk?

In the fridge.

Where's the fridge?

Callum!

Keep the heid, he said. I'm only kidding.

He came through with the tea and offered me a KitKat from a stack on the plate.

I just put them all out, he said.

I shouldn't really be drinking Earl Grey. It gives me a headache but I love the taste.

It *clears* my head, he said. What's in it?

Oil of bergamot.

What's that?

No idea.

It sounds exotic. Like something that should be smoked.

Do you smoke everyday?

I usually have one to get me started.

How can you work?

I can work fine.

But doing it every day must be bad for you.

It's not. Cannabis helps people with cancer. It's pain relief.

But you don't have cancer.

Aye, not yet. You should have a smoke. It would help your muscles.

I'd be too scared to smoke now. I feel stoned all the time anyway.

So what else has been happening?

Nothing. Jana thought she was pregnant but she's not. (The minute I'd said it, I regretted telling him. It seemed disloyal.)

Is that your friend I saw having sex? he said.

Yup.

She didn't like me.

No wonder. You were spying on her!

What about your pal next door? D'you still see him?

He's getting married in two weeks. He said your mum was in buying a carpet a while back.

Aye. She would've been.

I couldn't bring myself to mention the bruise. I changed the subject. Have you heard from Roquia?

Nah. She'll be onto better things. She's probably shagging some handsome prince in Stirling.

Are you not jealous?

Nah.

But you two were together since school, I said.

I know.

Was it not bitter when you finished?

Not really. She just went mad one time 'cos I went out to buy cigs and didn't come back for three hours.

What were you doing?

I met someone I knew and we went for a pint.

And that's why you finished?

She was leaving her job and going to uni anyway. It was on the cards. What about you? Do you not get jealous of Ivan being away?

No. I trust him a hundred percent. He's coming down for Richard's wedding. I can't wait.

That'll be a posh do.

Queen's Hotel.

I could do their photos cheap.

I laughed. I think they've got their photographer booked. It'll be like the royal wedding. If Ivan and I ever get hitched you can do ours. I want black and white. Colour's common.

You're on, doll. Listen, I better go. I've got another job to go to.

But you just got here.

I know, but I've to photograph a wee girl up at the

hospital. They've raised money for a dialysis machine.

Dead swans and ill children – all in a day's work for you.

He reached into his army bag. Here, you can borrow this, he said, handing me a home-made tape.

Violent Femmes? I've never heard of them.

They're supreme, he said.

Thanks a lot.

Your legs'll be fine if you dance to them.

He pecked me on the cheek. See you, doll. I'll take you for a wee spin next time.

I loved his ironic use of doll. It was sexy.

See you.

I watched him lope down the path. I could still feel his kiss, sticky on my cheek. I didn't want him to go. I watched his car turn right and disappear at the top of the road.

I got the dictionary out and looked up bergamot. I wanted to tell him it was a citrus fruit that grew in Italy and Africa.

12

A Wedding, a Graduation and Ganesh

CLARE IS STUNNING with piled up hair and her ivory dress. The five bridesmaids are in puffy cerise. I feel sexy with my new bra. I ask Ivan if he can tell the difference, see that I'm more lifted.

Beery uncles keep asking me to dance. *Are you not joining in with the young ones?/You don't want to be a wallflower!/You'll get up for the Gay Gordon, won't you?!*

I decline politely a hundred times. I'm saving my legs for Ivan.

Sean's brought Nellie (she's changed her mind about being just friends). She's too grown up looking for a nineteen-year-old. She says she loves my dress. I tell her I had to have it taken in. She says she loves Next but her mum says it's cheap rubbish.

It's my favourite shop, I say.

She puts her hand over her mouth. I'm sorry, I didn't

mean anything.

She says she likes my shoes.

I tell her that I'm annoyed they're scuffed already.

Cream marks so easily, doesn't it? she says.

Ivan is the most handsome man there.

We do the St Bernard's Waltz. *One, two, back two, side two, pause... up-down, side two, back two, twirl, twirl, twirl...* It's like riding a bike, it all comes back from school. My legs are trembling and I'll pay later but I force myself round the dance floor.

The two youngest bridesmaids dart around the tables like cerise goldfish.

Later, a drunk woman in a long tartan skirt cries in the toilets about fluffy towels. She'd wanted white ones for their present but she could only get pink. She says over and over again that they make a lovely couple.

I'd given them a huge Rosina Wachtmeister print, signed from Ivan as well. I loved her cats with big silver heads.

Rita and Nab whirl round doing Strip the Willow. Nab gets mixed up and ends up with the wrong partner. Rita is laughing.

Ivan dances with Clare. They look good together.

Richard says he'll always love me as the girl next door. I tell him I'll miss him.

I fantasise about cutting the cake, Ivan holding my arm. I want an ivory dress too. And a platinum ring. Or white gold.

*

We watched Scotland and Denmark in the opening rounds of the World Cup. The Scottish players looked as if they had rickets, and their strips looked like they were from C&A. Scotland lost, of course. Denmark got one. We slagged Nab about plundering Vikings. He smiled and said, The Danes definitely nabbed a goal from the Scots. He loved punning with his name.

Rita and Ivan had persuaded me to go to Dundee for a week while Rita decorated my room. (Ivan had moved back to his parents for the summer while he did his MSc project.)

I spent a week planning what to pack and seeking reassurance. *Are you sure your mum won't mind me sleeping for twelve hours every night?/Are you sure she'll understand that I have to lie down at the drop of a hat?/How will I manage the journey?*

Door to door, said Ivan. You'll be grand.

He came to collect me in his new yellow second-hand VW Beetle. He told me he hadn't had time to clean it and it still had the previous owner's – an old hill walker – grey curly hairs sticking out of the driver's seat.

Gross me out the door, I said as I clambered in.

There is nothing wrong with clichés: clichés come from life

and life is real. When Ivan told me he was going to India, MY HEART FROZE.

Square window. *Ivan's garden, overlooking the Tay.*

me   Why didn't you tell me?!

ivan   I didn't want to upset you. You know I've always wanted to go to India.

me   How long for?!

ivan   A few months. Once I've handed in my dissertation.

me   What'll I do without you? You'll never come back!

ivan   Of course I will! I have to come back for my PhD.

me   No you won't. You'll meet a beautiful Indian woman and stay there. Or an Australian. They're always travelling. Then you'll go back to Sydney with her.

ivan   Helen, stop being so dramatic! I just want to take a few months off. That's all.

me   When are you going?

ivan   Probably end of September, if I can get my

143

dissertation in early.

me   That's only three and half months away!

ivan   I want to see the Ganesh festival.

me   What's Ganesh?

ivan   He's an Indian god, a pot-bellied elephant with a broken tusk. They celebrate his birthday by carrying clay statues of him into the sea and leaving them there to dissolve. Rez says it's amazing to see.

me   I want to go home now. I'm not staying here.

ivan   You can't go home. You *are* staying here. You're on holiday.

me   I don't like Dundee. People are strange looking.

ivan   What are you talking about?!

me   They've got an in-bred look.

ivan   That's so childish. You're being ridiculous.

me   I don't care. It's what I think. We're spilling our beans today, aren't we?

ivan   I thought you were having a nice time here. My mum and dad are doing their best to

> look after you and make you feel at home.

me I know they are, and I'm grateful – I *was* having a nice time until you told me you were going round the world.

ivan I'm not going round the world. Stop being so infuriating.

me I don't want to speak to you anymore, my head feels like it's folding in. And don't call me Looby, I'm not a play-thing. [*She's trying to be tough, she secretly loves it when he calls her Looby*]

ivan You're not the only one – my head's folding in too.

She was lying in Ivan's dead sister's bedroom, thinking about how relaxing it would be to be a clay elephant dissolving in the sea, when Ivan came in with a cup of tea and a minty chocolate biscuit in green foil.

Here, he said. A peace offering.

These biscuits remind me of the plasma exchange, she said.

How come?

Remember I got addicted to cream eggs wrapped in green foil during the steroids and then I couldn't face

145

chocolate for ages.

Kind of, he said. Listen, I know it's shite for you that I'm going away and if I was the ill one I'd feel the same as you, but I *have* to go and I think it'd be worse for us if I didn't go.

I know, said Helen. I just got a shock. I'm sorry.

I'm sorry too.

And it should be 'if I *were* the ill one'. You need the subjunctive. Well, in French, you do.

He smiled and unwrapped the biscuit. Here. They're nice to dip in your tea.

Does your mum know you're going?

Yeah. She thinks it's great, but she's terrified I get some terrible Third World illness.

Well, you could get a terrible illness living in Balloch, couldn't you? said Helen. Will you need lots of vaccinations?

Hepatitis A, typhoid, polio booster, malaria tablets.

You've got it all planned!

You need to plan vaccinations, you can't have them the day before you go, can you?

Just promise me you'll come back, Ivan. Promise me.

I promise, he said. He'd twisted the green foil into the shape of a nail.

Is that another nail for my coffin?

I don't know what you're on about. He'd put the foil into his mouth and was chewing it.

Don't do that, she said. You'll hurt your fillings.

Are you coming downstairs? he said. Argentina's
playing.

When Ivan drove her back to Balloch at the end of her stay,
they had to stop in a lay-by. You can't let Rita and Nab see
you in this state, he said. You need to stop crying.

I know, she said between sobs.

I've never known anyone who cried so much.

I'm sick of it too, Ivan, she said. I'm so sick of hearing
myself. I hate being like this, *I hate it!*

They stopped at a Little Chef so that she could wash
her face.

I honestly can't help it. My hypothalamus is fucked.
You know it is.

Have you stopped for now? he said.

I've stopped, she said.

D'you want a doughnut?

Yes, please, she said, I'd love a doughnut.

Rita and Nab were standing in the driveway, grinning from
ear to ear.

Two people, one big smile.

They had sanded her bedroom floor and got her a new
sheepskin rug. The walls were white with a hint of a tint of
apple and she had new curtains from Habitat and a white
vase that Rita had filled with sweet peas from the garden.

Thank you so much, said Helen, hugging both of them. I love it! It's like a room in a magazine.

You're a lucky duck, said Ivan.

He was staying to eat but was going back to Dundee that night.

Helen lay down for an hour before dinner. She felt guilty for being so sad about Ivan when Rita and Nab had worked so hard to decorate her room. She hated Ivan for ruining everything.

So how was Dundee? Rita asked cheerfully when they sat down to eat.

It was lovely, said Helen. I rested lots and sat in the garden. Ivan's mum was great. She took me to the beach. I've got some blue shells.

And we went to an old Italian cafe for ice cream, said Ivan. It's the best ice cream in Scotland.

No, it's not. It's not as good as the ice cream here, said Helen. Gallini's is the best.

And we watched the World Cup, Ivan went on. Helen kept changing who she was supporting every five minutes.

I always want whoever's losing to win, said Helen.

How's your MSc coming along, Ivan? asked Nab.

Okay, he said. I'm doing a summer placement in a lab at Ninewells. Research into drugs for Alzheimer's. I think I'd like to get into that area.

How is your grandmother? said Rita.

She's getting worse. She keeps burning her cuffs on the cooker. I think she'll come to live with my parents soon.

I had a nice chat with her, said Helen, but she kept calling me Alison.

Such a shame, said Rita. She's not that old, is she?

Seventy-five, said Ivan, but if you ask her what age she is, she says: I'm seventy-five but I wish I was older so that I could die.

As soon as Ivan had gone Helen told them he was going to India.

We already know, said Rita. He told us when you were resting. He's worried about you. You'll need to try to be mature about it, she said, sighing.

How can I be mature? said Helen. I'm only twenty-two and I've got a mystery illness.

Well, you're nearly twenty-three and you can't tie Ivan to your apron strings, her mother went on. You have to be strong. He's been a huge support so far. You have to let him breathe. It might do you both good to have a break.

Helen went back upstairs to her magazine bedroom and stared at the hint of a tint of apple walls. Deep down she knew Rita was right. She also knew that everything came down to figures of speech in the end: she was a lucky duck and she couldn't tie Ivan to her apron strings.

Going to India was a great opportunity.

*

stranger	What are you ironing?
me	My polkadot dress for Jana's graduation next week. The dress I wore to Richard's wedding's got a stain on it.
stranger	Why are you doing it on the floor?
me	It's too tiring using the ironing board. It's better on the floor with a towel. Rita said she'd do it but I prefer to do things myself if I can.

*

Rita ran her up to Glasgow. They sat at the back of Bute Hall, watching the new graduates from Jana's (and Helen's) year parading by. Afterwards, everyone milling in the quads, sipping sherry in the sun. Helen had to sit down and found a bench under a cherry blossom.

Black sheep in her polkadot dress: no robe and no degree in a red tube.

Jana's dad came over and sat down beside her. It's so nice to meet you, he said. Now I can put a face to the name. Jana talks about you all the time.

It's lovely to meet you too, said Helen.

It's a beautiful day, isn't it?

Yeah, she said. We're lucky. It poured at my boyfriend's graduation last year. Not that I was actually there. I was too ill.

Jana's dad smiled and gestured to one of the doors in the cloisters. You can imagine Rapunzel imprisoned in there, can't you?

That's where we had our English tutorials, said Helen, way up in the turrets, metaphysical poets that no one could understand. It was freezing in winter.

He laughed. I thought you did French.

I did French and English. I was supposed to do Joint Honours.

I see, he said. Such a shame.

Jana was talking to Beryl (like a black mountain in her robe, her parents were like mountains too). She came over when she saw Helen with her dad.

Congratulations! Helen said, kissing her. You look gorgeous. She gave her the graduation present she'd got her, a book on David Hockney, Jana's favourite artist, wrapped in arty paper she'd got at the Third Eye Centre. She'd spent ages choosing it.

It's beautiful, honey, Jana said. I'll treasure this forever. You should have been graduating too today, she said. It's not fucking fair. She'd mimed the expletive in front of her father.

Wait 'til I'm a mature student, Helen said, and you'll all be jealous of me, with your nine to five jobs.

I'm sure they will, said Jana's dad.

After the milling with sherry, they went to the Ubiquitous Chip. The restaurant was full of black robes and proud parents.

Jana's dad was confident in an American way when he ordered even though he still had his Glasgow accent. Helen thought he was sexy and wished she was sitting beside him. She was having half a glass of champagne. Rita'd said, I don't think you should, but Helen didn't care if it made her ill. Her neck was in pliers anyway.

Jana had a summer job in the Grosvenor Cinema and was talking about going back to the States in October. Helen smiled, buffered by the champagne bubbles. Nothing seemed real. Real meant being terrified of Jana leaving. Ivan was already leaving at the end of September, Sean would be moving into his own flat in October, and Richard had moved five miles away with Clare.

Halfway through her *confit* of duck, Jana's granny put her hand on Helen's arm and said, Tell me, dear, how is your condition?

On the way home in the car, Helen fantasised that Jana's dad had fallen in love with her and taken her to California to look after her. Jana was funny about it at first until she got used to the idea. They all lived together in a big wooden house painted blue like the one Jana had shown her photos of.

13

India

I CAN'T BEAR to think of Ivan going so far away. I can't live without him, but I will have to. People drown themselves in work to get over things. My job is crying and baking and crocheting. My summer is measured out in tears and scones and white squares.

*

Nellie and Sean have gone to Venice. I'm reading one of Sean's psychology books, about traumas in childhood causing problems later on. I think of my childhood traumas and wonder if my immune system could've been damaged. Possible events were:

1. The sofa with the swirly brown and orange cover. I hated the feel of the nylon against my skin, but I would

make myself rub my hands along the cushions.

2. Shitting myself in primary one because I was too scared to tell the teacher that I needed the toilet – I sat at my desk playing with rods (the colourful wooden units we learned to count with) and said nothing. I waddled home, a navy gusset sticking to me.

3. Sean peeing on me from halfway up the Michael tree. I can still feel the warmth of my brother's urine on my scalp. He cried later and denied it.

4. Divorce of Rita and Peter.

Nellie and Sean bring me back a Murano glass dish. It looks like an ashtray, but I don't want to say anything. They are tanned and glowing. They say I would love Venice, though it smells and costs a fortune. They tell me about a hotel in Verona that has peacocks that chase you.

One night, they ask me if I want to see *Top Gun*. I don't really, but I'm not exactly busy, and it'll be a change from reading/baking/crocheting.

They drive to the cinema and I sit down inside while they queue for tickets outside. Nellie buys me a choc ice. I know she is trying to get in with me.

*

The weekend before he left for India, Ivan came to Balloch. We went to the bench and held hands. It's funny to think this time next week you'll be 4000 miles away and I'll still be here, I said. I could be sitting on the bench, remembering this conversation, and you won't even know.

You think too much, he replied.

I'd given him a Gustav Klimt card – *The Kiss* – with instructions to have a great cholera-free time and keep loving me. Take it on the plane with you to keep you safe, I said. He said he'd staple it to his passport. He'd given me a wee pewter Ganesh. He told me he was the God of Wisdom and Remover of Obstacles. Maybe he'll make me better, I said.

We discussed whether we could kiss other people while he was away. (We were being mature about it.) But what if you kiss other people and I don't? I said. It won't exactly be Even Stevens, will it? You'll have youth hostels of women after you and I'll have *no one*.

Don't upset yourself with stuff that hasn't happened, he replied.

He tightened his hand round mine and I stared at the loch, not really believing that he could be going so far away.

Rita and I were watching *The Way We Were*. Barbara Streisand and Robert Redford had split up and Barbara was saying, Why can't I have you?, and Robert had replied, Because you push too hard.

Ivan should be landing now, I said.

Yes, he will, replied Rita absent-mindedly.

It's funny that you can spend the day going to India, or just stay at home and make a banana and date loaf, I said.

Barbara was sobbing her heart down the phone now, trying to wangle Robert back into her bed. Rita said she thought Robert Redford was the most handsome actor next to Omar Sharif.

He's not as handsome as Ivan, I said, but I wouldn't throw him out the bed for eating biscuits.

She laughed. I've never heard that expression.

Ivan uses it all the time, I said.

Does he?

She was lost in Robert. I was lost in Ivan. I'd already written to him in my head and was counting the days 'til a pale blue letter landed on the mat.

Suddenly Rita said, Helen, don't move!

I knew that tone. I jumped up and fled to the bathroom. I locked the door and shuddered, shouting instructions through to my mother. Have you got it?! *Kill it!* Make sure it's dead!

I heard her banging her shoe on the floor. I waited until she called me through.

It's gone, she said. It was a big one. They're huge this year.

Is it definitely dead?!

Yes! Go and check in the bin if you don't believe me.

Did it nearly crawl over me?

I just saw it out of the corner of my eye, she said – it

was within an inch of your hand.

God, I hate them so much! They ruin your day – you're minding your own business and they dance across the floor like they own the place. *They plan it.*

She laughed. They're not exactly pleasant but they're harmless.

They're *not* harmless, Mum! If one of those garden spiders touched me, I would die. My heart would stop. I read that they've got eight eyes!

She shivered. Now you tell me – but they're supposed to be more scared of you than you are of them.

They just tell that to children so they're not scared, I said. I don't know how you can kill them, how you can get *near* enough them to kill them, and I don't know how you can pick them up when they're dead.

I use a tissue – I don't like them but I'm not phobic like you.

Jana's as scared as me, I said. I remember there was a huge one in our flat in Lawrence Street, and we were both laughing and crying at the same time. We put on washing up gloves and boots for protection, and Jana eventually killed it with an umbrella. Neither of us could look at it, even when it was flat. We had to go upstairs and get Ivan to bin it.

I can just imagine the pair of you, said Rita.

D'you know who's fearless? I said – Granny – she's amazing with spiders. She just picks them up and throws them outside.

157

She's a country girl at heart.

Last time I was there, Brian was slagging me for being scared, and Granny was in her philosopher's mode, saying you shouldn't be ashamed of your phobias. She was telling me about a woman in Fort William who was phobic about the hoot of an owl. Not owls themselves, just the hoot of an owl. It terrified her.

Would you like some tea? said Rita, laughing.

I'll make it, I said. You're missing the film.

Thanks, she said. I'll have some of your banana loaf too. It's lovely.

Is the spider *definitely* dead?

Yes!

I went through to the kitchen and filled the kettle. The bin made me shiver – knowing what was in it. I wished I could phone Ivan and tell him about the spider. I wished he could be sitting on the Chesterfield when I went back through. I'd been thinking about how missing people was really just about spaces and who was in them: last weekend, Ivan'd been in the space on the bench and in the space on the Chesterfield, but now he'd be in a space on a rickety chair in Bombay, and somebody else would be in the space on the bench, and Nab or Rita would be in the space on the Chesterfield.

We'd seen him off at Central Station. He'd taken the sleeper down to London.

Polaroid snapshot of the occasion: Ivan with a rucksack the size of a house. His mum and dad and Rita. Me clinging to him.

I love you.

Just over three years ago he'd seen me off to France from the same platform. Now, I was the mournful person waving and he was the person on the train with the great opportunity.

After his train had shunted out, I'd gone to the toilets. I'd breathed through my mouth, trying not to throw up from the watery smell of bowel movements that you get in public toilets. I put three sheets of toilet paper on top of the toilet seat before sitting down but they kept slipping off.

Nine sheets later I'd sat down. Peeing and gagging at the same time, my mouth was full of slippery saliva.

I'd curled my fingers round the Ganesh in Ivan's jacket pocket. It was only three months. It would fly by.

I didn't want to leave the cubicle, but I was getting pins and needles in my thighs and feet. I heard someone clacking in.

It's me, Helen. Are you okay? It was Rita.

Have you come to look under the doors and check I'm not slitting my wrists? I said.

Don't even joke about it! she'd said in her librarian's voice.

I'll be out in a minute, I said. My stomach's a bit dodgy.

When I'd come out she was re-applying her lipstick.

Why are you getting dolled up, Mum?

Just cheering myself up.

All the soap dispensers had been empty except the last one. The cream soap had spurted out like sperm.

What are you smiling at? she asked.

Nothing, I'd replied to her reflection above the sinks.

He'll be back before you know it, she said, you just have to concentrate on getting well now. She'd put her arm round me and we'd walked back to the car. Ivan's parents had already left. His mother had told me not to be a stranger. Halfway to the car, I had to go back to the toilets.

I'd dropped a few sheets of toilet paper into the toilet bowl so no one could hear.

*

Can't sleep for the wind howling round the house. I wish it would blow the birds away. Or concuss them (just slightly).

But five o'clock comes and still they start. There's one that sounds like a joiner, whistling and happy to be doing an honest day's work.

Which is more than can be said for me.

I feel for Ivan's letters under the pillow – his words are like jewels I've memorised: *the whole of India is stained red with paan.* I feel as if I'm there with him.

Me too, I've smoked bidis.

And tasted delicious chilli omelettes.

And bought sweet sickly chai in a clay cup from a chai-wallah at the train station.

I've seen the beauty of elephants immersed in the sea at Chowpatty beach.

I've smiled at the woman squeezing red glass bangles onto her arm 'til it bleeds, her circulation almost cut off by her sari.

I'm sick of the Swedish guy with blonde dreadlocks who thinks he's the son of Shiva. He was funny at first but now he's a pain in the arse.

I almost shat myself at the rustling in the dirt toilet in a Colva beach restaurant. It turned out to be a pig.

I try not to think about the rats.

Or the beggar with one arm and no legs, wheeling his torso along on a skateboard.

Or the children's outstretched arms as you get into a taxi in Bombay.

Or the homeless woman rubbing mustard oil on her naked baby.

Or the smell of farts on trains.

His last sentence, written in Goa: *The women here are beautiful but not as beautiful as you.*

Everything is bearable.

I get up and go downstairs. There are no bananas left. I'm glad – I'm sick of them, I only eat them for the potassium. I take a shiny Granny Smith. It has a rotten bit underneath that looks like a septic blister. I slice it off and take the apple back to bed.

I'm dying for a mango lassi.

*

November 1986

Today we're looking through the arched window. Maybe we should have a chat with Helen and try and cheer her up! She looks like she's been crying.

stranger   How are you today?

helen   I'm sick of these gales. You can't sleep a wink. The wind's like a bad-tempered wolf howling round the house all night.

stranger   Is that not a tautology, 'bad-tempered wolf'? You don't really get good-tempered ones, do you?

helen   You know what I mean. Anyway, I'm sure there are some pleasant, mild-mannered wolves.

stranger   I'm sorry, I'm being pedantic.

helen   It's okay. Tell me this: are you ever trying to read and you can't focus on the book 'cos you *know* that you're reading and you know that your eyes are sliding back and forth? Or when you're watching TV, you can't really focus 'cos you *know* you're watching it. You can see yourself sitting on the sofa, watching

162

Brookside. It's as if everything you do's been previewed. It's the same when you're having a shower, you can see yourself standing in the shower before you even go in.

stranger   Sounds like you're thinking too much.

helen   You do when you spend a lot of time on your own and your boyfriend's gone to India and you can't do aerobics.

stranger   What about a hobby?

helen   I've been writing poetry but it's terrible.

stranger   Can I see some?

helen   I'd rather not. Rita brought me an anthology of American poetry from the library and it put me in the mood. I've discovered Edna St Vincent Millay. I'd never heard of her before.

stranger   I have to confess I don't really like poetry. I can never understand it.

helen   Edna's easy to understand, you know what she means. She's all about the brittleness of love. I read she died after falling down the stairs. She left a glass of red wine on the landing.

stranger   She must've been drunk.

helen   No one really knows. She was addicted to morphine for a while. It's really sad.

stranger   [*bored with poetry discussion*] So, what happened to your photography lessons with Callum?

helen   I'm waiting 'til after I've had the ACTH injections. I'm going to buy a camera with my savings. I've got a catalogue.

stranger   What kind of camera?

helen   A Praktika, I think. Nothing too fancy.

stranger   Have you saved a lot of money?

helen   Not really. £500. I'm always buying books and tapes, and I give Rita a wee bit, a token gesture. I only get £50 a week.

stranger   What about your yoga? Are you still doing that?

helen   It's not real yoga. It's more stretching exercises that I make up. I'm still pretty flexible even though I'm weak.

stranger   Well, you don't want to seize up, do you?

helen   No, not really.

*

Dear Travelling Boy,

Did you know there are no woodpeckers in Ireland? The things you find out when you're an armchair traveller!

I can't believe it's only four weeks 'til you're home!!! Just cannot wait to spend New Year with you. Last night, I dreamt I was swimming in the loch with a black-faced sheep that had swum all the way from Goa. I woke myself up shouting, *What did Ivan say?!* The sheep said it was a secret!

So, I've had my first ACTH injection. I got a warm sense of well-being straight afterwards. It was lovely. That horrible clenching weakness in my muscles seemed less but it only lasted a few hours. I've to have another four jabs over the next couple of months. Fizza's getting them too. She seems to be getting worse again. It's awful. I don't know how she copes. Her mother's been praying for her with chickpeas. You pray over the chickpeas and on the third night you throw them in the river, so the fish eat them and can pray too. It's so magical, I love it.

I had a lovely birthday even though I wished you were here every minute. I pampered myself with a strawberry face mask and peppermint oil on my feet. Rita made lasagne. It was delicious but I kept thinking the pasta sheets looked like big flaps of skin. We had non-alcoholic sparkling wine. Rita and Nab got me that Diane Arbus book I told you about. I love it.

Jana and Callum came and Sean brought Nellie. I really don't like her. She's big-headed and I know she doesn't believe in ME. She thinks 'cos she's studying psychology she knows everything, but Sean is besotted and is now vegetarian. And my granny and grandad and Brian came. Brian got me a big box of Milk Tray and tried to deliver it like the advert. He was wearing a black polo and left the chocolates on the hall table.

I read out bits of your letters to everyone. My grandad said his usual, The young ones have a great life nowadays, as if he used to work down the mines. My granny entertained us with her recycled stories of swinging on trees and growing up in the Highlands.

Went to see *Withnail and I* at the ABC with Rita and Nab. It's so funny (I'll see it with you when you're home if you want) but the bastards wouldn't give me a concession with my sickness benefit book. They said I needed a UB40. I felt so humiliated, like I was scrounging.

I've been reading *The Third Policeman*, the Flann O'Brien book your mum lent me. Bicycles and humans interchange atoms, the bikes are so cheeky, they eat crumbs and sneak up to the fire to get warm. And the more time people spend on their bikes, the higher the percentage of bicycle they have in them. It cracks me up. You have to read it sometime!

Jana hates her IT course. She has to do Pascal programming and says it's too fucking hard. I think she wishes she'd gone back to San Fran after all but I'm SO glad she's still here. I couldn't do without her AND you at the same time.

I almost forgot, Rez phoned on my birthday, which was lovely. He's knackered working a hundred hours a week. He says he's so tired he wouldn't notice if his mother died.

And guess what – I finally finished that blanket for wee Zoe! (About time. I was sick of the sight of it.)

What else? I watched a documentary about a forty-year-old guy with Parkinson's. He feels like he's constantly got an electric current in his body and he alternates between being snaky and jerky. The poor guy used to be a climbing instructor and now he can hardly have a game of pool. (They used to think Parkinson's was psychosomatic in the '30s.)

Phone me as soon as you get back to London. I'm sending this to Delhi.

Lots and lots of love,

Looby-wallah xxx

PS. I love suffixing with 'wallah'.

Brian was looking at the Diane Arbus book, studying every page. These people are funny looking, he said.

They're not really funny looking, I said, just different.

It had never occurred – and would never occur – to Brian that he was funny looking too with his big squarish head and thick lips.

Look, he said, it's Valerie and Moira!

He was pointing to a photo of two women with Down's syndrome wearing Easter bonnets.

You're havering, I said. They're nothing like Valerie and Moira.

I think it's their double, he said.

How is Valerie, by the way? I said.

I think she's a lot better.

Are you sure? I didn't think she was going to get better.

Well, I think she's fine now. She's much better.

And is Moira still your girlfriend?

Don't be silly, Helen! he said. Moira's *Frank's* girlfriend! I told you that before.

Sorry, I said. I lose track. I can't keep up with your shenanigans.

What's shenanigans?

Just chopping and changing your mind all the time.

Well, is Ivan still *your* boyfriend?

I hope so, I said. He's in India just now. Remember I showed you on the map?

Will he be brown when he comes home?

Yeah, he'll have a great tan. It's boiling over there.

Is it as boiling as Alicante?

Much more boiling, I said.

Two weeks before Christmas, penguin count seven.

When the phone rang, I thought it would be Rita reminding me to defrost the chicken.

Long distance clicks and an operator with such a strong

Indian accent it sounded like a parody.

Then Ivan.

I can't believe it's you! I said. Where are you?! Are you okay?!

I'm back in Delhi. Did you get my letter?

I got one two weeks ago from Goa.

You haven't had the one since then?

No. What's wrong? You sound funny.

Listen, Looby, I'm not coming home at New Year. I'm travelling for longer. I wrote to you about it but I wanted to tell you properly... I've met a great crowd of people and we're going to Tibet. I want to do some trekking. I managed to change my ticket and my dad wired me some money.

Hollow/dull/solid air.

I stared at Nab's almanacs lined up on the hall shelf with their orange spines and black lettering: *Hvem, Hvad, Hvor.*

Are you still there? said Ivan.

Too hollow, too dull.

Helen?

I'm still here, I said, choking on tears the size of pears.

Listen to me, he said. Please don't cry. I'll be back at the end of March, beginning of April. It's not that long. I'll write all the time. I promise.

I've been looking forward to you coming home for the last ten weeks, I said, it's all I think about, it's what keeps me going! Why do you need another three months?!

I might nip to Thailand too.

Trapped under dry thick ice. No point speaking. The almanacs were chanting their black spines at me.

I can't hear you, he said. Listen, I'll call you tomorrow. It's really expensive to call if you're not speaking. I'll call you to tomorrow at the same time.

I made a noise, some numb word.

Bye, Looby.

Long distance click. Gone. He hadn't said he loved me.

Hollow

Hollow

Hollow

Hvem

Hvad

Hvor

Round window. *A thin girl is lying on the hall floor, sobbing and talking to herself.* She has just had a phone call from India. She is crying so much she is retching. She goes to the bathroom and spits acid saliva into the toilet bowl. She moves into the living room. She kneels down and sobs on the Chesterfield. She can taste salty tears against leather.

After a long time, she makes some tea.

After two sips she runs to the toilet and throws up. Her tongue feels like carpet. She goes upstairs and continues to wrack herself with tears.

Later, Agnes appears, nosing and purring into her face.

The bastard's not coming back, Agnes, she whimpers. He's not coming back. *What am I going to do?!*

Agnes climbs over her head, and Helen sees the lesion on the cat's abdomen for the first time. She forces the cat still and peers at the dried-in wound. She kisses her head and goes downstairs and looks for a vet in the phonebook. She is shaking.

The receptionist has a catarrhy voice and says it's probably just a scratch. They are fully booked for a week, but because of Helen's voice, which is woven with two-ply grief – Ivan grief AND Agnes grief – she gets an appointment for three days later.

Helen goes back upstairs and writes IVAN IS A CUNT in her diary.

What on earth's the matter? says Rita when she gets in from work. You look awful. Are you feeling ill?

Ivan's not coming back and Agnes has got a tumour, I say.

What are you talking about?!

I describe the afternoon's events and my mother sighs.

You have to be strong, she says for the *nth* time since I've been ill. You can't let yourself get upset, you'll undo the good the ACTH is doing. You *have* to get on with your life and let Ivan get on with his. That's all there is about it. When he phones tomorrow, no more tears. You can't afford to be this upset. You'll only make yourself ill.

I already *am* ill, I say. (My voice is husky from retching. I sound quite sexy.)

You know what I mean, she says, frowning. I'm going to unpack the groceries. Come and help me. It'll take your mind off things.

It's so fucking typical of Ivan, I say, following her into the kitchen. He's always chopping and changing his plans. I'm sick of it. I mean you don't *nip* to Thailand, do you?! You plan it. You plan ahead.

It's not really Ivan you're angry with, is it? Rita says more gently. It's your situation you're kicking against. But I wish you wouldn't swear. You know I don't like the *f* word.

How does he know I wouldn't have dumped him by now if I wasn't ill?! He's a cocky bastard, thinks he can gallivant round the world and I'll just be here waiting like the good little woman. Well, he can think again!

That's the spirit, says Rita. It's better to be angry than sad. Can you put the eggs away, please? The old ones will need to go out. It's ridiculous that we waste so many eggs in this house.

D'you think he's met someone else, Mum?

I don't know, Helen. I honestly don't know. All I do know is that your priority is to get well. You can't spend every minute worrying about what Ivan's doing. You have to concentrate on your friends here. Why don't you phone Callum and ask him for tea at the weekend?

You've changed your tune, I say. I thought you didn't like him.

Well, maybe I was wrong about him. I was very impressed with the way he spoke to Brian at your birthday. He treated him normally and didn't find it hard to talk to him like some people do.

He's a nice guy, I say, but what'll I do if Ivan's met someone?

You'll cope, says my mother. You have no choice. Is the chicken fully defrosted yet?

I think so, I say, but I can't eat anything. My stomach's unfolding.

Dear Looby,
It's the middle of the night, no birds yet. The gales have stopped and it's very quiet but I can't sleep. Ivan's not coming home for another three months. It's only him phoning tomorrow that's keeping me going. I've just been into the garden. It was bleak like a Beckett play. (*Waiting for Ivan*, ha ha.) The ground was frosty and the leaves looked hard but they were soft to walk on. I had on Nab's sheepskin and Rita's gardening shoes. She's a size smaller and I felt like I had Chinese bandaged feet. The moon looked like a cataract. Ivan said if you look at the moon on Ganesh day it's bad luck and you have to cross your arms and touch your ears. I looked at it deliberately tonight to piss Ganesh off. He doesn't remove obstacles, he makes them. I thought of going into the park to spite Ivan. I wanted to climb the Michael tree and sit in its huge branches, holding me safe

like a basket, but I couldn't even have jumped the ditch, and I'd have been terrified in the dark.

I've cut the buttons off his suede jacket and ripped up his last letter. I threw Ganesh away too but took him out of the bin later in case he puts a curse on me. Nab said that Ivan's not trying to hurt me, he's just a young man 'opening his wings'. Rita's mad at me and says she can't cope with me being so dramatic. She says I don't seem to realise how much my illness affects everyone else. I wish so much she didn't have to worry about me.

I am so afraid that I am never going to be well and this is my life forever. I could take paracetamol but it would kill Rita and they'd probably rescue me and I'd end up with brain damage *and* ME, dribbling all the time. And if it does work, your liver packs in and you go through agony before you die. I wish I'd paid more attention to poisonous plants at primary school. I just want to be in a deep sleep and wake up when Ivan kisses me. What will I do?

With best wishes
Helen.

Dear Helen,
All I can suggest is eating daffodil bulbs – they're toxic, can be fatal, especially to dogs – and lying in a glass coffin until Ivan gets back. Or you could try rhododendrons, they're toxic too, but maybe they need to be in flower.

With best wishes

Looby.

PS. Don't do anything I wouldn't do!

Lunchtime next day. All night, sleep broken by jagged truth.

She trudges down to the kitchen. A postcard of the Taj Mahal and a Christmas card with writing she half recognises are propped up against the marmalade jar.

Dear Looby,

Saw Taj Mahal glittering at sunrise. Mind-blowing but Agra is awful. It's all carpet factories and scams. Going back to Delhi. Will write properly soon.

Love, Ivan.

Helen rips up the postcard. The swing-bin is full. She scatters Ivan's words on top of Rita's grapefruit skins and presses down. (Grapefruit smells like sweat. She doesn't know how Rita can stand it. It's some diet she's on.) Scraps of card with 'love' and 'Looby' fall onto the floor. Helen thinks of the tins of words you got at primary school. You learned to read, just to cut up the words years later when your boyfriend breaks your heart.

She opens the Christmas card. It's from Rachel. Another fucking penguin (on skis with a stripy scarf tied round its neck).

Underneath JOY TO YOU AT CHRISTMAS, Rachel has written: How are you feeling these days? If you picked up the phone, you might fucking know, Helen says, throwing the card onto the table.

She makes some weak black tea. She looks at the hands of the kitchen clock.

They are slug-slow.

She needs to have a shower – she can smell herself – but she's scared she'll miss him phoning. She cleans her teeth at least. She can't bear the velvety coating of unbrushed teeth.

The bathroom window is open and she can hear Agnes miaowing. She rinses her mouth and goes to the back door. Agnes is stuck up the tree in Richard's garden again.

Helen sighs and puts on Nab's sheepskin and goes out to rescue Agnes, with Chinese bandaged feet. She hopes Richard's mum isn't in. She can't face anyone. She climbs onto the low iron fence that separates their gardens, leans against the shed and stretches into the tree. A branch stabs her in the face.

Come down, you stupid cat! It's freezing out here.

She gets dizzy and has to steady herself. She can feel her thighs pimpling. She reaches up to grab the cat again but Agnes is nailed to the tree.

Agnes, for fuck's sake, will you come down? My arms are knackered. I'm not a fireman.

She pleads and cajoles until Agnes gives in, allowing herself to be plucked. Helen clutches her with one arm, using the other to lean on the shed. As she climbs down, she skins her shin. Agnes is rigid with resistance but Helen manages to keep hold of her until she's inside the house.

The rescue of Agnes has taken eight minutes.

She goes into the bathroom and dabs her scraped leg with TCP. It's agony. She thinks of when her and Rachel used to spend hours skinning the bark off thick rhododendron branches, to see the shiny bone colour underneath.

She goes into Nab and Rita's room and lies down. She is still wearing Nab's sheepskin. She kicks off Rita's shoes. Her toes are numb and she's sure she'll get chilblains. She lifts the receiver on the phone next to the bed to check the dialling tone.

She feels calmer in here. It's a change of scene. She closes her eyes and tries not to look at the clock. She manages ten minutes. She rolls out of Nab's coat and throws it on the floor. There's a compact mirror and eyebrow tweezer on Rita's bedside cabinet. She starts plucking her eyebrows but her arms are burning from Agnes and she can't finish. She tries another ten minutes of not looking. She is staring at the Artex ceiling when the phone rings.

It's Rita to see if he's called yet.

Not yet, says Helen, but you have to hang up in case he's trying to get through! She is furious at her mother for calling and getting her hopes up.

Remember to stay cool, says Rita.

I will, says Helen. I have to go, Mum. She puts the receiver down and warns the phone not to ring again unless it's Ivan.

Agnes has come into the bedroom and is standing on Nab's coat. She looks retarded. Helen leans over and lifts her onto the bed. You shouldn't be in here, Agnes. You know

177

Nab doesn't like you on the bed, especially with wounds.

The cat climbs on top of her and starts kneading her with her paws as if she's standing in syrup. She still smells cold from being outdoors. You're not well, Helen says. You shouldn't be going up trees. You should be resting.

The kneading tickles Helen and makes her laugh – the minutes seem to drag less. When the phone rings (two on the dot, as good as his word) Agnes jumps off the bed.

Hi, it's me. Are you a bit calmer now? he says.

Not really, says Helen. (She is happy he sounds sheepish.) I threw up after you phoned and I didn't sleep last night. All I can eat is toast.

God, I'm so sorry. I'll make it up to you when I'm home. I promise.

Ivan, you've made a fool out of me. Here's me keeping your letters under my pillow and reciting them to everyone and you turn round and do this.

I haven't made a fool of you. I tell everyone I meet about you. What a fighter you are.

Fuck off, Ivan. (Into herself.)

Well, I don't feel like a fighter anymore. And, by the way, Agnes might have cancer.

Poor Agnes, he says, but she's old, isn't she? Listen, Rez is coming out to Delhi for a family wedding at the beginning of January. You can give him a letter if you want. It'll be quicker than the mail.

So Rez has known about this all along? He could have said – he's a bastard too!

It's not Rez's fault I'm staying, Helen.

She doesn't answer.

Are you still there?

Yup, she says.

How are you anyway?

I told you in my letter. I've started the ACTH injections.

Are they helping?

A little. Who exactly are you going to Tibet with?

Just some people I've met.

Some people? Do they not have names, these people?

Of course they have names.

Are they male or female?

A mixture, he says.

Have you met someone, Ivan?

I've met lots of people. I've told you in my letter.

Tell me the truth!

Listen, he says, stop getting yourself into a state again! I haven't met anyone in the way you mean. I'm travelling. I meet people all the time. I can't help it.

I have to go, Helen says.

Okay... I'll try and phone you at New Year. I'll be at Rez's uncle's.

I miss you so much. It's killing me.

I miss you too, he says.

I don't want to be without you. I love you.

There's no privacy here, he says. I'm in a plastic booth. Everyone can hear. He lowers his voice. I love you too.

I wish I believed you.

You know I do.

My mum says I've to keep my dignity but I obviously don't have any when it comes to you.

You've got lots of dignity. You have to try and eat something. Promise me.

I promise.

Bye, Looby.

Bye.

She listens for the click that's death and slowly puts the receiver down. She goes through to the kitchen and puts the kettle on. She is heartbroken that he didn't resist when she said she had to go. He should have known she was just trying to be tough. Of course she didn't *have to go,* she never has to go – busy people have to go! She has all the time in the world. She mashes up a banana with sugar and goes through to the living room and spoon-feeds herself at the window, dipping her ugliness and tears (like car headlights) whenever anyone passes by.

She imagines the gossip in the Co-op: *I saw the wee Fleet girl today. She was up at the window. She looked terrible. She was all contorted. She's got that funny virus.*

She takes her tea upstairs even though it's cold. She puts on *Astral Weeks* and gets into bed. There's a bloodstain on the quilt where Agnes has been lying. It looks like a miniature map of Africa. She's too exhausted to sponge it. She lies down and lets Van Morrison scrape away the pain. She loves *Ballerina*. She imagines herself like a ballerina.

Strong, sinewy legs, stretching her muscles at the bar.

She wants to be a dancer, not decaying in this bed.

It's dark when she wakes. Her 'thoughts are slow and brown' like Edna's. Everything's still hollow.

She goes downstairs. She puts the lights on in the living room. She goes into the kitchen and washes up the few dishes and wipes the table clean. She wishes Nab or Rita would come home, but they'll be home late tonight – they play badminton at the hospital on Thursdays after work. She feels comforted by their coats in the hall. It makes the house seem less empty.

She has to get clean. She has a shower and puts on a pair of Ivan's old jeans and his shirt. She heats up some tinned tomato soup. She slurps it deliberately for something to do, for something to hear other than the fridge humming.

She goes back to bed and waits for someone to come home and puncture the silence.

She is so tired of herself.

Well, did he phone? asks Rita, popping her head round the bedroom door.

Yup, I say. About twenty minutes after you.

Did you keep calm?

I think so, I say.

Good. What have you eaten today?

A banana and some tinned soup.

That's not enough, Helen.

I'll try and eat something before bed, I say. D'you know what I've got a craving for?

What?

Orange ice lollies.

Rita smiles. We don't have any but I'll get some tomorrow. How did you get that scratch on your face?

Rescuing Agnes from the tree.

Not again!

I'm coming with you to the vet's tomorrow. She definitely isn't herself.

I'm sure the lesion's just a scratch. She was probably in a fight.

I hope so. How was badminton?

I didn't play, my back was too sore. I chatted to Dr Seth's wife while Nab was playing. She was asking for you. One of her friends has ME. She's a nurse but she hasn't worked for a year and a half. She's not bedridden but she can't do more than potter about.

Who looks after her?

She's married to a consultant but I don't think he was very understanding to begin with.

Stupid bastard. Sorry for swearing.

She goes to a support group in Dumbarton. I can get the details if you want.

As long as there are no dreary women there, handing out digestives, I say.

I think this group has younger people in it, it wouldn't be as depressing for you as the Isobel woman.

One week, she interlaced the digestives with Jaffa Cakes.

You shouldn't mock, says Rita, she's a poor soul.

You could tell she'd been planning the biscuit arrangement all day.

You should be more understanding – you know what it's like to have so much time and nothing to fill it.

I know, I say, but she'd hog the whole evening. She talked about herself all the time and didn't listen to any of us.

You should give this other group a try. It might be more supportive.

I'll think about it – but you're not going to like people just 'cos they've got the same illness.

Right, I'm away to soak my weary bones.

Why are you weary – is it me?

Not really, she says. My back's really aching.

Why don't you take some painkillers?

You know me, I prefer not to.

I don't think an Anadin will kill you, Mum.

I'll be fine.

I almost forgot, Sean phoned. He's definitely going to Nellie's for Christmas but they'll both be here for New Year.

Good, I can tell Granny. Two less for her to cook for. Don't sit up here on your own moping.

I won't, I say. Deep down, I don't really blame Ivan for

not wanting to come home. What is there to come back for?

I know how hard it is for you, says Rita. We all do.

*

I think he could've met someone, babe, said Jana. You have to steel yourself for that.

Don't say that, Jana. Please. It's not bearable. Not on top of Agnes.

Why the big change of plan then?

You know how impulsive he is. He's always chopping and changing.

So when's he coming back?

Three months.

I guess it's not that long.

It'll pass, I said.

I knew I was defending him. I hadn't told her that I'd copied out an Edna poem – *Well, I Have Lost You* – and sent it via Rez.

Jana said she'd cancel her New Year plans and come to Balloch instead. Unless I wanted to go up to Glasgow.

I can't, I said. I'd need to get someone to bring me up. And I'd need to leave the party after an hour and I'd have nowhere proper to sleep. And how would I get back home on New Year's Day?

You can have my bed. Stay with me for a couple of days.

I'd love to but it's too much, Jana. I don't want to be exhausted for my next ACTH injection. And it might be my last Hogmanay with Agnes.

I know, she said. It was just a thought to get you away from the Ivan stuff.

I'd love it if you came here but it'll be the usual: Nab'll be on the Glenmorangie, reminiscing about Greenland and how the Inuits used urine as hairspray. Sean'll be wrapped round Princess Nellie, and my granny'll be wittering on about nothing.

She laughed. I'm not leaving you on your own, she said. It'll be fun to hang out with your family anyway.

You're an angel, I said. Happy Christmas tomorrow.

Happy Christmas, she said before hanging up and going back to bed with Pierce, the ex-policeman who was now doing an IT degree. He had sloping shoulders and kissed like a fish but he gave her great orgasms.

Why are you not wearing your Christmas hat, Helen? said Brian for the hundredth time.

Because it keeps slipping off, I said. Please stop asking.

Take that piece of cake, said my granny, pointing to the last piece of chocolate gateau.

I'm full, thanks, I said. I've had tons of turkey and stuffing.

If you get the last piece of cake you get a handsome husband!

I'll bear that in mind, I said, forcing a smile.

You really need to eat more, Helen, said Nab. You're thin like wire.

I excused myself from the table and went to lie on the couch. My grandad had already retired to his armchair with his pipe and his new James Herriot.

I don't like to see you so sad, Helen. Was Santa not good to you?

Sorry, Grandad. I'm trying my best. I'm sad about Agnes.

Nae herbs cure love, he said, eh?

That too, I said.

Brian came over and parked himself beside me. He took my hand and started stroking my palm. You could keep your hat on with kirbies, he said. That's what Rita does.

I'll do it next year, I said. I promise.

Arched Window. *Boxing Day*

Helen is hunched against the radiator, eating left-over turkey sandwiches and reading John Hedgecoe's *Introductory Photography Course*, her Christmas present from Rita and Nab. She looks up from the book and asks Brian to stop stroking Agnes's fur the wrong way. She doesn't like it when you do that, Helen says. She's not well.

*

Square window. *New Year's Eve*

Looby Loo's gone back in her basket! She's had a metallic headache since Boxing Day. Jana can't come after all, she's laid up with flu. Sean and Nellie are downstairs, glued to each other, wearing the Benetton sweaters they gave each other for Christmas.

Helen's thinking (again) of painless ways to kill herself that won't hurt her family. She wonders what she could write in her suicide note but knows there is nothing she could ever say that would compensate Rita. Maybe she could leave a bottle of claret on the landing.

At ten o'clock the phone rings and it's Ivan. His words are as powerful as a shot of ACTH. She won't have to kill herself after all.

She sits up with her family for the bells. They all wish her better health in 1987. Nellie is the picture of health with her big bones and rosy cheeks. Helen imagines her panting and blushing when she has sex with Sean. She will be on top, of course.

She toasts everyone's health and makes a New Year resolution to be nicer to Nellie. When she goes to bed she kisses Ganesh and puts him under her pillow. Please make Agnes okay, she whispers.

14

Callum

HIYA, PIGEONS! BRIAN was running up to the birds in George Square, screaming as they fluttered and blurred – coming back to scratch and peck round his feet.

Don't do that, said my granny, they're riddled with disease!

They're pushy, said Nab.

Ha ha! said Brian, rushing at them again. Pushy pigeons!

C'mon, I said. Don't dilly dally. Let's go back to the car.

Nab had driven me into town to help me choose a camera in the January sales. I'd been looking forward to just me and him but Brian had pleaded to come with us and then my granny had slotted herself into the arrangement too. While they were dredging the sales, Nab and I had gone to Jessops to get the camera. We also got a developing tank,

188

solutions, a thermometer, glossy photographic paper and a file for negatives. I was scared the assistant would ask me technical questions but I'd felt important, like a real photographer.

Afterwards, we'd gone to the Willow Tea Room. Nab loved the fake Rennie Mackintosh chairs but they were really uncomfy to sit on for any length of time. You felt like your head was bolted to your neck. Nab said he liked them because they helped his disc and 'squeezed out his spine'.

A man with a wart spreading over his nose like grey rice crispies had sat down at the next table. I felt sick and wanted to change seats but didn't want to offend him. He'd stared down at his plate, intent on his scone and jam. Ten minutes later a woman had joined him. I was glad that she was screening the wart, glad that he had a wife and wasn't on his own, spending a life of looking down. The woman was talking about her new gold taps and what kind of cleaner you could use on them.

On the way out, I got a Swatch watch for Ivan in the jeweller's downstairs. Not that he deserves it, I said to Nab. You're a sweet girl, he replied.

As we got into the car Brian was chuckling and saying 'pushy pigeons' over and over again in a sing-song way.

What did you get in the sales? I asked.

His face lit up and he rustled in his bags and flourished his purchases in front of me. *Ta-rra!* A Michael Jackson aldun! (He always said 'aldun' instead of album.) And an Abba tape!

Golden oldies, I said.

It's not golden oldies, Helen. It's *Abba*.

I'm teasing, I said.

What did you get?

My camera and some other stuff.

D'you like your camera?

I love it, I said.

Are you thrilled to bits?

I'm going to teach myself photography, I said, trying to sound breezy but all I cared about was my next blue letter and I couldn't pull the wool over my own eyes.

When we got home I laid out my camera and accessories. It was like a show of presents. I got into bed with my clothes on. I thought of the man with the wart and wondered how his wife could bare to touch his face. I wondered why they couldn't operate. I wondered if I could kiss Ivan if he had a growth like that.

His 'staying another three months' letter had arrived two weeks ago. It had been crumpled and marked as if it had been jammed in a machine. (I thought this was a bad omen.) He'd written that everyone he met in India seemed to be running away from something. (I'd written back, Are you running away from me, laddie?) I was sure that he was fucking Joyce, an Australian doctor he'd met in Goa. He said she'd been great when he'd had severe diarrhoea and all he could do for five days was eat bananas and lie still in the guest house. She'd thought it was amoebic dysentery and had given him Flagyl. India's full of pathogens, he'd written. (And Joyce is one of them, I thought.) I hated to think of him ill and shivering, and was jealous that she'd been looking after him. It should've been me. As if that wasn't bad enough, they'd swapped books. (You swap with everyone you meet, he said.) She'd given him *Hotel du Lac,* and he'd given her *A Bend in the River.* I was always trying to get him to read, and now he was reading everyone who'd ever been shortlisted.

*

I have a William Morris notebook with seductive blank pages: I write photography notes at the front and Buddhism notes at the back. I got a book on Buddhism from the library. If Ivan's coming back as a Buddhist, I want to know what he's on about.

Harsh negatives need soft printing, and *life is suffering.*

Glossy paper enhances blacks, and *'samsara'* means *endless wandering.*

Widening the aperture increases the depth of field, and *we have to accept change.*

I'm writing notes in a book with a chintz print cover, and Ivan's trekking in the Himalayas. We're just structuring our days differently.

*

My hands were shaking as I loaded the negatives into the developing tank. I'd been practising all week, feeling for sprocket holes in the dark, in the cupboard under the stairs. I sealed the tank and emerged from the cupboard, stubbing my toe on the Hoover. I called it a bastard.

I measured out the solutions in the kitchen, with the utmost care to get 68°. (It was like being back in chemistry, except I was the only one in the class.)

I sloshed the developer around the tank and counted the minutes, agitating every thirty seconds.

I poured out the developer; I stopped; and fixed; and rinsed.

I counted the minutes. Rinsing takes forever. You need to wash the film under water for half an hour.

When I finally took the negatives out of the tank I felt sick. I couldn't believe it had worked. They looked okay! I removed the excess water by sliding my fingers down the negatives (Callum's tip since I'd forgotten to buy a squeegee). I hung them up to dry with a clothes peg attached to a coat hanger on the shower rail. I fixed another clothes peg on the end of the strip to stop the negatives from curling up. I was smiling. I felt like a professional. I couldn't wait to show Rita and Nab.

*

I'm watching the wool cycle – I like the slow tumble and thud of the clothes. I had my last ACTH injection today. I felt like a drug addict, getting her last fix. I'm scared that I can't have any more – you can't keep having them – though they're not as good as they were at the beginning. I've posted a letter to Ivan, telling him that Callum's going to help me set up a darkroom. I hope he'll be jealous.

*

Callum sat cross-legged on the floor, holding the negatives up to the light. They're a bit overdeveloped, he said, but not bad for a first attempt.

They're suburban landscapes, I said. Bins in rain, squirrel in rain, squirrel on windowsill, DMs in rain...

You took a picture of DMs?

Yeah. Sean's old ones. I thought it was arty, raindrops against leather.

Could be, he said, smiling. The cat looks like bagpipes in this one.

I know, I said. That's why I took it. She was washing herself and lifted her back leg. She stayed like that for ages. It gave me time to focus.

What's this? he said.

Flake wrapper in a puddle.

And this?

A squirrel's tail.

He laughed. Just a wee bit blurred.

My arms get tired focusing. That's the problem... D'you think they're shite?

They're fine, he said. Now the good part. Come into the darkroom with me, little girl!

Behave yourself, I said. You're my teacher.

We'd pushed the single bed against the wall in the boxroom and set up the enlarger and all the trays. We'd blocked the light out completely with bin bags over the curtains. I'd handed him up masking tape and drawing pins like an apprentice. He'd been running up and downstairs with jugs of solutions. I told him he was like John Noakes.

Before we started, he said in a teachery voice, Have you acquainted yourself with the darkroom, Miss Fleet?

I think so, I said. Everything's on the floor.

He laughed. Okay. Lights off. Here goes.

I loved the soft redness of the safelight. It made you *feel* safe.

The enlarger looks like a lamp post, I said.

He showed me how you enlarge the print by cranking the handle up and down and how you frame the image with the easel.

Open the lens up to focus, he said, you need all the light you can get, and then stop down to F8 when it comes to printing.

It's amazing how the negative comes alive, I said.

Here, look into the focus finder, you can see the actual grain and really sharpen things up.

It's brilliant, I said.

Let's do the contact sheet now. Can you hand me some paper?

I opened the pack of Ilford and took out a sheet. It was like opening a condom, fumbling in the dark.

Remember, it's glossy side up. You can feel the glossy side if you get mixed up.

He laid out the strips of negatives on the paper and covered them with glass from an old clip frame. We're using a no. 2 filter and we'll go for fifteen seconds. He flicked the red safe filter aside. One elephant, two elephants, three elephants...

They did that in *Gregory's Girl*, I said.

I don't usually do that, I'm just spicing things up, he said.

He stopped counting and flicked the red tongue back. He handed me the paper.

In the developer now? I asked.

Slosh it for a minute. Keep sloshing and counting.

Fuck, some of it's spilled on the floor!

It's okay as long as the print's submerged. Keep calm.

I hope the developer doesn't stain the carpet.

Right that's long enough. Into the stop bath now. Don't get the tongs mixed up.

It looks black, I said. I don't think it's worked!

You can't see 'til the light's on... Right, fix it now. Another good slosh.

I counted elephants dutifully.

Now leave it for a bit. Is the paper away?

Yup.

Okay. Lights on.

I stood up and put the light on. We looked at the contact sheet.

A wee bit dark, said Callum.

I think it's lovely! I said. You can make them all out. I want to print 'Agnes Like Bagpipes'.

Let's do it again. We can do better than that.

Can I do it this time?

I put the light off and knelt down again.

Let's do ten seconds this time, he said. And filter no. 1. It'll soften things up.

I reached for the box of filters on the bed, dropping them as I handed them to Callum. They spread out on the floor like playing cards. I'm sorry, I said. I'm always dropping things. I'm a fucking butterfingers.

You need to relax, he said. It doesn't matter if you make a mistake. He put his arm round me as he changed the filter. I liked his sweater brushing my neck.

The second contact sheet was better. Can I print Agnes now? I said.

I think you should go for the Flake in the puddle. It's sharper.

You're the expert.

I put the Flake negative in the carrier. Can you do the lights, please? I said. I'm getting dizzy getting up and down.

He switched off the light and I saw that I'd put the

negative in upside down. I turned it round. It's too dark, I said. I can't see a thing.

Open it up to 4.5, he said.

I keep forgetting, I said. I'll never remember all this. Will it need soft printing because it's contrasty?

He laughed. Listen to David Bailey!

It's surreal in this light, I said. I feel like we're in a film.

He'd gone all serious. He showed me how to do a test strip and find the best exposure. Take a note of your final settings, he said. You can write them on the back of the print in pencil.

Finally, at F8/12 seconds/filter 1, I had a black and white print of a Flake wrapper in a puddle.

Your first print! he said.

I love it, I said. Good tonal range if I say so myself.

We should celebrate.

How?

With a wee snog on the bed.

Callum!

Only joshing. You just look very sexy in this light.

And you don't seem such a scallywag. You're a good teacher. Very patient.

Aye, my scallywagness is subdued in the darkroom. You see me in a different light, if you'll pardon the pun.

Can we have a break before we do another one? I said. My head feels weird.

Sure. I'm dying for a fag.

You can go downstairs and have a cigarette. I think we've got Jammie Dodgers.

As I turned off the light and closed the door to make sure Agnes wouldn't get in, I saw there was a dead moth in the fixer.

The second time we set up the darkroom, Callum told me the reason he hadn't come round with the interview contact sheets was his dad had hit his mum, and he'd hit his dad, and his mum and his sister had gone to stay with his granny. His dad had gone round crying and promised he would stop drinking and his mum had gone back even when she knew it was a lie. It'll be all cosy, ring-a-ring-a-rosie for a while, Callum said, and then he'll binge again. I feel I can tell you. I used to tell Roquia this stuff.

I'm sorry, I said. I don't know what to say. Rita hit my dad once but I know it's not remotely the same.

He hasn't hit her for years 'cos he knows I'll get him, he said. He threw a cup at her once and she had to go to Casualty.

Why doesn't she leave him?

She's tried. When we were wee, we'd go to stay in my auntie's in Crieff, but he'd come round whimpering like a dog. We even changed schools once. We went to a Catholic primary and had a green uniform. My mum says he's fine when he's not drinking, she says that's the real Duncan. Things get back to normal and you almost forget, then he comes home steaming and my mum reads the riot act and my wee sister's pleading with them to stop shouting.

I put my hand on his back. He bent his head forward and I walked my fingers up to the knobbly bit on his neck. He brought his head back and I cradled his neck in my hand.

It must be scary for your sister.

It is, but she's the apple of his eye. He'd never lay a finger on her. She's dying to move out but she doesn't want to leave my mum.

Your poor mum.

He always buys her presents after a raji. That's what the new carpet was all about. But he'll have had another ten rajis by the time it's paid up.

What does he do?

He's an electrician. Sometimes I hope he'll get killed at work.

It's good you can joke.

You have to, doll. D'you know what he did once when we were really wee? He opened all the doors on the advent calendar when he was drunk. My mum tried to close them all again, but they kept opening.

What a bastard!

I still remember that calendar. It was glittery.

Glittery ones are the best.

With swedgers behind the doors!

Nah, I don't like the ones with sweets, they look horrible when they're open, just an empty hole, no picture.

He laughed. I used to hate it when you got a crap picture like a robin or a drum.

Or a skate.

That bastard opened the whole fucking calendar, he said, shaking his head.

I'll get you a deluxe calendar next Christmas, I said.

With glitter and swedgers?

Of course!

I might just hold you to that.

Can I tell you something now? I said. It's really trivial compared to what you've told me but I want to tell you.

Aye.

It's *really, really* trivial.

Stop apologising, he said. Spit it out.

There's something about this light that makes you want to tell the truth, isn't there?

I suppose, he said.

I took my hand away from his neck. Remember you were asking if I missed Ivan and if I trusted him, and I said a hundred percent, well I was lying 'cos I don't. I'm always worried sick that he's away with someone else 'cos I'm ill. And I think he's shagging Joyce in India and that's why he's extended his trip.

Who's Joyce?

Some fucking superwoman doctor.

Callum didn't speak.

D'you think he has met someone else?!

I don't know, doll. He'd be daft to have someone else,

but you know what it's like when you're so far away. Boys will be boys. You shouldn't think about it.

I can't stop thinking about it. I torture myself with images of them. The only time I don't think about him is when I'm doing photography stuff. It's the only thing that absorbs me.

Well, we better get back to work then. Hand me the negs, Diane.

I sent copies of the best prints to Jana and Fizza. I'd written titles underneath in indelible ink: Agnes as Bagipes, DMs in the Rain, Ripped Bin Bag, Rita's Wedding Hat. I sent 'Flake in Puddle' to Delhi. I didn't even know where Ivan was. It was now the middle of March and I hadn't heard from him for three weeks. I *knew* he wouldn't be home by the end of the month. He'd drip-feed me the truth in his next letter. I didn't care just now: Agnes was at the top of my list of griefs. Sometimes she seemed to be in remission and sprang about the vegetable garden like a demented kitten. At others, she lay limp on the settee for days like a resident in an old folk's home. She couldn't jump in the window anymore. I massaged her gently between the ears. I wished she could tell me where it hurt.

*

Easter 1987

stranger	What did you do today?
me	I rescued our neighbours' child Zoe from snapdragons. I caught her in the front garden about to put them in her mouth.
stranger	You need eyes on the back of your head when they're that age.
me	Ask me what else I did!
stranger	What else did you do?
me	I learned to dodge and burn.
stranger	So, you're an expert in the darkroom now.
me	Yup. I say 'negs', and I use water instead of stop solution… Ask me what else I did!
stranger	What else?
me	I kissed Callum!
stranger	How did that happen?
me	We'd been in the darkroom all night, talking more than developing, and I felt really close to him. Then Nellie's hamster got out of its cage – we're looking after it while they're in London – and Callum was saying we could get another, black-eyed creams are ten a penny, and I was laughing so much I was

crying, and I couldn't stop crying, and he put his arms round me and kissed me and he tasted of cigarettes but I liked it and we had to keep looking for the hamster and we were both really shy of each other.

stranger   You've certainly had a busy day. When the cat's away the mice will play! Did you find the hamster, by the way?

me   Eventually. It was huddled under the bed behind a sweater. D'you think I should tell Ivan about Callum?

stranger   Well, they say honesty is the best policy!

15

An Orange Silk Dress

AGNES DIED TODAY. I feel like Camus. I only ever read the first line of *L'Étranger*, Jana was doing it for her final exam. I could never write a line like that – how can writers do that, write of terrible things? I'd be scared it really happened – *maman* dying – and a world without Rita is just not possible. But it's okay to write that Agnes died today, because it really happened and I can't tempt it by writing it.

We thought she'd die during the night, she was so weak. We took her to the vet first thing this morning. I haven't been up this early for months. I'm usually only up early for hospital appointments.

I stroked her head and they cut a chink in her fur and injected her with Euthatal. Then they took her away and incinerated her.

None of us spoke at dinner. We all had lumps in our throats.

You keep hoping her wee head will push round the door. You can't imagine her as NOT existing – you can't imagine her as dust. There are still tins of Whiskas in the cupboard – tuna and rabbit.

Brian phoned and said, It's terrible about the cat, isn't it?

Yeah, but it's good she's not suffering anymore. She was very ill.

I suppose so. Did you see *Top of the Pops?*

No.

Prince was on. He sang *Purple Rain.* It's my favourite.

Why can't we get another cat? I said to Rita a few days later.

Because they're too much of a responsibility, she said.

I knew she'd say this.

We could get one from the animal home, I said. No one wants the ones with three legs or one eye, but as long as it's a tortoiseshell, I don't mind.

That's all I need, she said, a handicapped cat. We're not getting another one. You can get one when you have your own flat.

Well, that'll be the year 2000, I said. I'll call it Mango. I think that's a lovely name for a cat, don't you?

Not really. It's a bit pretentious, calling your cat after fruit.

Chekhov named his dogs Bromine and Quinine, I said.

She laughed. Is Callum coming for tea tonight?

I think so. He might be a bit late though. He's taking photos of that Scout Hall that was set on fire.

You two seem very cosy these days.

I felt myself blushing. We're good friends, Mum, that's all.

I never said otherwise, replied my mother.

I'm just telling you, there's nothing going on. Anyway, it would be therapeutic for me to have another cat. It'd increase my chances of recovery.

We're not getting another one.

Stroking pets is supposed to reduce your blood pressure.

Stop blackmailing me, Helen.

We could get a diabetic one and give it injections.

No!

I'm only kidding, I said.

I never know with you, she replied.

He'd stay late and come into my bed when Nab and Rita were asleep. We'd try to be quiet so they wouldn't hear. I had to cover his mouth so he wouldn't groan too loudly. He'd asked me to go to his sister's twenty-first with him at the end of May. I said I'd try and was already worrying about what to wear.

*

I want to be asleep to get away from the pain in my spine, but the chemicals that let you sleep seem to be missing from my head. I try and think of what everyone I know is doing RIGHT NOW. Callum'll be having a joint. Jana might be laughing her sexy laugh and putting her hair behind her ear. Sean and Nellie will be entwined. Or they might be studying together in the main library or having a drink in Curlers. Fizza will be in bed, feeling vile. She might be crying. Brian will be doing a watercolour – it's his new thing. He got watercolour crayons for Christmas and has been painting cats non-stop since Agnes died. They're quite good. And Ivan – I have no idea what Ivan will be doing or where he will be doing it. He could have emigrated to Australia for all I know. Or he could be dead from dysentery.

*

Would you like some tea, Helen? Rita shouted up.

Yes, please. That would be lovely, thanks.

I was still half asleep. I drifted off again and was woken by the cup rattling on the saucer and Ivan saying, Here's your tea, Looby.

I sat up and grabbed at his arms and his clothes. *Is it you, is it really you?!*

Yeah, it's me. He was smiling.

But you didn't tell me you were coming home!

I wanted to surprise you, he said. He hugged me and I was crying and laughing and dreaming it all.

Rita came up with the tea. Who were you talking to?

I woke myself up shouting again. I was dreaming that Ivan was home. It was *so* real.

Afraid not. Just me. I'm off to work. See you later.

See you.

The dream had been so real I felt robbed. I was sad for the rest of the day.

I defrosted some beef and made chilli con carne for dinner as a surprise for Rita and Nab. I wondered if bay leaves actually did anything or if it was all just a con.

Ivan called from Heathrow two days after the dream. He sounded different, as if he were articulating his words for someone whose first language wasn't English. You sound like an American journalist in a film, I said.

I'll come to see you in a few days – as soon as I've got some decent sleep, he said.

When exactly?

When I'm not tired.

Can you not give me a day?

I'll call you when I get to my parents'.

You should've told me you were coming home. Your plane could've crashed and I would've had no idea you were on it.

My money's running out... I have to go, babe.

I was sick with excitement, and shaking. Ivan'd called me 'babe' – how American, how romantic!

My head was inflamed with the multi-tasking that lay ahead. First, I called Marion's salon. I'd like to make an appointment for highlights and a cut and blow-dry, please.

Marion's off for the week, the girl said. Jay could do you tomorrow at nine.

Is Jay good?

Jay trains the trainees, she said snootily.

Can you fit me in in the afternoon? Morning's no good.

Can you get away from your work for twelve?

I'll try, I said. (I'd need to set my alarm.)

Next, I phoned Clare and made an appointment for a leg waxing.

That night, I fantasised about picking Ivan up from the airport in his car – I'd been using it to get to my translator's job while he was away. I'd be a bit late 'cos I was held up at a meeting and I'd be putting lipstick on at the traffic lights. I'd be wearing my new charcoal grey suit.

Jay stood behind me, putting his fingers through my hair. I'd told him I wanted a choppy bob with blonde highlights – I had a picture from *Vogue*. Your hair's much thicker than the model's, he said. She's more flyaway. We don't want to go too layered or it could look frizzy when it's dried.

Whatever you think, I said. And I'd like the colour really subtle. I'm nervous. It's my first time.

Don't worry. You'll be a wee treat. Is it a special occasion?

My boyfriend's coming back from travelling. He's been away for seven months.

So you're getting all dolled up for him?

Yeah.

Quite right. We'll get you gowned up and started. Would you like a tea or a coffee?

Tea, please. Very weak.

My head was just bearable, although everything was vaguely hallucinated, and the music was too loud. The hairdresser next to me was asking her customer if her neighbour was still mental. The woman laughed and said yes.

Jay had just started dabbing in the colour when the questions started: *What is it you do anyway?*

I'm a student.

What are you studying?

French and English.

My pal's sister's doing German. She's in Frankfurt just now having a whale of a time.

I've already done my year abroad, but I've been ill so I'm not actually enrolled just now.

That's a shame – you could always work for the EEC when you've finished.

Maybe, I said.

The world's your oyster.

I looked at him in the mirror, so perky in his black shirt and Levi's. There was no point trying to explain so I just smiled.

When he'd finished, I felt like Boy George, with the mèche clips flapping in my hair. He'd twisted one in too tightly but I didn't want to say anything. He put me under the heat panels, and a boy goth with acne brought me tea and slapped a *Cosmopolitan* onto my lap.

I tried to read but Jay had told me not to move my head – reaching the tea was out of the question – and my arms were getting tired holding up the magazine. I got as far as my horoscope: *Scorpios are creatures of extremes, passionate and obsessive. Playing a waiting game is not your idea of fun. Use silver and grey to calm yourself down.*

After forty-five minutes, the timer wailed and the goth led me over to the sink to rinse out the chemicals. He scalded my head and asked me if this was my day off.

No, I said. I can't work just now. I have ME.

Is that where you're pure knackered all the time?

It's much more complex than that.

I think I had it last Christmas. I was in my bed for two weeks. My legs were like jelly. I'm not kidding.

I don't think it was ME, I said. Maybe you had a virus.

D'you want conditioner in your hair?

Please.

How long have you had it?

Three and a half years.

Will you ever get better?

It's supposed to burn itself out in five years.

It's not all gloom and doom then.

He turbaned my hair and took me back to the mirror.

211

My head felt like a boulder on my neck and my face was numb. He put the rubber thing that's like a car mat round my neck.

Jay re-appeared and chopped and layered without much more chat. I gave one word answers when he did. I tried to sip my tea but it was cold and had hair floating in it.

An hour later, he'd finished blow-drying me. The highlights glinted and I loved them. He held a mirror up so I could see the back – it didn't look like my head. It's lovely, I said. Thanks a lot! He was brushing the hair off my neck when I saw Rita come in. I felt the same relief I'd felt years ago when she'd meet me at the gates of primary school – she'd be two minutes late and I'd think she wasn't coming and then she'd suddenly be there and we'd beam at each other and everything would be fine.

The goth got my coat. I hope you feel better soon, he said.

Thanks, I said.

Your hair's gorgeous, said Rita. The honey colour really lifts your face up. What a difference!

I know – I love it. I can't wait for Ivan to see.

She half smiled. What time's the leg wax?

Four, I said. I think I was a bit ambitious booking it right after this. I feel crap.

We'll get some lunch and just relax for an hour. You'll be fine.

Rita. Lovely Rita.

*

I had golden hair and smooth legs but I had to do what I was dreading doing – I had to phone Callum and tell him Ivan was back. I was terrified he'd turn up the same day that Ivan was coming.

His mum answered and asked me how I was keeping. Up and down, I said. It's a terrible thing, she said. I wondered if she'd be so sympathetic if she knew I was about to dump her son.

Hi, doll.

I couldn't build up to it so I blurted it out – Ivan's back, I said.

That was quick. I thought he was gallivanting in Thailand.

He was but he's back.

Are you pleased?

Of course, I said.

Can I come over?

Just now? It's after nine.

I really want to see you.

Okay.

Are you going to tell him about us?

Of course not.

Why not?

I'll talk to you when you get here, I said. I don't like the phone.

Okay, he said.

*

You and Callum were midnight owls last night, said Nab.

Sorry, Nab, did we wake you? We were talking late. Callum was upset about something.

No, I was awake anyway. I was looking for Rennies.

I hoped he hadn't heard Callum crying.

He'd accused me of wanting to cheer myself up with a bit of rough while Ivan had been away.

I'm so sorry, I'd said. I didn't mean to hurt you. I thought we both knew it was a bit of fun all along.

His face was rigid with hurt. I thought it was more than fun, he said.

Please don't be so sad, Callum. You know how fond I am of you.

I'm fond of dogs. It means fuck all.

I'm sorry, I said.

Sorry is just shite.

I know but what else can I do to make you feel better?

You can tell Handsome Horace it's over.

You know I can't do that.

You can fuck off with your fondness then.

He'd sat on the bed with his hands over his eyes for half an hour. I made him two cups of Earl Grey but the bergamot had lost its charm.

*

Everything is so heavy. Agnes is gone and I seem to have broken Callum's heart. Ivan will make everything okay – he will be the magnificent rainbow after the non-stop drizzle for days.

*

I didn't sleep the night before. I was worrying about what to wear and just when I was falling asleep, the bastard magpies woke me.

Rita came up at midday to make sure I was up. It feels like my wedding day, I joked. I think your wedding would be less stressful, she said.

I had three hours to make myself beautiful.

I'd decided on my bright orange tracksuit bottoms (slightly flared) and black crew neck from Miss Selfridge. I showered with melon soap and washed my hair with seaweed shampoo. I sat on the floor and dried off and coated myself in cocoa butter.

I scrubbed my face with Japanese adzuki beans (which were going mouldy in the cardboard tub). I cleansed and toned and moisturised according to Clare's instructions. I combed my eyebrows and put Vaseline on my eyelashes with an old mascara brush. I pinched my cheeks and put on Rita's lipstick (pale amber). It was like a hook, moulded in the shape of her bottom lip, like all her lipsticks.

My arms felt like rags but I blow-dried my hair to bring out the highlights.

You look lovely, said Rita.

I'd already wrapped the Swatch watch in dark blue paper and silver ribbon and put it on my pillow for later.

I sat at the window, waiting for his yellow Beetle to come round the corner. I couldn't remember ever being so excited about anything. I felt like the terrier across the road that went berserk at the window every night when its owner came home from work.

He was right on time. That's him! I yelped, jumping up.

I stood beside the bins as his car crunched onto the gravel. I walked over as he got out. He was very tanned and thinner and wearing his thick glasses, which always made him a bit geeky. For a micro-second I felt disappointed and then he was holding me and I was leaning on him and he was back and he would never go away again and everything was bearable. We kissed shyly on the lips and I took his hand. Let's go in, I said.

Look who I found in the driveway! I said to Rita. They hugged awkwardly beside the fridge. You've lost weight, said Rita. That's amoebic dysentery for you, he replied.

Are you okay now? I said. Have the amoebas gone?

I hope so. It wasn't pleasant.

We'll need to feed you up. I still can't believe you're here. I have been dreaming of this – literally – for months!

He smiled but I didn't see any pity in his eyes and they should have been swimming in it.

He sat down in the living room and the space on the

216

couch was filled again. He looked so familiar, like a new pair of shoes I'd been lusting after but never thought I'd actually own. And here they were on the couch, bought at last, mine forever to covet and wear.

I sat beside him and he put his arm round me. There's so much to ask you, I don't know where to start! I said.

How are you? he said. Any improvements?

Small steps forward then a big step back. The ACTH was good.

It's heavy stuff.

It seemed to dilute the poison in my muscles.

That's good.

Don't you notice something different about me?

Your hair's nice. Have you had it cut?

Highlights, I've got highlights! Can you not see me glint? I stood up and went to the window. Can you see them now?

A little.

You can't, you're just saying that!

The light must be too flat, he said.

Rita came in with a tray of tea and sandwiches. How are your parents, Ivan?

They're fine, he said. I think they thought I was never coming back.

They're not the only ones, I said, sticking out my tongue.

And how's your grandmother? said Rita

Totally demented. The first thing she said to me was,

You smell like you've been in a cupboard. I told her I hadn't been in a cupboard, I'd been to India.

Maybe she thinks you were in Narnia, I said, sniffing his shoulder. You don't smell like a cupboard, you smell just like you.

Right, said Rita, that'll tide you both over 'til teatime. There's plenty in the freezer. I'm off to put my glad rags on.

Thanks, Mum, I said. Is it not a bit early for you leaving?

I want to drop in on Grandad, he's still not a hundred percent. I've got a Nevil Shute book for him.

My grandad's had a horrible flu, I said.

That's a shame, said Ivan. Where's Nab?

He's climbing the Ben with someone from the hospital. Rita's going to meet them at the guy's house for dinner. We'll have the place to ourselves. I can't wait to kiss you properly!

He smiled, and I glided along in the fairy tale.

I have something in the car for you, he said after Rita had gone.

Bring your bag in too, I said. Your overnight stuff.

He came back with a crumpled package that smelled of incense. I opened it. It was an orange silk dress. It's lovely, I said, grazing his cheek with a kiss. Thank you so much!

I hope it fits. I got medium.

It'll look great with a tan. I'm going to Madeira with Rita and Nab in the summer.

That's good, he said. Something to look forward to.

My first time abroad since France. You could come. There's plenty of room.

I can't. I'm just back.

Well, I might need to have a holiday romance then! I put my arms around him and tucked myself into him sideways like a cat. Where's your bag? I said.

I don't have one.

Why not?

I don't need one.

What do you mean?

I'm not staying, Looby.

What d'you mean you're not staying?!

I need to talk to you.

You're here to see me after seven months and you're not staying! You *have* to stay.

He took my hand. Listen to me, babe – you look lovely and I'm really happy to see you and it would be amazing to jump into bed with you but it wouldn't be fair... He explained in words made of felt how he'd had time to think when he was away and how it would be better if we were just friends and how he couldn't tell me on the phone, but I couldn't hear him properly because this was all happening through a window and the words weren't real, they were made of felt.

I clung to him and cried onto his shirt and his jeans and the orange dress.

I got highlights for you, I said! I blow-dried my stupid hair for you. I never blow-dry my hair. You've met someone.

It's Joyce isn't it?

No!

The sheep warned me.

What?

The sheep in my dream, that's what it was trying to do, warn me about this!

Don't be stupid.

You are my life.

Please don't say that – I can't be your life.

But you *are.*

I can't be. You're your own life.

You're dumping me because I'm ill.

I'm not *dumping* you.

Well it certainly feels like it! Which words do you prefer? *Destroying? Killing?*

Stop being so dramatic. Look this is hard for me too. I've worried myself sick wondering how I would tell you. I might be making a big mistake, I don't know, but I can't be with you just now, I just can't. I'm sorry.

Well, fuck off then!

D'you really want me to go?

Yes!

I don't think you should be on your own.

He was almost crying now.

Maybe you should have thought of that before delivering your grand monologue. I'm going to be on my own with this fucking illness for the rest of my life so I better get used to it!

You're hysterical.

I'm not!

Sit down. You need to calm down.

I don't need to calm down.

I'll make some more tea.

I don't want any more bastard tea. Do you know how many cups of tea I've had to drink since I got ill?! Every time it looks like things are getting a bit grim, someone makes me another cup of tea!

I'm sorry.

You haven't even noticed that Agnes is dead.

I knew what I had to do. He should have been folding me in kisses and instead he was telling me it was over. I went through to the kitchen and opened the cutlery drawer and raked for the chopping knife.

What are you doing, Helen?!

None of your business!

I found the knife and scored it across my left arm three times. I marched back through to Ivan. See what happens when you leave people because they're ill and you don't want them holding you back!

For fuck's sake! Are you mad?

No, I'm not mad. You know I'm not mad.

You need to wash your arm.

He propelled me through to the bathroom.

Ouch! I said as the water hit the cut. It hurts.

It's not deep, he said. It won't scar.

You know I'm not mad, I whispered.

The rage had gone, I was washed up and calm.

I'm hurt and terrified but I'm not mad, I said.

You can't let your mother and Nab see that.

I know. They'd have me sectioned.

I wish I had some Valium to give you. Does Rita have any?

Of course not. Rita doesn't even take Anadin. Why would she have Valium?

My mum's got some.

Well, Rita's *not* your mum. Rita doesn't need Valium.

What's that supposed to mean?

Nothing.

You're one to talk, you're like a fucking tsunami.

A what?

A big wave after an earthquake.

Well, you shouldn't have caused the earthquake, I said.

I'm sorry.

I'm sorry too, I said. I feel so stupid. I'm always mad and choppy with no sleep.

I'm going to make some tea. I need some even if you don't.

I've felt like doing it so often but never have. Tonight I snapped. It's weird, you get a kind of high from it.

It's the endorphins.

I thought you only got those from aerobics and sex.

No, endorphins block pain.

So it doesn't matter that you're leaving me! I'll just keep

222

cutting my arm. I won't feel a thing.

He shook his head and went into the kitchen.

I'm not going to kill myself, I shouted through. If I was going to do it, I'd have done it by now.

He came through with tea.

Don't tell anyone about my arm.

I won't.

Promise you won't.

I promise.

I'm not trying to blackmail you. I'm just upset.

I know.

We sipped our tea in silence (his) overlapping with grief (mine).

I've always known it would end like this, I said. Deep down I've always known.

Imagine I'd got ill, he said quietly. What would you have done?

I don't know, Ivan. How on earth could I know? I know I wouldn't have abandoned you though.

I'm not abandoning you. I'll phone you all the time.

We talked in circles for hours. It was dark but I didn't want the lights on. He kept denying that he'd met someone else. I wanted to hurt him with Callum, but I was too scared to tell him in case it made it easier for him to leave.

Can we put a lamp on, please? he said. It's depressing sitting in the dark.

I like the dark, I said. I'm too sad to have the lights on. We can go into the kitchen if you want. Are you hungry?

I'm starving.

We heated up oven chips and pizza and he told me about the Taj Mahal. He'd gone at sunrise when there was hardly anyone else there – he'd wanted to be first to charge through the gates and have a sense of being alone instead of sharing it with the thousands of other people.

It must've been amazing, I said.

It was amazing. All the semi-precious stones were sparkling, it was like a fairy-tale palace.

It makes me think of Hansel and Gretel, I said.

Why?

The witch tricks them with a fancy gingerbread house with diamond windows. It's so dazzling, she lures them in.

I'm lucky I got to see it so early in the morning.

You're lucky you got to see it, *full stop*.

I know.

I really loved all your letters, I said, I could imagine I was there with you – did you like getting mine – did you even read them?

Of course – it was lovely to get them.

Did you get my photos?

What photos?

The black and white photos I developed.

No.

You didn't get the bins or Agnes?

No.

I've got tons to show you.

Can I see them next time – it's getting late? I need to go.

I can't face your mum and Nab.

I better try on my dress before you go. If it doesn't fit you can give it to Dr Joyce.

Stop it, he said. You're like a pancake, flipping between calm and crazy.

Can you blame me?

Not really.

Please stay tonight. I'll try and be more Zen, I promise. *Please.* (Feminists would have shot me.)

I'll stay but I'm going first thing in the morning, okay?

We went to bed before Rita and Nab were back. I couldn't face them either. He borrowed my toothbrush after assuring me he was amoeba free. I hid the Swatch watch in my drawer. I'd lost enough dignity for one night.

We lay like spoons and he put his arm round me. I could feel him breathing on my neck. It was like agony iced with hundreds and thousands.

He left in the morning before Nab and Rita were up.

I put my fingers in my ears so I couldn't hear his car on the gravel. I went back to bed and wrapped my pillow in the orange dress and cried as quietly as I could. A microscopic part of me felt sorry for him for having the pain of telling me it was over, and if I was extra honest I could feel a *tiny* scrap of relief that I wouldn't have to worry myself to a pulp anymore, wondering if he still wanted me.

I managed to sleep until lunchtime. Before going

downstairs, I made sure my dressing gown sleeves were down.

I'm not really surprised, said Rita, who was dishing up bacon. At least he came and told you to your face. I admire him for that. It can't have been easy for him either.

He's going to phone tonight.

It'd be better if he didn't phone. You won't get over him if he keeps phoning. It'll just get your hopes up.

But I *need* him to phone, it helps me cope.

Well, it doesn't help *me* cope. I'm the one who has to listen to you crying your eyes out. Ivan has to do one thing or the other. He can't have his cake and eat it. I can't cope with your heartbreak.

He's just worried about me.

And Nab and I aren't?

I didn't say that. What do you want me to do, Mum, be banished to a nunnery because I'm ill?!

I don't know what to suggest anymore, Helen. I really don't.

Not having Ivan's like having my arm chopped off. I feel amputated.

Nab came through and cupped his hands round my head. Don't worry, these bleak feelings will fly away soon. He rubbed my ears. Your ears are soft and lovely, like your mum's.

I lifted my arms to touch his hands and remembered the red cross. Thanks, Nab, I said.

I hated them having to see my pain. I folded a piece of

dry toast in two and shoved a slice of bacon in.

I feel so stupid getting all done up for nothing.

You shouldn't feel stupid, said Nab.

I was like an advert for The Body Shop!

Rita sighed.

It was like being jilted, I said, all that build up to the big day then nothing.

You'll laugh about it all one day, said Rita.

I doubt it. How's Grandad anyway?

I'm not happy about his cough, said Rita. He was delighted with the Nevil Shute.

I hope it isn't lung cancer.

Please keep your morbid thoughts to yourself, Helen.

Well, he's always glued to his pipe.

She sighed again. I'm going out to the greenhouse later. You could come out.

Did you tell Grandad I was asking for him?

Yes.

I'll visit him when he's not infectious. I can't risk getting what he's got.

I know you can't. I'm doing a coloureds wash later, have you got anything?

Only the dress Ivan got me. I hope it shrinks.

Don't be silly. Ruining it won't help.

I wish I could go away somewhere. A long train journey to a remote island. I could come back when my grief was gone.

I'd like to go to a remote island too, Rita said.

Because of me?

Well, it's not always easy, Helen. We're all affected by your traumas because you can't contain them yourself.

I'm sorry.

There's no need to be sorry. I'm not blaming you – I'm just saying. Why don't you phone your friends later?

Jana's got exams. I don't want to be crying down the phone to her. Richard's too hen-pecked, he wouldn't be allowed to come over, and Callum appears to hate me.

Why don't you read then?

I'm too agitated. Anyway, there's dried-in snot on page 60 of *One Hundred Years of Solitude*. I can't read it anymore.

That's *disgusting*, said Rita.

Can you find out who had it out before me?

You don't know it was them.

You should fine them, I said.

Rita shuddered. It doesn't bear thinking about what people do with their library books.

I was getting fed up with all those Aurelianos and Arcadios anyway. It's too hard.

You can help me with my jigsaw later if you want, said Nab.

The last thing I felt like was creating a Greenlandic scene from 2000 pieces, but I didn't want to hurt Nab's feelings.

I'll need to have a shower first, I said. I feel horrible.

Kneeling in the bath, I tried to wring out all my tears to

spare Nab and Rita. The melon soap stung my arm.

Nab'd done half the jigsaw already. It had been on the dining table for weeks, he'd slide it carefully up to the end when we needed the table for eating.

We sorted out the remaining pieces by colour, and I grasped for words that would take me away from my agony.

How was the Ben, Nab?

Beautiful. Misty on the way down. Keith's son sprained his ankle. We had to help him down. It was not easy.

I climbed the Ben when I was sixteen. Richard and me.

Did you?

We had tomato soup in a flask.

Mmm.

We got eaten alive by midges – we were breathing them in, they were so thick.

That's a shame.

He was engrossed in sorting out the white pile from the blue-ish white. I tried to piece an Inuit together, all the time waiting for the phone.

It's wonderful to get a bit that fits, said Nab, as he snapped a husky's ear into place.

I lasted half an hour. I had to go upstairs to bawl.

The rest of the afternoon dragged by and he didn't phone.

In the evening, I watched a documentary on sea cows and waited. Sea cows are ugly and graceful and lumber about in the sunlit parts of the ocean. They seem so happy. I wanted to be one.

You better get it, said Rita, when the phone rang.

It was Brian. Hello, pet, how are you?

I'm okay. How are you?

I'm very excited. Your Auntie Ella from Canada's coming over.

Granny's cousin?

Yes.

The one who sent the Toronto pencils?

Yes!

Years ago, she'd sent him a packet of bright yellow pencils with TORONTO written on them in gold letters. He'd taken them everywhere. If you borrowed one and broke it you had to sharpen it before giving it back and if you lost one he went mad.

That's great, Brian. You should ask her to bring more.

I think I will. Can I have a word with my sister now?

I went back to the sea cows, praying that Rita and Brian wouldn't talk for too long, but I knew that Rita would want passed on to my granny and they would need to discuss my grandad's chest and then the Auntie Ella visit.

He didn't phone 'til after ten. I was scared your mum would answer, he said. Is she furious with me?

Not really, I said. I think she's more furious with me.

Did she see your arm?

No.

She'll kill you if she sees it.

I know. I'll need to get vitamin E oil for it.

It shouldn't scar. Are you okay?

I have to be.

I know.

I forgot to give you your Swatch watch – I got it for you in the January sales.

I don't deserve it.

I know you don't. I'll give it to Callum instead.

He didn't rise to the bait.

I have to go. I'll phone soon.

I love you.

I know.

Can I write to you?

Of course you can.

Bye... babe.

Bye, Looby.

The next day raw and unbearable with no phone call to rescue me. I'd been crying so much, my eyes were like slits. I looked like a snake. I wondered (again) how healthy people coped with heartbreak – I couldn't bake any more scones. I'd asked Rita how she coped when she got divorced. She said she'd painted the house from top to bottom and got a job at the library.

I rearranged my book shelf. The French novels were always getting on my nerves – you had to stack them upside down to get the titles on the spines running the same way as British and American books. I hated knowing they were upside down but hated the disorder of titles running in different directions even more.

I took my *Ferrar's* to bed and tried to revise some irregular verbs. The inside cover had the name of an Algerian student I'd met in Caen, scribbled in the corner. He'd pushed me round the campus in a supermarket trolley after too many kirs one night. That was the last time I'd been drunk and carefree.

Past historic of *être*: *fus, fus fut, fûmes, fûtes, furent.* Imperfect subjunctive takes stem from second person singular past historic minus the 's'. It was all coming back. *Fusse, fusses, fût, fussions, fussiez, fussent.* My brain felt like it was shimmering in a heat wave. I used to be able to go to lectures all day then study for three hours in the evenings and six hours on Saturdays and Sundays.

I missed my academic self. I missed Agnes at the bottom of the bed.

*

My darling boy, I am empty and lost without you...

Dear Ivan, I hate you and never want to see you again. You tricked me...

Dear Ivan, I love you so much. Please don't leave me...

*

I sent Callum a card of Man Ray's *Larmes*: Dear Callum,
I want to say again that I'm so sorry for hurting you but I
thought I'd write to tell you that Ivan has left me so I am
also in a mess. I hope you and I can still be friends. I'd still
like to come to your sister's twenty-first if you want me to.
Thank you again so much for teaching me photography. I'll
need to give you your enlarger back. Love, Helen.

*

Dear Looby,
You know how crap I am at writing but I got your three
letters and want so much to explain and try and take away
some of your hurt. I know this all seems unbearable for you
just now. It is not easy for me either to see you so sad. I still
care about you lots but I just can't be your boyfriend just
now. I think I have changed since travelling and I need some
time to re-adjust to things here. I think I am bit depressed.
I am so used to all the colours and smells of travelling and
back here everything seems so grey and bland. And I just
found out that one of the guys I travelled with has been
paralysed in a car crash in Gambia.

I also need to get my arse in gear and get my PhD
sorted out. My old professor at Glasgow may have a position
for me, which would be brilliant (testing a new Alzheimer's
drug, v. exciting). Anyway, what is most important is you

getting well, and you need ALL your energy for that, you can't waste it on me. I am thinking of you and will phone soon to see how you are.

Love, Ivan.

PS. You looked lovely when I saw you.

I wrote back immediately. I tried to be altruistic and said I was sorry about his friend in Gambia, as well as sending the usual words so powerless and pointless when the person does not love you back.

*

Scared to sleep in case I dream about him. *Can't be your boyfriend just now* – I have sucked onto these words like a leech and twisted them to mean that he could be my boyfriend *later*. I am like a bee, stunning itself against the window over and over, never fully understanding that there's an obstacle in the way of what it wants.

I wonder – not for the first time – what it would be like to have drawing pins pressed into your whole body. I wonder how many it would take to kill you.

I miss him so much.

I can't even make myself come. My arms are so fucked they should be in slings.

When I finally sleep, I dream of Toronto pencils.

16

Madeira

THE AIR HOSTESSES have silky hair and pillar-box red lips. The pretty ones have expensive engagement rings. The plain ones have bare wedding fingers and try extra hard to smile, to hide the disappointment sewn into their moon faces. I'm amazed they don't sweat in their nylon tunics, I'd have huge wet circles after five minutes.

When we take off, I dig my nails into Nab and Rita. Once we're up, the widow across the aisle takes photos of the clouds. She told me in the departure lounge that she'd been to Madeira with her husband Alec in the '60s and they'd gone to Reid's for afternoon tea and the sweat had been pouring off Alec because they'd been bombarded by waiters.

When we land, I dig my nails into Nab and Rita. The runway's on stilts in the water. By the time we get to the hotel, I am pummelled and dizzy and my ears are ringing. I feel as if the floor is sloping.

Our second week. Madeira is warm and beautiful, exotic flowers everywhere: bougainvillea, birds-of-paradise, mimosas and flowers that look like red toilet brushes. Yesterday, we got a taxi to the exotic bird garden. We saw an albino peacock – when it opened its feathers, it looked like a male bride.

I know I'm lucky to be here but Ivan burns into my head. I wanted to send him a postcard on the second day. I wrote it and hid it my case so that I wasn't tempted. I lasted 'til Day Five. I'm wearing the orange dress he gave me. You can see my nipples through it. It's been four months since he left me. I used to dread dreaming about him, but now I look forward to it.

He is all I want. And to be well.

Rita and Nab walk into Funchal every day. I keep hoping to get the bus in and meet them but haven't managed yet. I prefer to stay on the veranda and look at the beautiful garden. There are palm trees that remind me of Tina Turner.

Today at the poolside, I saw the headlines of an English newspaper. There'd been a bad train crash and Prince Charles was visiting the victims in hospital. It'd be bad enough being seriously hurt in an accident without waking up to find the royal family at your bedside. I can't think of anyone who'd be comforted by their presence – apart from

Brian. He collects royal souvenirs.

Tonight we're eating out. (Self-catering's all very well, says Rita, but all you're doing is washing dishes in a different sink.) Nab's pouring over the wine list, and Rita's holding her cigarette to the side so the smoke doesn't blow in my direction. I look round at the other tables. There's a hunchbacked woman with her elderly son – or husband, it's hard to tell – and there's an Anita Brookner woman on her own with a bottle of red wine. The waiter's Spanish, he looks like Hen Broon and says 'begetables'.

How can there be so much sadness in one dining room?

Part Two

17

FAQs

WHAT'S THIS?! WE'RE looking through the round window and it seems that Bob wasn't exactly honest when he told Helen she'd be better in five years: *Maybe he just didn't know!*

It's been five years and two weeks now, though she *is* improving. She's been volunteering at the adult literacy class at Rita's library, when she's able. Going back to uni's still out of the question though.

Even to do one class?

No way, Jose. (Nab's favourite joke: Did you hear about the Mexican twins who were firemen? Hose A and Hose B.)

*

Frequently asked questions by well-meaning strangers in the late '80s

stranger   I feel tired all the time. I think I've got the mystery illness.

me   It's much worse than feeling tired all the time. You feel like toxic waste and you have to have the symptoms for six months before they'll diagnose you.

*

stranger   Is it like flu?

me   It's like flu (without the mucus) PLUS glandular fever PLUS a vile hangover every day. You have to stay in bed. Your life stops and you can't function. There are subsets of symptoms within symptoms. You discover new kinds of pain, new kinds of weakness, neurological sensations you didn't think possible. And, if you're lucky, you might have irritable bowel syndrome, allergies and tinnitus throw in.

*

stranger   You don't feel better after a good night's sleep?

me   Don't be silly! You can sleep for twelve hours

and you're still exhausted when you wake up. And often you *can't* sleep.

stranger Why can't you sleep if you're so exhausted?

me They think there's disturbance in the hypothalamus, which controls the sleep cycle. Very vivid dreams is another symptom. Last night, I dreamt that Bruce Forsyth gave me a massage and wrapped me in Sellotape.

*

stranger Have you tried Bach Flower Remedies? Hornbeam's recommended for those who are floppy and tired.

me I've tried everything.

*

stranger Have you tried magnesium supplements? You can get muscle weakness and numbness and tingling if you're deficient.

me I've tried everything.

*

stranger Have you tried an anti-candida diet – cutting out foods with yeast and sugar? An overgrowth of yeast can make you tired all the time.

me I've tried everything.

*

stranger Can you not build up your strength with gentle exercise?

me No! Your muscles aren't producing energy normally. If you climb the stairs you feel like you've run a marathon – your muscles burn, they think they've done much more than they actually have. And they don't recover normally.

stranger You have too much lactic acid in your legs?

me Something like that. We have faulty glycolytic pathways. Did you know there are three pathways – one aerobic and two anaerobic – for producing energy? They're continuously operating in all our activities, though one is usually dominant. My ex-boyfriend told me – we're still really good friends.

stranger Who would have thought producing energy

was so complex?

me   I know, you take your body completely for granted, you don't care how it works until it stops working properly, and then you want to know all about it... I'm thinking of taking up the shot-put, it uses the anaerobic alactic pathway where huge amounts of energy are supplied very quickly and no lactic acid is produced.

stranger   I like your sense of humour.

*

stranger   What does ME actually stand for?

me   Myalgic encephalomyelitis. Myalgia is muscle pain. Encephalomyelitis is inflammation of the brain and spinal cord, though some medics say there is no inflammation present. But my brain certainly feels inflamed.

stranger   That's a bit of a mouthful – certainly sounds serious.

me   It's always getting new names. It's also been known as 'Icelandic Disease' and 'Royal Free Disease' – there were outbreaks in Iceland in 1949 and at the Royal Free Hospital in

245

1955. There have been outbreaks all over since then. It's being referred to as 'Raggedy Ann Syndrome' in the USA because you feel like a rag doll.

stranger   What about the term 'yuppie flu'?

me   What about it? It's referred to as 'yuppie flu' by those who don't know what the fuck they're talking about. I'm not a yuppie and I don't have flu, though I have asked for a Filofax for Christmas – a fake one.

stranger   What do you need a Filofax for?

me   Nothing. I just want to be fashionable.

*

stranger   Is it always triggered by a virus?

me   It often happens after a virus – we may be having an abnormal reaction to the virus, or the virus is persisting, but no one really knows. It can also happen after vaccinations and exposure to organophosphates – farmers have had a similar illness after using sheep-dip, but the government doesn't believe them either.

*

stranger   Why do some doctors not believe you?

me   I honestly have no idea. Maybe because there's no single diagnostic test and because they're arrogant. They don't understand it, so it's easier to blame the patient, label them as depressed, neurotic, lazy *etc*. They say people are jumping on the ME bandwagon, but how can you jump on a fucking bandwagon that you didn't know existed?!

stranger   I don't know, how can you?

me   I'd never heard of ME or Post-Viral Fatigue Syndrome or any other mystery illness until Bob diagnosed me... my GP dragged her heels for months, telling me I was imagining it. Thank God for the locum who believed I was ill – Rita called him out one day because I was in so much pain. And thank God for Bob.

stranger   No wonder people with ME get depressed, putting up with such disbelief.

me   Yes, no wonder.

stranger   No wonder they're prescribed antidepressants.

me   Yes, no wonder.

stranger   [*hesitantly*] But antidepressants can't cure ME, can they?

me   NO! NO! NO! Antidepressants are not curing the physical symptoms, they are just relieving secondary depression. But some doctors seem to think they can prescribe brisk walks and a handful of tricyclics, and send us on our way. It's fucking ridiculous: I would never take them.

stranger   I'm sorry. I didn't mean to upset you. It's just something I read.

me   I think there should be a mass crucifixion of all the GPs, psychiatrists and journalists who don't believe it is a physical illness. These people are so powerful and are causing so much damage by not believing us. They should be made to pay. They're making people *more* ill, forcing them to keep going.

stranger   Do you really feel that strongly?

me   Well, I'm against the death penalty but I'd be happy if they all got ME themselves. That would be enough. They would soon believe in it, within twenty-four hours of having it.

I'll tell you that for nothing.

*

stranger   Is there a lot of research going on?

me   The scientists who believe in it are
                 researching it, but the government isn't
                 funding anything. The ME charities – the
                 ME Association and Action for ME – are
                 trying to raise money and awareness, and
                 are lobbying the government. Clare Francis,
                 the round-the-world yachtswoman has it,
                 she was on *Wogan*.

*

stranger   Will you ever get better?

me   They keep saying it burns itself out in five
                 years, but that isn't true – I've been ill for
                 five years and one month. I'm really hoping
                 to get back to uni next year. I only need one
                 subject to graduate with an Ordinary degree,
                 but there's no way I could commute, and no
                 way I could live in a flat. My Honours degree
                 is out the window.

stranger   That's a shame.

me   I've been volunteering at the adult literacy class at the library, two hours a week. My head feels pumped up with chemicals by the time I've finished, and my glands are swollen, as if the actual effort of thinking is toxic, but it gives me a routine and I feel I'm doing something useful.

stranger   Do you ever feel sorry for yourself?

me   Not really sorry for myself, more powerless. I think you're more likely to feel sorry for yourself with short-term suffering. If you're healthy and you've got flu you feel sorry for yourself and need pampered. But if you're chronically ill you just survive it. You start to appreciate small things. It's what gets you through.

stranger   You seem very stoic.

me   Believe me, I have many days where I wish this wasn't happening, or that I was dead, but then I see those poor wee Romanian orphans – shitting themselves in their cots, babies who don't have a chance from the day they're born. I want to adopt them all.

stranger   [*uncomfortable with expressing emotion*]

Well, good luck anyway. I'll be interested to hear how you're doing.

me   I'll keep you posted.

18

Granny Fleet, Peter and Finn

WHEN YOU LOOK at your face in the mirror for a long time – just keep staring – you don't recognise yourself anymore. It's like when you say the same word over and over again until it loses its meaning. I have been staring for ages and I realise that my eyes are too high up. I'd never noticed before.

*

At first I thought it was a wrong number: no voice then a gravelly throat-clearing followed by Granny Fleet's accusing tones. We hadn't seen her for years, she'd taken Peter's side in their divorce and left Rita without a name – she'd never really accepted her son marrying someone from a council house. She still phoned us occasionally, when she was bored or in a bad mood. She looked like a man and was always crunching Oddfellows. She was much better off than my other granny but she used to give us jotters for Christmas and still sent us cheap Christmas cards that you could spit through. Why does she still bother with cards when she hates us? I asked Rita. She's lonely, said Rita. It makes her feel as if she's got friends.

Is that you, Helen?

Yes.

It's Granny Fleet.

I know.

I was just thinking about you, there was an article about your condition in the paper. I thought I'd send it to you. It's very interesting.

What does it say?

It suggests that if you had a more positive attitude to the illness, you would have more chance of getting better. You're in a vicious circle of thinking you'll never get better and that's what's keeping you ill.

Granny Fleet, the article is rubbish, I don't want it. I've explained my illness to you before!

You've sunk into a long depression without even knowing it, and your mother isn't helping by being at your constant beck and call.

Are you quite finished? I'm going to go, you're upsetting me.

There's no need for that tone, young lady, I'm just trying to help.

There's a lot of inaccurate stuff published about ME

– you have to have it to properly understand it.

She cleared her throat so the venom could get out: *Are you ever going to get a job, Helen?*

I can't work, you know I can't!

It's scandalous that you've thrown away the chance of a good education.

I'm going to phone Dad and tell him what you're saying. You're a poisonous old woman. Just leave me alone!

I slammed the phone down and picked it up to dial Peter, but Witchy Fleet hadn't hung up yet, she was still there, tutting and rasping. I slammed the phone down for a second time and waited for a couple of minutes before dialling Peter's surgery. His receptionist said he was with a patient. I told her it was important.

He called me back half an hour later. He said the receptionist had said I sounded terrible.

Your mother's been on the phone, dispensing her gems of wisdom, I said. She's so vicious, I hate her!

Helen, you know what she's like, why do you waste your energy getting upset?

I can't help it. She told me I should be working and that Rita's just encouraging me to stay ill.

Peter sighed. D'you want to go for lunch tomorrow? I've got the afternoon off.

Okay. A late lunch.

I'll pick you up about two.

I want to ask you about mercury amalgam toxicity – I might need my fillings drilled out.

I'll see you tomorrow. Just ignore my mother, she's off her head.

Bye, Dad... thanks.

Bye.

He took me to the garden centre in Helensburgh for lunch. They had a nice cafe with home-made tomato soup with fresh cream and parsley.

I asked him about mercury amalgam toxicity and ME. I'm not convinced of the link, he said. Why are dentists not more ill than the rest of the population since we're more exposed to mercury?

I thought you were, I said. I thought you were all suicidal.

No more than any other health professionals.

I'm joking, Dad.

Anyway, you've only got two fillings. I'll replace them with acrylic if you want, but drilling them out could just release more mercury and you'd have the trauma of the local anaesthetic. I've had ME patients who feel worse after anaesthetics.

Maybe I'll just leave it then, but if I need more fillings I'm not having mercury. I want white fillings.

It's a deal, he said.

They think it's the adrenaline that causes relapses, you need to use anaesthetic without adrenaline.

You're like an encyclopaedia, he said, smiling. He

looked like Sean when he smiled and for a second I could've hugged him.

So how's your mother?

You know Mum, I said, never sits down, always looking after everyone. I didn't tell her about Granny Fleet, she would've been furious. Can you believe she said that I've wasted a good education?! She knows fine I'll go back to uni as soon as I can. She doesn't consider how exhausting the commute would be – I'd have to go in three days a week – or how on earth I would manage in a flat on my own. I'd need a home help.

Ignore her.

I'm *desperate* to get back. I keep thinking it would be great if uni was right next door then I could stay in bed 'til my classes and come straight home and rest afterwards.

That would be handy.

People don't realise how much energy you need just getting to and from a place.

Calm down. You're getting worked up again. Let's just enjoy lunch. How's your brother?

He hardly comes home, he's always with Nellie. I think he'll move to London next year once he's graduated.

I can't believe Sean will be graduating next summer.

Will you go?

Of course I'll go.

You've got soup on your chin, Dad.

He dabbed it off and I felt sorry for him.

What are you doing for Christmas? I asked.

Probably go to Susan and her kids in the evening.

Are they friendly towards you?

Her daughters were a bit frosty at first but they're coming round. The son's okay.

Will you see Witchy Fleet?

I have to eat lunch with her, otherwise she'd be sitting on her own.

That's 'cos no one can stand her.

I know, but she's my mother.

Why doesn't Aunt Dorothy have her for Christmas?

She's got the excuse of being in Australia. She's invited her, but she knows she won't fly.

Our Australian cousins are lucky they've never had to meet her.

Is she really that bad?

Yup, I said.

When he dropped me off I noticed how thin and flat his hair was. He was only fifty-three but he looked like an old man from the back.

Penguin count five: they seemed (thankfully) to be out of fashion this festive season.

Nab and I were playing Scrabble. We allowed proper nouns when Nab was playing and I was trying to get away with DUNOON BATS.

Bats from Dunoon, I said.

Come on, Helen, that is not quite correct! he said.

257

Be a pal, Nab, it's Christmas.

Rita came through to the dining room and told us a plane had crashed into a petrol station in the Borders.

The next day, the grim truth and the ubiquitous image of the blue and white Pan Am cockpit lying on the ground like a broken neck. (It would take almost fourteen years to convict a Libyan guy for the bombing, based on the shaky evidence of a Maltese shopkeeper.)

Brian spent Christmas Day shaking his head and saying, It's terrible about that plane, the same way that he'd said, It's terrible about the cat, when Agnes died.

*

Dear Jana,

Glad you liked the 'baffies' I sent, I just saw them and knew you would love them. I hope they are keeping your feet cosy – is your heating working now? It's great about your job with Oracle – database manager trainee sounds very important, I am jealous. I am sorry that all the decent men are gay or married but I know you will not be short of someone to dibble with for long. I have some great dibbling news, but will keep it 'til the end.

God, I still shudder when I think of Lockerbie – I think of you, not that you would've been on that particular flight, but 'cos you used Pan Am back and forth all the time. Those poor students on their way home for Christmas, and the poor people on the ground, just wrapping their presents and checking their Christmas tree lights. I keep thinking of the pilots falling to earth in their broken-off cockpit. It's all too horrible to believe.

Everything else seems trivial by comparison.

But poor Sean – Nellie dumped him over the Christmas holidays! She went to some lawyers' ball and met someone. Sean had bought her a gorgeous choker to go with her ball-gown and the bitch dumped him. He is utterly heartbroken, but I am glad he can now meet someone who deserves him, she certainly doesn't.

My news – there's a private clinic in Edinburgh giving intravenous vitamin C to rag dolls. The doctor who runs it claims she has fully recovered from ME, but I want to read up on vitamin C more. It has amazing antiviral properties if you take mega doses. There's an American guy called Linus Pauling who's really into it, have you heard of him? It's also really expensive, £500, but Rita says it'll be worth it if she can 'get me back'. I visited Fizza last week, she was so bad, just lying in a darkened room. I don't know how she copes. I took her flowers and she couldn't even stand the crackling noise of the wrapping paper.

Still seeing Callum now and then. He took me up the loch last week and we held hands, I know he'd like more, but I can't give it, I still like holding hands though. He keeps saying he's going to Australia.

I know you disapprove, but I'm still having ambiguous friendship with Ivan. (He takes me up the loch too and we hold hands.) I would like more, but I know I can't ask. I think he still really cares about me and that is more important. But I could be totally wrong, both these men (or boys, they're still boys after all) are happy to hold my hand on the Bonnie Banks but maybe they don't really care a jot. I never ask Ivan about his love life and he is always very guarded. He knows I'd have an *eppie* if I knew what he was doing. He recently told me that he *had* had an affair with that Dr Joyce woman he met when he was in India. They wrote to each other for a while and she was going to visit last year but it all fell through. She's engaged to someone else now.

Now the juicy news! Nab's son Finn visited in January and we ended up having incestuous relations! Can you fucking believe it? He is twenty-eight and blonde and handsome and we drank cherry wine that he'd got at Copenhagen airport. It's really strong and sweet, I just had a tiny amount but he was knocking it back. I knew he liked me but couldn't tell if he was just being brotherly. We ended up making out as you would say, but there wasn't any nudity – that would've been too weird. He's just come out of a five yearer and is obviously on the rebound. He's a geologist and says he might go to work in the Middle East to get away from his memories. I think Nab and Rita knew there was a frisson between us but they didn't say anything – I mean it's not illegal, is it?

What else? My life is so boring compared to yours.

I was babysitting Zoe the other night. She is very sweet, three and a half. I plaited her flame red hair and read her a bedtime story. It's strange to have a child upstairs, knowing that its well-being depends entirely on you, even if just for a few hours.

I'm still volunteering at the literacy class. I really enjoy it. It's so rewarding – learning to read as an adult must be harder than learning Arabic.

So is anyone in San Francisco burning books? Rita thinks Salman should have known better than to offend a whole faith and culture, but I feel a bit sorry for him and wonder if having a fatwa is worse than having ME.

Well, 'baffied one' that is my news. Get your flashy new job to send you to Europe so you can visit me!

Lots of love,

Helen

*

Can't sleep. I keep worrying about my family being wiped out. I'd have to sell the house and live in a caravan, on sickness benefit. I'm like a Victorian woman, I need to find a lovely man to look after me, or be supported by my family forever.

19

Bees and Vitamin C

I'D NEVER BEEN in a private clinic. The doctor in charge was from Denmark. (Call me Helga, please!) She claimed to have made a full recovery from the mystery illness, although she still couldn't ski. Nab chatted to her in Danish. The other staff were serene and blonde and wore trendy white overalls. It was like being in some kind of Scandinavian heaven: New Age music ebbing and flowing, everything calm and white.

Helga was going to test my food allergies and design a special diet for me.

You got an infusion of twenty grams of vitamin C on alternate days over two weeks. One infusion was equivalent to two hundred oranges.

And a magnesium infusion for the muscle pain. (No skimping here.)

You were hooked up to the vitamin C drip for about an hour and a half with people on either side of you, also

262

hooked up. The nice blonde people brought you tea and *Cosmo* and *Vogue*.

The woman sitting next to me was a Christian. She told me how God had been a shining light throughout her illness. I told her how sore my legs were.

At the end of the fortnight, Helga told me I was allergic to everything except black tea, potatoes and lamb. (I'd given up coffee and alcohol almost completely in the first year of being ill. A sip of either and my muscles burned.) She wanted me to cut out yeast and sugar (*not that old chestnut!* – you couldn't open a magazine these days without reading about candida and ME), and she prescribed nystatin, an antifungal agent that tasted like rat poison. I was to go back in a month to be reviewed by the blonde angels.

Verdict on infusions: I got a whoosh of energy in my legs while I was hooked up, but don't tell Helga that I never stuck to the diet!

I also got some handy hints on vitamin C.

Cats (unlike humans) make their own vitamin C – Agnes obviously wasn't making enough.

Always buy vitamin C that contains bioflavonoids to help with the absorption.

And remember, large doses of vitamin C turn your urine bright yellow and your shit black.

*

I *have* to get back to university this autumn. I have five months to rest, rest, rest. Ivan's coming for dinner tonight. He was sceptical about the drips at first but is really happy they've helped. I think I'll get dressed up. Last night, I dreamt that I strangled myself with pink velvet ribbon.

*

Nab and I were watching a documentary about polar bears. They can smell baby seals from a mile away. In springtime, they sneak up on them and kill them.

The tension was unbearable. They kept cutting from the bear to the baby seal: the seal was clueless and minding its own business, you knew it was going to be swiped by the polar bear any minute. I covered my eyes. I just couldn't watch the blur of mauling and skin and blood.

How can the camera crew stand by and let it happen? I said. It's brutal to let that wee thing be murdered.

You're too emotional, said Nab. It's not, after all, as if it wouldn't happen if they weren't there. It's going to happen anyway. The camera people are like war photographers. They're waiting for it to happen, not *making* it happen.

Well, I can't watch, I said.

Arctic foxes also kill the baby seals.

Nab, don't tell me these things!

It's just nature – no seal, no meal.

I'm away to make Mum some tea. D'you want some?

No, thank you. The polar bears are not really evil,

Helen. You must not judge them.

They *are* evil, I shouted through, gushing the kitchen tap on so I wouldn't hear his reply.

Rita'd slipped her disc, lifting a big plant pot. She'd been in bed for nearly a week. Nab and I were just about holding the fort, but with our combined energies we couldn't do nearly as good a job as Rita – the house had a forlorn air about it as if someone had gone away for a long time. I'd caught her in her dressing gown the day before stirring the bolognese and wincing. Mum, you have to go back to bed – I can manage! I'd said. I wanted to look after her perfectly and be a bustling, efficient nurse but there was no one to help in the mornings when Nab was at work and I was still sleeping. She said I was doing a great job. Not really, I said – what kind of nurse is in bed as much as the patient? A nurse with very short shifts, she replied.

I took the tea into her and sat on the side of the bed. What are you reading?

Computers and Libraries.

Sounds boring.

It is. What are you and Nab doing?

Watching a documentary about polar bears. They're so cute when they're babies, and then they grow up to be big bastards.

Just like children, she said.

I can't watch, it's too violent.

I bet Nab's enjoying the scenery.

He is – but he's being a bit crabby.

265

Poor Nab, she said.

He was ten years older and I think she was beginning to feel the age gap.

He's tired, she said, he was ironing 'til after eleven last night. I told him only to do his work shirts but he did all my clothes too.

I know, I said, he's a star.

He's a New Man, she said.

The only New Man in this family.

That's not fair, she said. Sean tries. He's under a lot of pressure just now.

My brother had come home at the weekend with his laundry and we'd argued because he'd been hogging the washing machine (he'd been using Nellie's before), and I didn't think he was concerned enough about Rita. All he'd done was mope. It'd been five months since Nellie had dumped him, but he'd bumped into her in Byres Road with her new boyfriend. Why don't you make yourself useful and get your arse down to the supermarket? I'd said. Nab and I are knackered. I'm knackered too, he said. He'd made a face and snatched the shopping list I'd given him. At least you've got no studying, he shouted on his way out – you don't have to write a thesis on the impact of introversion-extraversion on a job interview! He'd been gone for ages and come back without the stock cubes. I'd begged him to go back and get them. We'd shielded Rita from the whole drama and he'd taken her roast chicken and new potatoes on a tray, lovingly prepared by her children, with a single tulip on the side.

*

Richard and Clare were having a cheese and wine. I hadn't seen Richard for ages. It was mostly going to be her friends. I'd asked if I could bring Callum, but she'd said no, the numbers were high enough and he wasn't officially my boyfriend. I was excited to be going to a social event and fantasised that I would meet a new shiny knight. Instead, I met Clare's new trainee, a big dollop of a girl, who told me with the conviction of a consultant neurologist that you could cure yourself of ME by drinking your own urine (pronounced yoor-*ine*). She also told me that my skin looked like it needed re-hydrated. Come into the salon, she said, I can give you a half-price facial.

Why has Clare taken that awful girl on? I asked Richard in the kitchen.

He rolled his eyes. She's her mum's cousin's daughter and she failed all her exams, he said. She needed a chance, but Clare's ready to stab her after two weeks.

No fucking wonder, I mouthed.

He smiled back and there was flirting in his eyes. I could've kissed him.

How's married life? I asked. Are you happy?

Sort of, he said.

Sort of?

Is anyone really ever happy? he said.

Clare's trainee is. She seems to think the world's her oyster.

267

It's good to see you, he said.

It's good to see you too.

With the wine warming my head, I wished I'd just married Richard. I would be safe – there could be worse things than living in a bungalow with top-quality carpeting and Ercol chairs.

Can you drink now? he said.

Not really – I'll feel crap tomorrow, even after half a glass, but it's nice to have a wee buzz, I said.

I don't think it's a good idea, said Rita.

We were lying in the garden on a beautiful July day. A bee was stuffing its head into a flower – occasionally the breeze would cause the flower to sway, and the bee would cling on, fastened in like it was on a fairground ride.

It's perfect, Mum, I said. I can stay in Rez's boxroom rent-free, and Ivan'll be there if I'm ill, and he can help me with my groceries. The flat's on the first floor, right on Gibson Street – three minutes' walk to my class. I couldn't have a better set-up!

I'm just afraid you'll end up getting hurt. You think you've armoured yourself against Ivan hurting you but you haven't. What if he brings a girlfriend back to the flat?

He wouldn't do that, he's not insensitive. And what if I bring someone back? It works both ways.

You're still in love with him, it's obvious.

I'm not! It's over two years since we split up – I love him

268

as a friend, that's all. Anyway, how could I not love him? Everyone loves Ivan. He's great.

Two years is nothing, she said, frowning.

I don't have the luxury of choosing who I live with, Mum. Who wants a flatmate with ME? I need people who understand.

Can you definitely stay on sickness benefit if you go back?

Yup. I'm only doing two lectures a week and one tutorial a fortnight. I just need to keep sending in my six-monthly sick notes.

Myra shouldn't have a problem with that.

No... they really *are* busy, aren't they?

Who are?

Bumble bees – they're so focused on what they're doing but so relaxed at the same time.

They're much less aggressive than honey bees, she said – they'd sting you as quick as look at you.

I think the phone's ringing, I said.

The sun's too gorgeous to answer.

Just leave it then.

It might be important, she said.

It's probably just Granny. D'you want me to go?

No, I'll get it, she said.

Don't run, you might trip in your flip-flops.

She was gone for a while and came back out with a jug of orange juice.

Who was it? I asked.

Finn looking for his father.

He was on for a long time, I said, cursing myself for not answering.

He wanted advice about the engineering company he's applying to in Saudi.

Did he not want to speak to me?

Afraid not.

Did he even ask for me?

No.

See if I care, I said, trying to be bolshie. I was embarrassed by the sudden lump in my throat.

He seemed a bit agitated, she said.

I didn't think he was serious about Saudi, I said. He seems a bit flighty, always changing his mind about his career. He reminds me of Ivan in that respect.

Maybe, she said.

He shouldn't be going to Saudi anyway. They behead people there.

I think he wants to get as far away from Denmark as possible, get over his broken heart.

I watched the bee – suspended over the gladioli, undecided where to go next – and wished I hadn't sent Finn the luxury photo-card of Loch Lomond to remind him of his visit. I poured some orange juice, and too many ice cubes tumbled into the glass. I fished them out and threw them on the grass, cursing myself again for not being the one to answer the phone. The bee hovered around the jug and tried to land on the rim. I brushed it away. It persisted for a bit before flying off and poking itself into another flower.

20

Wendy and Storm

CAN'T WAIT! MOVING in with Ivan and Rez at the weekend. Rez's flat is lovely, all magnolia, and cream carpets. I'll have a couple of weeks to settle in before term starts. I've decided on social anthropology. I've got the reading list already and have bought *Witchcraft, Oracles and Magic among the Azande*. The Azande are so cheeky – they believe that certain people have witchcraft in them and they send you a chicken wing if they suspect you. I can think of a few people who should get one: Granny Fleet would be first in line.

*

On 9th October 1989, I matriculated again. I was twenty-six. It was like my first day at school. I laid out all my clothes the night before.

Ivan had lain beside me on top of the quilt in our

strange limbo, platonic way – I didn't even know if I fancied him anymore. I'd kicked him out for breathing too heavily. The bed's too small, I said, and I have to sleep. He'd got up and kissed my forehead, Enjoy your first day back.

I had diarrhoea when I woke and could hardly eat.

I waited until late afternoon to matriculate so that the queues had gone down. After enrolling, I went to the union and got my diary. I was ecstatic not to need my sickness benefit book for ID anymore: I was a student again (albeit a student with a secret, a student with a pension book)!

My first lecture was the next day. It didn't start 'til two, so I could sleep 'til noon. I took ages getting ready. I had a new navy beret and spent twenty minutes getting it to sit at the right angle.

Anthropology was on the eight floor of the Social Sciences Department. I wondered what I'd do if the lifts were ever broken. Most of the class were just out of school, seventeen, eighteen. A lot of the girls were wearing jeans and short black military-style jackets. They'd already made friends, bonded at Freshers' Week, getting pissed and throwing up in the union, crying mascara down their faces. You could spot the mature students a mile away – they were old and had anoraks or flowery skirts. I was trendy with my beret and baby Doc Martens (I loved them, they made my legs feel supported) but I felt like I didn't belong: I wasn't a new student and I wasn't a mature student. I was a recently released hostage trying to get back to normal. I scanned the lecture theatre for nice men but there were none.

The lecturer appeared and apologised for being 'bunged up'. He said he'd had a severe sinus infection and was on his third course of antibiotics. He still had his bicycle clips on. I wanted to tell him he shouldn't be cycling in his state unless he wanted weak legs for the rest of his life. He said he'd keep things short and sketched out the year's coursework. I was disappointed, I'd wanted a proper lecture – I was dying to take notes in my new pad with my deluxe rollerball felt pen. I thought of my first day at secondary school when I'd been gutted 'cos we got no homework, just a tour of the buildings.

A short guy in his late thirties came in, unfazed by the attention latecomers get. He looked like a male version of Lulu and was wearing jeans, cowboy boots, a denim jacket and a red and white Palestinian scarf. He sat beside me and smiled. I smiled back. He stank of smoke and his roots were showing.

By the end of the lecture my head was numb, my neck caned. See you next time, said Lulu. Yeah, I said, grateful for the camaraderie. He shot his hand out. I'm Mo, by the way.

I love having the place to myself. Rez is hardly here and when he is he's knackered with bloodshot eyes (he's a senior houseman, about to specialise in paediatrics). I love the thick carpets and central heating. Jana and I only had a gas fire in the living room when we were students. I feel so safe. I want to stay here forever. Me and Ivan and Rez. All I

need is a cat – and the boys to put the toilet seat down – and
things would be perfect.

My wee sister had a beret like that for school, said Ivan.
We were slumped on the sofa, my leg flung over his. Does it
make you sad to see it? I said.

Not really, he said. Can I try it on?

No, you'll stretch it.

You suit it, he said.

I think I look better with a hat than without one. It
would be good if you were born with a hat.

As long as it wasn't a bowler hat. Are you hungry?

Don't know, I said. I'm too tired to know.

Will we get an Indian?

If you want, I'm skint though.

I'll get it.

Are you sure?

Yup.

I'll make spaghetti tomorrow, I said. Rez should be
here.

Would be good to eat with him, said Ivan.

That nurse he's seeing left a toothbrush in the bathroom.
It's got a peanut skin in the bristles. It makes me feel sick.

Run it under the tap then.

I can't, I said. I'll throw up.

Can we eat late tomorrow? I'm going swimming after
work.

If you want, I said.

Why don't you come to the pool?

Nah, I'll need my energy for cooking.

You don't have to swim, he said, you can just float. Wendy might come.

Who's Wendy?

Girl in my lab. She's depressed, her boyfriend's gone to London.

Why?

Research post in colo-rectal cancer.

Lovely.

Move your leg, he said, I'm going to get the food.

Maybe we could just lie on our stomachs instead.

What are you on about?

Sean had a flatmate who lay on his stomach when he was hungry and his grant had run out.

I think I'd rather have a chicken korma, said Ivan.

I wake up feeling as if I've been rolled up in a heavy blanket and can't move my limbs: my punishment for swimming three lengths yesterday.

Wendy is plain (I am thrilled), but she has delineated calf muscles, and sliced up and down the pool in her Speedo costume and goggles while I stayed at the shallow end, hooking my ankles to the side, stretching my legs and floating. Ivan kept coming up to me and peering, *Is that you?* (he won't wear his contacts in the pool, he lost one before).

You're like Helen Keller, I said. Why aren't you wearing your glasses?

I hate swimming in glasses, he said. You feel like a prick.

I think it's 'cos you don't want Wendy to see you looking geeky.

That's crap! he said. She sees them at work all the time.

You don't need to be so hostile.

He swam away in the huff and was quiet for the rest of the night.

I have another two hours before I have to get up (noon). I set the alarm for an extra half hour.

*

Sometimes when I'm walking to my lectures, I wonder if I'm the only one on campus with weak legs, pushing through water. I wonder what it feels like to walk to your class with normal legs.

Sometimes, I wonder what everyone would look like with horses' heads.

*

We were sitting up late, Rez and Ivan were slagging off *The Clangers*. They'd had a bottle of wine each.

I hated them, said Ivan. They sounded like fucking pan

pipes the way they were always hooting

They didn't *hoot*, they whistled, I said. They were adorable.

That's right, said Rez, snorting – all they did was hoot!

Clangers are beyond reproach, I said.

Mr Benn was the best, said Rez. He was the man!

He was a pervert, said Ivan.

No, he wasn't, I said. He was just a wee man who liked to escape his drab life by dressing up.

Why are you defending him? said Ivan.

Because he needs defending, I said.

Rez and Ivan were laughing idiotically: *Mr Benn needs defending, ha ha ha!*

It's not that funny, I said.

Captain Pugwash was a pervert too, said Ivan.

I must admit, he *was* shite, I said. I never liked him.

I've got to tend a baby with a necrotic leg in six hours, said Rez, yawning.

How on earth will you get up? I said.

Fuck knows. Auto-pilot.

I looked at my watch. It's half one, I said. I have to go to bed too. I've got a class in twelve hours.

No goodnight kisses for your flatmates? said Ivan, mock-pleading as I left the kitchen.

I went back and pecked his cheek, and Rez's too – I didn't want him to feel left out.

While I was brushing my teeth, their voices became conspicuously quiet as they tried to whisper. I knew they were talking about me. Their voices got loud again because they were drunk and forgot. I strained my ears but still couldn't make out what they were saying. When I came out of the bathroom, Rez was trying to whistle like a clanger. It pissed me off that Ivan'd been so aggressive about children's programmes. I knew it was to do with his sister and too much wine.

Mo had made a beeline for me since the first day – I couldn't get out of sitting next to him. Five weeks into term, I was still changing my mind about him. When I'd told him I had ME, he'd said, Is that the middle class illness?, and I'd said, No, it's the neurological illness. But he made me laugh. He used to be a taxi driver and his fucking wife had custody of the wean and he hated her. He was reading *Mrs Dalloway* for his English class and hated all the brackets. He thought I was crazy living with Ivan. Men and women can never be friends, he said, there's always one who wants to shag the other.

The lecturer was telling us about the Nuer, a polygynous cattle-loving people in the southern Sudan. I wondered if it would be easier if Ivan and I were Nuer: that way, he could have me and other wives (who weren't ill) and everybody would be happy. I'd have my own hut and he'd come and sleep with me when it was my turn.

*

The phone woke me (it never stopped ringing, I was always taking messages for Ivan and Rez). I stumbled from bed into the hall, my calves felt injected with poison. It was an American girl for Ivan. She'd met him at Glastonbury and she was going to be in Glasgow next weekend, did he want to meet up?

He's not here, I said.

Can you let him know Storm called.

Storm?

That's right.

As in thunder?

Yeah.

Ivan's at work, I said.

I'll call again later... Are you his room-mate?

No, I'm his girlfriend, I said.

When's good to call?

He often works late. It depends on his mice, I said.

His mice?

His research.

Okay, I'll call later.

Bye, I said, hanging up in a way that might have been too hasty.

I have done a terrible thing, *I have lied.* Maybe it's not my fault, maybe I have witchcraft (*mangu*) in me. Witches don't know they are witches, after all. They're born with it – it's not their fault.

*

The minute Ivan was in from work, I handed him a mug of tea. I've done something terrible, I said. I was half asleep and her name threw me, I mean who the fuck's called Storm? She said she met you at Glastonbury.

What happened? he said, frowning.

I told her I was your girlfriend.

She's just someone I met at the Stone Roses, he said.

Why's she coming to see you then?

She's not coming to see me, she's coming to Glasgow. You know what Americans are like, they keep in touch with everyone.

Are you not mad that I told her I'm your girlfriend?

Doesn't matter.

But even if something *had* happened with her, you wouldn't be able to tell me, would you?

I'm sorry, he said, I can't drink this tea, it's far too weak.

Dunk another bag in then.

It's *homeopathic,* it's so weak. How can you drink it like that, Helen?

Stop changing the subject.

Nothing happened!

Sometimes I think I'll unravel, I said. I'm finding it so hard coping with all these women.

What women?!

Wendy, for a start. It's obvious she fancies you.

Wendy's crazy about her boyfriend, he said, sighing.

I don't think I can keep living here.

Don't be ridiculous, he said. Where else would you live?

I can cope with you not being my boyfriend but I can't cope with you having a girlfriend right in front of my eyes.

I don't have a girlfriend right in front of your eyes.

I know but I'm constantly afraid of it happening.

We've been through this, he said.

How would you feel if I was parading men around? I said. That'll be the test. I'll bring someone back. I quite fancy Rez's friend, Lawrence.

Ivan laughed sarcastically. Dr Stuck-Up Wanker Lawrence? He's a prick.

He's got his private pilot's licence, I said.

I know. Rez has been up with him. They flew over Loch Lomond.

That'd be our first date, I said, we'd do loop the loops over my mum and Nab.

I can just see you in a Piper Aztec, he said. You shit yourself in a 747.

I'd be fine. Lawrence'd look after me.

You've got some imagination. I think you'd change your mind if you knew his views on ME.

Are they dodgy?

Extremely, he's a non-believer.

Bastard.

All that glitters is not gold, Looby.

How d'you know he doesn't believe?

He said something to Rez.

He better not show his face here again. I won't let him in.

You can't really vet Rez's friends in his own house, you're not a bouncer.

I just feel violent towards him now, I said. I'll give him the cold shoulder next time.

Is there any chilli left from last night? said Ivan. I'm starving.

Tons. I'll re-heat you some. Not that you deserve it.

I haven't actually done anything.

I'm sorry, I said. I should rub off my eyelashes in shame.

He came over to the microwave and hugged me. You've got to calm down, he said. You're causing a storm in a teacup, don't you think?

We both smiled at his pun.

I can't help it, I said. You should send me a poisoned chicken wing, that'd sort me out. I'd deny the charges of course.

Is that your witchcraft stuff?

Yeah, all I need to do is blow water over it and say: 'If I possess *mangu* in my belly I am unaware of it; may it cool. It is thus that I blow out water'.

And that's you off the hook?

Yup.

Seems a bit jammy to me.

It's just their way of dealing with bad things.

Have you already eaten?

Yeah, I ate at four. You know how I get hungry at odd times. I'll be starving again by eight.

Chilli's brilliant, he said, digging into the leftovers noisily.

It's always better the second night, I said, checking myself from commenting on his chomping.

I didn't want to unravel in front of Rez and I couldn't trust myself not to, so I went home the weekend Storm was coming. Ivan gave me a lift to the station. He kept saying I didn't have to leave but I think he was relieved that I was. She's sleeping on the couch, he said for the hundredth time, as I got out of the car. I believe you, I said, you don't need to keep telling me.

Before getting on the train, I went to the health food store next to the station. I got some Royal Jelly bath oil for Rita and Bach Rescue Remedy for myself. I couldn't see anything for Nab.

You're supposed to have a few drops of Rescue Remedy during times of stress. I kept thinking of Ivan making Storm come with his beautiful fingers and had drunk half the bottle by the time I got to Balloch.

I stayed with Rita and Nab for five days, my first time home since term had started. It's lovely to have you back in the nest, said Nab.

I slept for twelve hours every night. It was luxury, not having to cook or do dishes. I did more than my fair share of dishes in the flat. Even when I was exhausted with spaghetti legs, I felt I *should* be doing them – I felt I should compensate for not paying rent. I cleaned the toilet most of the time too.

Rita quizzed me about the flat and I said it was working out fine, Ivan was great.

He makes me laugh, I said. Whenever I'm clumsy, he says, Mind the gap!

I don't get it, she said.

Mind the *synaptic* gap – the tiny fluid filled gap between neurons. It's only 0.00002 mm.

I know what the synaptic gap is, Helen.

Ivan jokes that mine are too wide and the chemicals can't jump, that's why I'm always dropping things.

Have you met any nice men? she said.

Not really. Rez's got a gorgeous friend but he's a Tory and he doesn't believe in ME.

We can do without him, she said.

Sean phoned when I was there. He'd been temping in London since graduating and was excited 'cos he had a second interview for a job with a charity that helped brain-injured people back into employment. Rita was over the moon. It'll be the making of him if he gets it, she said. Fingers crossed, I'd said to him.

I felt myself becoming cocooned again, part of me didn't want to leave. Nab and Rita were like a big soft sling.

*

Rita gave me a lift back up to Glasgow. Before we left, she asked if I was okay for money. We've got a huge gas bill, I said, but I can use my savings.

I'd rather you didn't, she said. You need them for Christmas and holidays. Once you start dipping in for bills, it's a slippery slope. Nab and I will help you.

Thanks a lot, Mum, I said. What would I do without you?

When we got to the flat, Ivan and Rez were out and the sink was full of dishes. Rita offered to do them. It won't take me long, she said.

No, it's not fair, I said. You shouldn't be doing their dishes!

It's better I do them than you. Do you have rubber gloves?

Under the sink, I said.

I can't see any.

Maybe they're in the bathroom.

I went to look and found a Durex wrapper on the floor, it had missed the bin. I knew that Rez didn't use condoms, his nurse was on the pill.

Did you find the gloves? Rita shouted through.

It's fine, Mum. I'll do them later.

I've started now, it's no bother, she said.

I locked the door and pretended to be using the toilet. *Could he not have destroyed the evidence, the stupid bastard?!* Maybe he was trying to harden me up. I wrapped the broken foil in toilet paper and put it in my pocket. It still smelled of rubber. I sat there for as long as I could, banishing my tears and composing myself. I flushed the toilet – it even sounded like a pretend flush – and went back into the kitchen.

Would you like some tea, Mum? I asked. My throat was closing up, jamming the words.

I reached up to the cupboard and was glad Rita couldn't see my face. She was still up to her elbows in Ivan and Rez's dirty plates: I was furious with both of them now, treating me like a drudge.

I found the gloves, she said.

Where?

In the cutlery drawer. Brand new, still in the packet.

One of them must've put them in there, I said. I don't know why they bother, they won't actually use them.

Do you always do their dishes? she said.

Not always, I said. (I felt myself defending them.)

She frowned. Don't overdo it. I'm sure they don't expect it.

They don't, I said.

I just wanted her to go so that I could mull over the condom and cry.

Can I smoke in here? she asked, peeling off the gloves and sitting down.

I suppose so. Rez smokes occasionally.

I gave her a chipped saucer for an ashtray.

So what have you got planned for the rest of the week?

Just classes and grocery shopping. I'll ask Ivan to take me in the car so I can stock up on heavy stuff.

It's good he can help you, she said. I'm glad it's working out, I was worried you'd just end up in bits again.

She stubbed out her cigarette halfway. Right, I'm off. I don't want to get home too late.

You haven't finished your tea, I said.

I've had enough, thanks.

I'll come outside and wave you off, I said. Now that she was going, I didn't want her to go.

We hugged before she got into the car. If I don't see you through the week, I'll see you through the window, I said.

She smiled. I'll phone you when we hear about Sean's job.

I really hope he gets it, I said.

I waited 'til her car had disappeared from sight, before going back upstairs. I was crying before I was inside the flat. All the pain of Ivan had come back, compressed into a single moment of finding a condom under the sink.

I went into his room. There were three juggling balls on the bed. They had yellow and blue harlequin skin. I'd never seen them before. I picked them up. They were suede. I knew Storm had brought them. I wanted to gore them, slice them open. I threw them on the floor. One of them rolled under his desk. I smelled his pillows for traces of her and kicked the bed.

I went back into the kitchen. I cleaned the ashtray and sat down. I stared at the clock, watching the second hand jump from notch to notch. I couldn't bear the hours ahead, the seconds, the length of the evening.

I laid my head on the table and wept myself into a lull.

I wished I could get rid of the pain aerobically, go running, or go to the gym and punch a bag, but I had to work it all out in my head. I wondered what tears do for you biochemically, why you feel better after them.

I ran a bath. While it was cooling, I left my share of the gas bill on the kitchen table and a pointy note about the dishes.

The water was still too hot and burned circles round my ankles when I stepped in. I gushed on the cold tap and knelt down. I could only stay in for five minutes, the heat was too exhausting. I went to bed with a towel wrapped round me and listened to Sade in the dark.

The bed was damp from the towel and my muscles were vibrating. I got up and put pyjamas on. I lay back down and listened to the noises of late evening. Every time a door banged, my heart started to race.

I couldn't sleep and got up again. I went into the living room and turned on the TV. I watched a documentary about a baby girl with spina bifida. Her parents were strong and optimistic and said they wouldn't swap her for the world. The doctors'd had to operate on her when she was just born. I turned away. She was at risk from hydrocephalus and they'd inserted a shunt into her brain to drain the excess fluid.

She'd have this for the rest of her life. It was unbearable to think of such a tiny being having these horrors.

Before trying to sleep again, I retrieved the juggling balls and put them back on Ivan's bed. They lay on his quilt like trophies.

When he finally got in after midnight I was lying in bed wide awake, but I didn't get up.

The next day, I bought a man's jacket from Oxfam (olive green) to cheer me up. One arm was longer than the other but if you rolled the sleeves up you couldn't tell. When I reached down to get my bag in the changing room, I thought I was going to faint. I knelt down and stayed behind the makeshift curtain until I felt less dizzy. When I came out, the woman who was waiting glared.

That evening, both Ivan and Rez seemed sheepish and said sorry about the dishes. It's your flat, Rez, I said, you can do what you want, but sometimes I feel like a cleaner, that's all. I wanted to get him on his own and ask him about the condom – maybe it was his – but he'd just cover up for Ivan so there was no point.

Ivan brought the harlequin trophies into the living room to show me. D'you like my new balls?

Ha ha, I said.

D'you want a shot?

No, I said. Where did you get them?

Storm brought them, he said. We were practising all

weekend. It's good fun. You should try it.

*

stranger	How are you? It's a while since we chatted – you look pale.
me	My essay on the Azande's due in a week. I can only type with two fingers and my arms burn, and you can never get a Mac free, you have to reserve them. Ivan's got a computer but it's an IBM.
stranger	You couldn't just write it by hand?
me	No one writes stuff by hand anymore. I wish I could type properly – I should've done typing at school instead of physics. It would've been a lot more useful than knowing that Velocity = Frequency x Wavelength.
stranger	Why didn't you do typing?
me	Bright pupils didn't do secretarial studies. It wasn't on the academic timetable. I didn't actually want to do it at the time, but looking back it would have made much more sense.
stranger	How's everything else going?
me	Don't ask.

stranger   Ivan?

me   It's my own fault – I should've known it would be like this. He's such a good friend to me and I keep putting pressure on him about other women. He's so calm, he hardly gets angry when I'm being emotional and choppy. Can you believe I kept a condom wrapper to confront him with? I ended up throwing it away – I just couldn't bear a big fight, it saps me, leaves me like jelly for days.

stranger   He's not exactly blameless though. You've said he's still quite flirtatious with you.

me   He is, but I think it's more affectionate than sexual. It's hard to tell. I think he sees me like a sister.

stranger   His sister died, didn't she?

me   Yup, and he still thinks it was his fault. She was running across the road to the ice cream van. His mum had asked him to go and he sent Molly instead. I think he's missing what she would be like now. He talks about her more than he ever did.

stranger   It's good he's got you then.

me   His family's going through a lot just now.

His granny's got Alzheimer's and is wreaking havoc at his parents'. And his dad's got no emotions. I feel sorry for his mum, she's got no one to talk to, his dad's so remote. Ivan thinks he's autistic. No wonder his mum drinks sometimes.

stranger   Everyone's got their problems.

me   I know.

stranger   Still, you can't put all your eggs in one basket – you don't want to invest all your emotions in Ivan again.

me   You sound like my mother! I just have to get through my essay and end of term exam. That's what's most important.

stranger   Good luck then. And enjoy the Christmas break.

me   You too.

*

Got my first Christmas card today: a glittery robin from Callum. It made me laugh. He said he'll phone me over the holidays. I put the card up in the kitchen for Ivan to see. Last night, I dreamt that Granny Fleet was chasing me with giant plastic cocktail sticks. I woke myself up shouting, *Why don't you believe that I'm ill?!*

*

New Year's Day 1990

We've all got flu, I'm terrified: ME + FLU = DEATH. Back to twenty-four hours a day in bed, no life. I'm scared Rita and Nab don't get better.

My nose drips onto the pillow all night, and my ears are squeaking with catarrh.

Sean's the only one not ill, he has to go back to London tomorrow for work. I wish he could stay longer. He's living in Ilford with graduates who work for Ford. He travels into the centre of London for his job. He knows the Tube stations off by heart and talks about the Central line as if he grew up there.

I'm worried I won't be well enough for the start of term. I'll need to borrow Mo's notes and his writing's impossible to read. It's like code, he writes in tiny letters with arrows and asterisks all over the place. I could ask the mature student in my tutorial, his writing's perfect, but he blushes whenever I speak to him. He probably wouldn't want to lend his notes anyway, he'd be too nervous that I'd lose them.

My granny's coming over later to make stovies. She'll tell us (again) about the time she was almost dead with flu and my grandad was doing the cooking and boiled the pork chops.

21

MA, ME!

SOMETIMES I GO to the careers office. I feel in awe of all the opportunities, looking through the toyshop window at treasures I can never have: glittering jobs, glamorous placements, exotic Master's degrees.

I always check, but there are no jobs for four hours a week.

*

Callum phoned out of the blue (I hadn't heard anything since the robin) and asked if I wanted to see *The Unbearable Lightness of Being* at the GFT. He asked if he could stay over. It's shite going for the last train, he said. I thought you'd gone to Australia, I said.

The weekend he came, Ivan was in Dundee – his granny had poured a boiling kettle over the floor and scalded the skin off her feet, and his mum was crying all the time. I'd asked if he wanted me to go with him, but he said it'd be better if he went on his own.

When we got back from the film, we sat in my room and Callum lit a joint. Rez'll kill you, I said, he'll get struck off if he's got drugs in his flat. You have to sit at the window.

You've landed on your feet, doll, he said, inhaling loudly and grinning.

How?

Living in such a toasty pad.

I'm lucky the way it's worked out, I said, even though my room's tiny.

Cosy and toasty. Extremely toasty.

He offered me the joint and I had a couple of draws. I was fed up being so careful about my health – it didn't make any difference, I still felt crap, even with all my abstaining.

What you doing tomorrow? he asked.

Starting my essay on potlatching.

What's potlatching?

The Pacific Northwest Indians had wild ceremonies where they sang and danced and ate tons – they gave away their property as gifts and got prestige in return.

Big feasts and presents, sounds brilliant!

It's a lovely word, isn't it? I said.

Pot... latch. He said it slowly with delight on his face, like a toddler who'd just completed a puzzle.

It means 'to give' in Chinook Jargon which was the trade language then.

Chinook! Another lovely word. Is that all they do on your course, teach you lovely words?

I heard a noise and went into the living room to check it wasn't Rez's car. When I came back, Callum was lying on the floor, wedged against the wall like a draft excluder. So if you wanted a canoe for nothing, you could go to a potlatch? he said.

I laughed and sat down on the floor, leaning against the bed.

It was a kind of trading as well, I said, a way to get rid of surplus stock. Sometimes they burned blankets if they had too many, just to show off – the more they destroyed or gave away, the more social status for the chief.

My head felt pointed and my lips were going numb. I felt as if it was someone else with my voice who was talking.

You know what would be good, he said, if you had a potlatch instead of a twenty-first. You'd get invitations saying: YOU ARE INVITED TO MY POTLATCH IN THE SWAN HOTEL ON 10th MAY.

But you wouldn't get any presents, you'd have to give other people presents.

Right enough, he said... you could give them all blankets.

I'd rather get shells or beads. Is the tenth of May your birthday?

Yup.

What age will you be?

Twenty-eight.

I'll need to remember to send you a card. It's terrible I don't even know when your birthday is.

It's sinful, he said.

Ivan's is in a couple of weeks. He'll be twenty-nine, it seems so fucking old.

Where is the handsome brute anyway?

I told you, he's gone to Dundee, there's a family crisis with his granny.

Aye, grannies can be bedlam.

There are good grannies and bad grannies, I said.

There's good and bad everything, he said, sitting up. He leaned over and kissed me.

I kissed him back without really meaning to. He told me he wanted me. You can't have me, I said, we've got no condoms.

There must be some in the flat.

I'm not rummaging through Rez and Ivan's stuff, I said.

I'll do it, he said.

Behave yourself, you will not.

Let's just lie down and be cosy then.

We went to bed and made each other come. My arm got tired quickly. Callum was in his element. Use your mouth, he gasped.

I ran to the bathroom and spat out his sperm and brushed my teeth.

I hope you've not got AIDS, I said. You can get it from oral sex if you've got lesions in your mouth.

I'm riddled with it, he said.

I sincerely hope you're joking.

You need to relax, doll, take a chill pill. (He pronounced it *cheel peel*.)

I don't need a chill pill, I just don't want AIDS. My immune system's fucked as it is.

I think it's time for some shut-eye, he said. I'm knackered.

I'll sleep in Ivan's bed. You stay in here.

Can I not come in with you?

No, Rez'll clipe on me.

Fuck's sake, it's like the police in here.

We can't both sleep in Ivan's bed, you know we can't.

Has he got a double?

You know he's got a double bed.

Lovely jubbly.

I'm sorry, I said. I just want to be discreet.

He stood up. Have you got a toothbrush I can use, if it's not too much to ask?

I'm sure I can find you one, I said.

He followed me into the bathroom. There's a forest of them in here, he said, examining the toothbrush mug.

I'll sterilise one for you, I said, plucking one that I knew wasn't Ivan's or Rez's.

I'll just rinse it, he said. No need to sterilise.

You don't want me to pour boiling water over it?

It's too much. You're hyper-clean.

I'm funny about toothbrushes, I said.

You should live in a bubble and wear white gloves.

I'm a dentist's daughter.

That's no excuse.

I kissed him on the forehead and ruffled his hair. Sorry to be so clinical about everything. It's just how I am.

Have you got a nightie I can borrow? he said.

I've got a big T-shirt you can have. It's ancient, it says RELAX on it.

I left him in the bathroom, singing Frankie Goes To Hollywood and cleaning his teeth with God knows whose toothbrush. I found the T-shirt, crumpled in a ball at the back of my wardrobe, but it had a huge blood stain on it. It had been there for weeks. I was horrified at myself for forgetting. I found him a T-shirt of Ivan's instead.

Couldn't find mine, take Ivan's, I said.

Thanks, doll. I'm not allowed in his bed but I get to wear his T-shirt!

I'm sorry, I said.

Only joshing. Nighty night. Sleep tight.

I got changed and went into Ivan's room and got into bed. I felt something on my foot. There was a rolled-up elastoplast stuck to the sheets. It looked like a moth. I got up and put it in the bin and washed my hands. I could hear Callum moving around, I knew he was having another smoke. I prayed that Rez wouldn't come back.

Ivan's pillows were musty. I lay awake for ages. Eventually, I fell asleep wondering what the gap between your eyelashes and your face is when your eyes are shut.

*

Ivan looked done in when he got back from Dundee. I just wish she'd die, he said. For everyone's sake. Her brain's a black hole. It's a fucking nightmare.

How's your mum? I said

She's at the end of her tether, she does everything. My dad's sister does fuck all. My granny's in hospital with no skin on her feet and that bitch is hardly in touch. Too busy having dinner parties in London.

It's always like that in families. One person does all the caring. D'you not think it's time your granny went into a home? I said gently.

I think my dad's come round to the fact. They're going to start looking.

You poor boy, I said. What can I do to make you feel better?

Nothing, he said. No one can do anything.

I'd never seen him so demoralised.

And we're fucking around in the lab with mice, he said – it'll take years to get these cognitive enhancers on the market – and meanwhile demented old people are eating plants and smearing shit everywhere.

Was your mum drinking at all? I said.

She only had one glass of wine on Saturday with dinner.

Well, that's good, isn't it?

I think she gets tipsy more out of loneliness than an

301

inability to cope.

I didn't want to tell him that when she'd phoned for him last week in the afternoon, she'd been slurring her words.

Anyway, how was your weekend – did Callum come?

Yeah. We saw the film, it was brilliant. It had the same actor as *My Beautiful Laundrette*. Callum stayed over, I slept in your bed and he had mine. I changed your sheets for you.

Thanks, he said.

You should sleep, you look exhausted, I said.

I'll have an early night. I've got a meeting with my principal investigator first thing.

D'you want some tea?

Yeah, but not homeopathic, a bit of colour in it, please.

I put the kettle on and hugged him. Is that a new polo neck? I said.

Yeah, my mum got it. The neck's funny, isn't it? It doesn't sit right, it juts out.

You look like a Tudor.

He laughed. You're a cheeky brat.

I got you to laugh though, didn't I?

I felt guilty that I'd been taking drugs and having sex while he'd been in Dundee having a crap weekend.

I got tickets for the Robert Cray Band for Ivan's birthday. They were playing in the QM. Rez and Dr Wanker Lawrence came too. I tried standing but had to sit down after one song. I wondered if Dr Wanker thought I was putting it on. Ivan (my hero) made a point of telling him I had to find a seat. The seats in the balcony were already taken so I sat on the tables at the side, jammed between sweaty undergraduates, hardly able to see a thing. The music was brilliant though, the band was pooled in pink and purple light. At the end, Ivan came and found me and grabbed me and kissed me on the lips. Thanks for such a great present, Looby. You're a star. He was drunk and his kiss was wet and studenty. I hugged him, and it reminded me of years ago when we'd be in the union, drinking and dancing all night.

When we got home he took his trainers off and got into my bed fully dressed. I want to sleep in your bed, he said.

But you smell drunk and you'll snore.

I've got a semi.

Go to bed you cheeky chemist.

I'm not a chemist, I'm a biochemist.

I sat on the bed and stroked the back of his head.

D'you want some Irish in you? he said.

Not tonight, thank you.

I've got a condom, he said, mumbling into the pillow, but it's been through the washing machine in my jeans.

D'you want some coffee?

Yes, please.

When I came back with the coffee, he was sitting up and looked a bit like he'd been crying.

*

I was studying for my end of term exam the week before Easter. Ivan came into my room and asked if I wanted toasted cheese. My head's a sieve, I said tearfully, I can't remember anything.

You'll be grand, he said.

I loved it when he used Irish expressions.

I told him that if I got seventy percent in my exam and an 'A' in my next essay, I'd get an exemption and wouldn't have to sit the final exam in June.

Fingers crossed, he said. Do you want toasted cheese or not?

Please, I said. At least I don't have to look after those leopards.

What leopards?

I dreamt you gave me two baby leopards to look after and they kept running away. I was knackered. I was so relieved to wake up.

*

In June 1990, I graduated. *Hurrah! Hurrah! Hurrah!*

Helen Fleet, MA, ME.

I felt sexy with my hair up, important in my new black suit, my graduation present from Rita and Nab.

Everyone beaming their heads off in the photos.

Nab and Rita were sophisticated in their pale grey

suits. My grandad was tall and too thin in his navy blue suit – he looked like a Giacometti sculpture. I couldn't take my eyes off my granny's brooch, a hideous rolled-gold deer with diamond antlers, a present from the Toronto pencils woman. Brian was wearing his suit for special occasions and kept fiddling with his collar.

Sean couldn't make it but sent an Interflora bouquet. Peter came but left straight after the ceremony.

We went to the Ubiquitous Chip.

Brian begged to be allowed some champagne. We all clinked to my achievement. My granny said she'd stormed the gates of heaven with prayers for me. Uncle Donnie, her cousin, came up in the conversation. He's not keeping well, she said, he can't take cheese because of his pills.

Ivan joined us for coffee afterwards. I'd wanted him at the whole lunch but he'd said it should just be my family. He had a single white rose for me. I'll dry it and keep it forever, I said. When we'd finished, Brian asked if he could have his photo taken wearing my graduation robe. I like that purple hood, he said. It's lovely.

Later, I asked Ivan what drugs reacted with cheese.

MAOIs, he said. They're a kind of antidepressant.

Uncle Donnie must be depressed then, I said.

Is he the guy who cuts your mum's grass?

Yeah, he was always so cheery – who'd have thought it?

Cheese and red wine are both dodgy – they can cause your blood pressure to soar.

Poor man, I said. He lives on his own, he's got no one to look after him.

You should phone him.

I should, I said, but I've never phoned him before – I don't really know him.

22

London

A COUPLE OF weeks after graduating, I went to London to see
Sean. The last time I'd been on the train to Euston I'd been
going to France with Jana. Seven years ago.

The guy sitting opposite was handsome, in his early
thirties. He only had one leg. I tried not to look when he
was laying his crutches on the luggage rack above. He was
wearing shorts which made his stump more obvious, the
denim fringe against his skin. He had cheese sandwiches in
a Tupperware box. They were cut in triangles.

He got off at Preston. A girl with a dog met him and
they kissed.

At Crewe, an old woman with a yellow face asked me to
get her case down for her. It was huge. I told her I was sorry,
I couldn't, I'd hurt my back. I knew she didn't believe me.

At Euston, I panicked when I couldn't see Sean. I
searched frantically for his face in the crowd. I'd told him

what carriage I was in. I didn't know whether to stay put or get a trolley and start walking up the platform. My holdall weighed a ton even though I was only visiting for a week. Nab had carried it onto the train for me. Suddenly Sean was behind me. Hey there, sister with the degree! He hugged me and grabbed my bag. It's heavy, I said. You know me, I can't travel light. It's fine, he said, throwing it onto his shoulder. C'mon, I've got you a ticket already.

Descending into the Tube was like going into another country. I steadied myself on the escalator. Take my arm if you want, said Sean.

It feels so international here, I said. It even *smells* international.

Sean smiled, he was trying to be blasé about the fact he knew his way round.

Even the buskers are more sophisticated, I said.

We didn't have to wait long for our train, but there were no seats.

It's only three stops, said Sean. We change at Holborn.

I shut my eyes and hung from the hand-grip, thinking of soft pillows. How can you do this every day? I asked.

You get used to it, he said.

You love it, don't you?

Yeah, he said, grinning. Are you knackered?

I feel jet-lagged, I said. I was up at 7 a.m.

You can lie down when we get in. Are you hungry?

A bit. I had horrible sandwiches on the train. Mum made me some but I had to buy more.

I stocked up for you coming, he said. We'll get a carry-out tonight, there's a good Chinese place near us. Amber's looking forward to meeting you.

Who's Amber?

She's one of my flatmates and we're kind of going out.

Does she work for Ford?

Nah, she works with the deaf.

I thought all of your flatmates work for Ford.

Two of them do. This is us, he said, yanking my arm.

He led the way and we battered our way through Holborn and changed from the black line to the red line. The train jolted off and I hung with my arm burning, wanting more than anything to lie down. Do we have to change again after this? I said.

We could stay on 'til Newbury Park but it's too far for you to walk. We'll just change at Stratford and get the main line to Seven Kings. The house is a hop and a skip from there.

Can we not get a taxi from Newbury Park? I said. I'll pay.

If you want, but you always have to wait for ages.

I'd rather wait than change again.

Okay, it's up to you, he said.

I tried to study the Tube map through the swaying of the train. What's the yellow and green line? I said.

That's two different lines, he said. Circle and District.

God, I must seem like a hillbilly, I said. It looks like the earth wire on a plug.

It takes a while to absorb it all, he said.

I closed my eyes and hung and thought again of soft pillows. I prayed I'd get a seat by Bethnal Green.

We can come back into town tomorrow night if you feel up to it, said Sean.

I think I'll be happy just staying in your flat.

See how you feel, he said. Or we could leave it 'til Sunday.

Sean didn't mean it, but the pressure was already on to be okay to go out.

By the time we got to his house, I felt as if the balls of my feet had been caned. The street reminded me of Festive Road, where Mr Benn lived.

The house seemed tiny inside compared to the flats in Glasgow I was used to. The hall had a swirly carpet and a teak telephone table. Bubble glass doors led into the other rooms. I went into the living room and sank into the brown fake velvet couch.

I'll just put your bag upstairs, said Sean. You're in my room.

Wait a minute, I said, I've got something for you. I dug into the side zip compartment and gave him the small silver package: the silver ribbon I'd curled was flat and lifeless.

Is it a tape?

Open it and see.

He ripped it open. Thanks a lot! I really like The Fall. So does Amber.

I was slightly hurt that he hadn't noticed the funky wrapping paper. Ivan's into them too, I said.

They're brilliant, aren't they? he said, galloping off upstairs.

I took my DMs off and lay down. I could smell wine on the arm of the couch. I closed my eyes. I could see brash, hallucinated images, faces like exclamation marks – patterns invented by my hyped-up, exhausted brain.

Sean galloped back down. I asked him why there was a fridge in the living room.

Dunno. We don't use it. It's just there.

I closed my eyes again. I could hear mugs being taken out of the cupboard and a spoon bouncing off the work surface, reassuring noises, the kettle getting louder.

By the way, don't drink the tap water, he shouted through. There's bottled stuff in the fridge.

Okay, I said. I wanted to lie undisturbed on the couch forever.

Sean appeared in the doorway, holding two mugs of tea. Let's go into the garden, he said.

I got up but felt dizzy and had to sit down again. I had faint purple zigzags on the fringes of my vision.

Are you okay?

I must've got up too fast. Happens all the time.

Come and get some sun on your face. Can you bring the biscuits?

I got up more slowly and followed him outside. You're so lucky to have a garden, I said.

It's a bit overgrown, but it's handy. It's been boiling since May. The weather's much better down here.

311

He handed me my tea and I sat the mug down on the springy grass.

You seem really happy, I said. You're like Dick Whittington, all settled down, seeking your fortune.

I love it here. You need a lot of energy though. You could never live here.

How's your job?

I work with great people. That's how I met Amber, she's an advocacy worker and knows one of our advocacy workers.

What's she like?

She's gorgeous, he said, blushing. She's half Surinamese and half Dutch. She just moved in a month ago and we really hit it off.

D'you ever hear from Nellie the elephant?

Nah – you never liked her, did you?

I really tried to like her, but she was very unlikable, and telling Mum she thought I should try antidepressants was the tin lid.

I know.

Is she in London too?

I think so, I don't know where though. I don't want to know.

It's funny how you're part of someone and then you're not.

Bronwen and Paul, my other flatmates, used to go out but now they're both seeing other people. They get on fine though.

How long did they go out for?

Not that long. How's it going with Ivan?

Completely fucked. I shouldn't be living with him, but who else could I live with? Who'd help me like he does? Don't say anything to Mum. She thinks everything's hunky dory.

You like living at Rez's though, don't you?

I love it, but I can't stay there rent-free forever. Rez's been dropping hints. I don't know what's going to happen.

Can you not apply for housing benefit?

I'm going to try, but it's just a boxroom.

But it's a really nice flat, all mod cons. You should see what some landlords get away with!

I suppose.

It's brilliant you got your degree though.

I'm going to look for voluntary work when I get back, maybe do a night class in October. There's one called 'Understanding Flying' I quite fancy, aeronautical engineering for beginners

You're crazy, he said.

I worry sick if Mum's flying, I can't watch the news 'cos I'm sure her plane will have crashed. Nab's taking her to Paris for a long weekend for their anniversary. I'm really glad for her, she needs a break, but I'm dreading it.

You can't worry about things that are out of your control, he said. It's a waste of energy.

I just think it's amazing that people are as unscathed as they are, given that the world is so physically dangerous, I said.

I think that's someone home, said Sean, leaping up. He came back with a tall girl with thin hair and a black suit. Bronwen, this is my sister Helen. Helen, this is Bronwen.

We shook hands and I was terrified she'd ask me what I did.

Sunday night, Freud's, a trendy basement bar, all minimalist and wooden. I've got a stool, everyone else is standing. We had to leave the last place because I couldn't get a seat. My legs are fucked.

I really like Amber, she's down to earth and pretty in a quirky way. She has coffee skin and corkscrew hair. She said she liked my Oxfam jacket and showed me how to say my name in sign language. Bronwen and her friend, whose name I can't remember, are wearing sexy little dresses and Jigsaw jackets and strappy shoes I could never walk in. I feel like Cinderella with my second-hand jacket and the dress I wore to Richard's wedding. Bronwen's nice, but I don't like her friend. She's from Portsmouth. She's in a bad mood 'cos she wanted to stay in the last bar 'cos an Iranian guy she fancies was supposed to come in later. Her and Bronwen could have stayed there, but Bronwen wanted to come to Freud's with us.

I was worried about not being able to afford a round for everyone but Sean and Amber are skint too and we're in our own round. I've had one glass of wine, and am on Aqua Libra now. I love being out in London. I wish I could live here. I feel proud of Sean, he's so kind and grown up. You can tell Amber really likes him, but she's not clingy, she's cool.

During the week, I sunbathed and listened to *GLR*, waiting for them all to come home from work. I read a Dennis Potter novel.

I peeked in all of their rooms. Amber's was stashed with candles and incense and Indian scarves, her clothes all over the floor. Bronwen's was anally tidy, the way mine would be if I hadn't got ill. (When I was growing up, my jewellery box had to be at the right angle or I couldn't sleep.) She had lots of shoes lined up and her wardrobe was full of padded hangers and lovely clothes. She had a diary beside her bed, with a purple velvet cover. I brushed my fingers over it. She didn't seem the type to keep a diary. Paul's room smelled stale; he had weights on the floor and a poster of Betty Blue.

Sean finished work early one day and I met him in Covent Garden. I got a taxi to Newbury Park. I was nervous on the Tube myself but after a few stops I felt cosmopolitan. I loved the adverts for museums and events – stretching dizzyingly in a diagonal down the escalators.

I bought a David Hockney postcard for Fizza. After I'd posted it, I worried that a naked man in the shower might offend her parents.

Sean told me he'd miss me when I'd gone and thanked

me for doing their breakfast dishes. We went to a cheap
Nepalese restaurant. I was glad to see he was eating meat
again – he didn't look so pasty. He talked about work
– the guy he was helping just now had lost his ability to
recognise people, after a car crash. After dinner, we went to
see *Sweetie*. I loved it when the mad sister ate the ceramic
horses out of spite.

*

Back in Glasgow, can't stop crying, but I'll rescue myself,
I always do. London emphasised how fucked my life is: I
saw what normal graduates do. I felt so outside everyone,
so *unemployed*. Bronwen was telling me about her second
interview with Ford and how she got lost in the lifts and was
in a huge panic in case she was late, and I realised that I've
never even *had* an interview, not since the Swan Hotel. And
I'm fed up looking like a student. Amber said she liked my
bohemian look, but there's a thin line between bohemian
and tinker. I wonder if I'll ever have another chance to wear
my graduation suit. I'm so shielded living here with Ivan
and Rez: the reality is that Ivan's researching a drug for
Alzheimer's, Rez's saving children with leukaemia, and I'm
writing a shopping list for Hoover bags and shampoo. The
last time I had a position of responsibility was when I was
head girl, confiscating cigarettes from first years.

*

Anxieties nail themselves into my head when I'm trying to sleep: what will I do if anything happens to Rita and Nab, how the fuck will I manage? I need to find a GP in Glasgow who believes in ME. I can't stay registered with Myra forever, but I need her for my sick notes. She's a believer.

Sat up late talking to Jab last night. He cheered me up. Jab (short for Jabril) works with Rez. He's Jordanian. I like him because he's so passionate and enthusiastic about everything. Words rush out of his mouth and his sentences collide as he interrupts himself. He won't let you finish your sentences. He's crazy about bagging Munros. He almost killed himself once, retrieving an expensive rucksack from the edge of a precipice – he said he'd rather have cut his hands off than leave his new rucksack on Ben Oss. A few years ago, he was doing post-graduate medical studies in America and was expelled for throwing a stapler at a poster of Israel in the campus travel agent's. He said it wasn't Israel, it was Palestine. (His parents fled to Jordan before he was born.) He thinks the Holocaust was exaggerated. *You can't say that*, I said, *you know it's not true!* I'm shocked at you, Jab. It's so wrong to say what you're saying! Helen, you don't understand, he replied, they treat us like cockroaches, even lower than cockroaches. They want to exterminate us. He told me the proper name – *keffiyeh* – for the ubiquitous chequered scarves as worn by Mo. Like every good student, I supported the Palestinians and had voted for Yasser to be university rector, but he'd been beaten by the Glasgow Lord Provost. Jab doesn't know much about ME but he's a believer. Rita loves him, she's met him twice. Why can't you fancy him? she said, he's a delightful young man. He's really sweet, I replied, but he's too hyper and he looks a bit like a hamster. He's just not my type.

*

The tangerines moved along the supermarket belt. I could see myself peeling one later and eating it. The preview filled me with dread.

I was trying not to think about Rita flying, especially as I'd read Bronwen's diary when I was in London. I knew that she'd never had an orgasm with anyone until Paul, and I was sure I'd be punished for this knowledge by my mother in a plane crash.

The woman in front was paying, her wallet had fallen open at a photo of her and her husband. I wished I had a happy couple photo in my wallet for people to see at the checkout. All I had was a photo of Agnes. I'd recently dreamt that I was carrying her around dead in a knapsack. The Azande think that a bad dream is an experience of witchcraft. I *was* a witch, I shouldn't have read Bronwen's diary.

I got a taxi back to the flat.

Ivan and Rez and Jab had gone to Skye to climb the Cuillins. They'd all be showing off, and Jab would be rushing them along the ridges, *Yella! Yella!* Because of the rock type, compasses don't always work properly so I was worried they'd get lost and die.

In a way, I liked having the weekend to myself, I could rest as much as I needed, no one would disturb me, and I could watch what I wanted on TV, though there was nothing much on except cricket. I thought I might visit Jana's granny on Sunday. I hadn't seen her for ages.

On Saturday night, I microwaved a fish and potato pie and watched a documentary about dancing bears in Bulgaria: they'd been captured when they were cubs and were undernourished and constantly chained. Their noses and mouths were shredded by the rings. Stupid bastard tourists paid to see them dance (the tourists should have been chained and made to dance for bread and water). The head of the gypsies said one bear supported ten people. The gypsies had been persecuted but they had no fucking right to brutalise the poor bears. I couldn't stop thinking about the shredded, infected flesh round their noses. I wished I didn't know. (There are some things you just don't want in your head.) There was a sanctuary for released bears in Turkey. I wished I could work for them.

I felt utterly sad and decided to give myself a facial. I tore my room apart, searching for my hair-band, cursing myself for being so scatty – I was so tired of losing things – and steamed my face over a Pyrex bowl in the kitchen.

I squeezed out the last of my Dead Sea facial clay and smeared it on. I lay on the couch 'til my face stung. I rinsed off the mask, leaving smears of green all over the sink and towel. I felt scrubbed and lovely, but my loveliness was wasted, there was no one to see me, no one to kiss my breasts.

I started to shave my bikini line, for no particular reason, probably out of boredom, and ended up shaving off all my pubic hair. I didn't like the effect, it looked childlike and pornographic.

Afterwards, it itched like crazy.

*

stranger   You look cheered up, what's happened? You've had a face like a wet weekend recently.

me   I know, I've been quite sad since graduating. When I look at jobs in the *Guardian* and *Glasgow Herald*, I get demoralised that I can't apply for them. I feel like an impostor when I go into the careers office. I'm scared I'll be found out.

stranger   What job would you do if you were well?

me   I'm not sure. Maybe something in the NHS, or something in arts administration. I keep changing my mind.

stranger   It must be difficult.

me   Seven years of ME takes its toll. I've also
realised how much time I've spent on my
own since getting ill. You're either in bed
being ill, or sleeping extra hours, or staying
at home because you can't join in what every
one else is doing.

stranger   So what's cheered you up?

me   A letter from Jana, she's had a bonus at
work and has offered to pay my fare to San
Francisco as a graduation present! I'd love
to go, I miss her a lot.

stranger   How will you manage an eleven hour flight?

me   I have no idea. I'm trying not to worry about
it.

*

Dear Jana,

You are my very own 'deus ex machina'! You have rescued
me from despair. Thanks so much for your lovely card and
offer to pay my fare over! I would love to come and visit you.
How about October? That gives me about six weeks to rest,

I'm still recovering from London. I would probably come for three weeks to make it worth it.

Your stories of the men you are dating make me howl, especially the herring party with the morose Finnish software engineer with his arm in a cast! My sex life is non-existent. Sexual experiences of last eighteen months: feeling my stepbrother's penis through his jeans; having Callum's not so fragrant penis in my mouth; being asked out by Mo, a divorced guy in my class, who hates woman and is often aggressive, I think he's an alcoholic. I invited him for dinner one night and he was surly to Ivan because he said he likes Woody Allen – Mo said his films are one big middle class wank.

Yesterday, I went to see a French film, it's cheap on Wednesdays – thank God, I have my student ID 'til October, I hate using that fucking pension book for concessions. Anyway, I felt self-conscious being at the film on my own and the guy selling tickets was really good-looking which made it worse. I bought Opal Fruits from the machine and they got stuck, just dangled, wouldn't drop down, and I had to ask him for help. You can imagine my humiliation.

On the way back from the film, the polkadot boy doctor who took my blood years ago was sitting opposite me on the Underground. It took me a while to realise who he was. He looked away, I think he was shy. If we'd been in a film, I would've told him he'd taken my blood when he was a junior doctor, and he would've stayed on 'til my stop and fallen in love with me.

I've had to apply for housing benefit as I can't keep staying here for nothing. Rez had to write a letter saying he was my landlord, and I had to go for an interview. A woman with whiskers asked me why I hadn't needed rent before and I had to explain that Rez hadn't charged me before. A guy in a grey anorak came to look at the flat. Both Rez and Ivan have double beds and I know he thought I was sleeping with one of them. I was expecting a long battle but amazingly my claim was processed, and I got the first cheque yesterday. I feel much better paying my way. There are very few people like Rez who would have let me stay a whole year for nothing. I rely so much on the goodwill of my friends and family. I'd be fucked without them, I'd be living on the breadline. I don't know how other ill people who don't have family to help them manage. I've applied for a Visa card, they hand them out to graduates these days, though if they knew I was a rag doll they would never give me one!

Glad your job is going well and that your insane psychiatrist flatmate has left. Hope the gay banker is better. I will get to meet him and can judge for myself.

Cannot wait to see you! What can I bring you – Pan Drops, cheese and onion crisps, a few sheep? Rez has a fax machine now, he loves gadgets, so you can fax me confirmation of flights if you want.

Lots of love,

Helen xxx

PS. I will never go to Bulgaria, they have chained dancing bears. It's obscene.

*

Worried sick. How can I possibly travel anywhere, never mind California, with legs with no power in them? They've been awful the last two weeks. I don't want to let Jana down by cancelling, she is so excited about me going, and the ticket is non-refundable. I have three weeks to go. I've practised packing to see how heavy my case is. I won't be able to bear the disappointment if I can't go. I'm thinking of having a one-off vitamin C drip if Helga will do it.

A week later, a fax came from Jana: Great news, my new room-mate has moved in, but he will be away for the time you are here and is fine about you using his room! He's going to Europe to get over his ex. His dog died the week he moved in with me, it ate extra strength Tylenol. I can't say I felt too sad as I wasn't crazy about having a dog in the apartment. Hope you are feeling stronger, just get your skinny ass over here! Love you, Jana.

I faxed her back that I was going for a vitamin C boost.

The week before travelling I went home to Balloch to rest properly. One afternoon I got a taxi to Marion's on impulse, she'd fitted me in at the last minute. I asked her to cut my hair really short, I couldn't be bothered with it anymore.

She wanted to re-do my highlights but it was too expensive, and I didn't care that they'd grown out.

23

San Francisco

I SAT IN the pen at the airport with Jean, the other passenger who needed special assistance, a breathless woman in her sixties with dyed red hair and bald patches. I was in a 2.5 mg Valium haze – I was scared to take more and halved the bitter yellow 5 mg tablets with my thumbnail. Myra had prescribed them, I'd been in such a state about feeling ill and travelling.

Rita had kept my place in the queue 'til it was my turn to check in. She'd lifted my case onto the luggage belt. It weighed 25 kilos. Watch you don't wreck your back, Mum, I'd said. I was horrified to see that my boarding pass had a wheelchair symbol on it. I'd asked if I could just have the assistance at Heathrow, where there would be tons of walking, but it was in their regulations that I had to take the wheelchair for the whole journey. It'll be great, said Rita, you won't have to queue, and you'll get on the plane first. There's no way I'm letting Jana see me like this, I said, shaking my head.

My mother hugged me goodbye and I was wheeled off with my pink Head bag on my lap. Phone me when you get there, even if it's late! she said. Her eyes had filled up. Bye, Mum, thanks for everything, I said, waving and struggling not to weep with exhaustion and gratitude (and excitement).

Jean smiled after me with complicity.

The chair was great, I had to admit, it was luxury not having to waste weak legs on queuing and walking, but I kept moving my feet so no one would think I was paralysed. The guy took me to the domestic departures lounge. I got out and sat with the other passengers, most of them commuters in business suits. I crossed my legs and uncrossed them to highlight my able-bodiedness.

I hadn't slept properly for days – I felt like one of those cats they'd done sleep deprivation experiments on: they knocked out their serotonin with a drug so that they staggered around, unable to fall asleep, eventually dying of exhaustion after a couple of weeks.

When they called the flight, I was allowed to board first. I was too tired to worry properly about the plane crashing, but when we took off I still expected to plummet seconds later.

At Heathrow, an Asian man with a wheelchair met me. He smiled and said, In you get, duckie. He pushed me through a maze of carpeted grey corridors. We had to get a lift to a different level (doubling the mortification, being wheeled into a lift); he dropped me at the shuttle bus for Terminal Four.

The shuttle took about twenty minutes. I waited 'til last to get off and this time was met by a thin African man. I was beginning to feel guilty about being chauffeured around by immigrant workers.

We got straight through security and passport control without having to queue. My plane didn't leave for another two hours. I told the man I could walk a bit and he tipped me out of the wheelchair and told me to be back at the pen at least an hour before the flight. I went to the toilets. I smelled faintly of sweat so I washed under my arms. A beautiful S-shaped pregnant woman was putting her hair in a ponytail. She looked Italian. I wanted to be her, so glowing and functioning. I cleansed my face, brushed my teeth and put on some lipstick.

My legs were weak and my skull was tight, I would've loved some tea but the queues were too long. I went to the newsagents and bought a can of Coke and *Vogue* – which added another kilo to my hand luggage – and some barley sugar sweets for my ears.

I passed Tie Rack and went in and caressed some boxers. They made me want to phone Ivan. I got Ystasis for Jana in Duty Free. I was lucky to get a till without a queue.

I made my way back, I had tons of time but I was scared I'd miss my pick up slot. I sat down in the wheelchair zone and took another half Valium. There was a young man with cerebral palsy, he must have wondered what the fuck I was doing there. I shuffled through my travel documents and checked them for the hundredth time. I had a wad of dollars rolled up in a bumbag which I had refused to wear. Rita had got it for me. It's leather, she'd said. They're bang in fashion.

I wanted to have a shower and lie down in the Club Class lounge. I curled up on the seats and used my Head bag as a pillow. I smelled of antiperspirant.

I was taken to the San Francisco flight on a buggy like the ones they use on golf courses. It was much less embarrassing than a wheelchair – I felt like a celebrity who was late for her flight. I could see the planes lined up at the gates with their pointy black and white cockpit heads; they looked like a row of cats drinking milk.

I felt that everyone was looking at me when the buggy dropped me off. I sat down and closed my eyes. All around me I could hear the elastic vowels of Americans.

They called the toddlers and frail people to board first. I walked slowly behind an old woman with a walking stick and pearls and too much rouge. An S-shaped woman was also boarding early. I felt relieved, the plane couldn't possibly crash with a pregnant woman on board, it would be too cruel.

I had asked for an aisle seat, I knew I would need to pee lots and didn't want to be clambering over other passengers. I put my bag in the locker and got settled in. I put my *Vogue* and *Oscar and Lucinda* in the seat pocket in front. They bulged out and left me hardly any room.

I hoped a handsome man would sit beside me but I got a very small Indian woman. Her bones looked like they would break if you touched her. I got up to let her in and she beamed gratefully. She had a bag she wanted put up in the locker and signalled to me to do it for her. It was heavy so I got one of the stewardesses to do it, I didn't know how the old woman had carried it herself. She gestured for help with her seatbelt. I clicked her in and she rubbed my hands to thank me. Her fingers were like brown velvet claws. I thought she must be cold, wearing just her sari with a cardigan on top. I hoped she had a coat with her.

A woman with an arse like a shelf was wedging herself into the seat in front. She hated me from the start. I accidentally dunted her seat and she turned round and glared with shark eyes.

The plane was huge – it took an age for everyone to be boarded and strapped in. When we finally lumbered along the runway, I had the thought that when we plummeted I would die between a small-boned brown woman and a pale pink fat woman. The old woman had slipped her hand into mine when the plane lifted off. It was nice to feel needed even though I was probably more afraid than her. Her palms weren't even sweating.

The fat woman put her seat back immediately and fell asleep and snored. I dropped my toilet bag, looking for my lip balm, and a lipstick rolled under her seat. I almost sprained my neck retrieving it.

Somehow, the hours passed, with meals and drinks being placed in front of you by beautifully manicured hands, and films and cartoons, if you didn't mind constantly having to rearrange your headphones to get rid of the crackling. I'd never liked *Mr Bean* much but it passed the time, and I'd seen *Tom and Jerry* a thousand times, but I'd never noticed the beauty of the drawings before – the sharp, bold outlines made me feel optimistic.

The old woman and I held hands again when there was bad turbulence over Greenland. Both our palms were sweating. I told myself I was flying over Nab's birthplace so nothing bad could happen. I'd kept two flight-size bottles of Merlot for Jana, but I opened one after the turbulence.

The Valium and wine made me feel benevolent, I wanted to smile at everyone, except the fat woman – she licked the foil lid of her trifle and I wanted to kill her.

I was constantly getting up to pee and slap out pins and needles. The old woman slept most of the time and got up twice during the whole flight. Both times she asked me to keep her seat.

Towards the end of the flight, they handed out immigration cards for non-Americans. A steward came round and checked if I needed assistance when we landed. He ticked me off on his list.

Everyone was queuing to freshen their sour breaths and underarms before landing. The toilets were choked with paper and stank, and there was only a dribble of water to wash in. The light made you green with enlarged pores. It was better not to look. When I got back to my seat, the fat woman was cleaning her ears with cotton buds and looking at the wax.

The pilot, unbelievably crisp and awake, pointed out Alcatraz and the Golden Gate Bridge. I could see brown crinkled velvet hills as we came into land. The plane dipped steeply several times – at this rate we'd end up in the fucking bay. When the stewardess announced, Welcome to San Francisco International Airport, I had tears of relief.

The Indian woman couldn't understand why I wasn't getting off with her. I have to wait 'til last, I explained, but she was confused and looked sad when I stayed in my seat. She looked so fragile, I felt I should take her with me, put her on my lap. I wondered if the wheelchair guy would be blonde-haired and blue-eyed, but, of course, he was Mexican. There were about six wheelchair passengers, it was like a parade.

The luggage carousels were mobbed. People with bloodshot, jet-lagged eyes, crowding and pushing, dragging their cases off the moving belts. I kept thinking I'd spotted mine, but there were a lot of black Samsonites. When it finally came, I got out of the chair and pointed to it. The guy grabbed it and put it on a trolley. I got back into the wheelchair and he pushed me with one hand and pulled the trolley behind him with the other. I felt sorry for him, but I couldn't have managed without him.

Immigration was next. You heard so many stories of how ruthless they were, always deporting people. I dreaded being turned back, I couldn't go through another eleven hour flight, I'd die of exhaustion. We bypassed the zoo of queues, and the guy wheeled me straight to a booth. I stood up to give the immigration officer my passport. My hands and legs were shaking. He asked me how long I was staying and asked to see my return ticket. I was sure he'd think I was here to work, pretending to be disabled. He scrutinised my ticket and handed it back without a word. He stapled something to my passport and told me to have a nice stay. We continued through customs without being stopped.

I turned round and told the Mexican guy I could manage on my own now and thanked him. I didn't want Jana to see me in a wheelchair. He looked perplexed. I would've liked him to keep pushing the trolley for me, but I didn't like to ask. I wondered if I should tip him, but I had no money, it was all rolled up in the bumbag at the bottom of my other bag. I'm okay now, I said, standing up. Really. Thank you.

I was totally disorientated and sick with excitement. I pointed the trolley through some sliding doors and saw a wall of people. At first I couldn't see Jana, then she hurled herself towards me, screaming, *Helen!* We were both crying. I can't fucking believe you're here, she said.

Me neither, I said. Don't hug me too tightly, I think I smell.

I thought you were getting a wheelchair! she said.

I did, but I shooed the wee man away after customs, he must've thought I was crazy. I just didn't want you to see me.

She lifted the case from the trolley, it was almost the same size as her.

It's on wheels, I said, but it's heavy. She manoeuvred it behind her. I'll need to take your arm, I said. My legs are like jelly.

The car's not far, can you last?

Just about, I said.

Your car's like a wagon, I said, when we reached it.

It's an Oldsmobile, I love it, don't want to part with it. Everyone gives me shit about it, it's not very Silicon Valley.

I love it, I said. It's like a sofa at the front.

We got into the car and grinned at each other. You look amazing, I said. Tanned and lovely.

Thanks, she said. You look exhausted but gorgeous as ever. Your hair's so short!

I don't feel very gorgeous, I said. I had a huge spot on my chin last week and dabbed it with Dettol and all my skin peeled off. It still feels tight.

Is Dettol not for cleaning toilets?

Yeah, but you can use it as antiseptic, but I didn't dilute it.

Crazy girl, she said.

We turned out of the airport and passed a billboard that said: BE HERE FOR THE CURE.

Rush-hour traffic had started. I marvelled at the way Jana changed lanes and zoomed in and out of the other cars, cursing other drivers.

By the way, my dad's invited us for dinner next weekend

if you feel up to it. He's got a new girlfriend, Kim, she's a holistic healer. She's cool.

You sound so American, I said, laughing.

I *am* American, she said. I'm a dumb American. I faked it all those years in Scotland. God, I've missed you. How the hell are you?

When we got to her flat, it was getting dark. The view was stunning. You could see the Bay Bridge and its blinking red lights. I got out of the car and took a deep breath, I felt like I was inhaling the whole San Francisco skyline.

I think I'm dreaming this, I said. I'm not really here.

You surely are, she said. View's great isn't it?

It's breathtaking, I said.

I shouldn't tell you this, but a guy killed himself last week in my neighbour's garden, shot himself in the chest with a .38 pearl-handled revolver. We think he chose this street 'cos of the view. I missed it all, I was in Seattle.

That's grim, I said.

Jana'd said .38 revolver as if everyone knew what it meant. I was too tired to ask.

What the hell have you got in here? she said, lugging my case up the flight of stairs to her apartment.

It's all presents for you, I said.

It's a good thing I've been working out.

Her flat was huge with hardwood floors. This is amazing! I said. Very Armistead Maupin.

I was so lucky to get it, renting's a nightmare in this city.

She put my case in her flatmate's room. I've put sheets on Jeff's futon, and you can use my comforter.

I've never slept on a futon, I said.

They're hard to begin with but you get used to them. There are more blankets if you want, I know you like lots of weight.

That's funny that you remember.

I always think of you under a mountain of bedclothes, even in summer.

I should lie down, I said. I feel like the floor's slanting and I'm walking uphill.

You're bound to be out of it, she said. It's midnight your time. Would you like some tea?

I'd love some.

Come through and lie on the couch. Are you hungry? I can make something or we can have leftover pizza.

Pizza's fine, I said.

I went into the living room and lay down. My neck felt like it had been whipped. The blinking red lights of the bridge were visible through the open blinds. I could see why you would want them as your last view, they were very soothing.

Jana brought through cold pizza and green tea.

We should have a toast, she said. D'you want some Zinfandel?

What's Zinfandel?

Californian wine, it's pink.

336

Just a sip, I said.

She brought me half a glass.

It's a gorgeous colour, I said.

It's called white Zinfandel, even though it's pink. You get red too.

It reminds me of Mateus Rosé, I said.

That stuff was disgusting!

We used to love it, I said. I clinked her glass. Here's to us! Thanks so much again for sending me a ticket.

I was so scared you wouldn't make it, she said. Thank God you did! Let's toast the men who pushed you here. She thrust her glass up high in front of her and threw her head back, laughing. To the wheelchair men!

To the wheelchair men! I said.

I couldn't stop yawning but it was only 5 p.m.

You should try and stay up, said Jana, have a bath.

I get too hot in baths, I said. I can't stay in for more than five minutes – I'd rather have a shower.

It's a great shower, she said, it'll wake you up, give you a fine pummelling.

I'll give you your presents first, I said.

I went through to my room and wrestled with the labels the airport had put on my case. I gave Jana the perfume, an Aztec Camera CD, Pan Drops, a *Broons* annual and the sweater Rita had knitted. Rita's gone a bit mad, I said, she's knitting stripy sweaters for everyone.

I love it, she said.

She put the CD on straight away.

I wasn't even sure if you had a CD player, I said.

I've only got six CDs, she said mournfully.

Well, now you've got seven, I said.

The shower pressure was majestic. I sat down on the tiles, hugging my knees, I could've stayed in there forever.

When I came out, Jana was wearing the sweater and singing along to *Walk Out To Winter*. This makes me so sad, she said. I miss Glasgow! I miss the seasons. There are *no* seasons here. It's flat.

You don't miss the rain though, I said. No one could miss the rain.

I guess it does rain a lot over there.

It never fucking stops, I said.

I really miss autumn though, she said, it's so dark and leafy and orange.

More like dark and leafy and damp, I said, lying down on the couch again.

So tell me, how is Mr Cox doing?

Ivan's fine, I said. His grandmother's very ill though and they're close.

You're still crazy about him, she said. I can tell from your letters, reading between the lines.

No, I'm not!

Is he seeing anyone?

I don't think so, not seriously, I think Wendy, the girl he works with, is after him though.

How would you feel if he got serious with someone?

I think I'd be okay if I was with someone else, but if I was still on my own I'd be devastated.

You *are* still crazy about him.

It's just hard to meet other people.

I guess you never really get over the last 'til you meet the next.

It's easier here, I said, you all go on dates. Are you still seeing the Finnish man with the broken arm?

Lasse? Not really, he's so anal and uptight. Can you believe he made me have an HIV test before he'd have sex with me! I got the fast 'result in three days' test. They sent the blood to a clinic in Minnesota. It cost seventy-five dollars!

Did he get tested too?

No, he said he'd already been tested last year.

And you believed him?

She made a typical Jana pout. If he was infected, he wouldn't have wanted me to take the test, would he?

I suppose not. Were you nervous getting the results?

A little, you start to think about some risks you may have taken, but I was fine. I gave a false name though, you don't want that stuff on record... but it was a waste of money, sex with Lasse was horrible, he was so clinical and still insisted we use a condom.

Condoms aren't that bad, I said.

Yeah, but it kept slipping off on account of his button mushroom penis.

You haven't changed, I said, giggling.

Well, what about you, Missy, at least I haven't seen my stepbrother's penis!

I didn't see it! I felt it through his jeans, that's all.

Well, if Lasse is typical of the Scandinavian man, you didn't miss much.

I can assure you that Finn seemed to be very well endowed.

Another toast, she said... to the genitalia of Lasse and Finn!

We clinked glasses again, and I had another sip of pink wine. Jana lit a cigarette and opened the window. She made smoking look sexy, I almost wanted one.

Lasse said I have a sexy voice. He said I sound like an actress.

You do, I said. You have a lovely voice.

Really, she said, it's not easy to meet men here, there's a huge shortage of single straight men.

What's Jeff like?

Very handsome, but also very gay.

I know, you said in your fax. What exactly does he do?

I'm not sure. He's in banking.

I think of 'Jeff' as a name for a farm-boy with dungarees and a checked shirt.

Not this Jeff, he's very dapper.

It's nice of him to let me use his room.

He's a sweet guy.

What would you have done if his dog hadn't died?

It wasn't really his dog, it was his ex's, Jeff just had custody for a while. It wouldn't have been living here for very long.

I would never share a flat with a dog. They're too noisy and they smell of ham.

They do not smell of ham! she said, guffawing. They smell of dog.

Maybe I should get that Minnesota test, I said, sometimes I worry that I got AIDS from the plasma exchange. They weren't screening blood then.

You worry too much, she said.

You don't worry enough, I replied.

By the way, no one here has heard of ME, she said, they call it chronic fatigue syndrome, and most people haven't heard of that either. They still talk about yuppie flu.

They can fuck right off then, I said.

They surely can.

I think I'll have a Valium to help me sleep, d'you want one?

Sure, I could do with a buzz.

It doesn't really buzz you, just makes you feel suspended and benevolent.

Suspended and benevolent's fine, she said.

I stood up stiffly and painfully, my legs were dead. I stamped the pins and needles out.

We'll need to go to my shiatsu guy in Palo Alto and get you ironed out, said Jana. He walks on your spine and bends you in half.

Sounds a bit brutal.

He's excellent, she said. I go whenever I'm stressed out at work.

I came back with half a Valium for her.

Thanks, she said. D'you want a Zinfandel refill?

No, I have to sleep now or I'll die. What will I do if there's an earthquake when you're at work?

Just stand under the doorway and pray, that's all you can do, she said, laughing.

I hugged her goodnight. It's so brilliant to see you.

You too, honey, she said. Sleep well.

Jet lag's like every thought you've ever had, compressed into one big thought, and you can't sleep even though you've been awake for thirty hours.

I've been tossing and turning forever, listening to the foghorns. There's no way I can sleep. I need earplugs and I'm hungry. I get up and look at my watch, it's 4 a.m. I open the blind. I can see the neon lights of a Diet Coke sign and the pyramid of the Transamerica building through the thick layers of fog. I remember with a jolt that I was supposed to phone Rita.

I go into the kitchen. Jana's fridge is huge and buzzing. She has four kinds of bread in the freezer, and she's covered the door in as many photos, postcards and magnets as you can fit on. She has the postcard I sent her from London and a photo of her and me and Ivan. It's funny to see him here.

(I used to have the same photo but I'd ripped it up when he said he was going to Thailand.)

I make some toast. I spread the jam on as quietly as possible, scared that the scraping will wake Jana, she has to get up at 6.30. I eat the toast at the kitchen table with my eyes shut.

When I go back to bed, the fog's beginning to shred and I can just make out a Safeway and a Bank of America.

I find my orange foam earplugs and lie down. I can still hear the foghorns, but they are padded and distant. I am exhausted and happy.

I am in San Francisco.

24

Jana

THE FIRST FEW days, I could only sleep in snatches. I staggered round Jana's flat like a cat without enough serotonin. I got hooked on *The Young and the Restless* (a daytime soap) and listened to *KUSF,* a university radio station that played brilliant music.

On my third day, I walked to a cafe two blocks away. I made the mistake of ordering tea.

Hot tea?

Yes, please. (What other kind was there?)

Is English Breakfast okay?

Fine, thanks.

We also have Prince of Wales.

English Breakfast's fine. (I had no idea of the difference.)

While I waited, two cops came in and ordered coffee to take away. They were scary with their guns but they were undeniably cool. At home the police were so uptight, with dandruff on their black lapels.

The waitress brought me a cup of microwaved water with a tea bag on the side. I dipped it in and it floated miserably on the surface, barely colouring the lukewarm water.

The walk back to the flat was uphill all the way. I stopped to rest in a tiny second-hand bookshop. I sat on a stool and picked up some Ray Bradbury stories to make it look like I was in there to browse. I bought the book before I left. The man serving had something wrong with his arms, they extended from his shoulders like Meccano, he couldn't bend them properly.

When I got back I lay down, I wanted to be okay for City Lights bookstore. Jana was taking me after work, my first venture downtown.

*

Second week in San Francisco. *Blue wooden house in Cole Valley. Jana, her dad, Kim and Helen are eating pumpkin soup. Kim is a hippy in her late forties with hollowed-out blue eyes and turquoise rings.*

jana's dad   So are you enjoying San Francisco?

helen   Yeah, I love being in Jana's flat, just hanging out and reading, looking at the view.

jana's dad   Have you managed to do much?

helen   We went to hot tubs in Palo Alto. I loved them. You'd never get anything like that in Glasgow... and yesterday we went to the Japanese tea garden. It's beautiful, so peaceful. Makes you want to be Zen and calm.

jana   [*laughing*] You couldn't be Zen if you tried.

kim   [*widening her eyes*] Do you ever meditate, Helen?

helen   I've tried but I just can't empty my head. I went to a Buddhist class for a while, but I found I was just looking forward to the tea break – they had a giant teapot that did the whole class.

[*Jana's dad smiles*]

kim   Have you tried yoga? It helps restore your energy. I had very weak wrists until I started doing yoga. I have much more strength now.

helen   I don't think yoga would strengthen my muscles.

kim   Really, the Salutation of the Sun is a wonderfully strengthening   exercise... you should try it.

helen   I did and it made me dizzy.

jana   Helen's tried everything, Kim, really she has.

kim   I use yoga and meditation with a lot of my clients, some of them are really sick with HIV, and cancer, you would be surprised at how energised they can be after our sessions.

helen   I feel weak and horrible after yoga, it doesn't energise me.

jana's dad   [*sensing the tension*] So what are you reading these days, Helen?

helen   *Oscar and Lucinda,* but I can't really get into it.

kim   Have you read *The Joy Luck Club* by Amy Tan? It's a wonderful book, I'll lend it to you while you're here. She's a Bay Area writer.

[*Jana's dad makes a face*]

kim   Robert, don't be rude, honey... [*turning to Helen*]... he doesn't like it because it's all about women.

jana's dad   That's not true. I like books about women. I just didn't like the style. You should read

Mating by Norman Rush, it's excellent, written from a woman's point of view.

kim   Yeah, by a man.

helen   I just read a short story by Ray Bradbury. It's called *A Flight of Ravens*. I really liked the tone, the hysteria. The man who sold it to me couldn't bend his arms properly.

jana   You always notice these strange things about people. No one else would.

helen   I know.

kim   There are some *great* bookstores here, new and second-hand.

helen   We've already been to City Lights – I could live there! – and there's a great second-hand place near Jana. That's where I got Ray Bradbury.

jana   [*yawning*] I'd like to read more, but I just don't have time.

jana's dad   Who are your favourite writers?

helen   I don't really have any, though I tend to read men more than women. And I hate books about childhoods. I'm more interested in reading about 'now', I don't care about childhoods. One or two lines is enough.

jana   Childhoods suck.

[*Jana's dad frowns but recovers quickly and smiles*]

kim   Have you ever tried fasting, Helen? It's a wonderful way to get rid of the toxins that make us sick. Last year, I fasted for a whole weekend and when I went into the bank on Monday morning, people let me go to the front of the line, it was like I had an aura about me. It was *amazing,* I could feel a light around me, protecting me.

helen   I don't think fasting's a good idea for me, personally. *Have you got that, you stupid hollow-eyed hippy?* (Into herself.)

[*No one speaks for a while*]

helen   The soup's lovely, Kim, how did you make it?

kim   I can give you the recipe, I'll write it out for you.

Sorry about Kim, said Jana on the drive home. She's got a good heart, she just wants to help.

How she heals people is beyond me, I said. You would *need* holistic healing after seeing her.

She lost her husband a few years ago, he drowned, I think that's why she's so intense.

I know, she told me when you were in the kitchen with your dad.

And she's from Bolinas.

Where's that?

A tiny town over the Golden Gate Bridge, everyone's a little crazy there – they all live by their crystals.

She asked me how being fatigued affected my sex life.

She did not!

How did your dad meet her anyway?

She took his writing class in summer.

What does he see in her? She seems too New Agey for him.

Great sex, what else?

Don't you think there's something weird about a fifty-year-old woman wearing plaits? I said.

I guess.

We pulled into her driveway, the red lights blinking behind us. We stayed in the car, neither of us could be bothered moving.

I wish I could live here, I said. I wish I could transfer my sickness benefit. I'm sure I could find interesting voluntary work.

That would be so great! said Jana. There are lots of good training programmes – I think volunteers are more respected here.

I know, at home it's mostly Oxfam or serving tea in hospital cafes.

We'll need to find you an American husband, then you could stay.

We need to find us both American husbands, I said.

Let's go in, she said. It's late.

Jana went straight to bed. I sat in the living room in the dark, the red lights through the blinds so comforting and peaceful. I counted the days I had left. Ten seemed a lot, but they would blur away to nothing soon enough and I'd be packing to go home. I closed my eyes and imagined kissing Jana's dad.

When I went to bed he asked me what I wanted. *Your fingers inside me, please, then fuck me, I'll plait my hair for you, Robert, YES... YES...YES!*

My arm would be useless tomorrow.

One evening, Jana dropped me at a shopping centre downtown while she went to her advanced Spanish conversation class.

I got the escalator up to Mango. An assistant pounced on me immediately and asked me how I was, and if I'd like help in starting a dressing room.

I'm sorry I don't know what you mean, I said.

You're not American, are you?

No, I said.

I can tell from what you're wearing. Americans are all grey and black but you have your own style. If you want me to start a dressing room, be sure to let me know.

Thanks, I said. I still didn't know what she meant.

I began to browse – I wanted to buy everything – and picked up a few things and hung them over my arm.

Let me take those for you, she said, appearing from nowhere, and I'll put them in the dressing room.

Thanks, I said, glad to be able to rest my arm. It was dawning on me that they hang stuff up in the changing room for you to save you carrying it around.

I tried the clothes on – everything looked horrible apart from a lilac skirt.

I bought the skirt and paid for it by Visa, the first time I'd ever used it. I felt experienced and international.

Next I went into Anne Taylor. The clothes were elegant, exactly what I'd wear if I had a career. I was looking at gorgeous black trousers when I started to feel vile, numbness and weakness cloaking over me, toxins injected into my head. There was nowhere to go, the shopping mall was huge and sterile, fluorescent lights and chrome everywhere. Jana wasn't picking me up for another hour and a half. I wanted to tell the shop assistant that I felt like my organs were going to pack in, but she'd just think I was a drug addict.

I took the trousers into the changing room and sat down on the wooden stool. I pinched my face, it was numb. It was my own fault for overdoing it – we'd gone to Berkeley for Ethiopian food the night before (delicious flat breads and

THE STATE OF ME

spicy meat, no cutlery) and I should've just stayed in.

I sat for as long as I could and came out again, leaving the untried trousers behind. Everything seemed exaggerated, hallucinated. I asked the assistant if there was somewhere I could get a glass of water and she gave me directions to a cafe three floors up. I got lost twice and had to keep asking for directions. I hated this place. I ended up in the restrooms at Nordstrom's. They were like toilets in a fancy hotel, a far cry from the toilets in department stores at home (ripped toilet paper stuck to the floor, unflushed toilets with murky, half-dissolved shits).

I sat in an elegant, padded chair 'til the awfulness had begun to ease. I pinched my face again.

I eventually found the cafe and bought some water. A man with a staircase of fat from his neck to his groin was eating ice cream at the next table. I wondered how often he thought of killing himself.

A few nights later we were meeting Lori and Ansel and some others Jana worked with, for cocktails. I still wasn't feeling good but I didn't want to ruin her plans. According to Jana, Lori was a sweetheart and her boyfriend Ansel was an asshole. He goes everywhere with her, she said. He wears thick white socks and Birkenstocks. All sock and no shoe, I said. Jana giggled.

There were about eight people, I forgot their names as soon as I was introduced. I was sitting between Ansel

353

and Jana. Ansel looked like an Osmond, his teeth were too tightly packed together, and you knew that when he flossed them he'd find shreds of chicken.

Have you seen much of the city? he asked politely.

Yeah, quite a bit.

What do you like best?

Hard to say, I love it all... maybe North Beach.

It's great, isn't it?

Yeah.

I like cilantro too.

Cilantro?! That's funny.

I've never had it before. We call it coriander but we buy it as seeds or it's ground up. I love fresh cilantro, I could eat bunches of it.

D'you hear that, honey, said Ansel, leaning over to Lori, Helen's never had cilantro!

Wow, said Lori in a baby voice.

Is this your first time in the.US? said Lori.

Yeah.

Is it different from Scotland?

Very.

What's different?

Lots of things: the weather, the ethnic diversity, the choice of restaurants. And you get such good service here. Everywhere you go, there's the potential to be pampered. You get back rubs in the supermarket, they bag your groceries for you, they carry your clothes into changing rooms, they call you to remind you that you have a dental appointment...

Americans work hard, said Ansel, we need to be pampered. Do they not work hard in England?

I suppose so, I said... though I actually live in Scotland.

I could feel myself blushing.

Don't be a cunt, Ansel, don't ask me what I do. (Into myself.)

It's just different here, I said, steering him away from jobs. Everyone expects good service. At home it's a bonus if you get it.

Wow, said Ansel, looking baffled.

And no one tells you to have a nice day.

He looked even more baffled, he looked almost *hurt*.

So what is it you do for work exactly?

I'm not working just now, I said. I've been ill.

That's too bad.

I dreaded more questions so I asked him where the toilets were. When I came back I tried to get a look at his white-socked feet but they were hidden under the table.

They were talking about Halloween now.

Will you be here for the parade? asked Ansel.

No, I said. I'm leaving next week.

That's a pity. It's a blast. My room-mate's dressing up as a table.

How can you dress up as a table?

Did I tell you that, honey? said Ansel, leaning over to Lori. Walt's dressing up as a table for the parade.

No, said Lori, barely audible, you didn't.

Jana was guffawing, caught up in conversation with the guy on her right.

What are you laughing at? I asked.

We were talking about when we went camping in Yosemite in the summer and I forgot to put my toothpaste in the locker and Ansel was afraid a bear would come. He gave me such a hard time, I thought he was going to make me eat it!

Ansel tried to smile at the memory but you could tell he was still annoyed. You can't be too careful with those bears, Jana. I've done a lot of camping.

Ansel, honey, it was pretty funny, said Lori.

Sounds hysterical, I said.

Anyone for another cocktail? someone asked.

Are we running a tab? said Ansel.

I'll have another cosmopolitan, said Jana.

Will you be okay to drive? I said.

Of course, she replied. It's just two cocktails. Loosen up, *chica!*

I could tell she was annoyed. We were getting on each other's nerves a bit, after two weeks together.

Everyone ordered another cocktail and started chatting about stocks and options. I had no idea what they were on about. My head was clamped and I was on mineral water. I wanted to lie down.

Lori was opening up with her margarita. I could see why Jana liked her. I couldn't understand why she was with

Ansel.

After the second round everyone suddenly got up to leave. People didn't sit and drink all night the way they did at home.

Back in the flat, Jana seemed subdued.

If I were Lori, I'd cancel Ansel, I said, yawning.

Yeah, she could do much better.

Are you okay?

There's something I need to tell you, she said, patting the kitchen table. Sit down. I don't know if there's any point telling you, it was so long ago, but it's been on my mind... I'll just come out and say it.

What is it, you're freaking me out?!

She took a deep breath. I slept with Ivan once, the night of your twenty-first, when he gave me a lift back up to Glasgow. We were both upset about you being so sick and we ended up in bed. It only happened once and I'm so sorry. And now you'll hate me.

I looked at her incredulously. *You and Ivan!* But you were my best friends, and I was so ill!

I know. It sucks.

I'm dazed, Jana. Why are you telling me now, six years on?

She looked completely forlorn.

I don't know, guilt... and maybe you guys'll get back together, so it's better that you know.

Who seduced who?

I can't remember. It was clumsy and messy.

I was bedridden, Jana.

I know.

He couldn't fuck me, so he fucked you.

She put her head in her hands.

You know what, I said – at the time, I actually wondered if you two were a possibility, but I dismissed it, I thought I was being paranoid, torturing myself with the worst thing that could happen.

Ivan felt terrible about it. We both did.

That makes it okay then?

It wasn't okay, it was wrong.

What d'you want me to say?

I don't know.

I don't know either, I said.

I just had to tell you. I'm so sorry.

I'm glad you told me.

Can I make you some tea?

I think I'll just go to bed.

I'm glad tomorrow's Friday, she said. We can talk about this at the weekend.

I don't want to talk about it again. There's no point.

I'm so sorry.

Anyway, I thought you wanted me to get over Ivan, now you think I'll get back with him!

Not really, I just know how much you love him and that's why I told you. You deserve someone you can trust, someone amazing.

It's not that easy, Jana! You forget I've got a big black

mark against my name before the relationship's even off the ground. Who wants a girlfriend with ME?

You've still got a lot to offer, you know you have.

Like what – blow jobs and home-baking?!

I know it's difficult for you, but it's not exactly a tea party for me either, she said – her voice was breaking.

I didn't say it was.

Sometimes I think that you think it's all so easy for me.

Of course I don't, I just think you take risks.

Like what?!

Well, you have unsafe sex... you drink and drive... sometimes I think you've got a death wish.

Everyone here drinks and drives, doesn't mean we're not safe. I had two drinks, Helen. I would never drive drunk. When did you turn into Miss Goody Two Shoes?

That's not fair.

I'm sorry, she said.

I get the feeling you want to argue with me – is that why you told me about Ivan, just to engineer a fight?

She was sobbing now.

What's wrong, Jana?

I don't know, everything... I'm dreading you leaving.

I'm dreading leaving too.

She was sobbing harder and harder. I hated seeing her so sad.

I got up and hugged her.

You need to calm down, d'you want some Valium?

Sure, she said. Are you having one?

No, I want to keep them for travelling.

I'm a mess. My fucking mascara's in my eyes, she said.

I got her a tablet and a glass of water.

Thanks, she said.

Let's just forget about you and Ivan, I said, it doesn't matter.

Will you tell him that I told you?

I don't know, there seems little point.

Are we still friends?

Of course, I said.

How can you forgive me?

I don't know.

I've let you down in the worst way.

I know, I said, but you're still my saviour.

You're mine too, she said.

I'd go mad without you.

Me too.

I'm going to get ready for bed, I said. In a way I'm relieved, I thought you were going to tell me you were HIV positive.

No, but I'm a harlot.

Ivan's to blame too, I said. Let's not talk about it anymore.

Okay, she said, half smiling. You're right, Lori should cancel Ansel.

He's an arse, I said.

In bed I thought back to the night of my twenty-first,

straining to remember what Ivan and Jana had been like. I couldn't even cry, it was too long ago. I realised, maybe for the first time, how my getting ill had fucked things up for everyone.

I lay awake, listening to the foghorns. I'd grown to like them. They made me feel at home.

D'you want to go to Point Reyes today and look at whales? said Jana, leafing through my guide book. It was my last weekend.

Nah, I said.

We were both still a bit subdued.

Who the fuck goes to see whales anyway? she said. I don't know anyone.

Whale lovers, I said.

She laughed.

Last night I dreamt I was torturing penguins, I said. It was horrible.

Wasn't penguins you were torturing, it was me.

I was skinning them and they were screaming.

That's creepy. What about Napa?

Nah, let's just stay here.

A movie?

A movie's okay.

She picked up the pink pages. Let's see what's on... what about *Sex, Lies and Videotape*? James Spader's in it.

Who's James Spader?

He's cute, you'll like him.

We went to a matinee. The film was great, Jana was right, James Spader was sexy. We were reunited by our lust for him.

Afterwards, we went to Cafe Flore in the Castro, Jana's favourite cafe. I'd started drinking coffee again since I'd been here, it was too hard to resist. The guy cleaning the tables was wearing lipstick and had budding breasts.

The next day, we went to the Cliff House and had coffee with Baileys and watched the sun set over the ocean.

In the evening, I made chicken curry. I was excited to have cilantro. Jana invited her dad and Kim over. Kim diplomatically picked out the chicken and put it on the side of her plate. She'd given me a Californian cookbook with the recipe for pumpkin soup. I felt I'd judged her too harshly before. She was much more mellow and there wasn't a peep out of her about the Salutation of the Sun.

I had two days of resting and looking at the blinking lights before leaving.

The airport was awful. Jana couldn't stop weeping.

Come to Glasgow next year, I said.

I only get two weeks' vacation, she wailed.

Use it for Glasgow then, I said, letting go of her hand so that I could check in.

I told the woman at the BA desk I didn't need a wheelchair 'til Heathrow, and she didn't force me to use one.

It was dark when we took off. The Japanese man across the aisle was folding straws and putting them in his shirt pocket.

Jana had given me a package and made me promise not to open it 'til I was on the plane. I waited 'til we were up and the seatbelt sign was off: it was a tiny silver box with a compass embedded in the lid. Inside, she'd folded gold paper and written: So that you can find your way back to San Francisco.

By the time the plane landed in London, I was back in rag doll mode, the wheelchair was essential. Rita picked me up in Glasgow and took me back to Balloch. For days, I was nocturnal, asleep all day, awake all night. I missed Jana and looked at my holiday photos over and over again.

I didn't want to go back to the flat but after a week I prised myself away from the comfort of Rita and Nab. They took me up to Glasgow and helped with my case and got me groceries. I was still sleeping 'til late afternoon and was glad to be in a different time zone to Ivan – I wanted to be cold to him but couldn't because of his granny. She had died when I was away. Wendy seemed to be around a lot but I was too washed out for it to really register.

Q. What has Wendy got that I haven't? (I have nicer hair, nicer eyes, nicer ankles, nicer everything. In a roomful of men, I'm the one they'd be looking at, until someone asked, What do you do?, and my cover would be blown.)

A. She has a career and she can run marathons.

*

Wendy came round one night with a handful of schedules. Ivan was buying a flat with the money he had inherited. I was just passing the estate agents and thought I'd pick these up for you, she said.

Rez said I could move into Ivan's old room when he moved out.

It gave me something to look forward to.

25

A Seduction

FINN WAS ON the news last night! (Gulf War I was being brought to our television screens – ex-pat women and children had already been sent home. It was thrilling, the threat of Scuds and chemical warfare, but the special effects were not as good as Gulf War II would turn out to be.) Finn was standing in a queue in Jubail, waiting to be given his gas mask, just a glimpse of him, but it was definitely him. I'd jumped up and screeched to Ivan to come through: Finn's on TV, my stepbrother's on the news! By the time he'd come through – eating cold beans from a glass – Finn had gone. God, I hope he's okay, I said.

The phone rang almost immediately, it was Rita. Did you see Finn on the news?!

Is Nab okay? He must be worried sick, I said.

You know Nab, said Rita, he's very philosophical about these things. He tries not to worry.

I'm going to watch the late news, I said, he might be on again.

What's Finn doing in Saudi? asked Ivan when I went back through.

He's a geologist, I said. Why are you eating cold beans?

They were in the fridge, I couldn't be arsed heating them up.

Why are you in a bad mood?

I'm not, he said, I'm just tired.

Ivan and Rez both wanted to watch the football highlights, but I'd pleaded with them to let me watch the late night news.

They won't show him again, said Ivan.

They will, I said, they often repeat clips.

Why do you care so much? said Ivan. You hardly know the guy.

He's Nab's son and he's in a war zone for God's sake! Don't be so insensitive.

At ten o'clock, I'd sat right up at the television, waiting for the Gulf report. I'd seen Finn and touched the screen where he'd been. It had crackled with static.

I told you they'd show him again, I said to Ivan.

Can I have the remote now? he'd said, I want to watch Arsenal.

My granny was saying that Saddam should be boiled in oil for what he'd done to his own people. I'd met her and

Rita in town for late night shopping and dinner. I know, Granny, but it's not black and white, I said. The West are only helping because of the oil, they don't care about the Kurds. She pursed her lips, she hated people disagreeing with her, and repeated that he should be boiled in oil. She was getting worked up so Rita changed the subject. Would you like to have coffee, Mother? My granny replied that she couldn't drink coffee anymore because of the 'caff-*aine*'. She said the last time she'd had it she'd woken up during the night and thought she was in Africa.

*

Mock interview, *March 1991*

interviewer   Good morning, Miss Fleet. Thank you for coming. Did you have a difficult journey? You look very tired.

me   I'm always very tired, Mr Interviewer.

interviewer   Let's get started. [*clearing throat*] I'm a little confused looking at your CV: you got the dux medal at school, but then had a seven-year gap before getting your degree. I'm curious about what you were doing in between.

me   I was travelling.

interviewer   Seven years is a long time to travel.

me   I was in Madeira then London then San Francisco.

interviewer   Were you working while you travelled?

me   [*bowing head in shame*] I'm sorry, I have to come clean, Mr Interviewer, I wasn't travelling, I was ill.

interviewer   For seven years?!

me   Yup. In fact, I'm still ill, but I thought I'd chance my arm and come for an interview. I need the experience. By the way, in Canada you wouldn't be allowed to ask about gaps in my CV, you'd have to concentrate on the positives.

interviewer   Very well then, what skills make you suitable for this job?

me   I get exhausted at the drop of a hat and my concentration's terrible.

interviewer   And how do you handle pressure? You would be working to deadlines, after all.

me   Very badly. People with my illness have a poor stress response – I could never work to deadlines. And to be honest, as I can't depend on my physical well-being, I would need a lot of sick days. In fact, I'd only be here for a few hours a week – if you were lucky. Your job description said the hours were flexible, that's why I applied.

interviewer   [*forcing a smile*] I admire your cheek, Miss Fleet. We'll be in touch. By the way, I like your suit, very smart.

me   Thank you. I got it in San Francisco.

*

Ivan's moved out, he's bought a place. I love having his room, it's so much bigger, I can spread out, and I now have a view of a beautiful spire. (The boxroom looked onto a dreary bit of grass and washing poles that no one ever used.)

Ivan's new flat's in Hillhead. It's gorgeous. I took some tapes over last night that he'd left at Rez's. You're so lucky to have your own place, I said.

He told me that Wendy was moving in with him for a while 'cos she was having problems with her flatmate and couldn't find anywhere decent.

Where will she sleep? I asked, throwing the question at him like a dart.

Spare room, he said.

You don't need to lie, I said.

I'll still help you get heavy groceries, he said. I'm having some wine, d'you want some?

I only drink Californian now.

Wait a minute and I'll check my cellar, he said.

He went to the kitchen and came back with two tumblers. It's French, I'm afraid. It's all I've got. Cheers, he said. Thanks for bringing the tapes over.

We were sitting on the floor, he had no furniture yet. He put his arm round me. Are you okay?

I'd be more okay if Wendy wasn't moving in.

She's just a lodger, she'll be paying rent.

You've got no furniture, how can she pay rent?

Bills then. She won't be here for long.

I might have to send her a chicken wing, I said.

How many people do you actually send chicken wings to? You seem to have a file.

I could gift-wrap one and bring it to your house-warming. Expose her as a witch to the whole party.

Why don't you just throw her in the Clyde and see if she floats?

Sorry, I said. I lay my head in his lap. This was all I wanted, this was enough. He stroked my hair.

Will there be any nice men at your house-warming?

Just boring biochemists.

What do you want as a present?

Anything, he said. Whatever you want.

I think I'll get wine glasses. Jana had gorgeous ones, so big and roomy, you just wanted to press them against your face.

Wine glasses would be nice.

I broke two when I was there, beheaded them when I was washing up. They're so fragile.

Nothing to do with you being clumsy.

Anyone can break glasses, I said.

You more than most, Looby.

Your ceiling's filthy, I said. It could do with a lick of paint.

I know. My mother said she'd help.

I can help too.

How can you help?

I can do the skirting. The whole room needs tarted up.

Skirting's harder than it looks, he said, you have to watch for drips.

I love when you get a skin over the paint and you have to pop it.

Very Freudian, he said. Can you shift a bit? My leg's numb.

I slid over.

What did you do today? he asked.

I was in the French Department. I like to drop in, see what's happening. It smells exactly like it did when Jana and I were there. I keep expecting to see her come out of the Common Room.

Remember I used to meet you there every Friday at four?

Seems like another lifetime, I said.

Are you still applying for that counselling course?

I phoned them for an application. It's two evenings a

week, six hours, and you get coffee breaks. My energy's always better at night.

Sounds ideal.

It's £500.

Can you not get a grant?

Most people who do it work full-time. Their jobs pay.

Will Rita and Nab help?

How else could I afford it?

By the way, he said, I've been accepted for that research post.

What research post?

Post-doc at UCSF, I thought I told you about it.

I sat up like a shot – *UCSF!*

Careful – you almost spilled my wine.

You didn't tell me! How long for?!

A year. I applied in October, it must've been when you were away.

A year?!

It's not that long, he said, and I'm not going 'til the end of the summer.

I know the UCSF hospital, it's near Jana's dad, I said wistfully. Will you see her?

I don't know, haven't really thought about it. I might ask her to help me find a flat.

Or you could just move in with her.

I thought she had a flatmate.

I know you slept with her the night of my twenty-first, Ivan.

He shook his head slowly, frowning... When did she tell you?

When I was over there.

I can't believe her. It was *years* ago, it meant nothing.

People always say that.

We were comforting each other, it was fucking hard watching you so ill.

You poor lambs, it must've been awful for you.

Why did the stupid bitch tell you?

Don't call Jana a stupid bitch!

What kind of friend would tell you something like that?

What kind of *boyfriend* would DO something like that?!

Let's not dig it all up, there's no point.

I've tried not to torture myself – Jana was so sorry and guilty about the whole thing, but now you're going over there it might happen again.

Of course, it won't. Don't be ridiculous. Lie back down, he said, gently pushing my head.

We stayed like that for ages, not speaking, me raising my head occasionally to slug the wine.

What's your research post?

More of the same. Developing cognitive enhancers for people with dementia. I'll be a post-doc researcher in drug metabolism.

Why can't you stay here and test them on me? My memory's crap – I'll be your guinea pig. Anyway, you can't go away, you've just bought a flat.

I'll rent it out.

I'll come with you, I'll hide in your luggage.

You'll be fine. You'll be doing your counselling course.

I'd rather be doing it in San Francisco.

You'll need to move your head, he said.

Why?

Because.

The wine had made me bold.

I don't want to move, I said.

He shifted a bit.

I wondered if I should, then began to stroke him.

No, Helen, *don't*, he said.

I ignored him and kept stroking.

We shouldn't be doing this, he said, curling over me.

I unzipped him and he barely resisted. He found my mouth and I kissed him back with every bone. I'd wanted this for so long, but now it was happening I felt I was outside it – round window – watching us making love, but not feeling it. I wanted to tell him I loved him, but I was scared he wouldn't say it back.

I felt like Jana – to hell with the consequences – but at the last minute I asked him to pull out – It's not safe, I said, we have to be careful!

He called me his sexiest babe and came all over my breasts. I'll get you a towel, he said when he'd recovered. I lay on the floor, shivering slightly, cold without the exertion. He came back and wiped his sperm off me.

You look sad, he said.

I feel sad.

And beautiful.

There's no point being beautiful, I said. It doesn't get you anywhere.

I'm sorry about Jana, he said.

You should be.

And I'm sorry about now.

Do you regret we did it? I said.

I'm just scared you'll get all emotional and torn.

I feel flat, like it should've been better, I said.

You know what they say about sex with an ex, he said.

Don't call it sex with an ex, it was sex with *me!*

I'm joking.

D'you think it was empty? I said.

See, you're getting emotional and analysing everything.

No, I'm not, but you're being cold to me.

I'm not being cold. I just don't want a big saga.

Will you tell Wendy?

Tell her what?

That we had sex.

It's none of her business.

I want to tell everyone.

Why?

I just do.

Get dressed, he said, before you catch cold.

My legs are trembling, I said.

D'you want some coffee to pep you up?

Please. (I didn't want any, but said yes just to prolong my time with him.)

I got dressed. He brought me coffee and I drank it as slowly as I could.

I've only got myself to blame, I said. I shouldn't have seduced you.

Stop analysing things.

I'm my own worst enemy. No matter what I do, whether I'm hot or cold to you, it always backfires.

He took my hands. Helen, it felt great, he said softly, but we can't get carried away. You know we can't.

I always end up losing you, I said.

Don't be sad, he said. Please don't be sad.

You're like sand, I said. No matter how many handfuls I take, I still lose you through my fingers.

What are you doing tomorrow?

Meeting the girl with Down's Syndrome that I befriend. I might take her to the cinema.

What's her name again?

Morag.

Did you know that people with Down's are more likely to develop Alzheimer's?

Why?

After forty, they get beta-amyloid deposits in their brains, same as people with Alzheimer's, but they don't always develop the symptoms.

That's so cruel! At least if you were normal and started

losing it, you'd know you were losing it, at the beginning anyway, but if you had Down's it would be terrifying.

It's pretty fucked, he said.

I'd nursed the last few millimetres of coffee for as long as possible. I wanted to ask him if I could stay over, but instead I said, I wonder what age Morag is.

It's getting late, he said. I'll walk you home.

I suppose that's your flat christened, I said as I stood up.

It was a ten minute walk to Rez's. We walked slowly, I linked my arm into his. When we got there, he wouldn't come up. He hugged me tightly and kissed me on the cheek. Have a good time with Morag, he said. I didn't hug him back. I watched him walk away, hoping he'd turn round, but he didn't.

I trudged upstairs. I felt like I'd been doing gymnastics.

Rez was watching TV. There's a fax from Jana, he said. It just came in. How's Ivan doing?

Fine, I said sharply.

I went into the hall and ripped the fax from the machine and took it into my room. Jana was on a high, she'd been on her third date with Kavi, an English software engineer. He'd just taken her to the hot springs in Sonoma for the weekend and they'd had mud baths and champagne. She wanted to tell me how happy she was and that she missed me lots. I knew it meant she wouldn't be coming over in the summer. I ripped the fax up. Then I looked for the rose Ivan'd given me for my graduation and crumbled it over the floor. I stifled my sobs, I didn't want Rez to hear me crying.

I went into the shower, cried more and washed Ivan off me. I was sore and swollen from him. When I came out, I listened to Frank Zappa. He always cheered me up.

I went to bed with the curtains open: the moon was hanging behind the spire, blatantly poetic, sad and beautiful.

I was sitting with Morag in the first row. We'll get cricks in our necks, I said.

I always sit in the first row, she replied.

Can we not sit in the second or third?

No, I always sit in the first.

She'd taken her jacket off, but insisted on keeping her bag on. It was glued to her, slung diagonally over her shoulder. She'd lost her bus pass once and was terrified of it happening again. She kept it in a wallet inside a bigger purse inside her bag. Your purse is like a Russian doll, I said.

She was lost in the moment, relishing every flicker from the screen, even though we were still at the adverts. I was watching my own film, *Sex With Ivan,* every frame frozen in my head. I wished I hadn't crumbled the rose.

It's all wrong, I should be living with Ivan, rushing around in the mornings to dry my hair before work. I'll go to his house-warming party, dressed to kill and if anyone asks me what I do I'll say I'm an acrobat.

26

Fabio

FABIO HAD BLONDE hair and a padded cord jacket with leather trims. He looked a bit like James Spader, but he wasn't my type. He was too stocky. The first time we had sex, it was like having a tree trunk on top of me.

I met him at Ivan's party. He was going into the fridge for beer and I asked him if there was any cheese.

For God's sake, woman, are you a mouse?!

I just need some cheese, I said, laughing, I'm starving.

He rummaged around. There's no cheese, but I've found some spring onions.

I think I'll pass, I said. They're a bit limp.

Are there no party nibbles left?

They're all gone, I said. (I was horrified he'd said 'nibbles'.)

I'm Fabio, by the way.

I'm Helen, I said.

That's my mother's name. Means 'light'.

I know, I said.

So who do you know here?

Ivan. He's my best friend, well, best male friend.

I'm a friend of Wendy's, he said.

Oh.

Are her and Ivan not having a thing?

Ivan has a lot of casual girlfriends, I said – it's hard to keep track.

But she's just moved in with him.

Only 'til she gets another flat, I said. She was having problems in her old place.

He nodded. Are you a biochemist too?

No, I said, shaking my head.

So, what do you do then?

I work in salad distribution.

Salad distribution?

It's boring, I said, I don't want to talk about it.

Sounds fascinating, he said, making a face.

What do you do? I asked.

I analyse bridges.

Sounds fascinating, I said.

I was working on the Forth Road Bridge last week.

What were you doing – painting it?

Cheeky, he said, I was measuring the width of the cable saddles, actually.

It's the same design as the Golden Gate, isn't it?

Yeah.

I was there in October, I said. It's so scary, those big choppy waves below. I still have nightmares that they're lapping over the bridge and I can't get across.

It's a feat of engineering, he said – the towers are 746 feet high.

Did you know that more than a thousand people have jumped off since it was built?

Funnily enough, I didn't, he said.

I shuddered. Imagine jumping into all that shrouding fog. People have jumped off with children in their arms.

You're a cheery one. Are you really a distributor of salads?

No.

What are you then?

I felt my cheeks pulsing – I'm not working just now, I have ME.

God, my mother thought she had that, she's *such* a hypochondriac!

It's not a hypochondriac's illness, I said, it's a serious neurological syndrome.

To be honest, I don't know much about it, he said.

There are 150 000 sufferers in the UK just now.

Must be serious then.

I think I'll go and find Ivan, I said. I've hardly seen him tonight.

Sorry, he said, you seem upset. I didn't mean to offend you.

Don't worry, I said, ignorance about my illness is

endemic, I'm used to it. (*You stupid bastard with your leather trims.*)

I found Ivan in the living room with the biochemistry set. One guy was saying that he thought central heating had contributed to the breakdown of the family because people didn't huddle together in the living room anymore. Wendy was talking about liver toxicity in mice. I looked as bored as I could. How are you doing, Looby? asked Ivan, draping his arm round me. Wendy's glance nicked me like a paper-cut.

I'm okay, I said, but I'm going to go soon. I'm getting a lift back with Jab.

You *can't* leave, it's too early!

It's midnight, I said. I want to go home and make toasted cheese.

I'll make you some, he said.

You can't, you don't have any cheese.

We're low on basics, chipped in Wendy, we're doing a big shopping tomorrow.

Good, I said, I'll come with you, if that's okay.

Sure, said Ivan. We'll pick you up.

I felt someone prod me gently. It was Fabio. Sorry about what I said in the kitchen, Helen. I didn't mean anything by it. Let me take you for dinner next week to make it up to you.

That would be nice, I said.

What's your number?

I asked Ivan for a pen. There's one in my room, he said.

383

Come with me if you want.

I followed him through.

Looby, you can't go out with Fabio, he said.

Can I have the pen, please? I'm just going for dinner, I'm not going to marry him.

Wendy says he kisses his mother on the lips.

Wendy's a witch, she makes things up. Anyway, I like men that look after their mothers.

Ivan took my hand and pulled me towards him. I would like to kiss *you* on the lips.

Don't! I said. You're such an imp. A big drunk bastard imp.

He kissed me on the forehead. Sorry.

I'm going to go for dinner with Fabio, I said. Maybe he'll redeem himself.

What did he say to offend you?

Just the usual, I said.

A non-believer, Looby. Just what you need.

You're in no position to judge anyone, I said.

I'm just the big bastard imp who helps you all the time.

That's not fair, you know how grateful I am. Just tell me the truth, are you screwing Wendy?

We've slept together a few times, he said, but she's more serious about me than I am about her.

I knew you were sleeping with her, I said.

I still don't think she's over her old boyfriend.

Well, we all know how that feels, don't we? I said,

snatching the pen from him and going back through to the living room. Ivan followed a few minutes later.

You were a long time getting a pen, said Wendy.

Fuck off, Wendy. (Into myself.)

While Fabio was writing my number on the back of his hand, Jab appeared with his coat on and said he was leaving. He asked me if I was coming.

I'll call you next week, said Fabio, putting his hand on my shoulder.

Ivan saw me to the door and tried to hug me. Go back to your girlfriend, I said.

I felt on a high as I got into Jab's car, but by the time we got back to the flat the high was punctured. You and Ivan have a strange relationship, said Jab as I was getting out.

I know, I said.

Is he with Wendy now?

Kind of. I don't know.

She is so pasty and white, said Jab. Not my type at all.

'Night, Jab, thanks for the lift, I said.

I went to bed, slightly excited about Fabio but torturing myself with Wendy. I couldn't sleep for ages.

When I woke up the next day I was happy because I'd see Ivan when he took me to the supermarket.

He phoned at three to say he was too hung-over to shop, but Wendy would still take me if I wanted. I needed to get heavy stuff and Rez wasn't around, so I accepted her offer.

She barely spoke to me in the car. I'll just get you at the exit, she said as the automatic doors of the supermarket snapped shut behind us.

She shopped like a robot, she knew where everything was. I felt rushed. I just couldn't imagine her having sex with Ivan, or being sexually excited by anyone. She was just too *deft*.

I can't believe I'm nervous about going on a date with a man who has a cord jacket with leather trims. I've quizzed Rez about him, but he doesn't know anything, and I can't ask Ivan, and certainly not Wendy.

I'm meeting him for pizza after work. My legs are weak.

I'm ten minutes early. I've brought a book to appear nonchalant but I can't absorb the words. I play with the carnation in the centre of the table, twirling the stem between my thumb and fingers. I check my lipstick (again) to make sure there's none on my teeth. My heart's pounding.

I feel myself blushing when I see him come in. He's early too. He looks good in his suit, but as he gets closer I see he has a golf magazine under his arm. My heart sinks.

He seems nervous. Hi, he says. He has just brushed his teeth.

Hi.

Been here long?

Ten minutes, I say. I'm always too early for things. I

dread being late.

Me too. I see you've brought a book – did you think I was going to be boring?!

Of course not. (I say nothing about the golf magazine, I don't want to get off on the wrong foot.)

He smiles. Would you like a drink?

Sparkling mineral water, please.

His hands are shaking when he picks up the menu. I can't bear it. He's less confident than he was at the party but he has warm eyes.

I tried to fix the table before you got here, I say. It's really shoogly.

Fabio folds up the napkin again, more tightly, and puts it back under the leg. Statically indeterminate, he says, as he sits down.

Is that engineering speak for shoogly?

He laughs. That's better, he says, checking that the table is steady.

The waitress comes over and takes the drinks order. Fabio orders a Stella Artois and my water.

What are you having to eat? he asks.

Think I'll have the Neopolitan.

Pizzas here are great, he says, very authentic.

Do you have Italian blood? I ask.

My dad was Italian. He died when I was five. My mum's Scottish.

That's sad, I say. What happened?

Brain haemorrhage. I hardly remember him.

You don't look Italian, I say, you seem too blonde, though you have dark eyes.

I take after my mother more.

Fabio's a lovely name. What's your last name?

Pucci.

Fabio Pucci – you sound like a film star!

What's yours?

Fleet.

Helen Fleet. You sound like a detective, he says, smiling.

I smile back. So how are your bridges?

I'm going to be involved in the new Skye bridge in a few months, it's an exciting project. How's your salad distribution?

I don't know why I lied, I say. I just get so fed up explaining what I do, I've decided to make stuff up.

Everyone should have their secrets, he says. He takes a sip of beer – I didn't know you went out with Ivan for five years.

You're the detective! I say. Did Wendy tell you?

My lips are sealed, he says.

Wendy must've told you.

What happened, why did you break up? he asks.

I got ill, and he went travelling, we just drifted apart.

You still seem really close.

We are, I say. It's complicated.

The waitress comes back with the drinks and takes the food order.

You and Wendy don't really get on, do you? says Fabio.

No, we don't.

She said you had a huge fight once about fox hunting.

Why did she tell you that? It was ages ago.

She's probably jealous of your history with Ivan.

She was going on about neurological damage to boxers, and I said it was more important to ban fox hunting than boxing – I'm not saying boxing's good, it's not, it's horrible, but I have more sympathy for the foxes, that's all. Foxes don't have a choice, but Wendy thinks it's more important to ban boxing.

Wendy loves to quote studies and statistics, says Fabio. She can get a bit carried away sometimes.

I'm much more emotional than her, I say. The argument got out of hand.

I wouldn't worry about it.

I'm not. Anyway, how do you know her?

Swimming club at uni. We just hit it off, been friends for years.

She came swimming with Ivan and me once, that's how I met her.

Do you like swimming?

I like it, but it's exhausting.

It's good for depression, he says.

I'm not depressed, I reply.

Sorry, I just meant swimming's good for depression, that's all.

I can't think of anything to say and panic for a topic. So will you need to go to Skye for work? I ask.

Not for a while. I'm more on the design side of things. The surveyors are up there just now analysing the rock and soil.

People take bridges for granted, I say, they don't think about all the design and planning behind them.

People take most things for granted, he says.

We went to Skye when I was wee. It rained the whole weekend, and there was a labrador in the hotel that smelled horrible.

I hate the smell of dogs, he says. I prefer cats.

Me too, I say. I would love one, but it's difficult in a flat. I hate litter trays.

A tortoise would be easier.

Tortoises are grotesque, they're like dinosaurs!

I had one when I was a kid, he says. I used to polish its shell with olive oil.

You did not!

Why's that so funny?

I don't know, it's just absurd, I say.

You have such white teeth, he says. They're amazing.

My brother's are really white too.

This is a porcelain veneer, he says, pinging his front tooth. The tooth's dead.

It looks really natural, I say. You can't tell.

It's good, but I'd rather it was real.

Did you know there are twenty-eight natural shades of tooth, from near white to grey?

You're full of eccentric facts.

My dad's a dentist, that's how I know.

What does your brother do?

He's in London, he works with head-injured people. He went to London after graduating.

I went to London too.

Why on earth did you come back?

He blushes. A relationship didn't work out. I was in a bad way. I stopped work for three months.

How long were you together for?

Six years. Since uni.

Are you still in touch?

No. I hate her. We were going to buy a flat together and everything, and then she met someone else.

Must've been awful for you.

It was.

When did you move back up?

Two years ago.

And you're still at home?

Yeah. I'm going to get my own place soon. I think my mum enjoys having me around. She's been lonely since she retired, and I have no brothers or sisters.

What did she retire from?

She was a home economics teacher.

You can't have much privacy living at home though.

It works out okay.

But you can never run about naked and listen to loud music.

He laughs. I wouldn't really want to.

After the pizza, I go to the toilet. I could definitely fancy him – hopefully the golf magazine's a one-off. I think Wendy has primed him about ME, 'cos he's barely mentioned it. I'm surprised that I felt slightly jealous when he mentioned his ex-girlfriend in London. I hope we'll have a goodnight kiss. When I go to touch up my lipstick, I'm horrified to see I have basil on my teeth.

He'd walked me to the Underground and we'd kissed. It was nice but strange – a different mouth always is – and I just thanked God I'd intercepted the basil. When I got home, I'd made a list of pros and cons.

pros	cons
kind	had breakdown
sexy smile	leather trims
makes me laugh	golf magazine
good kisser	polished tortoise
has car	says 'nibbles'

I felt mercenary including his car, but it was much better to have a boyfriend with a car, no point pretending otherwise. When I told Morag about him, she said, That's a funny name, I don't like that name.

*

On our third date, he was wearing his padded jacket and I went off him again until he took it off in the cinema and was himself. We saw *My Own Private Idaho*. I loved it, he hated it. I knew we'd have different taste in films. (His favourite film was *Ghost*.)

On the way out, we met Ivan and Wendy in the foyer. I was ecstatic that they weren't holding hands. Fabio was holding mine. Ivan said he'd loved the film. Wendy was feeling sick because she couldn't stand the 'dreadful smell of popcorn'. We were all embarrassed.

A couple of weeks later, Fabio took me to his house for Sunday dinner. They had a tartan carpet and there were golf clubs and a ginger cat in the hall.

His mother was tall and brittle. She asked me if I'd tried echinacea. I told her I'd tried everything. It boosts your immune system, dear, she said – I wouldn't be without it.

Later, she told Fabio I had a lovely figure and she wanted to make me a skirt. It's really kind of her, I said, and I thought back to the time I'd crocheted a baby blanket for Zoe and it had been the main thing in my life.

*

Summer flew by. I measured out my weeks, saving energy for Fabio: Wednesday was Fabio night, Saturday was Fabio night, Sunday was going to Fabio's mum's for dinner.

By Monday, I was shattered.
I thought less about Ivan than I'd ever done.

27

A Dream About Cocktail Sticks

MY WRISTS ARE used up with lipstick: the backs of my hands bruised with PLUM, CONGA and BRAZIL. There are too many choices, I can't decide. The make-up girl's pressurising me with her vacuous comments.

I end up with PLUSH PLUM.

I want to phone Fabio at work and tell him I'm in town, ask him to meet me later. He was really moody at the weekend, like a teenager.

As the make-up girl wraps the lipstick, all I can think about is dialling him.

*

Hey Missy,
Happy, Happy Birthday! Hope you like the lipstick and it's not too dark, I spent ages choosing it!

Thank you for your enquiries about Fabio – yes, he does fold his clothes before sex, but he is a GREAT lover and has an excellent penis, I am pleased to report, hard to believe we've been together for four months! His mother is sweet, she made me a lovely skirt, I've worn it a couple of times. Am excited, my counselling classes start next week – did you know the counsellor is the constant and the client is the variable?! Ivan's leaving for SF in two weeks, I'm really fine about it. I'll give him your tel. number and I'm sure he'll be in touch once he's settled. He's renting his flat to Wendy and another biochemist when he's gone. Glad things are going well with Kavi, do you really think he is THE ONE? Hope you like the card – I love Modigliani's women. Fabio said I remind him of one with my green eyes (that are really grey).

PS. Have you seen that film *Bagdad Cafe*, I absolutely loved it, I loved the music. Fabio hated it. I drag him to all my films and in return I have to go and see crap with Tom Hanks – please tell me how anyone can like Tom Hanks, his lips are always moist.

Lots of love,

Helen xxx

I'm dreading Ivan leaving. He's coming over to say goodbye on Wednesday – Fabio night. I'll tell Fabio I'm not feeling well, I can't have them clashing.

*

We didn't really know what to say, he gave me a long hug and kissed me on the lips, the kind of kiss that could have led to more. Make sure Fabulous Fabio takes care of you, he said.

I bet you'll fall in love with a Californian woman who wants to name her children after herbs, I said.

I have to go, babe.

Remember to stand under the doorway if there's an earthquake.

Bye, he said. I'll write, I promise.

I don't want you to go.

He unlaced his fingers from mine.

A final kiss on the lips.

*

Things to do: visit Fizza; find someone to role-play the client in my counselling assignment; birthday present for Rita's fiftieth.

*

Fabio's being weird. He's almost annoyed that I can't have him stay over mid-week anymore. I've explained that I need to rest on Wednesdays 'cos of my classes on Tuesdays and Thursdays. And I wish we didn't have to go to his mum's for dinner almost every Sunday, but if I tell him he'll be offended. I don't know why he doesn't just buy a house next door to her.

pros	cons
good sex	moody/lives with mother
pleasant weekends	clicks fingers all the time
generous	got me sheepskin mittens for my birthday

I feel guilty for not liking the mittens, they are actually lambskin and quite nice, but I feel sorry for the lambs. He also got me perfume and took me for a lovely dinner, but sometimes I am bored, I feel we have nothing to talk about, but I don't want to be without him.

*

I'm obsessed with getting a leather briefcase. A woman in my class has one, she's a teacher. I've been back to look at one twice, but it's too expensive. I like the way I look carrying it. Very professional. I am so tempted to put it on Visa.

*

A Christmas card from Ivan with the Golden Gate Bridge. I put the card up – prominently – in my room for Fabio to see. I'm getting him a black polo neck for Christmas, he looks great in black against his blonde hair. I've been invited to his mum's for New Year dinner. I wonder who Ivan's spending Christmas with, but I don't want to ask Jana if she knows.

*

Stayed with Fabio for two nights at Hogmanay. He sneaked into my room after the bells. I don't like their shower, the curtain laps round your legs and clings, and I always feel sad seeing Fabio's toiletries beside his mum's. There's special liquid soap for dry skin.

*

Saw the briefcase again in the January sales, it was half price, but I'd got it out of my system, and half price makes you think there's something wrong with it anyway.

*

Got two Valentines, one from Brian and one from Fabio. Fabio's card had a cute kitten, he doesn't realise that I hate cute cats. I sent him a Modigliani card.

I'm a bastard for being so ungrateful. He came over with chocolates and flowers after work. Birthdays are also important to him, he makes a huge effort – I should be pleased.

*

Feeling crap after walking too much at the weekend. I had to miss both classes this week. Rez said I looked grey. He usually doesn't notice.

*

Had a brilliant lecture on Gestalt today. It's my favourite school of therapy, developed by Fritz Perls. It's about *wholeness* and focuses on the here and now – only the present is significant. (Jana saw a Gestalt therapist for a while. One time, she lay on cushions on the floor and screamed at her father.) Role-playing and dreams are an important part of the sessions. Every part of your dream is a contradictory aspect of yourself: you act the dream out, inventing dialogue for every 'character' – animate and inanimate. It's a bit like writing a play. Freud said dreams were 'the royal road to the unconscious', Perls said they were 'the royal road to integration'.

So when I dream (recurrently) that my bad granny is chasing me with giant cocktail sticks, in order to resolve my anger I have to become myself, the bad granny, *and* the cocktail stick.

Cocktail stick dream. *April 1992*

me   Granny Fleet, I am furious that you still don't believe that I am physically ill! I am also furious that the government doesn't believe

400

that soldiers with Gulf War Syndrome are genuinely ill. I'm hardly a fan of the army, but these poor guys are so ill and getting zero support from the very people responsible, the people who gave them dangerous vaccination cocktails, and sprayed them with neurotoxic pesticides to kill sand-flies and mosquitoes. (And let's not forget the exposure to depleted uranium from exploded ammunition.)

granny fleet   When are you going to stop all this nonsense, my girl? It's all in your head. You are a MALINGERER, you don't want to work, God only knows why, and you've got your mother and Nab wrapped round your little finger. When will you get tired of all this acting? You deserve an Oscar! You managed to go to San Francisco, but people who are genuinely ill don't hop on long-haul flights. You are a millstone round your family's neck. I am ashamed of you.

cocktail stick   If I jab you, maybe that will hurt you, and prick some sense into you, make you realise you are not really ill. But, even though I am a brightly coloured giant cocktail stick, I am also made of plastic – you could easily deflect me and snap me in half. You could easily win the fight.

When I tell Fabio the cocktail stick dream, he just rolls his eyes. He thinks dreams are random, nothing to do with anything.

I know he is depressed, I wish I could help him. I don't know if he had antidepressants in London, he won't tell me. Sometimes he just wants to lie on the couch all weekend, he says I should understand, and when I tell him that I can't help lying on the couch – there's no cure for me – he says there's no cure for him either. I tell him to go and play golf, but he says he has no energy. And if I suggest counselling, he gets angry and says I think counselling is the answer to everything just 'cos I'm doing a course.

But he can be so funny without realising it. We were driving back from the pine shop – we were picking up a bookcase I'd ordered – and we got stuck behind a lorry with a heavy load, it had a police escort. That's a nodal joint for an oil rig, said Fabio, referring to the huge structure on the back of the lorry, matter-of-factly, as if everyone would have known what a nodal joint for an oil rig is. He didn't understand why I thought it was so funny.

I think it's sexy that he knows these things.

28

Rome Then Cystitis

CAN'T BELIEVE I forgot Ivan's birthday. First time ever. I've sent him a belated card – I didn't really forget, it just passed by and I didn't notice.

I had to stay in bed today. Fabio took me out for dinner for our one year anniversary last night. I got really dressed up and we flirted a lot and had amazing sex afterwards. I'm mortified, I think Rez heard us.

Fabio seems less down, in a good phase, but when he's in a dip he is cold. He doesn't care about things unless they affect him directly. We argue about politics – he doesn't vote. When I tell him that we're lucky to live in a democracy, that it's criminal not to vote, that people in Sierra Leone are having their limbs amputated, he just puts his fingers in his ears. I think depression makes you selfish, or maybe it just makes you numb – he's not selfish about the people he's close to and maybe that's what counts.

*

Postcard from Ivan from Napa Valley, he went up in a hot air balloon for his birthday – I wonder who with. I'm not sure how much I miss him, Fabio uses up all my emotions just now.

*

I've passed my counselling course, *Hurrah! Hurrah! Hurrah!* I'll be looking for one afternoon a week jobs again. I wonder if I could manage two afternoons, but there'd need to be two days in between to rest. Maybe I could do Tuesdays and Fridays, one to five, but I think that would be overdoing it. I've been thinking about the people who make up names for lipstick – maybe I could do that. I'd name a range after states of mind: WHY HASN'T HE PHONED?/IS HE FUCKING SOMEONE ELSE?/ONE NIGHT STAND.

I am so fed up, most part-time jobs are for twenty hours a week or more. I saw one job for data entry, ten hours a week. I could never do that – after an hour at a keyboard, my arms ache, my eyes are bloodshot and I can't think straight. Looks like my career is going to be in serial volunteering.

stranger   What do you do?

me   I'm a serial volunteer.

404

*

Fabio wants to take me to Rome for a long weekend for my birthday. He is so kind to me. It'll be so romantic – I can't wait! I haven't been on holiday with a boyfriend since I went to Zakynthos with Ivan when we were in second year. There are very few people I would go away with, people who don't mind me going at my own pace, who don't expect me to traipse round the sights.

Am so happy! I've found a volunteer job as a receptionist at a centre for counselling with sliding scale fees. Five hours a week, three hours on Tuesday and two on Friday, it's ideal. The therapists are from diverse disciplines, I love explaining the different schools to people who call up. One of them does holistic healing and wants to give me an Indian head massage. There's a kettle and a Tupperware box of tea bags in the waiting room, and a sign reminding you to wash your mugs. Sometimes, people forget, or are called for their appointments, so I wash them for them.

I'm so excited: I feel I'm doing something useful, and earning my sickness benefit.

*

I loved Rome, but we didn't get on.

We had a fight on the first day because I was too tired

to get up for breakfast. Neither of us had slept well because of the Vespas, and the room was too hot. It's a shame to miss out on breakfast, Fabio said, especially since it's paid for – you can go back to bed afterwards. I can't believe you said that! I'd replied tearfully. You can't put pressure on me to get up, you know you can't! Can you not just bring me something when you've finished? I just want us to enjoy Rome together, he said. We will, I said, but not in the mornings. As a peace offering, he'd brought me bread and cheese and ham and coffee (all delicious) and gone out for a walk and left me to rest. I'd tried to get back to sleep but it was impossible because of the maid singing and clattering her way along the corridor. By the time she got to our room, it was after eleven and she looked at me as if she couldn't believe there was still a stupid tourist in bed. I apologised to her and put the DO NOT DISTURB sign on the door. I just wanted to sleep for a week and wake up repaired.

I had a bath and thought that if Ivan'd been here he would've slapped some ham on a roll for me and buggered off round Rome on his own, without any fuss – he was so much more independent than Fabio.

I felt like hell but got dressed and used lipstick as blusher to try and perk my face up.

Fabio came back and we went for lunch near the hotel. I wanted to lie down afterwards but didn't want Fabio to be peeved so I trailed round for a bit. I kept having to stop and sit on the sides of fountains. I was relieved when he said he wanted to go back to the hotel. He said he was disappointed by the amount of graffiti we'd seen.

That night we went for dinner near the hotel, on the Via Cavour, a shabby street that reminded me of Glasgow. Fabio explained the menu to me, the courses were endless and the food just kept coming. When we'd finished, the owner brought out a beautiful black puppy and put her on the table for us to pat, as if she were an after-dinner ritual like brandy and cigars. They love their dogs here, said Fabio, apologetically. It's not very hygienic, I said – a dog's bum on the place mats. Fabio laughed out loud, only now recovered from this morning's fight. Please let me pay my share, I said. I hate you paying for everything.

On our second afternoon, we had lunch sitting outside a tiny cafe opposite the Colosseum. There was a giant basket of oranges on the pavement. Afterwards, Fabio went to the Colosseum while I stayed in the cafe and read the guidebook. Are you sure you'll be okay? he said. You don't mind me going without you? Of course not, I replied, I'm perfectly happy to stay here. The sun's lovely.

The slack-jawed American couple at the next table chewed their *panini* like cud and didn't say a word to one another. I wondered if they loved each other in their own way. Fabio came back an hour and a half later and asked me if I'd pose for a photo with a centurion.

That night we kissed at the Trevi fountain and I bought a bag of peaches. I loved how everything closed in the afternoon and opened again at night, it suited my energy. When we got back to the hotel, Fabio made me laugh with his impersonation of a *pietà*, Mary stretching her arms out in a ludicrous pose, holding Jesus in her lap. Then we had sex.

On our third day, I tried to find a second-hand bookshop in Trastevere while Fabio queued for the Sistine chapel. He couldn't understand that I wasn't more disappointed that I couldn't queue and walk the distance. I'm *happy* sitting in cafes and reading, I said. It's my favourite thing to do.

I got on the wrong bus and ended up in the suburbs, stranded at a small bus depot. I felt panicky and wished I hadn't left Fabio. It took me an hour to get back and when I found the Trastevere bookshop it was shut. I got a bus back to the hotel and collapsed into bed. After a couple of hours, I became convinced that something had happened to Fabio and prayed the next echoes in the corridor would be him. I wondered how I'd manage if he didn't come back.

When he finally appeared, we lay together and he described in detail the frescos he'd seen. I wish you could've come, he said, I got you some postcards. That was sweet, I said, thank you. Later, we got a bus to Gianicolo hill and watched the sun set. Fabio wanted to walk back down, my legs felt like elastic, but I said okay. At the bottom, we sat on a wall and ate pizza slices. We got a taxi back to the hotel. The guy drove like a maniac. Rome streaked by, it felt like a film.

On our last night we went to a fancy restaurant in the Piazza Navona. Fabio was in a dip again. He wasn't even trying to hide it.

This is all lovely, I said, but to be honest I'd be happier eating pizza on a wall, with you in a better mood.

They say you don't really know someone 'til you live with them or go on holiday with them, he said quietly, almost to himself.

Exactly, I said.

Your illness affects everything, Helen, doesn't it?

What do you mean?!

Do you think you'll ever be well enough to have children?

Why are you asking me that now? I said.

All the cute wee kids here – just makes me wonder if you'll be well enough.

Please don't put me on the spot like this.

Just tell me, will you be well enough?

No, I don't think so. Probably not.

Okay, at least I know.

Are you giving me an ultimatum?

No, I just wanted to ask.

Do you think *you'll* ever be well enough to have children? I said.

What do you mean by that?

Should depressed people have children?

I'm not depressed.

Well, what the hell's wrong with you, Fabio? If you're not depressed, why are you still living at home?

You know why, he said – my mother's lonely, I'm looking after her.

I know she's lonely, and it's great you care, but you could still see her lots and have your own place. She's not disabled.

His lips were tight and thin, he had no colour. I thought he was going to cry.

Why did you even bring me here? I said.

It got a good write-up.

I don't mean the restaurant, I mean Rome, why did you bring me?

For your birthday.

But you've been so moody most of the time, neither of us has really enjoyed it. You've ruined your lovely gift to me.

You said you liked sitting in cafes – I thought you were enjoying it.

I just never know what you're going to be like from one minute to the next.

I never know what *you're* going to be like from one minute to the next, if you'll be able to walk somewhere or not.

I can't do anything about it, I said, but you can get help, you don't have to be depressed, it's unnecessary!

You don't know what you're talking about, he said. You know nothing.

I think you actually like being depressed – because it makes you numb and you don't have to face things.

You don't understand.

You're right – I don't understand that you're happy to

stay sad. I'm *tired* trying to understand, but you put up with me so I try to put up with you.

Enough, he said. You've said enough.

We ate in silence, with frozen, aching faces. The asparagus risotto was wasted on us. Whenever the waiter came to the table, we tried to paper over the cracks.

Fabio asked if I wanted to keep the beautifully hand-written bill as a souvenir.

What's the point? I said.

We walked back, he offered me a taxi, but I wanted to walk. I lagged behind him, fantasising that we would make up at the hotel and have sex in the shower, rammed against the white tiles.

We turned our backs on each other in bed. I couldn't stop crying.

You forget that I lived at home for a long time when I was ill, I said, I *know* what it's like to be dependent – I was hideously dependent – but as soon as I was able I left again.

I just want to sleep, he said. Please. Just let me sleep.

The next day, we were grim and polite. I'd decided that when we got to Glasgow I'd be dramatic and get my own taxi, but when we were changing planes at Heathrow I got the first stabs of cystitis. I got Cymalon from Boots and had a sachet before boarding and another one during the flight. By the time we got to Glasgow, I was in agony, having to pee constantly, and there was blood. Fabio said he'd stay with me and called his mother to say he wouldn't be back. It was one of the worst nights of my life, the sachets weren't working, the constant burning urge to pee was vile, and when I did it was like needles. I had a hot water bottle clamped between my legs. Why do men not get cystitis? I wailed – it's not fucking fair. I'm never having sex again. I'm so sorry, said Fabio, I hate to see you in so much pain.

The next morning, I got an emergency appointment at a nearby practice. I had to register as a temporary patient as Myra was still my GP. Please stop clicking your fingers, I said to Fabio as we sat in the waiting room. It's really annoying.

The GP smiled and said, Honeymoon cystitis, not pleasant, is it? She gave me a prescription for antibiotics and the symptoms abated within a few hours.

I liked her and thought I'd register with her permanently.

Rita called me that evening, desperate to hear my news. Well, how was Rome, she asked, was it very romantic? I was going to phone you last night, but wanted to give you a chance to rest.

I'm still feeling really tired, Mum, I said, can I phone you back tomorrow?

An hour later, Brian called. He wanted to know if I'd met the Pope.

After Rome, we limped along, knowing it was just a matter of time. Neither of us was strong enough to end it, especially not with Christmas coming up – it was too sad.

*

In January, I made a breaking up dinner. Remember the first time we met, I said – I was looking for cheese at Ivan's.

You were the sexiest girl at the party.

You had on your cord jacket with leather trims, I said.

You've always hated my clothes.

Not all of them, I like your polo necks.

I'm still happy I met you, he said, taking my hand.

Me too, I said.

You're right, he said. My situation isn't normal either, it's not fair of me to blame you.

Maybe that's what brought us together, I said, we're both odd.

Maybe.

When he left, he had tears in his eyes. I went to sleep with a photo of him and the Roman centurion under my pillow. He was smiling in it, that's why I liked it. So often he had looked miserable, wearing his depression like a shroud.

*

Postcard from Callum, he's gone to Sydney for six months, I'm amazed he's finally got his act together. I'm happy for him. He's written in a giant scrawl, Oz is a blast, doll. Hope you are fine. xxx

*

Fabio phoned a month after the break-up dinner. My heart leapt. I'd had to stop myself from phoning him almost every night. He missed me. Maybe we shouldn't have finished, he said. It's not as if we fight all the time, maybe it was just a bad patch.

My voice was shaking. It wasn't a bad patch, I said. We're too different.

I just wanted to make sure, he said.

I miss you too, I said. I hate it without you.

Why don't we get back together then?

We can't, I said, we'd just be burying our heads, limping along with our own secrets.

You're right.

Maybe we can have coffee soon.

Okay, he said.

I'll phone you.

I'll be in Skye next week, he said, I wanted to talk to you before I left.

I'm glad you phoned me.

I'm glad too, he said.

As soon as he'd hung up, I wanted to phone him back and ask him to come over, but I didn't.

*

Fabio brought me an Easter egg last night, we've had coffee

a few times and are trying to be friends. I had to get the morning-after pill today. I'm cloaked in nausea. He might be moving to Inverness. I told him it was a great opportunity.

*

stranger	How are you? It's ages since we've spoken.
me	Jana called me, Kavi and her are getting married!
stranger	Will you go to her wedding?
me	I'd love to go, she wants me to be her bridesmaid but it's not practical. I can't wait to meet Kavi Kavi!
stranger	Why d'you call him Kavi Kavi?
me	After kava kava – it's a herbal ingredient derived from a Polynesian plant with heart-shaped leaves. It's good for anxiety and tension.
stranger	Will Fabio go with you?
me	Fabio and I broke up ages ago, just after New Year.
stranger	I'm sorry, I didn't know. You seem okay about it.

me	We weren't right for each other from the beginning, but we still got really involved. It was very passionate. We had sex at Easter.
stranger	It happens.
me	It was awful, the condom broke, I had to get the morning-after pill. I felt so ill after taking it.
stranger	How's your health generally?
me	Good days and bad days. In between days. I still sleep for eleven or twelve hours, but I'd say I'm a bit better than a year ago, though I still feel grim if I overdo it. And when I have a cold, my symptoms get much worse, my legs are horrible for weeks. But I'm managing my voluntary job, I've only been off a few times. They're really understanding and don't pressure me. If I can't go in, it doesn't matter – no employer would be that understanding.
stranger	Do you still see Bob?
me	No, my appointments with him tailed off after the ACTH injections.
stranger	What about your friend Fizza?
me	She's improved a bit. She's not in bed so

much, but she still uses a wheelchair for being out and about. She's got great spirit, though she's mortified 'cos her wee brother's married and she's not.

stranger   What about Ivan?

me   What about him?

stranger   Why so coy?

me   I wasn't aware I was being coy.

stranger   Will you see him at Jana's wedding?

me   I don't know if he'll be invited, but I'll definitely see him if I go over there. They've extended his contract for another year.

stranger   By the way, I read that the World Health Organization has classified ME as a neurological illness since 1969. You must be happy.

me   It's good, I suppose, but a lot of doctors still don't believe in it. I changed GPs recently, but I felt like I was on trial. The first one I spoke to was so nice when I had cystitis, but when I went back she said she didn't believe in ME, but she couldn't speak for her colleagues. I think she thinks 'cos I went to Rome I'm fine.

stranger	It's bizarre you still have to fight to be believed.
me	If I had MS or lupus I wouldn't have to go through this. Still, I've got a really nice Indian guy now, he has no problem with my sick notes. It just wasn't practical to stay with Myra.
stranger	Nice to see you again and catch up. Say hello to Ivan.
me	It won't be 'til the end of the year, Jana wants to get married in December.

*

4th July 1993
Hey Jana,
Happy Independence Day to you!

Am a bit fed up so thought I'd write – ME has been crap to be honest, such a struggle doing reception work at the counselling centre. I missed four weeks and I've cut down my hours from five to two, it's all so pathetic. Would be so good to see you for a night – could do with some Jana therapy! Have to admit that I'm missing Ivan since Fabio and I broke up, I find myself thinking about him more than ever. I miss Fab too, we had a good time – when he wasn't depressed – but I think he was really just sandbagging me from Ivan,

418

though at the time I didn't realise it. Anyway, Fab has to get himself sorted out. I think I held back from criticising his living at home because I'm not exactly leading a dynamic, independent life, but I think a more healthy girlfriend would have been unhappy about his lifestyle. At least we are still friends, maybe because we knew all along it wasn't the be all and end all. Anyway, he's moving up north with work. I hope he can be happy, he's a good boy, if a little fragile.

There's a cute Gestalt therapist where I volunteer, I've been to his house for dinner, but of course he has an equally cute girlfriend – they always do! Anyway, how are things with Kavi Kavi? Are you still very much in love? I hope so! Am glad you've postponed getting married 'til springtime, December is dreary, better to be a bride in the sun. Did I tell you Rez and his girlfriend are very serious? I think she will move in and I'll be moving out. Everyone's nesting up! I just don't have energy to look for somewhere else, would be ideal if I could move into Ivan's and kick Wendy out.

By the way, I finally saw *The Piano*, I loved it, I think there is always a moment when you want to chop off your lover's fingers, though I had to look away. Dare I ask, have you seen Ivan recently? Is he still dating that Stanford med student, he was very sketchy in his last letter. He knows I'm not with Fab anymore and doesn't want to rub in his happiness.

Write soon with news of lovely things,

Lots of love,

Helen xxx

*

I'm lying on my bed, wearing my new grey sweater, thinking that Ivan would like it, he always liked my breasts best. I'm going to be thirty in a month. I think about what I've achieved, what I can put on my CV. I don't see why you can't include your relationships, let your potential boss know that you've been through hell, *you have experience.*

NAME

Helen Fleet

WORK EXPERIENCE

Waitress

Serial volunteer

EDUCATION

Four Highers: French (A), English (A), Maths (A), Chemistry (A), 1981

Mystery illness (has taught me a lot), 1983 – present

Ordinary Arts degree, MA, 1990

Certificate in Counselling Skills and Theory, 1992

TRAVEL

London, France, Zakynthos, Madeira, San Francisco, Rome. (And inter-railing in 1981, but we got homesick and came home early.)

RELATIONSHIP EXPERIENCE

Penetrative sex with three men: Hadi, Ivan and Fabio. Still in love with Ivan.

ADDITIONAL INFORMATION

I have a mini hi-fi and a pine bookcase, and an expensive leather briefcase (got it in the January sales after Fabio and I had finished) and a suit I haven't worn since my graduation.

I need to go out, I've been in all day. It's brightened up after raining for most of the afternoon.

I put on my coat.

I walk to the delicatessen on the corner, happy in my grey sweater, and buy some over-priced chocolate peanuts.

Part Three

29

A Pale Blue Dress

JANA'S GETTING MARRIED today. She will just be waking up. She's marrying a man I've never met.

I just couldn't have managed the flight.

I've come to the bench. It's May, but you still need a coat. The sky and the loch are the same colour – they are grey, the colour of fish.

I'm phoning her in an hour, at four my time.

A couple of months ago, I bought a pale blue dress for her wedding. I kept trying it on in the flat, hoping I could go, *imagining* myself there, but I didn't dare book – it was too much money to lose and you're not covered for pre-existing conditions.

She's getting married in the Chinese Pavilion in Golden Gate Park.

I've had a lump in my throat all day. Rita's trying to cheer me up. She asked if I'd like a video tonight and an

Indian takeaway.

Ivan's going.

A few days later, I'm back in Rez's flat, waiting for the washing machine repair man. I'm wearing leggings and an old sweater of Nab's, my hair needs washed: I feel like a dart player's wife. The pale blue dress is hanging in the cupboard as if the woman it belonged to died before she got a chance to wear it.

Rez'd called on Monday and asked if I could come back for Wednesday 'cos the repair guy was coming. I should've said – No, I can't come, my head's compressed and my arms and legs feel like chopped meat, but I didn't want to let him down.

The guy was supposed to be here at ten – a hideously early start for me, I had to set the alarm for nine – but he's late, it's quarter to eleven and he's not here yet. I'm angry that I had to get up early for nothing. At quarter past eleven there's a knock at the door. You've got a faulty washing machine, he says, as if it's my fault.

I thought you were coming at ten, I say.

I got held up at the last job. And I couldn't get the van parked. Sorry.

I show him into the kitchen.

What's the problem then?

It's overheating, I say. It's shrinking delicates and woollens.

He opens the washing machine, grips it from inside and inches it out slowly from under the work surface, dragging it across the lino. He's flushed with the effort – I'm scared he'll ask me to help. His gold chain bracelet has left a mark on his arm.

You've got a mothball in here, he says, holding out a white pellet.

My flatmate must've had it in with his clothes, I say.

You'd be surprised at what gets left in, he says, standing up and taking the lid off the machine. It's probably a new thermostat you're needing.

Can you do it today?

Depends on whether I've got the part in my van, he says. Have you got an old towel for the floor? I'll need to start a cycle so I can get a temperature reading.

I get him a towel and ask if he wants some tea.

Two sugars and no milk, he says, starting the machine. So have you got no classes today?

No, I say. (I can't be bothered explaining.)

The students have an easy life of it, he says.

It's a lot of work, I say. Getting a degree is a lot of work.

I'm not much of a reader myself, but I like to go to the library.

Why do you like libraries if you don't like reading?

I love browsing, he says, I can spend a couple of hours just browsing – I wouldn't read a novel though. When I was younger, I used to read James Bond books – I can still remember the description of a scorpion and a spider, it was so clear, I thought I was there.

There's nothing better than a book that pulls you in, I say.

But I wouldn't read a novel, he repeats emphatically. I prefer browsing.

You prefer non-fiction, I say, handing him his tea. Sorry, there are no biscuits.

I prefer stuff that's real, he says.

I'll just leave you to it. I'll be in the living room if you need anything.

We'll just wait for the temperature to peak, he says.

I go into the living room and lie on the couch. I close my eyes and wonder what Jana's doing. She'll be on a beach in Maui with Kavi Kavi, having great sex and cocktails. Ivan phoned me after the wedding. He said I was greatly missed. He said he'd get the photos developed at a 24-hour place and send me copies.

He sounded sad.

I just wish the repair man would go, so I could go back to bed. I am close to tears.

A week later, the photos arrive. I've been looking out for them everyday. I tear open the padded envelope and devour them. Jana is beautiful. I look through them quickly, searching for Ivan. He's only in three. I scan the group photo, wondering if he's with anyone, then I go back and study Jana, feeling guilty that I'm more interested in Ivan.

I'll need to get a frame for her.

*

I can't take another ten years of this: being ill is too lonely.

I am fed up having no money and weak legs.

I think again of how it would be better simply not to *be*, but then I think of the stories you hear of how everything leaks out of you when you're dead, even your spinal fluid.

And the body bag. Apart from anything else, it would all be so humiliating.

30

A Death

I'M HALF ASLEEP. There's a glass of water at the side of the bed, I keep meaning to lean over and pick it up, I'm so thirsty, but I'm too tired to move and then I think I *have* picked it up, but I haven't, I just imagined I had – like thinking you've got up to pee when you haven't, you just hoped you had – and I'm still thirsty and my thumb's throbbing. I snagged it on a knife in the sink tonight and it bled for an hour. I went through half a toilet roll. It wasn't even that deep. Rez said hands bleed for ages because they are so fleshy.

I don't know why I'm so thirsty. I force myself to lean over and lift the glass and drink. It's solid and comforting in my hand. I lie back down and amuse myself again with the impossibility of flying to San Francisco and surprising Ivan, arriving fresh and beautiful (no jet lag), and phoning him from the airport. He'll leave work early to pick me up, incredulous (and delighted) that I have come.

I'm wondering if we'll kiss madly at the airport or wait 'til his apartment to tear our clothes off, when the phone rings. It's after midnight and I wait for Rez to answer, it'll be the hospital, but he doesn't answer and I get up, scared something has happened to Rita. I pick up the phone and Ivan is crying. His mother has died.

God, what happened?! I hear myself ask. My question seems lame and pointless.

She was drinking and took a lot of stuff, he says.

I'm so sorry, Ivan.

I say it again, almost whispering.

Can you meet me at the airport? he says. I'm coming back tomorrow.

Of course, babe.

Even in this awful moment, I wonder if it's okay to be calling him babe.

It'll be the day after tomorrow that I actually arrive, he says.

I'll be there.

It was Molly's birthday, she'd have been twenty-eight, he says.

God, I didn't know. D'you think that's why —

I don't know.

Your poor dad.

He'll cave in when it hits him, he says, letting go of a huge sob.

Come home, Ivan, I say. Just come home.

I'll call you with my flights.

D'you want me to get Rez?

No, you tell him. I have to go.

Bye, babe. I'll see you when you get home.

It's a fucking mess.

I'm so sorry.

I know.

You know I love you, I say. Whatever you need, tell me.

Bye... I love you too.

I put the phone down and start to dial Rita but decide to wait 'til morning – there's nothing she can do, and I don't want to alarm her. I feel guilty, like I'm somehow responsible for what's happened – I've got what I wanted, Ivan saying he loves me, but his mum had to die first.

I knock Rez's door, but there's no response. I go in and touch the quilt mound, he's not there. He must've gone out after I'd gone to bed. He always goes out at strange times. The room smells of him. I don't want to be alone. I curl up on his bed and sink into tears for Ivan and his mum. I wonder what drugs she overdosed on, if she meant it. I think of the last time I saw her: she'd dropped in on her way back from Glasgow Airport a few years ago. She'd given Ivan a red and green plate from a Spanish marketplace and later he'd used it for crisps at his house-warming and someone had used it as an ashtray. I wish he was home and I could hold him and shield him from it all. I think about calling Jana, maybe she can help him, take care of him 'til he comes home. I sit up, wondering where I've put her new number. She sent me a change of address card months ago. I devastate my room searching for it, finally finding it behind the laundry basket.

I go into the hall to dial. My hands are shaking. I get Jana's answering machine. She's not there, it's the weekend, she's out with Kavi doing sunny things.

I leave a message and can't stop my voice from breaking.

Fizza would say that everything happens for a reason, everything's God's will. Obviously, I don't agree – I think everything is random and cruel, but sometimes you look back and you think it couldn't have been any other way.

Thirty-six hours later, Rita and I meet Ivan at the airport. He is tanned, but the strain of his mother is stamped on his face. We take him back to Rez's, and Rita asks if there's anything else she can do.

When she's gone, I hold Ivan and his grief crashes against me like waves.

Rez is driving him to Dundee later tonight.

*

When the coffin slides away behind the red curtain, you assume it's going straight into the furnace, but it can be put into a holding pattern – like a plane waiting to land. You

433

just have to hope the ashes you get are the ones you want, and not a stranger's, someone you may have hated had you known them.

Ivan is stoic at the service, even more handsome in his grief and black clothes, but the pain on his face is like skin stretched on a drum. The last time he'd seen her was when his parents had visited him six months ago. She'd loved Haight Street and said it made her feel young again.

His dad shakes people's hands professionally, like an actor playing the part of a widower. Every time I look his way, I'm afraid I'll see him crying.

The reception is in an upmarket hotel. The sandwiches, brown and white, are not dry and curled up like the usual buffets. The waitresses pour tea and coffee from huge pots, and I wonder how they can lift them without their arms collapsing.

There are lots of Irish accents, Ivan's mum's side over from Dublin. Everyone assumes I'm his girlfriend. (I held his hand during the whole service and wept with him when her coffin disappeared.) I overhear an old woman, her twisting mouth full of sandwich, telling another old woman, her face marbled with lilac broken veins, that 'Liam's schizophrenic but he's well read'.

Later, Nab and Rita ask if I'm going back with them, but Ivan wants me to stay.

Are you sure? I say – I don't want to intrude on your dad's grief.

I want you with me tonight, he replies.

*

For seven nights, Ivan's dad has slept alone. I wonder now if he's lying awake, touching the empty sheet beside him with a flattened hand, wondering stupidly and pointlessly why his wife isn't there.

Across the landing, Ivan and I make love, soundlessly, and I am happy, inside his sadness.

I keep asking him if he's okay. He says he is. He has no mother now, but there are things to be done, things to sort out.

*

Everything's accelerated.

Ivan's gone back to San Francisco 'til October to finish his contract. Then he's coming back. He says California's la-la land, he's tired of it. He applied for a post at Dundee Uni when he was home, he got his application in just before the deadline. They're doing lots of Alzheimer's research there. He's in with a good chance.

I'm moving into his flat, Wendy and the other girl are moving out. Rez will be glad to be rid of me. I don't blame him. He can be all cosy with his girlfriend now.

I don't know if Ivan and I are really back together, but I don't want to question him too much, he wants me in his flat and that is enough. Maybe he's just being sentimental – he won't know what he wants 'til his mother's sunk in.

I so much want to help him. I have a second-hand book on grief from my counselling course, but I never actually used it. The previous owner had highlighted sections in pink, but they make no sense.

I can't read someone else's highlights.

31

Fizza and a Swollen Eye

WHEN I MOVE into Ivan's, the fridge light isn't working. I replace the bulb and feel manly, and proficient in DIY. The fridge reminds me of Fabio, our first conversation. I've been meaning to phone him – I don't know if he knows from Wendy that I'm moving back with Ivan. When I was moving in, she was still moving out. We were polite and walked around each other like traffic islands.

After three years of tenants, the flat is shabby. I wonder if Ivan'll want to decorate and imagine us going to Habitat together. His mother helped him gloss the hall. Sometimes I shudder and feel she's watching me. I get up to pee during the night, and run through and run back, scared she'll be in the mirror when I look.

I'm woken by journals thudding through the door, redirected from San Francisco. Ivan gets more post than me and he doesn't even live here yet.

He'll be home in a week. He'll have two weeks before he starts the job in Dundee.

I'm counting the days.

Rita's been giving me the same advice she gave me seven years ago when he came home from India – *Don't put all your eggs in one basket!* – and as I mark his new job on my Egon Schiele calendar, I realise that nothing has really changed.

*

I don't sleep the night before, I'm far too excited. He's due at four. I've made bolognese sauce and bought a single pink gerbera. I've put it in a glass in the living room.

I'm brushing my teeth when I hear a black cab pull up. I look outside. Ivan is paying. He has two suitcases and a rucksack and his guitar. He looks forlorn.

My legs are shaking. I spit out the toothpaste and rush out to meet him.

We hug for a long time. He has a stale smell from travelling.

I didn't realise how much I've missed you, he says, pressing me to him.

I take his guitar from him. I try to pick his rucksack up too.

That's too heavy for you, he says, leave it.

You're worth it, I say.

Leave it. I'll come back for it.

When we get inside, he kisses me and tells me I have toothpaste on my face.

I've noticed changes I didn't notice before. He has American intonation. He says 'garbage' and 'backpack' – without irony – and *'yeah, right!'* all the time. He doesn't leave the toilet seat up anymore. I think his American girlfriend(s) must've rubbed off on him. Jana says American men don't leave the toilet seat up as much as European men. They're too polite.

He is so busy, he has so much to do. I try to stay in the background, let him settle down – but when he says one night that American women are demanding and talk in baby voices and want to be put on a pedestal, I ask, Are there going to be any turning up heartbroken on the doorstep?

Of course not, he says. There was a woman at Stanford, it was intense, but it's been over for months – since before Jana's wedding. You know that.

That's why you sounded sad on the phone on the day of Jana's wedding – I thought it was because you missed me, but it was because of that woman.

Let's not analyse, he says.

I'm sorry.

Let's just be.

I'll try.

I bite my tongue and try to get off the subject, but I have to say my piece: If this awful thing hadn't happened with your mother, you wouldn't have come home, Ivan, I'm sure of it – it's only because of her that you're here.

Everything's because of something, he says, if you think about it.

But I'm afraid that I'm just a by-product of what happened.

You're not a by-product.

How can you be sure?

Let's just be, he says again. You and me.

But there are practicalities to sort out: I can't stay on sickness benefit if we are going to be properly living together. I'll wait 'til New Year to broach this, I don't want to assume too much. Maybe I'll end up in the spare room, applying for rent again.

We have sex a lot. I am terrified of getting pregnant. I worry when he's putting the condom on, because he is so short-sighted: I have to check it and re-check it or put it on myself.

*

One Thursday, Fizza came to visit. She'd had to cancel the last time.

Her dad brought her – he was coming back for her in

an hour. She was wearing lipstick, but I knew how weak her legs had been when she'd been in front of the mirror applying it.

Lie down, I said, if you're too tired to sit up.

The sofa swallowed her up.

You're so lucky to have all this, she said. There's no way I'd be well enough to live with someone.

I know, I said, I am lucky.

I hate still being at my parents.

It must be hard, I said. I hate it when I'm forced to go back to my mum and Nab's for spells. You just sink back into invalid mode.

But you've got Ivan now, she said.

Well, things are still very new with us. I don't know what's going to happen.

Is he coming back this weekend?

Yeah, he's been coming back on Fridays.

She sighed. In my community, I'm the strange unmarried girl with the weird illness.

You're only thirty-two! I said. You've still got time to meet someone.

It's not as simple as that.

Can I cheer you up with some chocolate gateau?

She smiled.

I brought the tea and cake through on a tray (I'd laid it out already).

Does that not kill your arms? she asked.

They're trembling, I said.

She sat up. It's really good to see you. I've been looking forward to this for ages.

Me too, I said.

These are lovely mugs. They're very delicate.

They're china, I said, I got them in a sale. The others were old and chipped.

I wish I could be doing simple things like that, she said, buying mugs for my flat.

Did I put enough sugar in your tea?

It's perfect.

I'm crap at making tea for others, I said, I make it too weak and never know how much milk and sugar to put in. I've never taken sugar.

Even when you were wee?

I stopped when I was ten, I thought it was grown up not to have sugar.

She laughed. So are you still doing your voluntary work?

Only three hours a week. I was doing six hours but it was too much, so I cut it down to two, then three.

At least you're doing something, she said.

It shapes my week, I said, but it's a struggle sometimes.

Don't you get lonely, though, the days you're on your own?

Sometimes I get weary if I haven't seen anyone for a few days.

I couldn't handle a whole day on my own, she said.

My ideal is to have an event or a task every other day – one day on, one day off – even if it's just going out to buy shampoo or have a cup of coffee.

I don't think it's good to be too much on your own, said Fizza. You go crazy.

When I was really ill, I used to force myself to go downstairs just to have the comfort of people around me, but I felt as if I was dying and had to go back upstairs after five minutes.

I'm still like that, she said. I remember when I was really ill I couldn't even bear the posters in my room, they were too much for my head, and my mum had to take them down.

That's awful, I said.

Sometimes, I still can't believe that I've got this illness, even after all these years it can still shock me.

I know what you mean, I said.

I honestly can't remember what it feels like to be normal.

I can remember doing normal things, I said, but I can't remember what being well feels like.

Do you think they'll ever get to the bottom of it?

Not unless they get more money for research, I said. Someone really important has to get it, then maybe they'll take it more seriously. All the world leaders. All the doctors. All the politicians.

The world would descend into chaos, said Fizza. They'd have to find a cure!

Until then all we've got is these fucking psychiatrists with their cognitive behavioural therapy and graded exercise.

They're evil, said Fizza. Making people more ill, forcing them to exercise. It's like a witch-hunt – *they're* the ones that need psychiatrists. Why can't they just leave us alone?

Did you see that article in the *Glasgow Herald* last week by the journalist who diagnosed herself? She's married now and plays tennis and reviews holiday destinations.

I saw it, said Fizza.

It pisses me off when people *claim* they had ME, but now they're fine and they can go on safaris.

I'm sure she did have some post-viral thing for a few months, said Fizza, but to say it was ME is irresponsible. She says she hid it from her friends and family, but how could you *possibly* hide this illness from anyone?

People with genuine ME don't make her kind of recovery.

But now people will have read her article and think: So that's what ME is like.

Exactly, I said. More misinformation.

Fizza looked suddenly grey.

Are you okay? I asked.

It's just my head, it's all the talking. My dad should be here soon.

There's still tons I can't do, I said, trying to make her feel better. I missed Jana's wedding. I was too ill to travel.

I know.

That reminds me, d'you want to see the photos or are you too tired?

I can look at them.

I dug them out and sat beside her. I handed her the photos, one by one. Her hands were shaking as she took them.

Your poor hands, I said.

They always shake, said Fizza. Jana's gorgeous. She hasn't changed.

Do you remember her from all those years ago?

Yeah, she visited you in hospital a few times. God, I'd love to go to San Francisco.

It's beautiful, I said. I fantasise that Ivan and I will go there for our honeymoon.

Do you think Ivan would marry you?!

I don't know, I said. I still can't believe I am enough for him.

He wouldn't get your hopes up again, would he?

Not deliberately, but he must be all over the place after his mum and moving back here so suddenly.

I hope I'm well enough for your wedding, she said.

I hope *I'm* well enough for my wedding, I said.

We'll both be well, she said. *Inshallah.*

When Fizza had gone, I wept for her. I knew she'd never lived in a flat or even had a boyfriend.

445

*

We spent Christmas in Dundee with Ivan's dad. It was my first Christmas away from Rita and Nab. On the way up, we got a real tree.

Ivan scratched his cornea while he was underneath the tree on Christmas Eve, peering at the gift labels without his glasses on. His eye swelled up; he looked injured and I loved him even more. He had to go to Casualty for a tetanus and antibiotics.

At bedtime, I kissed his swollen eye.

By Christmas Day, he looked like the Elephant Man.

Are you still able to cook the turkey? I asked.

You only need one eye to cook a turkey, he replied.

I'd never cooked one before, it seemed complicated and scary. Ivan said he was a dab-hand after spending three Thanksgivings in California.

Someone must've shown you, I said – all those women you ate yams and turkey with.

You have to keep basting, he said. Every twenty minutes. As long as you baste, you can't go wrong.

I'm sure, I said.

The innuendo was lost on him, he wasn't really listening.

When the turkey had cooked and cooled, I started carving it without asking him – I had no idea what I was doing.

You're destroying my turkey! he said when he found

me. You're supposed to do the legs and wings first – go and put the crackers out or something!

His dad smiled when I told him what I'd done. I think he appreciated me being there. Your son's merciless in the kitchen, I said. I went into the dining room and finished laying the table. We'd bought luxury crackers, gold and white crêpe. I'd been dreading the forced merriment and the space where his mother should have been, but it was fine. His dad seemed more gentle than before.

On Boxing Day, we visited the spot by the river where they'd scattered her ashes. Ivan had joked that we should take tinsel. I knew he was just trying to be brave. On the way back, he said he was thinking about going skiing with Rez in March. You don't mind, do you? Of course not, I said, of course you should go, but already I was fretting about the gorgeous women with lip salve and navy skiing pants.

32

The Silvery Tay

I SQUEEZE THE washing-up liquid bottle, it coughs like a dog. Nothing comes out. That will be today's jaunt, going out to buy more.

We had a big talk in January – since we are living together properly as a couple, I've had to come off sickness benefit. We now have a joint account. It feels so strange. I joke with him that I'll spend all his money on toiletries.

*

When Ivan was skiing, I found out that Amber was pregnant. I was glad she couldn't see my face. I told her it was lovely news and congratulated her. Rita told me later that Amber'd been worried about telling me in case I got upset. I was pleased for them, but it felt odd.

I was glad Ivan was away.

I sat up late waiting for a French film, but it wasn't showing on BBC Scotland. Instead we got curling championships with big grunting women. It was midnight, but I didn't want to go to bed. I turned over and watched a repeat documentary about a woman who'd survived a plane crash in Chile when she was a child. She'd been asleep and woken up to find herself spinning to the ground like a sycamore leaf, still strapped into her seat. When she'd regained consciousness, she'd seen a row of seats sticking out of the mud and recognised her mother's feet.

I went to bed thinking of the girl spinning to the ground, but something else was niggling: I knew it would be hard for me to actually see Amber S-shaped and pregnant. We were supposed to be visiting them at Easter in their new house in Cambridge. I wondered if she'd be showing after four months.

Ivan was restless when he got back from skiing. How d'you feel about moving to Dundee? he said, a few days after his return.

Dundee?! Are you serious?

I've been thinking about it a lot. I can't keep commuting and staying with my dad for the next three years. You and I hardly see each other. The sooner we do it the better.

Sounds like you've already decided, I said.

It just makes sense. We should move in summer, it's less bleak.

Will you sell this place?

Probably, he said. Or rent it out. Stop making that face.

Sorry.

Dundee's not that bad. There are some beautiful houses by the Tay. I've been to see one.

You've been house hunting already?!

Just browsing.

I don't really have a choice, do I?

I guess not, babe.

I'm not ecstatic about it, I said, but of course I'll move.

You can find interesting voluntary work there, I'm sure.

Will we have to cancel Cambridge?

Why would we?

Seems a lot to do when we're moving house.

We're not moving tomorrow. We'll start looking properly after Easter.

Can we have a garden?

Definitely.

A cat?

Don't get your hopes up, I think I'm still allergic.

I sighed. Amber's pregnant, by the way.

You're going to be an auntie.

Yup.

That's nice.

You'll be an uncle – if you want to be, that is.

So I will.

I hope it's a girl, I said – boys just grow up to be bastards.

Thanks a lot, he said.

Well, I'm just getting used to us living here and now we have to move.

That's the real world, Looby. Work dictates where you live. You can't just live somewhere because you like it.

I'm just a bit peeved, I said. I have no power in these things and it's no one's fault, it's just the way it is.

They say you know your house the moment you walk in. I was lucky – in the end I only had to see one. Ivan came home with handfuls for me to look at. He viewed them during the week and was often disappointed. One Friday, he called and told me to get the train up straight away. I've found our house, Looby, he said, sounding so excited. It's south-facing, five minutes' walk from the shops. You'll love the garden. It's perfect.

In the West End?

No, Broughty Ferry, but you'll love it. Five minutes from the beach.

But it's full of pensioners.

There are young people too, he said, and arty shops springing up. *Please*, you have to see this house. It's owned by an artist.

*

451

It was described as a cottage but was a small hundred-year-old stone bungalow with a slate roof. The owner was moving to Spain and she wanted a quick sale.

There was a blue velvet cinema seat in the hall.

My favourite room was the separate toilet, panelled in turquoise stained wood – it made me think of New Mexico, though Ivan thought it was gaudy. There was a huge kitchen and dining area with French doors onto the garden, a gorgeous bedroom, a study and a smallish living room with varnished floorboards. The bathroom had hand-painted tiles.

The garden was untamed, tangled with sweet peas and flowers I didn't know. I love it, I said to the owner. I've been very happy here, she said.

She was old but she had lovely skin.

Afterwards, we drove to the beach and yabbered like children about the pros and cons.

D'you think the living room's too small? said Ivan.

We can make it cosy. And the kitchen's huge. That makes up for it.

Only one bedroom, said Ivan.

The study can easily take the sofa bed, I said.

She's leaving the garden furniture. Her late husband made it.

You have to make an offer! I said. You have to! Or someone else'll snap it up.

We went to see it one more time and arranged for a survey. I went back to Glasgow.

I felt sick waiting for him to phone.

By Friday, he had made an offer and over the weekend the woman accepted.

I'd had the job of showing Ivan's flat to prospective buyers as he was away all week. At first it was exhausting making sure the toilet was sparkling and the cushions plumped, rehearsing what to say, but after a string of viewers I let them walk through the flat themselves and only talked to them if they asked questions. In the sixth week, the flat was bought by a lecturer in film and television. I vaguely recognised him and it turned out we'd been in the same English class in 1982.

*

At the end of August, we moved. I was packing a final box of glasses, wrapping them in newspaper, putting them in a box, when I heard on the radio that a Norwegian had been beheaded by Kashmiri separatists. I felt sick and couldn't stop thinking about it. I didn't mention it to Ivan, he got mad when I dwelled on these things. He took the box of glasses down to the car, oblivious to what was in my head. I unplugged the radio, I wanted to leave it – it was old and splashed with paint – but it would be handy for the new house.

We took a final electricity reading and left.

Are you sad? I said, as we drove away, looking back one last time.

Kind of.

But you never really lived in that flat.

I still feel a bit odd leaving.

A new chapter, I said. I hope it's a good one.

It will be, he said. You won't be able to put the book down.

It was still light when we arrived.

Should you not carry me over the threshold? I said.

D'you want me to?

No, people'll think we're crazy. The curtains'll be twitching.

Welcome to your new home, he said, as he opened the door. In you go.

Welcome to your new home too, I said.

His furniture had already been brought up by the removal people. It was strange seeing it here.

It feels funny, doesn't it? I said.

Do you still love it?

I still love it, I said, following him from room to room, my fingertips trailing his.

The artist had left the cinema seat in the study. Cool! said Ivan.

It's not cool, I said. It's ugly. It's not staying.

You've got no taste, he said.

We unloaded the car slowly, Ivan taking most of it.

I made some tea, boiling the water in a pan because I couldn't find the kettle.

Ivan wanted his in the study. I took it through to him. It's black, I'm afraid, there's no milk.

As long as it's not homeopathic, he said, slumped in the blue velvet seat.

During the night he woke me shouting in his sleep: *Why are there circles of water round the house?!*

When I told him the next day, he couldn't remember. You must be anxious, I said.

I don't feel anxious, it's all gone so smoothly, he said. Buying a cottage and selling a flat in two months. Pretty jammy.

I thought it would have been more traumatic, I said.

I'm not complaining, said Ivan. We deserve some good luck, don't you think?

Our first evening, we sat in the garden and had fish suppers. You could smell the sea.

It's bliss eating outside, isn't it?

Ivan nodded.

D'you see how silvery those flowers are? I said.

What are they? he asked.

No idea, but blue and white flowers look silver at dusk.

Rita told me.

We'll need to learn about gardening, said Ivan, before things get out of control.

Things are already out of control, I said. We'll need to trim those coppery bushes at the front.

That can be your job.

A cat from next door appeared, smelling the fish.

Scat! said Ivan.

You're welcome here anytime you want, wee cat, I said. Just ignore him.

We'll need to get the cat flap filled in, said Ivan. A cat flap's a bit pointless with no cat.

We'll need it for visiting cats, I said. You'll just need to take antihistamines.

It looks like a madman's calendar, said Ivan, looking at my asterisks and arrows for September's deliveries and tradesmen. He'd taken a week off to work on the house. We were living on pasta and tuna fish. It was like being students again.

We painted the living room white to make it seem bigger. It had been peach and needed three coats. Ivan rolled the paint on with ease. I painted as much as I could, but afterwards I felt pummelled and arthritic, I could hardly move my hands. I decided it was better if I did the preparatory work and the cleaning of brushes, but I couldn't stop touching up parts of the wall that still looked a bit patchy. You're addicted to dabbing, said Ivan.

We got bright pink cushions.

Ivan's dad bought us a beautiful dining table from John Lewis. It's too nice to use, I said. I'm scared to touch it.

Don't be silly, said his dad. It's *for* using.

I was glad for him that we were nearby, it gave him somewhere else to visit. He looked so thin these days, his shoulders were like a coat hanger.

Nab and Rita came up to help. The water pressure in the bathroom was a bit high and Nab said we had 'violent taps'. Rita did lots in the garden. She said all it needed was a good cutting back and told me the blue and white flowers were lobelia.

*

By winter, the house felt completely ours, as if we'd always lived there, though council tax bills for the previous owner were still coming through the door like confetti.

33

Pearl

PEARL IS EXQUISITE with brown skin and green eyes. Her feet
are like triangles of rubber, I could spend all day stroking
them. I dreamt I dropped her against the fireplace. Her feet
were singed and she was screaming. I can't tell anyone in
case they're scared to let me hold her.

It's strange having a baby in the house, she rules the
roost. Every moment of the day is governed by what she
wants or needs. Christmas is out the window. All everyone
wants is their turn of her.

Ivan looks gorgeous with a baby on his lap.

At first, Rita thought Sean and Amber were too young
to have a child (they are both twenty-eight) but now she's in
love with Pearl and can't stop buying baby clothes.

I know facts about babies now: they are all born with
blue eyes, and they grow at approximately 0.5 mm a day
in the first year. I notice babies more too, they never really

registered before. Women with prams are quite often rude, they expect you to open doors for them and they don't say thank you.

Sean and Amber come up to Dundee for New Year. They think our house is lovely. Amber is too exhausted to stay up for the bells. Pearl squeaks and squawks all night, they take turns at getting up.

More than ever, I know I could never do it.

*

In spring, we went to Arran with Rez and his girlfriend. We hadn't been away since we'd moved house, apart from Balloch at Christmas. The guy on the ferry was camp with a honey-coloured wig, you could tell he felt important with his white shirt and epaulettes, even though his duties didn't extend beyond announcing that the bar was adjacent to the gift shop.

The owner of the hotel met us off the ferry in a minibus. He was wild-eyed and aristocratic with a hat with a peacock feather.

The next day while the others were climbing Goat Fell, I walked along the beach. I saw seals in the distance, their heads pointing through the freezing purple and grey water. They reminded me of Nab. I made a circle of stones on the beach and stood inside and made a wish. On the way back,

I passed a dead rabbit embedded in the side of the road.

I lay down for an hour. I was meeting everyone in the hotel bar later.

They were rosy with exercise and well-being. A couple of Australians had joined them during the climb. One asked why I hadn't climbed too, and just I was about to explain, Ivan intervened: Because she has a fatiguing illness, he said, putting his arm round me. She can't do tiring stuff.

I wish you could have seen the seals, I said – they were so cheeky – and the stones were such gorgeous colours.

What did you wish for? he asked.

I'm not telling you, I said, it's a secret.

The next day it poured. Everyone was bored and listless but I was quite happy, it meant Ivan would be with me all day. Rez's girlfriend bought a miniature Highland cow embroidery set to pass the time, but she didn't read the instructions and her cross stitches were too tight. She threw it away in disgust.

*

I woke with period pains like swords. They'd been getting heavier over the last few months, I dreaded them now, huge clots slipping out of me. I think your body starts to punish you if you're over thirty and not yet pregnant. I got up and raked through the medicine cabinet for my prescription painkillers. I took double the dose and curled up on the couch 'til they'd worked. I didn't want to wake Ivan with my groaning. He'd come to bed late after a leaving do at work.

*

I don't mind housework, it's my equivalent of going to the gym, though I hate dishes and ironing, and emptying the coffee pot – the grounds going everywhere, falling behind the bin.

I like cleaning the bathroom: I love the gleaming taps and the shiny floor and the smell of bleach, though I hate when you're cleaning the sink and the same hair keeps turning up, no matter how often you've cleaned it off. I hate hair on soap too, and I hate the towels falling off the rail when you've just arranged them neatly. (It's a bit strong calling them cunts, says Ivan.)

Cleaning the toilet is my favourite task (it's positively aerobic!). Last week, I accidentally melted the toilet brush, a turquoise one I'd bought to match the decor. I poured boiling water on it to get rid of the flecks of shit, but the brush had melted and the shit had stayed. I was trying to clean it, I explained to Ivan later – it was disgusting. It's a toilet brush, he replied, it's supposed to be disgusting.

When I'm hoovering, I find his disposable contacts at the side of the bed, crisped up and dehydrated. I keep meaning to hand-wash his good sweater for him. Jana's gay flatmate gave her a tip: you roll the soaking garment up in a towel and twist it to wring out the excess water.

It works, but it's tiring on my arms.

*

In January 1996, I started my first paid job since the Swan Hotel: one afternoon a week for an organisation that helped people with dementia. Ivan knew the son of the woman who'd set up the charity. She was impressed by my volunteering history and twelve years of ME. You'll be able to fully empathise, she said. And you've got your counselling credential. She'd given me a hefty manual to take home and study.

On my first day, a woman called and said her husband couldn't stop eating cherry cake and got violent if he couldn't have any. He had Pick's Disease, they often have a craving for sweet things.

When my first payslip arrived, Ivan said I should frame it.

You better be good to me, I said, this'll be keeping us in toilet roll.

Mostly, I listen and refer carers onto other services. Sometimes people just phone and weep. The office is a ten minute bus journey into town. I start at one so set the alarm for eleven. If he isn't working late, Ivan picks me up, though he's often working late.

*

Brian came to visit, he'd been asking for ages. Rita drove him up.

He ran up to the door and hugged me. You're like a big python, I said. You're squeezing the life out of me.

I've brought you After Eights, he said. It's a luxury box.

What's that clinking in your bag – have you brought a carry-out with you?!

It's aftershave, said Rita. It's his latest thing. He's brought two bottles.

I'd made mushroom soup.

Brian licked the back of his spoon after every mouthful. After dinner, Rita had a cigarette in the garden. She hardly smoked in front of me anymore, it caused too many fights. Your mum'll be freezing out there, said Ivan.

I feel bad, I said, but even if she hangs out the window we'll still get the smell.

I went out to the car with her when she was leaving. Thanks so much for bringing Brian through.

Don't let him exhaust you, she said.

I won't.

Your house is lovely. It really seems to be working out with you and Ivan.

It is, I said, hugging her goodbye.

The next day, Ivan took Brian into town, he was reeking of aftershave. They looked at videos and CDs. Brian said he had the time of his life.

We got a takeaway for dinner. Brian said he wanted

a chinky. I explained that it was horrible to say chinky, unacceptable. He said he was sorry, that he was just showing off. Afterwards, we watched a video and made ourselves sick with After Eights. Brian sat in the cinema chair. I love it when you think there are no After Eights left, but then you find one slotted into the corner, I said to Ivan.

On Sunday, after cajoling Brian into *not* going to Mass, we went for a drive along the coast. We skimmed stones on the water, our hands were freezing. Brian bought a postcard with a lighthouse for my granny and grandad. On the way back, a motorcyclist overtook us, he must've be doing a hundred. He'll be killed at the next bend, said Ivan.

On Monday – after Brian had eaten a mountain of French toast – Ivan drove him back to Glasgow. Rita's meeting you there, I told him. She'll take you home to Balloch.

I'm getting handed over like a parcel, said Brian.

It's been lovely to see you, I said.

You know what the next time'll be, don't you?

Your fortieth.

That's right, he said. The big 'four O'!

We'll be there, I said. Don't you worry.

When they'd left, I stripped the sofa bed. There were stains on the sheets. It was too sad to think about.

By the time Ivan got back, it was late. I was in the bath. I'd run it twice, the first time I'd left the cold running and forgotten – I'd had to drain most of it away. I was glad Ivan hadn't seen the waste.

He came in and sat on the side of the bath.

Thanks for using your holiday to take Brian back, I said. You're an angel.

No problem. It was nice to have him.

Was my mum there on time?

It worked out fine.

He was funny when he said he felt like a parcel, he's so insightful sometimes.

I stopped in and saw Rez, said Ivan.

How is he?

Fine. He's going to propose to his girlfriend.

Is he?!

Yup. Says she's the one.

I'm not crazy about her, I said.

Me neither, but Rez probably sees a different side.

I think she's a cold fish. Are you coming in?

Nah, save the water though. I feel like sloshing around on my own. It's too tangled when we're both in.

Spoilsport.

You must be exhausted.

I am, I said. Brian's lovely, but he's hard work. You must be tired too.

Not really. It was an easy weekend. By the way, I found these on the passenger seat, he said, holding out hair clips. If you ever get lost, I'll find you by your trail of kirbies.

I'm always losing them, I said.

I'm always finding them, said Ivan. They're everywhere.

*

Have you seen the paper? They've printed my letter! I squealed down the phone.

That's great, said Ivan.

I'll read it out. Are you listening?

I'll see it when I come home, Looby. I'm really busy.

That bastard doctor'll have to eat his words. They've printed another two letters as well as mine. I feel so vindicated!

See you later. It's great news.

As I hung up I could feel myself grinning. I felt as if I'd won a major prize. I re-read my letter.

How I wish it were psychosomatic

As a thirty-three-year-old ME sufferer for almost thirteen years, I resented the unprofessional, arrogant tone of Dr C Fox's letter (31 March) declaring the condition to be not physical. How does he know?

A lot of research is being done into disturbed muscle energy metabolism and persisting viral infection in people with ME. In my case, it was triggered by an aggressive case of Coxsackie B4 virus in 1983.

When I was diagnosed with ME by a consultant neurologist in 1984, I had never even heard of it. After an array of blood tests and muscle-function tests, the consultant told me I had a full-house of abnormalities. I assume he meant physical.

I was a straight 'A' student and have a university degree but have never been able to start a career as a result of having this illness. How I wish my symptoms were psychosomatic!

If Dr Fox were bedridden with ME for just one day, he would know beyond doubt that the disease is physical and he would perhaps cease to be 'irritated by the ME lobby'. He might be extremely grateful for it.

I suggest he get in touch with the Persistent Virus Disease Research Foundation – a group committed to researching the causes and pathology of ME. I'm sure they'd be delighted to have him on their mailing list.

I'm aware that I may be incorrect in assuming that Dr Fox is male.

Helen Fleet, Dundee.

One of the other letters was from a woman whose ten-year-old son was ill. He'd missed two years of school.

I'd take the whole page into work next week and photocopy it to send to everyone.

*

On election night we sat up whooping as the Tories fell like skittles. Ivan went to work after only two hours' sleep. I made a celebration dinner.

Things can only get better!

34

More Questions

stranger	Why can't you have children if people affected by thalidomide can?
me	I can't believe you're asking such an insensitive, ignorant question – how many conversations about my illness do we have to have?! I haven't heard from you for years and you turn up like a bad penny with absurd questions.
stranger	Just tell me, if a woman with no arms can look after a child, why can't you?
me	*You know why* – because of the MASSIVE fatigue and muscle weakness! I'm in tatters after a couple of hours with my niece. It takes me days to recover. How on earth

could I look after my own?

stranger   Does it not make you sad you won't have any?

me   Of course it does, but I've just accepted it. If I got pregnant I could end up being bedridden again. I just can't risk that. It wouldn't be fair to the child or Ivan or me. It might be more upsetting if I were actually infertile, which is bizarre because the end result is the same, but maybe I've tricked myself into believing that I still have the choice, even though I don't – not really. Sometimes I think if we were rich and had a nanny and cook and cleaner, I would consider it... but I am just so afraid of having a baby I can't look after. It would be wrong.

stranger   Sorry, I didn't realise.

me   I have a recurrent dream where my baby turns into a tulip and I crush its head. It's always a relief to wake up.

stranger   Does Ivan not mind?

me   Ivan says he doesn't want to have children, but I don't like to get into it too much. I'm scared he changes his mind. I know his ex at Stanford had an abortion, but he doesn't talk about it.

stranger   At least you've got your niece.

me   I know. And Ivan adores her. I hope Sean and Amber have another one!

*

stranger   What's the most you can do these days?

me   On a good day, I can walk a mile, but my legs will be burning afterwards – I need a few days to recover. I've occasionally pushed myself to do two miles – it's always tempting to try and do a bit more – but you end up paying for it. It's not worth it.

stranger   You still have to be strict with yourself.

me   I'm always measuring out my energy behind the scenes, but people don't see it. They see you at a party and think you're fine, they don't see you resting all day to be able to go, and being wrecked all next day because you went. They don't see you leaning on walls at bus stops because you can't stand for more than five minutes. They don't see how tired your arm gets after beating an egg. They don't know you almost always have poison in your calves when you wake up. They don't see you weeping because you're so tired of it all. Last week, a nun with bulbous eyes called me a lazy girl because I was sitting down on the bus.

stranger   She doesn't sounds like a very happy nun. What's your worst day like?

me   I can't leave the flat, having a shower and making a cup of tea are utterly taxing. I wake up with unbearably weak legs and they stay like that for days or weeks. I haven't done anything to cause it, it just happens. And the headaches like helmets follow you everywhere.

stranger   But you're still managing to work one afternoon a week?

me   I've been working for a year now! I've been off five times. My week revolves around being well enough for Thursdays, I go in from one 'til five. I am fit for nothing afterwards. Thank God for Ivan. He is my shining knight.

*

stranger   A lot of people are calling it chronic fatigue syndrome (CFS), aren't they?

me   Yes, especially in the USA, but chronic fatigue goes nowhere near describing the complexity of this condition. A lot of people have chronic fatigue, especially if they are depressed, but they *don't* have ME. But nowadays you often see it referred to as ME/CFS. The terms have become interchangeable. People with ME are very angry about this.

stranger   Would you say there is more acceptance now than in the '80s?

me   There is definitely more awareness, and a little more acceptance, you wouldn't see the term 'yuppie flu' now, but there are still psychiatrists who are hell-bent on the CBT and graded exercise approach. They have conceded we are actually ill, but are still convinced our muscles are weak due to deconditioning, and not due to the disease process. However, as I've said a hundred times, if any of these blinkered fools were to have ME for a day they would soon change their tunes. Sadly, these are the people who advise the government on my illness.

*

stranger   I was in Waterstone's yesterday. There seemed to be quite a few books about it.

me   When I first got ill, there was nothing, now the health sections are full of books. Some are good, others are crap. Meditating and aromatherapy won't cure you. Neither will learning to love yourself or drinking nettle tea. The best book was written in 1986 by Dr Melvin Ramsay: *Post-Viral Fatigue Syndrome – The Saga of Royal Free Disease.* It explores the history of ME and the lack of belief.

stranger   What do you think of support groups?

me   I think they can be helpful, especially at the beginning when the illness is so unknown and terrifying, but these days there are groups for everyone with ME – bisexual Christians and Jehovah's Witnesses. It's like everything, it can get a bit indulgent.

*

stranger   What's the latest research showing?

me   There are more and more research teams springing up, but they desperately need money to develop their theories. Certain viruses and cytokines – proteins involved in immunity – can alter the permeability of the blood brain barrier. They think toxins may be getting through and causing damage.

stranger   So that funny virus you had – Coxsackie – could have caused damage to the blood brain barrier?

me   Maybe. Also a deficiency in fatty acids may cause the barrier to 'leak'.

stranger   I also read somewhere they've found reduced levels of cortisol.

me   Yup, that would make sense – I think that's why the ACTH injections helped me. They've found many things, a reduced blood flow to the brain, for example – things you can't fake. There are still crucial pieces of the jigsaw missing, but the powers that be are not providing adequate money for research. It all comes down to funding.

stranger   Or lack of it.

me   Exactly.

35

A Seagull, 1998

IVAN PHONED AT lunchtime to say the seagull had gone. I drove past this morning, he said, it wasn't there.

I'm glad, I said. The poor thing had no dignity lying there.

How are you feeling?

My head's still inflamed, I said. I cancelled work after you left, there's no way I could help anyone today.

Okay, see you later. Don't paint anything.

Hardly.

I know what you're like dabbing everything that takes your fancy.

I won't dab. I'll make dinner though.

Are you sure?

There's frozen haddock I forgot we had, I quite fancy kedgeree.

I've got to go, someone needs me.

See you later.

Bye.

One less thing to worry about: the seagull had gone, and Ivan was in a better mood. I went into the kitchen to make some coffee. The coffee pot – an Alessi, a gift from Lucia when she came back after Christmas, a thank you for staying with us – was lying on the worktop, drying from last night, its dome head unscrewed like a detached cockpit. It reminded me of Lockerbie.

I drink too much coffee now, it used to make me ill, but now I am immune to it. I love the gurgling noise the Alessi makes when the coffee's ready.

I know I shouldn't feel threatened by Lucia, Ivan's not interested. He says European PhD students are ten a penny, the hospital's crawling with them. They're both going to a conference in Cambridge next week. Ivan's staying with Sean and Amber. I'm glad he's not staying in a hotel, then he might be tempted.

I am worn out with doubting. He stormed out last week and said, *When will you believe I love you?!*

He knows when.

36

Vélos and Blue Wasps

Ivan was eating salad from a bag, picking out the good bits.

Can you leave some for dinner, please? I said.

I don't like the red bits, what are they?

Lollo rosso.

It's a bit frilly and pointless, don't you think?

I made a face.

Do you like it? he asked.

It's nice mixed with the other leaves but there'll be no other leaves left if you keep eating.

I'll put it in a bowl, he said.

Can you dress it too, please? Not too much oil, you always drown it.

Did you get out of bed on the wrong side today, Looby?

Sorry, I said, I've got cramps, and I'm just thinking about something I read.

Another grim story you're letting flower in your head.

A Somalian boy.

Don't tell me.

He was roasted on a spit by Belgian soldiers.

Fuck's sake.

And his mother was forced to watch.

Jesus.

He survived, but I keep thinking about his agony.

Well, stop thinking about it, please! Let's just have dinner and talk about nothing important.

That old man phoned again.

What old man?

He phoned last week and said, *Is that the Italian?* I told you, do you not remember?

Sorry, I don't.

It was definitely him. He was havering and wouldn't hang up. Every time I lifted the phone he was still there.

Has he gone now? said Ivan, pouring too much oil over the salad, which was mainly lollo rosso now.

I hope so.

I've been thinking, said Ivan.

What?

I know what'll cheer you up.

You're not allergic to cats anymore.

Better than that.

What could be better than that?

I think we should get married.

Don't tease me!

478

I'm not. I think we should. You're right.

But you said people always get divorced when they get married after living together.

Not always.

I couldn't bear it. I just couldn't go through it.

I thought you wanted a husband, you like the word.

I do like the word, it's a sexy word. Boyfriend just sounds so childish.

Well, Miss Arsey Lollo Rosso, can I be your husband?

Don't mock.

I'm serious.

Ask me properly then.

Will you marry me? he said, getting down on one knee.

Really?

Really.

A hundred times over! I said, throwing my arms round him as he stood up.

You're like a Scud missile, he said, laughing, trying to keep his balance.

Is there a long waiting list?

No idea.

We'll need to phone the registry office, I said. I don't want a big fiasco, just a wee affair. Are we really going to do this?

We really are, Looby. Consider yourself wed.

After dinner we celebrated our betrothal – *comme une sucette*, like a lollipop!

Later, I phoned Jana to tell her what I'd always hoped to tell her.

Arched window. *Next day. Research lab.*

ivan   I have some news. Helen and I are getting married. Helen really wants to.

lucia   You must really love her.

ivan   Of course I love her.

lucia   I mean marrying someone who's ill.

ivan   I knew her before she got ill. We have a long history.

lucia   You don't mind not having children.

ivan   No, I don't mind. There are enough children.

lucia   You say that now, you might feel different when you're forty.

ivan   There's more to life than having kids.

lucia   Does she not want a child?

ivan   There's no way she could do it.

            [*Lucia kisses Ivan on the cheek tentatively, lingers then quickly kisses him on the mouth*]

lucia	Sorry. I've wanted to do that for ages. I won't have another chance now that you're getting married, will I?
	[*Ivan doesn't say anything*]
lucia	Helen knows I like you, doesn't she?
ivan	Helen tortures herself with things that aren't real.
lucia	And she knows you like me too.
ivan	Nothing ever happened, Lucia. I have nothing to hide. Can you go and check on those tissue cultures, please?
lucia	I'm happy for you both. Congratulations!

You only needed fifteen days' notice to get married. And £72. And original copies of your birth certificates. Ivan picked up the forms from the registry office.

Neither of us knew where our birth certificates were and we argued about who to have as witnesses.

You had to fill in a section about your parents – IS YOUR MOTHER STILL LIVING? I wished Ivan could've skipped that part.

A week later, we took the forms back and the ceremony was booked for four weeks' time. They showed us the marriage room. It wasn't exactly the Chinese Pavilion, but it had a couple of Matisse prints and white lights like globes to jazz it up. Ivan wrote a cheque to the registrar and went back to work. I got the bus home. The woman beside me had a pineapple on her lap.

The jeweller told us that men get broader rings because a thin ring can look effeminate. I couldn't believe all the sizes.

I felt it was greedy to have a wedding list (we were only inviting twelve to the actual ceremony, and we were having an evening reception at the end of the summer in a converted church in Glasgow) but people had been putting pressure on us to make one, so we placed one at Debenhams. We got a free cappuccino. We chose gifts that weren't too expensive, although what I really wanted was a Bondi blue iMac. Jana had one.

I bought bridal magazines and went shopping a couple of times but everything I tried on was horrible. One shop had a pile of mannequins outside on the pavement, some were missing arms and legs. It looked so brutal, like the scene of an accident. I wondered if it was a bad omen.

Ivan had booked a surprise honeymoon but he couldn't keep it secret. He told me we were going to France and I screamed.

Whereabouts?! You must tell me!

Cassis.

Where is it?

A tranquil beach town near Aix-en-Provence, he said, sounding like a travel agent. Someone at work recommended it.

You are a lovely man, I said, taking me to France.

You'll need to do all the talking. You'll be in charge.

That'll make a change, I said. Me in charge.

I look forward to it, said Ivan.

A week before the ceremony, I had my hair cut and highlighted. The trainee boy who washed my hair asked if I liked sausages.

The day before, I had a facial and a massage.

That night Ivan stayed with his dad.

I did my own make-up: morello cherry lipstick, mascara and a hint of blusher. Rita did my nails. I wore the pale blue dress and Helen Fleet became Helen Cox. The sun was shining and we basked in confetti on the steps of the registry office.

We went to Auchmithie for lunch, a tiny coastal village north of Dundee. Nab took photos of us on the cliffs. He was our official photographer. My grandad was too ill for the photos, he had vertigo and stayed inside. (How are your dizzy swirls, Father?, Nab was always asking.)

After lunch, Nab made a speech that made us all cry.

I kept looking at my left hand. It was beautiful.

stranger	Congratulations!
me	Thank you.
stranger	Are you all packed?
me	Just about.
stranger	You're glowing.
me	Ask me what I do, as if you've just met me for the first time!
stranger	What do you do?
me	I'm a housewife!

Ivan felt queasy on the flight. The air hostess gave him tonic water.

When we got to Marseille, they'd lost our luggage and I had to give them the hotel address. I felt shy speaking French in front of Ivan.

His face was tripping him. They said they'd deliver our cases in the morning and gave us emergency night packs with a T-shirt, a facecloth and a toothbrush. Are you well enough to drive? I asked. Yup, he said, but you'll need to navigate. My head's killing me.

I felt guilty that I couldn't drive instead of him, but I wasn't safe not even at home. My head would go numb and I couldn't process everything you have to process in order to drive safely.

The roadside was a mass of poppies and purple gorse and pink daisies. It's like driving through a Monet painting, isn't it? I said, hoping to make him feel better.

When our luggage arrived the next day, I was so happy, it was almost worth the delay. Ivan was still queasy and I got a taste of my own medicine. He wasn't able to do much and hardly ate. You're fading away, you must eat more than cherries, I said, skirting my hand over his head, the way you would with a child.

His inertia didn't bother me for myself. I was happy to stay in Cassis and walk to the nearby creeks or sit in cafes or bob on the pier. I saw insects that looked like blue wasps.

At night we stayed in and watch French television. I could only understand half of it. Ivan kept changing over to football.

The man in the room opposite was Canadian and had a hearing aid. He was on his own. Ivan couldn't understand why it made me sad. He's probably having a great time, Ivan said.

By the third day, Ivan felt better and we went to Aix. We sat under plane trees on Cours Mirabeau and read the *New York Times* and drank coffee. I bought a book of short stories in French and two yellow plates. We stuffed ourselves with *moules*. You must be feeling better if you can face *moules*, Mr Cox, I said. You're sexy, when you speak French, he replied. That night we made love for the first time on our honeymoon. Come here, Helen Coxsackie, he said.

The next day he brought me breakfast back to the room (we'd both skipped it the first couple of days). We'd been planning to go to St Tropez but the guidebook said it was all designer stores and tack so we went to Bormes-les-Mimosas instead, a hilltop town. On our way out, I glimpsed the Canadian man in his vest and pants, his door was half open. D'you think I should tell him his door's open, I said, maybe he doesn't realise 'cos he can't hear? Please don't spend all day worrying about him, said Ivan. He's fine.

Bormes-les-Mimosas was beautiful, full of flowers and twisty streets and red-topped houses. We ate *cabillaud* at a posh seafood restaurant. The drive back was long and we got lost. I hate these bastard green signs with white arrows, said Ivan – they make no fucking sense!

Calm down, I said. We should stop and look at the map.

I was scared we'd have a fight, I wanted the honeymoon to be totally argument-free, and had been rescuing us from even the smallest frictions.

Back at the hotel we lay on the bed, too tired to get undressed.

Let's just stay in Cassis tomorrow and do nothing, I said.

You'll need to rest up for Porquerolles anyway.

I know.

Are you sure you're up to it?

I want to try.

It's supposed to be stunning.

How long is the ferry? I asked.

About an hour and a half from Toulon. And an hour to get to Toulon from here. We'll need to be up very early to make it worth it.

I'll rest completely tomorrow.

I'm feeling hungry again, said Ivan. The cod didn't exactly fill me up.

It was a bit bland.

I'd never order cod at home, he said, it just sounded better in French.

Everything sounds better in French. You can open the *crème de marron* if you want. There's bread.

Crème de what?

Chestnut jam. I got it for Rita, but you can open it. I'll get more.

He kissed me on his way to the jam.

I watched him unscrew the lid and stick his finger in.

It's delicious – here, taste it, he said, putting his finger to my lips.

You finger's bitter, I said.

Crème de marron, said Ivan, exaggerating a French accent and getting crumbs all over the floor as he fished for the bread.

I used to worry they were teaching us the wrong words at school, I said. I remember thinking: How do they really know that *poisson* is fish and *chien* is dog? Maybe they've got it all wrong and it's a trick, they're not really teaching us French after all.

I know what you mean, said Ivan, I used to think the same in chemistry. I thought they were making it all up.

Porquerolles is one of the Îles d'Hyères. It has a stunning landscape of pine glades and remote beaches. The only way to get around is by bike or on foot.

I hadn't been on a bike for years. I knew that my legs would be ruined the next day but I didn't want to let Ivan down.

You can stop and rest as soon as you want, he said as we got off the ferry and walked towards the vélos for hire.

There was a hill right at the start.

I'll never get up this, I said. There's no way I can pedal. I'll need to walk.

Lean on your bike, said Ivan, use it like a zimmer.

Don't make me laugh, I said. I can't push and laugh at the same time.

He rode on ahead and waited for me at the top.

Get on your bike, wife, he said. It's nice and flat now.

My legs were burning already. I got on and it all came back so easily. I pedalled along the flat, gathering speed so I could rest my legs, the sun and wind on my face. I can't believe I'm doing this! I shouted.

Don't overdo it, he shouted back. He was getting way ahead of me again.

I love this! It's brilliant! I gasped.

After fifteen minutes I had to stop.

I shouted to Ivan but he couldn't hear me. Eventually, he turned round and realised I was no longer pedalling. He circled round effortlessly and came back.

We lay down the bikes and found a beautiful cove to ourselves. Ivan unhooked his rucksack.

I'm starving, I said. I need a piece of bread.

I started unpacking the food.

The cheese is melting, I said. It's oozing out.

Put it in the shade, he said. Behind that rock.

Are you hungry?

I want to see more of the island. I want to keep going.

Okay, I said, but don't be reckless. I know what you're like.

Are you sure you'll be okay on your own?

I'll be fine, I said, I've got the picnic. Have you got water?

Yup.

You should be careful, I said. You won't realise how strong the sun is when you're cycling.

I'll put my hat on. Okay, I'm away.

I watched him disappear, secretly disappointed that he hadn't stayed a bit longer, but I didn't want to nag.

I spread out and settled into the cove. This was as good as it got: sun-bathing topless in a pine grove by the sea, French short stories I could understand, and the anticipation of Ivan returning.

I went down to the water and dipped my feet in. It was freezing, but there were beautiful fish. I went back to my spot and lay down, trying to get comfy again on the pebbles. My legs were buzzing and burning inside.

An hour and a half had passed and he wasn't back, I felt uneasy. I went back down to the water and crouched down, trailing my hand in the waves, trying to ignore the hole that was forming in a perfect day.

Another half hour passed. I was beginning to feel real panic, when he appeared from nowhere saying he had a vélo-gubbed arse.

I was worried! I said. I thought something had happened.

Sorry, he said. I lost track of time. He kissed me as he sat down. We should go to one of the bars in the harbour on the way back and have a drink.

If you want, I said, irked that he was so casual about being late.

Are you going to cycle more? he asked.

Of course not, I need my energy to cycle back, I said, trying not to snap.

There'll be no yellow jersey for you, Looby.

Those guys must be amazingly fit, I said.

I think they're the fittest athletes of all. It's a real endurance test, cycling over mountains.

You should eat something, I said.

I'd kill for a beer.

Do you not worry about my restrictions? I said.

He was rummaging in the backpack. What?

I'm restricted, I said – I couldn't have come looking for you if something had happened.

But nothing happened – you didn't have to come looking.

But what if I had?

I don't spend too much time analysing your potential in emergencies.

I'd be crap.

Probably, he said. Everyone would perish. He lay on his side, propped up by his elbow, eating the rest of the bread and cheese.

You're very handsome in those sunglasses, I said.

Everyone's handsome in sunglasses.

That's not true, some people look worse.

He didn't answer, he'd turned his attention to *Gravity's Rainbow*, his third attempt.

I thought you'd given up on that.

I'm not really taking it in, he said.

I lay perpendicular to him and used his back as a pillow.

I wish you could get a job in the south of France, I said. I definitely have more energy in the sun.

You'll need to settle for the east of Scotland for another few years with all the Wellcome funding we're getting.

East of Scotland's fine, I said. As long as you're there.

Good.

Anywhere's fine. I'd go to Japan.

We lazed for another couple of hours. A yacht dropped its anchor and the people on board were drinking and laughing.

I'd love a yacht, said Ivan. Just bugger off at the weekends.

You'd freeze to death on the Tay, I said. You'd need a duffel coat.

He laughed.

We should go, I said. Time to pack up.

I can't be bothered moving, said Ivan.

If we miss the boat, we're fucked.

He stood up and yawned.

I'm dreading getting back on my vélo, I said.

You'll be grand, he said. It's not that far.

I felt my ear sting, something had buzzed inside. I shook my head as if to rattle it out.

Is it away? said Ivan.

It's dead, I said, wiping the tiny insect off my finger with a tissue. Why would you fly right into someone's ear?

That's their job, said Ivan, that's what insects do.

I walked over to where the bikes lay. Please don't ride so far ahead of me this time.

I'll try not to. It's quite hard to pedal slowly though.

The ride back seemed shorter – I loved free-wheeling down the hill at the end, but I was glad to get rid of the bike.

We sat in the Bar de la Marine and drank kirs royals while we waited for the ferry.

Let's toast Jana, I said. She'd love it here.

To Jana, said Ivan.

And Kavi too. I hope they can come to our party.

I hope so, he said. Why are you laughing?

I'm thinking back to Jana and I missing the ferry to Cherbourg. It was hysterical. I remember it like yesterday.

A long time ago, said Ivan.

We were children.

Some of us are still children, he said.

You mean me.

I'm teasing.

And Fizza too, I said. Let's toast Fizza.

The kir was going to my head.

Back in Cassis, I collapsed into bed. Ivan lifted the sheet back and started kissing my breasts. I'm no good to you, I

493

said. I've got vélo-gubbed legs. Don't worry, he said, I'll do all the work.

Afterwards, he went out for bread and cheese and olives. We ate on the veranda. Dusk slipped over us and I had a glass of wine.

You feel folded up in velvet when it gets dark here, don't you?

Yeah, he said.

It's comforting.

I suppose.

Are you sad about tomorrow? I asked, stroking his wrist.

A bit.

D'you want to be on your own?

I might hike into the big creek. I can't believe it's been four years.

Me neither.

She was always very fond of you, he said.

I just wish I'd known her better.

We sat for ages in the warm darkness, not speaking, our arms just touching, each with our own thoughts. I didn't want it to end.

Before going to sleep, he turned to me and said, Have you removed the insects from your ears?

On the flight home, Ivan was falling asleep before the plane had even taken off. *Please* don't sleep 'til we're up, I said. I need you to be awake.

It'll be fine, he said, leaning his head back on my shoulder.

The engines might stall, I said.

They won't, said Ivan. Read your French book. It'll be fine.

Epilogue

On 11th January 2002, the Chief Medical Officer's Working Group produced a long report for the government, saying that ME is real, debilitating and distressing, imposing a substantial burden on patients, families and carers. Doctors were no longer allowed to tell patients they didn't believe in it.

Three cheers for the Chief Medical Officer! *Hurrah! Hurrah! Hurrah!*

*

If we look through the round window, and *really* strain our eyes, we can see some of the powerful people who didn't believe in the illness – GPs, psychiatrists, journalists – standing shamefaced in the corner. They are wearing dunce hats and stuttering apologies.

*

Author's note: In August 2007, the National Institute of Health and Clinical Excellence (NICE) published guidelines for the management of ME, which – while acknowledging it can be as disabling as MS or lupus – indicate cognitive behaviour therapy (CBT) and graded exercise (GET) as the primary treatment. In doing so, NICE has blatantly disregarded the biomedical model of the illness in favour of the psychosocial model. There has been widespread condemnation of these guidelines and, at the time of writing, the One Click ME Pressure Group is in the process of taking NICE to court.

About the Author

Nasim Marie Jafry was born in the west of Scotland in 1963 to a Scottish mother and Pakistani father. She has an MA and MSc from Glasgow University, but her studies were severely disrupted when she became ill with ME. She has lived in San Francisco and currently resides in Edinburgh. Her short stories have appeared in various publications. *The State of Me* is her first novel. She blogs at http://www. velo-gubbed-legs.blogspot.com.

Acknowledgements

I wish to thank:

My family for their love and support, with special thanks to my mother and step-father for their exceptional kindness and understanding, Pauline for showing me a different way, and my nephews for sparkling. Anne Boyle for always believing. Joanna and Tom Kane for their calmness. Friends near and far: Anna MR, Anne Tice, Anne-Sofie Laegran, Barbara Sabbadini, Cath Duguid, CL, Cheryl Minto, Ciara MacLaverty, Graeme Smith, Graham Spinardi, Helen Boden, Jamie M, Jennifer Murphy, Joanne Limburg, Keith Marrison, Laura Francescangeli, Summera Shaheen, Tess Biddington, Trisha Harbord and Vikram Chaudhary. My very fine blog friends. All those who helped with research, even the tiniest detail. Bernard MacLaverty for his advice. Caroline Smailes for her generosity of spirit. The gem that is The Friday Project, with special thanks to Clare Christian,

Clare Weber and Madeleine James. And thanks also to Joanna Chisholm for her valuable input.

The poem by Eeva Kilpi on page vii is from *A Treasury of Finnish Love: poems, quotations and proverbs in Swedish, Finnish and English*, translated and edited by Börje Vähämäki (New York: Hippocrene Books, 1996). Copyright © 1996, Börje Vähämäki. Reprinted by kind permission.

The eternal problem of the human being is how to structure his waking hours radio quotation on page 110 from the psychiatrist Eric Berne is from his book *Games People Play* (New York: Grove Press, 1964).

'thoughts are slow and brown' on page 181 is taken from Edna St Vincent Millay's poem 'Sorrow'. Copyright © 1917, 1945 by Edna St Vincent Millay. Reprinted by kind permission of Edna St Vincent Millay Society.